Wicked**DIX**

Wicked DIX

International Bestselling Author

MONICA JAMES

Cover Design: Perfect Pear Creative Covers
Cover Models: David Tomasic and Michelle Lancaster
Photographer: Monica James
Formatting: E.M. Tippetts Book Designs

Follow me on:
authormonicajames.com

OTHER BOOKS BY
MONICA JAMES

THE I SURRENDER SERIES

I Surrender

Surrender to Me

Surrendered

White

SOMETHING LIKE NORMAL SERIES

Something like Normal

Something like Redemption

Something like Love

A HARD LOVE ROMANCE

Dirty Dix

Wicked Dix

The Hunt

MEMORIES FROM YESTERDAY DUET

Forgetting You, Forgetting Me

Forgetting You, Remembering Me

SINS OF THE HEART DUET

Absinthe of the Heart

Defiance of the Heart

ALL THE PRETTY THINGS TRILOGY
Bad Saint
Fallen Saint
Forever My Saint
The Devil's Crown-Part One (Spin-Off)
The Devil's Crown-Part Two (Spin-Off)

THE MONSTERS WITHIN DUET
Bullseye
Blowback

DELIVER US FROM EVIL TRILOGY
Thy Kingdom Come
Into Temptation
Deliver Us From Evil

IN LOVE AND WAR
North of the Stars
Fall of the Stars

STANDALONE
Mr. Write
Chase the Butterflies
Beyond the Roses
Someone Else's Shadow

Now...

"How could you?" gasps the girl, whose heart I've just shattered into smithereens.

"I can explain." But I can't. There is no explanation worthy enough to excuse why I'm here.

"Well?" The single, slow-falling tear that traces a path down her porcelain cheek highlights what a true bastard I really am.

"I-I..." Fuck! What am I even trying to say? Where do I start? When was the exact moment this all turned to shit?

"Just like I thought." She spins on her heel and scampers toward the door.

"Madison, wait! Please hear me out."

"Why, Dixon? To hear more of your lies!"

"Maddy, please," I plead, reaching out and latching onto her arm like the desperate man I am.

"No!" she shrieks, recoiling, my touch appearing to repulse her.

"Don't do this. Please don't do this."

My feeble voice betrays my fear. But I don't care. The only good, decent thing in my life is about to walk out that door, and I wouldn't blame her if she never came back. I'll grovel, beg at her feet if I need to, but a small part of me knows it was bound to come to this.

"Don't do what?" she cries, her fingers unsteady as she

brushes back her long hair.

I deserve this.

I'm a manwhore.

And I'm a coward.

I don't deserve this beautiful *angelo*'s love. I never did. But I wanted it so badly I thought consequences be damned. But now, now I've gone and fucked it all up.

"I'm sorry. It's not what you think." But it is.

I *was* meeting up in this fleabag motel to conspire with her sister—a sister who truly represents sin.

"I hope it's not what I think because if it is, then I don't know who you are."

Words have never hurt more than those just spoken.

"I'm the same man I was this morning. I'm the same man who loves you more than life itself. That hasn't changed. That'll never change," I press, stepping forward, needing to touch her. But she steps away with nothing but disgust in her eyes.

"Just tell me one thing…what are you doing here?"

I could lie. I mean, that's all I've been doing. But when you can no longer distinguish between the lies you've told and the truth, it's time to come clean.

My silence is cementing my guilt.

"Tell me this isn't what I think it is, and I'll forget I ever saw you here."

Everything at this moment is heightened—the clock on the discolored wall sounds in time with my lashing heart, my heavy breathing is in sync with the wild wind thrashing about outside, but most of all, the torrent of tears streaming down Madison's cheeks are in concert with my drowning soul.

"Dixon?" Her lower lip trembles as she waits for me to

remedy this situation.

Every inch of my body tells me to lie, but I can't. I do the only decent thing I've ever done in my entire life.

I say nothing at all.

"I thought so," she whispers brokenly after a minute of silence.

Her beautiful green eyes reveal nothing but betrayal as she yanks open the door. "Goodbye, Dr. Mathews. Thank you for being the biggest regret of my life," she sobs, her voice stuck in her throat.

I want to say so many things, but I don't. I simply stand numbly and watch the best thing in my life walk out on me. And for once, I do the right thing.

I let her go.

One

Dixon

Then...

"And then he said...sorry, I need a minute," snuffles Goldilocks as she unfurls an unsteady hand.

"Take all the time you need, Ms. Kibard." I'll just continue with my morbid doodle of a teddy bear getting his stuffing blown out.

When she finally regains her composure, she continues. "And then he said...if I bought one more teddy bear, he was going to leave me." She clutches onto her eyeless, scraggly, diseased-looking teddy bear like it's Lord Jesus himself. "Can you believe that?"

You bet your crazy ass I can. But I calmly nod, appearing stone-faced. This is my job, after all.

"I'm not here to pass judgment, Ms. Kibard. Let's talk about why you have a...fascination with teddy bears."

Yes, this *is* as ridiculous as it sounds, but her crazy makes me forget the madness of my own.

It's been ten days. Ten whole days during which I've lied to the most innocent, most honorable person I've ever met. For ten days, I've hated myself more than I thought I possibly could.

I'm not a good person, I know that. Before meeting Madison Roberts, I was questioning my humanity, questioning if I actually ever had any morals, ethics, or a soul. But for a split second, she made me feel as if maybe there was hope for me. As if maybe I could be a good man.

But that hope got shot to hell when the sins of my past blackmailed me into being her little lapdog. And now, my hands are tied. Tied by Juliet Harte—the Antichrist in heels.

This is my karma for succumbing to her sinful ways. But contracting Ebola while covered in smallpox and listening to Celine Dion on repeat would be preferable and less painful than what Juliet proposes I do. My cock curls in on itself and goes into retreat when thinking about touching that harlot ever again.

"Dr. Mathews, do you agree?"

Focusing on the train wreck in front of me, I try to backtrack to the last thing I remember her saying.

"Blah, blah, bear. Blah, blah, teddy. Blah, blah, Daddy."

Pushing my miserable woes aside, I steeple my fingers under my chin. "I'd like to talk about your bear." I drop my gaze to the diabolic fluff ball, hoping this works because I have not listened to a word she's said. "Who gave you that little…" *roadkill*, I internally offer, but instead settle for, "that little guy?"

We human beings, we are such expressive creatures, and the smallest change in facial expressions usually reveals what's lurking beneath the surface. And now is no exception.

As Goldie's jaw begins to tremble, I know what her answer will be. "My father." She draws the dirty teddy into her chest, hugging it tight.

How'd I know her answer was going to be just that? Well, I know because I'm a man. We men, we are right royal bastards. If we don't fuck our daughters up, then someone else's son will do it for us.

The thought has my stomach churning because if what Juliet says is true and she *is* carrying my child, then that child is doomed to grow up to be a conniving bastard or a psychotic, manipulative, batshit-crazy bitch.

The fact Juliet has slept with half of Manhattan and their dog makes me feel a touch better that this poor child might not be mine. But if it is…

I shudder.

I can't deal with this. I need to focus on one drama at a time. And Goldie weeping about how her father used this bear as his scapegoat to touch her inappropriately is not one of them.

Tonight, I'm having dinner with Sebastian and Rachel at their lavish home in Westchester County. I liked them both instantly when we first met ten days ago, and under normal circumstances, I would be thrilled to spend an evening with Madison's parents. But there is nothing normal about tonight's proceedings.

The heavy cell in my pocket taunts me, reminding me that some twenty minutes ago, I received a text message from the bitchface herself. A text which shattered all hope that maybe she was joking.

It said, *I've got an itch only you can scratch.* It's a line she's used before.

But this time, I replied with, **There's a cream you can get for that.**

I thought *suck on that, you smug, presumptuous she-devil*, but she made it known just who was in charge and running this freak show when she countered a second later.

The only cream I want is the one that comes from your cock.

Romance truly is dead. Juliet Harte killed it the day she opened her venomous mouth and I happily stuck my dick into it.

I remove my glasses and massage the bridge of my nose with two fingers. How the fuck am I going to do this? I'll have the woman I worship on one side of me, while the woman I despise will be on the other side, no doubt trying to give me a discreet hand job under the table.

I'm fucked. And not in a good way.

"It's okay, Tracey. You know it'll feel good."

Steadily lifting my head, I'm baffled as to why it sounds like Regan MacNeil from *The Exorcist*, post possession, has just crawled into my office. What I'm confronted with just highlights the kind of week I've had.

"Ms. Kibard?" I ask, pulling back in utter confusion when I'm now faced with the eyeless bear instead of Goldie.

The bear dances in front of Goldie's face, each word enunciated with an improper thrust. "Tracey isn't here. You're talking to Johnny now. Do you want to fuck her pussy?"

"*Excuse me?*" I question the...bear in horror, but also, part humor.

"You heard me. She likes it hard." The bear gyrates robustly, just to emphasize his point in case I missed the disturbing memo.

I run a hand down my face.

As Johnny the bear details Tracey's abusive childhood, I sink further and further into my seat. But I listen and pretend to care because I know this will be the only normalcy to my day.

"You can touch her. She wants it." It appears this bear can not only talk, but he's also a pimp.

Oh dear God.

I throw my head back in defeat.

What have I done to deserve this? However, it's not a what but rather a who. And that who totally outplayed a player. She beat me at my own game. A game that I foolishly believed I had mastered.

But now I realize, this entire time, I was the one getting played. I played straight into her hands. And now that my balls are in her court, I'm afraid of what she'll do to them once it's her turn to serve.

Two

Dixon

Walking through the hallway of Madison's apartment block usually gives me the warm fuzzies.

But tonight, it's giving me heartburn. I pull at the collar of my white shirt. It feels like hands are squeezing off my air supply the closer I get to Maddy's front door.

How am I supposed to pull this off? Lying to Maddy's face is one thing, but lying in front of her parents, with the source of the lie sitting mere inches from me, is something else. My walls are already crumbling, and I don't know how much longer I'll be able to keep this up.

Pulling it together, I take a deep breath before knocking on her front door. She opens it a second later, and when she does, I feel like an even bigger asshole.

"Dixon," she gushes, curling a soft lock of hair behind her ear. Her cheeks flush a soft pink, and she nervously nibbles on her tempting lower lip.

10

If anything has ever looked this sweet, then I don't remember seeing it.

I was spellbound by Madison Roberts the moment I saw her, and I'm not embarrassed to confess I have been ever since. I came to her rescue after some Neanderthal was manhandling her. I don't know why I felt the need to intervene, but I'm glad I did.

After I made some god-awful decisions—like screwing Juliet on more than one occasion—I came to my senses and knew that this amazing, beautiful woman was the only woman I wanted. Even when I was "seeing" Juliet, Madison was always on my mind. I just wish I had listened to common sense sooner.

I was happy with friendship, if that was all she could offer, but once I got to know the real her, I knew I needed her more than I needed air to breathe. I'm a lucky son of a bitch that she felt the same way.

Her strengths and weaknesses inspire me to become a better man.

"Madison." As she continues gnawing on her lip, I step forward and slip my hand around her slender waist. "You look incredible."

She blushes further, a shade akin to the color of her summer dress. "Thank you."

"No, thank…" I lean forward and nuzzle her cheek. "You," I conclude in her ear. A small whimper catches in her throat, and the sound has my alpha dog beating his chest in pride. I love that after everything she's been through, she trusts me enough to allow this closeness between us.

As I look over her shoulder and see her overnight bag sitting innocently by the door, I can't help but frown. The sight would usually give me the warm and fuzzies, but due to obvious circumstances, I now feel undeserving. And Maddy can sense my shift immediately.

"I just thought I could stay over because your house is closer to my parents'. But I don't have to. I'm sorry for assuming," she quickly adds, peering down at her shoes.

"Hey," I coo, using two fingers to raise her chin. I drown in those big, innocent emerald eyes. "Never apologize for wanting to stay the night. You know you're always welcome in my home. And bed."

She swallows hard at my bold statement. "I just, I didn't want to assume. I mean lately…" But she pauses.

"What?" I prompt softly.

"Lately, you've just been distracted. I've hardly seen you all week. Have I done something wrong?" She looks regretful that she's said too much, while I'm regretful that I've said too little.

As hard as I've tried to mask my shame, it obviously hasn't been hard enough. She's seen through my bullshit, just like I knew she would.

"No, Maddy, no. You've done nothing wrong." I cup her cheeks, searching her eyes. "It's me who's done wrong." She looks at me, waiting for me to explain. But I can't.

"I'm sorry, you're completely right. I've just been busy with…work." She hears me break but doesn't press.

"Okay. As long as you're sure."

I stroke my thumb over her lower lip. "Yes, *angelo*, with you, I'm always sure. You're the only stable thing in my life." Her smile lights up the darkest night.

I kiss her forehead a second later. "C'mon, let's go."

I reach for her bag and shrug it onto my shoulder. "Jesus,

12

what have you got in here? A dead body?"

She laughs. "Not yet." I know she's referring to Juliet, and I can't help but smirk at her comment.

If only my life were that easy.

We walk to my car hand in hand, and I listen to Madison fill me in on her week. I really have been a horrible boyfriend because when I ask her certain questions, she informs me I asked her the same ones last week.

"Are you sure everything is all right?" Madison asks as we're waiting at the lights.

"Yes, why?"

She reaches over and stills my drumming fingers on the steering wheel as her response.

Looking over, I smile. "I'm fine. I just had a hard day today. I counseled my first teddy bear."

"Pardon?" She retreats, pulling a similar face to mine when I was witnessing the debacle.

I grin at her adorability. "You don't want to know."

When she toys with her seat belt, I wonder what's troubling her. She answers my question a moment later. "I had my session today."

"Oh?" Of course she did. It's Tuesday today. Get it together, you damn fool.

"Yeah." She leaves the word hanging, waiting for me to lead the conversation.

"How'd it go?" We have an unspoken rule that we don't discuss her sessions. Ever. So I'm curious to know why she brought it up.

"Dr. Canetti thinks I'm making real progress. She suggested that I write my feelings down."

"That's a good idea," I reply, pulling onto the freeway.

"So I have."

"And that's helped?"

"Yeah, a little. I want to confront Beth. I mean, Juliet."

Her name is like a swift kick to my balls. "Confront her about what exactly?"

She shuffles in her seat, her breathing turning ragged. "For, for being so…mean to me while we were growing up."

Why did she halt? What was she intending to say?

"Maddy…" I keep my eyes focused on the road. "I don't know Juliet…" *Lies! Lies! Lies!* "But from what I can tell, she would be mean to her own mother."

"Her mother is dead."

"Precisely. That option is far better than having to deal with a devil child."

"Dixon!" she admonished. "That's awful." But her muted chuckles reveal she agrees.

"Are you going to be okay seeing her this evening?"

Her tiny shoulders lift. "I don't know. She doesn't bother me as much anymore. It's my bro—her fiancé," she corrects quickly, "who does."

I grip the steering wheel, my knuckles turning white.

I'm pleased her lowlife, vermin brother isn't going to be in attendance, as this dinner would have turned into a barbecue—a barbecue of me grilling his ass before I sliced him up into teeny tiny pieces.

I have never loathed two people more than I do Juliet Harte and her cocksucker partner, Dylan Roberts. No other couple has deserved each other more. They say misery loves company; well, these two individuals are the most miserable bastards I

14

know.

"You never have to see him again. And if you do, I'll be your personal bodyguard."

She smiles, and the sight has me falling over myself like a slobbering, lovestruck fool.

"I like your body, so it's a deal," she cheekily says.

I get giddier than a schoolgirl at a One Direction concert. "Well, in that case, it's yours any time you want it."

"Tonight?"

I almost sideswipe a semi traveling on the other side of the road. Correcting quickly, I look over at the giggling vixen next to me. "A little warning next time."

"How would you like to be warned?" She bats those impossibly long lashes my way. "I'm in desperate need of urgent medical attention, Dr. Mathews, which only you can provide." She has the gall to wink.

I want to kiss that smart mouth before I watch it open in passion as I eat her out.

"Careful. Otherwise, I'll turn this car around, and the only thing I'll be eating…is you." I give her a wink of my own. Her giggles die in her throat instantly.

As her pink tongue nervously darts out to wet her bottom lip, I smother my moan. The sight reminds me that because of my lie, I am now a fucking monk. The few times I have seen Madison over the course of this nightmare, I've been so incredibly guilt-ridden, I haven't been able to touch her without wanting to cut off my own hands. I don't deserve her, but I want her—so, so bad.

And by the way she's pressing her thighs together and clawing at the seat, I dare say she wants me—so, so bad.

Suddenly, my BMW has become as stifling as the sun, and I focus on nothing but the road, afraid of what I'll do if I look at her and she looks at me in return.

Thankfully, moments later, I turn into the gated community and see the impressive, thirty-two-acre lakefront estate. The widespread, three-story white home is impressive, to say the least. The gravel crunches under my tires as we ascend the long driveway. The front lawn is enormous and beautifully green, and as we get closer to the gigantic home, I begin to understand why Juliet is the way she is.

Her entire life, it would appear she's had everything she could ever wish for, and in turn, this wealth has turned her into a spoiled little brat. What happens when someone has everything they could ever want? They want more because *more* is never enough.

Unlike Madison.

Madison has experienced many hardships throughout her life, and before Sebastian came into her world, she and her mom were doing it tough. She knows what it's like to be hungry. She appreciates her fortune because she's not an ungrateful she-devil. And she has a soul.

I park the car, taking a moment to appreciate the eye-catching sight before me. "So you said it has many bedrooms again?"

Madison unbuckles her belt and looks out the windshield also. "Seven. Not to mention five bathrooms, a saltwater swimming pool, a theater room, a two-thousand-square-foot guesthouse, and just for fun, a full-size tennis court."

"No *wonder* Sebastian is in such good shape," I say as if solving a riddle. Madison playfully slaps my arm.

When we exit the car, I feel like the luckiest man alive when she slips her tiny hand in mine. The marbled stairway is immaculately polished, and the large alcove shelters two glass doors. Madison doesn't have time to sound the doorbell because her mother opens the door the moment we climb the last step.

"You made it!" Rachel clucks, racing forward and embracing Madison in a tight hug.

"Mom!" Maddy exclaims, the embarrassment apparent in her tone.

"Sorry, but I can't remember the last time I saw you twice within a month. I'm just so happy to have you here." She winks at me over Maddy's shoulder, and I can't help but smile.

She finally pulls away, beaming in my direction. "It's so nice to see you, Dixon. Thank you for coming."

"Thank you for having me, Rachel."

She leans in to give me a kiss, but my mother would be rolling in her grave if I didn't grace both her cheeks with a kiss. She blushes a lovely shade of pink. A pink that reminds me of her daughter's...

"Please, won't you come inside?" Rachel signals with her hand, mercifully interrupting my train of perverted thoughts.

She welcomes us into her remarkable home, and I won't lie, this home is probably the nicest abode I have ever seen. The large foyer opens up to five different passages one can take, but to transport them to where, I don't know. But I can't wait to find out.

We follow Rachel through the extravagant living room and down the hallway. "Come through. Sebastian is just in the kitchen cooking."

I raise my eyebrow while Rachel laughs. "He is a much better cook than I am. Trust me, if I was cooking, we would be having pizza."

The moment we step into the kitchen, I smell fresh tomato sauce, oregano, and golden mozzarella—three of my favorite smells in the world. Smells that remind me of my mother.

"Look who I found at our front door," Rachel teases, while Sebastian turns from the stove with a big smile on his face.

"Button. You look beautiful." He wipes his hands on a dishcloth before wrapping Maddy in a tight embrace.

"Thank you. Whatever you're cooking smells absolutely delicious." She stands on her tippy-toes to look over his shoulder as they break apart.

"Seeing as Dr. Mathews is Italian"—his eyes flick my way—"I figured I'd try my hand with some Italian cuisine." He extends his palm, and we shake firmly.

A man with a good handshake is a man who has balls.

"Madison is right. It does smell delicious. But please, call me Dixon." Sebastian happily nods. "I hope you like red wine." I pass him the six-hundred-dollar bottle of Cabernet Sauvignon.

He whistles, perusing the label. "You've got good taste. But we already knew that." He glances lovingly at Maddy, who beams. "This will go wonderfully with dinner. Honey, would you open this bottle for me? My tomato sauce is about to boil over."

Rachel nods as Sebastian goes back to the stove. "So how was traffic?" he asks, his back turned as he busily adds in some fresh basil leaves.

"It was fine. With Dixon behind the wheel, we're lucky we got here in one piece," Maddy quips, grinning at me as she

18

reaches across the counter to steal a slice of tomato.

I'm utterly captivated as she pops it into her mouth, licking the stray juices from her lips.

"Oh, I don't believe that. I bet Dixon is a wonderful driver," I vaguely hear Rachel say in the background. I can't keep my eyes off Madison as she innocently licks her fingers clean.

My dick chooses this moment to come out of hibernation. How typical.

"Isn't that right, Dixon? Dixon?"

My name being repeated is a sure sign I've missed something important. But the only important thing to me is Madison recreating that entire performance, but this time, I'll volunteer to be the tomato.

Only Madison's flushed cheeks and bashful smirk alert me to the fact that someone is expecting me to talk. But how can I speak? I'm rendered speechless by the beauty in front of me. All that long, soft hair and those supple, pink lips—all I can think about is what those lips could do, and how I could use that hair as reins.

Because I'm a masochist, I drop my gaze to her spectacular chest, which is steadily swelling with every coarse breath she takes. Thoughts of what I've done to those amazing, full breasts have me wishing I wasn't in a room with her parents—her parents, who are probably seconds away from throwing me out because I'm clearly undressing their baby daughter with my heated eyes.

"That's absolutely right, Rachel. Your daughter is in good hands." My gaze never wavers from Maddy's as I respond, thankful I was half listening.

Her red glow alerts me to the fact that she's just as turned

19

on as I am.

"I have no doubt about that," Rachel says, placing a glass of wine on the counter in front of me. She seems oblivious to the fact I'm considering we skip dinner and I head straight for dessert—the dessert between Madison's thighs.

"I'm so happy we can all be together. It's just a shame Dylan has to work. But Juliet should be here any minute."

And just like that, my dick shrivels into a prune. Juliet is like the opposite of Viagra.

Madison shuffles uncomfortably.

"Maddy, do you want to show Dixon into the dining room? Dinner is almost done," Sebastian says over his shoulder while Rachel is busily pulling out the good china.

She nods but doesn't speak. How can they not see her retreat?

I follow as she nervously leads me into a huge dining room that overlooks the pool. The minute she stops walking, I scoop her up into my arms.

"Are you all right?" I ask, kissing her temple lightly.

Turning into my embrace, she replies, "I'm fine. I just wish we could have one dinner without the mention of him."

"I know, *angelo.*" We stay hugging for a while, both needing the comfort.

I'm lost in the stillness of the pool when Maddy whispers, "So what were you thinking about?" She quickly clarifies, "In the kitchen."

Deciding to ask her what she thinks, I put forward, "What do you think I was thinking about?"

Her breathing begins to mount. "I-I think you were thinking what I was," she reveals in that small voice, which I've come to learn means a fire is building in her belly.

"Oh yeah? And what's that?" I can feel her heart soaring about in her chest. The air is charged with a palpable tension, and we're both ready to explode.

She bravely looks up. "That we should pay a visit to the guesthouse."

My cock stands in salute and high-fives my raging need to get laid.

"You"—I tap the end of her nose—"are a mind reader. Shall we sneak off before appetizers are served?"

She giggles but turns serious. "No. But maybe before dessert?"

I grunt when she shyly slides a hand between us. She surprises me as she brushes over the bulge that appears whenever I'm in her presence.

"That suits me just fine because I already know what I'm having."

Her pupils darken, and she swallows nervously. "Maybe…" She groans when I bend forward to suck her earlobe into my hungry mouth. "We could just skip dinner altogether then?" she suggests, voicing my exact thoughts.

"You'll have no complaints from me."

Her tiny whimpers swathe us in a blanket of bliss as I kiss down the length of her arched, elongated neck. My self-control is diminishing, and it's taking every ounce of strength I have not to take her outside and make good on my word right now. I have a serious semi, and if she keeps making those little sounds, I'll be able to slice through the meatloaf with my rock-hard dick.

"Ah, Dixon," she cries when I bite over her frantic pulse. But I can't stop.

I'm moments away from getting caught with my hand underneath her dress, and that's not the impression I want to leave on her parents. I need a distraction or at least an ice-cold shower.

I sadly get one of the two. I really would have preferred the cold shower.

"Is this a private party? Or can anyone join?"

Madison pulls away, horrified, while I glare at the woman destroying my life.

"Oh, please don't stop on my account." Juliet's shrill voice is comparable to that of a dying hyena with flatulence.

"Be…Juliet," Maddy hastily corrects, standing closer to my side.

Juliet nods her greeting, her impish gaze locked with mine. "How lovely to see you again, Dr. Mathews." Her ruby lips tip up into a secretive smile—a secret I'm sadly privy to.

If looks could kill, Juliet would be a smoldering pile of ashes where she stands. However, I choose to ignore her and glance over at the elegantly set table. I'm thankful when I see two seats sitting opposite the other while a place is set at the head of the table.

"Here," I say, pulling the chair out for Maddy.

She adjusts her dress before taking a seat. "Thank you."

I kiss the top of her head and take the seat next to her, leaving Juliet standing awkwardly in the middle of the room. She gets the hint and unhappily sinks into the seat across from me.

"I hope you're hungry," announces Rachel, who enters bearing an assortment of food, Sebastian trailing close behind.

The moment he sees Juliet, his eyes light up. "Bonbon, I

didn't hear you come in."

"Sorry, Daddy, I let myself in."

He places the huge tray of lasagna in the middle of the table before bending forward and kissing Juliet on the head. "There's no need to apologize. This will always be your home. Yours too, Button." Juliet looks like she's about to launch over the table and claw out Madison's eyes.

I think back to our first session where I originally thought Juliet's father may be the root of her addiction; however, getting to know Sebastian better, I realize he has nothing to do with his daughter's deviancy. I now can't help but wonder who is. This house may be rich in possessions, but what was lacking emotionally for Juliet to turn out the way she has?

"How's the morning sickness going? Still having problems keeping anything down?" Rachel innocently asks, taking her seat.

When Juliet cups her small belly, I actually feel like I'm the one having problems keeping anything down. The bile rises, and I feel even more disgusted with myself that there is any possibility that the baby is mine.

"Oh, Rachel," Juliet fawns, looking pointedly at me. "If this baby is anything like his father, he'll give me trouble right till the very end."

Rachel chuckles while I glare at a grinning Juliet.

"Dig in, everyone," Sebastian says, waving his hands out to the feast in front of him. Sadly, I've lost my appetite.

Madison's stillness reveals that she's still uncomfortable, but she reaches for my plate and smiles. "What would you like?"

"You don't have to serve me."

"I want to." The blush on her cheeks has me thinking about

23

our earlier conversation.

Subtly gathering up the hem of her dress, I lightly rub my fingers along her inner soft thigh. "I'll have anything you think I'll enjoy," I reply, relishing the sensation of her skin prickling at my touch.

"H-How about one of everything?" The plate wavers slightly in her unsteady hold.

"Sounds good to me. It all looks too delicious to deny." I accentuate my sentence by giving her thigh a gentle squeeze.

Only I can hear her muted moan as Sebastian and Rachel are chatting to Juliet about the baby. She serves up a decent serving of lasagna, meatloaf, salad, and some garlic bread while I continue stroking her scorching skin.

"Dixon, tell me, is that lasagna as good as your mom's?" Sebastian teases when Maddy places my colossal plate in front of me.

I look down at my meal and smile. "From smells alone, it'll come close. She would have been proud."

My use of the past tense alerts him to my mother's passing. "Oh, I'm sorry. She's passed?"

I nod. "It's okay." I wave my hand, as there's no need for apologies. "She did. Close to a year ago now from breast cancer."

Rachel's kind face softens. "Oh, dear. That's awful. I'm so sorry to hear that. What about your father?" she asks, reaching for her wine.

I shuffle in my seat. My father is an extremely touchy subject for me. I've barely detailed his condition to Maddy. "My father is still living," I reply, picking up my fork, hoping to disguise my discomfort. "He's in New Jersey." I exclude where exactly in New Jersey he is.

"Are you close?" Rachel asks, oblivious to how uncomfortable I am. The entire table is quiet, awaiting my response.

There is no way I can avoid this, and I've done enough lying this week. "We were, but he suffered a breakdown after my mother and now—" But I can't say it. I can't say now he resembles someone I no longer know.

Madison slips her hand into mine. "I'd love to meet him one day."

No, you really don't. But I smile at her kindness. "Yeah. One day," I reply half-heartedly, letting go of her hand.

Thanks to my obvious retreat, the room becomes as comfortable as a turkey before Thanksgiving.

Sebastian clears his throat. "So Button, have you decided what you're doing for your birthday?"

And that's exactly the change of subject I need. "It's your birthday? When?" I turn to look at her, cocking a surprised brow.

"It's not until late next month," she replies, brushing it off.

"The thirtieth, to be precise," Rachel adds, sipping her wine.

Madison narrows her eyes playfully at her mom.

"Remember when you were younger; all you wanted for your birthday was to go to Rome?" Sebastian reveals while slicing through his meatloaf.

"It was?" Again, this is news to me.

"Yeah." She shrugs. "It always looked like such a nice place to visit. And I've heard their biscotti are to die for." Her teasing grin hints at the first time we had biscotti together at Dolci's, the first time I actually felt like a gentleman and not a complete scoundrel.

I've missed those feelings, and I want to relive them. With

that thought in mind, I declare, "Then it's settled. For your birthday, we're going to Rome."

Maddy laughs, but her humor catches in her throat when she sees I'm dead serious. "No. I can't accept. That's too much."

I shake my head, as I won't hear otherwise. "Nonsense. We're going, *angelo*. All you need is your passport and a suitcase. I'll take care of the rest."

"Dixon—" But I silence her with a smug smirk that tells her this is a losing battle.

She turns to look at Rachel. "Mom!"

But she only raises her hands, not taking any blame for spilling the beans.

These pleasantries have almost made me forget Juliet is sitting across from me—almost.

"Since you're so generously offering trips to Rome, what's one more? I pack light." She teasingly laughs, appearing to be joking, but I know better.

I turn slowly, fixing my annoyed stare on her. "Three's a crowd."

"There are some circumstances when three can be fun." She cockily grins while I turn my lip up in disgust.

"Well, this isn't one of them." Maddy nervously sips her wine, but I make no attempt to hide my contempt for her stepsibling.

I can't believe I actually liked fucking this woman once upon a time. Her blonde hair sits in a harsh bun, exposing her sharp, pointy, annoying features. Her body, baby bump aside, is not at all feminine and soft like Maddy's. Not to mention she's a right royal bitch who has me wishing I was neutered every time I look at her.

I must have been fucking nuts.

In no way, shape, or form do I find myself attracted to her, and if I could erase all memories of her, I would. But sadly, I can't. She's just a reminder of what a jackass I am.

We go on eating our meal, keeping the conversation light. Whenever Juliet speaks, I ignore her or whisper into Maddy's ear. Most times, it's trivial things like, "How do you like the wine?" or "This meal is delicious," but I make sure to stroke her leg or graze my lips over the shell of her ear. I do things that'll make her blush or squirm. Things that'll make Juliet turn her own shade of red, but not the happy kind.

Who knew annoying her would become my new favorite pastime?

"Who's ready for dessert?" Rachel sing-songs while I brush my fingers dangerously close to Madison's delicious heat.

"I know I am," I whisper. Her soft intake of breath has my very interested cock stirring and doing push-ups in my pants.

Just as I'm going to concoct a lame-ass excuse that'll give Maddy and me the escape plan we need, Rachel asks, "Maddy, can you help me work the new coffee machine? Sebastian says it's too high-tech for him."

Sebastian laughs, playfully smacking his wife on the ass as she heads for the kitchen.

Maddy looks at me with nothing but apology in her eyes, but I smile, kissing her quickly on the lips. "Lucky you packed your pj's."

She leans into my mouth and whispers, "I didn't."

I almost choke on my excitement while Maddy smugly rises. My gaze falls to her lengthy legs, and very vivid images of those legs spread open before me invade my brain. I need this woman on my tongue and in my mouth this instant.

But I play it cool and stand also, as I have no intention of being in a room with Juliet for any longer than I have to. "I'm just going out for a smoke."

"Okay. See you soon." She leans forward and kisses me briefly on the lips. It's too brief, but it'll have to tide me over for now.

Sebastian is talking to a non-enthused Juliet about the baby while I excuse myself and head outside. I can feel her eagle eyes on me the entire time.

Walking down the paved path, I decide to take a tour around the grounds, as I have no idea how long Maddy will be. Tonight hasn't been too painful, but I suppose it's only just begun.

As I pensively smoke my Marlboro, I look out into the vastness, the murky blackness of the lake hiding the secrets of what went on here. This house holds so many secrets. Ones I wish I knew. And others, I wish I didn't.

"I'm going to make all your dreams come true."

And just like that, my peace shatters, and I'm surrounded with clamor. "You're going to run away from home and join the circus?" I bluntly reply, not even bothering to turn around.

"You don't mean that." Her shoes crunch over the pebbles, indicating she's getting closer and closer—which is my cue to move the fuck away.

Without a second thought, I openly reveal, "I have absolutely no qualms about running you over with my car."

Her floral smell, a scent I used to crave, catches on the light breeze and fetches so many memories—memories I wish I could dig out of my brain. But I can't.

"Why are you being so cruel?"

I take a long drag before replying, "What can I say...you bring out the best in me. You always have."

She ignores my insolence. "You're not serious about Pollyanna, are you?"

"If you're referring to Madison, then yes, I'm very serious." I keep my back turned because the sight of her makes me sick.

"Dixon..."

The moment I feel her hand on my shoulder, I spin around and snarl, "Do *not* touch me."

She appears taken back by my hostility. "What the hell is the matter with you? There was a time when you actually enjoyed being with me. Enjoyed fucking me," she adds, running a sharp fingernail down my arm.

I feel as if she's slicing a knife through my flesh. I slap her hand off me. "I plead insanity for that period of my life."

Her face twists in confusion. "I must have been fucking nuts to touch you voluntarily." Watching her mouth drop, I add, "As interesting as this little catch-up has been, I have better things to do—like not look at you."

I butt out my smoke and attempt to shove past her, but she stops me. "You seem to be forgetting our little secret. A certain secret which could destroy your career." She smugly folds her arms across her busty chest, challenging me.

The action infuriates me further, and what little resolve I have left explodes. "You know what?" I lunge into her face. "Tell whoever you want." I spread my arms out wide. "I don't care anymore. I'd prefer that than being blackmailed into being your little gopher boy."

I've caught her completely off guard, and it's a sight to

celebrate. But my celebration is short-lived.

"I'll tell your precious *angelo*," she threatens, verbally shitting on my term of endearment.

I narrow my eyes. "Go ahead. Actually, you know what? I'll tell her. That option is far better than what you propose I do."

The frantic pounding of her carotid pulse reveals that she's either frightened or, God forbid, turned on by our exchange. "And what exactly is that?" she asks, licking her lips quickly.

"I have no fucking clue! Ten days ago, you cornered me, and you know what happens when you corner a rabid dog?" She shakes her head, her chest beginning to rise. "It bites."

Her hand flutters over her throat. "I'm quite accustomed to your biting, Dr. Mathews. I recall every single one."

Pinning her with my glare, I state, "Get out of my way before I act on impulse and drown you in that lake." I'm surprised when she calmly steps aside. But I don't waste any time getting away from her.

"Oh, by the way." Her self-righteous voice, however, stops me in my tracks. "Did you hear the good news?"

"You're moving to Africa?"

She disregards my snide remark. "Dylan will be moving in with me next weekend. I know it's sooner than everyone expected. Shall I ask sweet Madison to help us get settled?"

And there it is—the clincher. The one thing she'll always have over me.

Unluckily for me, she's the only person who can keep Maddy's bastard brother away from her, and she knows it. I couldn't give a damn about a tarnished reputation, but a tarnished Maddy—I'll do anything to stop that from happening.

I turn slowly, taking three deep breaths before I speak. "So help me God—if either of you touch her, I'll end you both."

Her lips tip up into a wicked grin. "I don't think you're in a position to be making any threats."

Charging over to her, I grip her upper arms. "That isn't a threat. It's a promise," I affirm, shaking her roughly.

My actions only stoke her depravity. "Ooh, I like it when you play rough."

"This isn't a joke. It's my life. It's *Maddy's* life you're fucking up because of some damn game you're playing." I can't help myself and squeeze her biceps harder, hoping she'll see reason.

But of course, she doesn't. "I'm playing the game you taught me."

I drop my hands, disgusted because she's right.

She taps her lip, cocking her head to the side. "You know, your devotion is really commendable, but I call bullshit. I think if I were to tell the innocent Maddy about your after-hours activities with your patients, she wouldn't be so eager to hop on the first plane with you to Rome. I think she'd drop your manwhore ass instantly. I also think, deep down, you do really care about your career. If the media or your colleagues got wind of this, you'd be ruined. Everything you've worked so hard for would be destroyed. We both know you won't tell Madison, Dixon. I call your bluff."

That…*bitch*.

"What do you want?" I grind out between clenched teeth, hating that she's right.

With an air of confidence, she states, "You know what I want."

Just her insinuation of what she has in mind turns my stomach. "Well, that's not going to happen, so what's option B?"

31

She scoffs, appearing annoyed that I'm still fighting her. "This isn't a game show. You play by my rules—otherwise, you lose."

How can she think I will ever come out the winner when she's got me by the balls? "I already lose if I participate in what you propose I do!"

She waves off my concerns with a sweep of her hand. "Oh, stop being such a crybaby. You've turned soft. But I know"—she strides forward and cups my dick—"how hard you can be."

Swallowing down my revulsion, I choose to be frank. "So what…if I fuck you and become your little bitch, you'll keep that psycho away from Maddy?" I try to breathe past the pain of her fondling my balls.

She nods as her massaging strokes get harder and harder—unlike my cock. "Yes, and not to mention your secret will remain under lock and key." She motions to her mouth while throwing away the invisible key. "No one has to know what a manwhore you really are. You can go on playing happy families with Little Bo Peep, and she'll be none the wiser that you're fucking for her freedom. And yours."

I couldn't give a rat's ass about my freedom. I'll happily pay for my sins if it means sparing Maddy the pain of ever seeing her brother again.

I know it'll shatter her. She's finally found a place she can call home. A place she feels safe, where she doesn't feel the need to lock her bedroom door at night. But if that maniac moves into her building, it'll drag up the past, and I know it'll ruin her.

But I *won't* be Juliet's personal blow-up doll, and I *will* figure out another way. No matter what, I refuse to be driven to sin by this woman, who only wants me because she can't have me.

This isn't about physical gratification. It's all about control.

So for now, I'll let her believe she's won. "Fine," I snarl, pulling out of her grip.

Juliet smiles a winner's grin. "Did I say Dylan was moving in next week? Silly me, these baby hormones are making my brain mush. I meant he was thinking about it, but I told him no. I mean, I wouldn't want to live in sin."

I can't help but laugh a bitter, sarcastic snicker. "It's a little too late for that." I drop my eyes to her belly.

She cups her swelling stomach proudly. "Well, technically it's *our* sin, not Dylan's. I'm trying to make amends for my past, to wipe the slate clean with my husband-to-be."

I run a hand through my snarled hair, yanking at the longer locks. "There aren't enough lifetimes for either of us to make amends, Juliet."

She purses her lips, appearing to digest my statement. "I suppose you're right." She steps forward and runs her pointer down my cheek. "In that case, pick me up Saturday morning."

I slap her hand away. Although I don't want to meet her anywhere, I can tell by her resolve that this isn't optional. "You do realize you live in the same apartment block as Maddy, right? That's not going to happen. If I'm to play along with this charade, then we'll do it my way."

"Fine then. You choose the location, and I'll do the rest."

Thinking of an area Madison rarely visits, I state, "Meet me *on the corner of Warren Street and West Broadway, Tribeca.*"

She happily nods. "I love it when you get all controlling. It shows me that underneath this boring, pussy-whipped exterior lies the man who fucked me until I forgot my own name."

I turn my head away, ashamed.

Juliet steps closer and I close my eyes, sickened by what she says next. "You need to find him again because that man is the *real* you, not this neutered little bitch she's turned you into. One way or another, I'm going to help find that man because deep down…we both know you'll like it. You're addicted to sin, Dixon. We both are."

Just as she raises her hand and attempts to stroke my cheek, I hear an uncertain voice behind me that tears out my heart.

"Is everything all right?"

I quickly latch onto Juliet's wrist and drop it by her side. She smirks.

"Yes, everything is fine." I pull my shit together and turn around to face a baffled Madison. Before she has a chance to question me again, I suggest, "Shall we go in?"

She looks lost, confused and angry but nods.

"I'll be right in," Juliet sing-songs smugly behind me. "I'm just going to call Dylan. He was going to drop by, but I'll tell him not to bother."

I close my eyes for the briefest of seconds but remain calm. Madison, on the other hand, looks weak at the knees at the mere mention of her brother. Wrapping my arm around her quivering shoulders, I lead her away from the scheming whore who is far smarter than I took her for. This deliberate ploy is to demonstrate who's calling the shots. How easily she can break everything I care for.

"Are you sure everything is o-okay?" Maddy asks in a small voice as we walk toward the house.

"Yes, everything is fine." I tighten my hold around her.

"What did Juliet want?"

My dick still hurts from her touch. "Nothing important.

Are you ready for dessert?" I ask, needing to scrub every trace of her off me.

She subtly shrugs out from my hold. "I've lost my appetite."

Before I can question if *she's* all right, she steps inside. I follow blindly a second later, taking my seat and engaging in small talk, but all I can focus on is what the hell I just agreed to.

Have I just sold my soul to the devil?

Three

Dixon

The next day, I'm irritated, impatient, and highly strung.

Thanks to basically being caught red-handed with Juliet, Madison asked me to take her home, complaining of a headache. I knew she was lying, but who am I to judge?

That's all I've been doing.

Contrary to what Juliet thinks, I am not addicted to sin. I'm no longer that man, thanks to Maddy.

Riddled with guilt, I reach for my cell.

How's the head?

It's a lame attempt, but I need to know she's still talking to me.

Fine. Her clipped response just told me to go fuck myself.

I need to fix this. **Let's do something fun this weekend.**

I'm thankful when she replies, *Like what?*

I don't know. You choose.

Spending Sat through to Sun with you sounds fun to me.

Usually, her reply would have me happier than a pig in shit, but now I feel like a complete asshole.

I can't Saturday morning, but Saturday evening and all day Sunday, I'm yours.

What's going on Sat morning?

I groan while typing out my bullshit reply. **Nothing important.**

I get a simple *Okay* in return.

I'm ruining my relationship, but I remind myself I'm doing this for Maddy.

I'll pick you up around 4? I'm still staring at my phone ten minutes later, awaiting her reply.

I thump my forehead against the desk just as Ms. Vale knocks on my door. "Dr. Mathews. I have the coffee and painkillers you asked for. Oh dear, are you all right?" she asks when she steps inside my office.

"Fine. Just leave it on my desk, Ms. Vale," I reply, not even bothering to raise my head. Her cautious footsteps reveal she's approaching me as she would a caged tiger. "Will there be anything else?" I ask when those footsteps aren't directing her back toward the door.

She clears her throat. "I, just…I'm sorry to pry, but are you okay?"

"Never been better."

She doesn't believe a word, but she doesn't press. "If you say so but…" She unexpectedly pauses. "You may want to change your shirt before Chad arrives." She then whispers, "You've got last week's tuna salad on the front right pocket."

"I was saving it for later," I reply, failing to disguise my disgust at my sloppy appearance. "Please reschedule my appointment to next week."

There is no way I can face Chad, looking and smelling the way I do. I have no idea what this meeting is about, but it can wait. My head isn't in the game, and I'd only end up fucking things up.

"Okay, Dr. Mathews. Your ten a.m. is waiting for you in reception."

It's only ten o'clock? Surely I've been here longer than an hour.

Finally raising my head, I meet her concerned gaze. "Who is it?"

By her poor attempt at masking her smile, I know it's bad. "Paul Childs."

Groaning, I drop my head back down onto my desk. "Great.

Please bring in the Febreze once we're done."

"Of course. I'll give you a couple of minutes before I send him in." The door closes, announcing her departure.

I raise my head, but slump back down a few moments later when Paul strolls into my office, sucking on a pacifier and appearing to be wearing an adult diaper underneath his slacks.

Today can blow me.

When Finch asked to meet tonight instead of our usual Friday night, I was more than happy to oblige. It beats drinking alone, which I've been doing since this whole fiasco started.

"Holy shit! What's your new cologne? Eau de dog shit?"

"Hello to you too, Hunter." I finish my sentence by flipping him off.

"It's not my fault you smell like a Tijuana hooker's cooch on a Sunday morning."

Choosing to talk to the adult, I turn to Finch. "Hey, man, how's the family?"

"They're good, Dix. Gabriella just took her first step," he replies, unable to wipe the smile from his face.

"That's awesome. You must be so proud." I motion to our regular server that I'll have my usual. Scotch. Neat.

Hunter, as usual, ruins our pleasantries. "Yeah, unlike you, Dix, Gabriella is actually standing on her own two feet."

I look down the bar, wondering where my damn scotch is. But of course he gets into my line of vision.

I finally cave. "What's that supposed to mean?"

"It means"—he tips his Budweiser my way—"you need to

grow some balls and tell that cunt to fuck off and die."

Finch splutters up his Coke. I'm convinced Hunter was a poet in his former life.

"It's not that simple. I've explained to you why I can't do that," I grumble, beginning to get sick of my own voice.

He stubbornly shakes his head. "No, all you've done is given me lame-ass excuses," he refutes. "Cherry Pie will understand that—" I find it amusing that Hunter still refers to Madison this way. The nickname came about when in true Hunter fashion he decided to give a ridiculous, yet frightening accurate analogy which somehow compared my relationship woes to food.

"That what?" I interrupt. "That before I met her I was fucking anything that moved? And that anything included my patients, and oh yeah, her diabolical stepsister, who just may be carrying my child."

"Maybe you could lead in with something a little more subtle?" he suggests, scratching over his stubble.

"Like?" I ask, waiting for his ingenious speech.

He shrugs. "Like, I dunno, 'Hey, Honey Cakes, did you cut your hair? No? Well, whatever you did, you look so pretty, and wow, you look so beautiful today. By the way, love your shoes.'"

I can't help but laugh at his foolishness. "That's not going to cut it."

"Why not? Girls love that shit," he claims, sipping his beer.

"Maddy isn't just any girl. She'll call me out on my bullshit. I'm certain she already knows something is up."

Hunter blows out a loud breath and nods. "True. That's why you need to tell her."

I run a hand down my face.

Hunter is right. I know I need to tell her, but I'm not

prepared to lose her. And I know that'll happen if I tell her the truth. Yesterday, I told Juliet I would tell Madison myself, but if push came to shove, would I? She's right. She did call my bluff. I'm stuck between a rock and a horny woman. And I hate it.

"What do you think, Finch?" He's been awfully quiet, which usually means he's thinking.

He taps the rim of his glass. "Bad language aside, I agree with Hunter for once."

Hunter fist-pumps a loud, "Hell yeah," and adds, "Can I have that in writing?"

Once again, I ignore Hunter's theatrics. "You think I should tell her?"

"I think you should tell them *both*," Finch replies wisely.

I pull a pained face, not liking that option in the slightest.

"I know you're trying to be honorable, Dix, but there is nothing honorable about that woman. She says she won't tell anyone your secrets, but do you actually believe her? I mean, she doesn't have a very good track record."

"Not to mention her pussy would eat you for breakfast," Hunter pipes in, trying to be helpful. But he's not. Both Finch and I turn to look at him, revolted.

He raises his hands. "What? I'm just saying…"

"Well, stop saying…anything," I retort playfully.

He humphs and sinks low, nursing his beer.

"So you don't think she'll stick to her word?"

His incredulous look explains it all. "I'm sorry, but you're better off telling Maddy and dealing with the consequences than tiptoeing around a ticking time bomb. I mean, she's blackmailing you into having sex with her. That right there is your answer."

I sigh, hating that he's right.

Hunter chooses this moment to intervene. "You must have been some fuck, dude. Most of the girls I've slept with would rather abstain from sex forever than blackmail me into sleeping with them ever again."

I roll my eyes. "This has nothing to do with sex. It has to do with power."

"Well, in that case, why don't you use your psychobabble bullshit and hypnotize her to stop wanting your cock?"

"I'm not a hypnotist, you moron. But you do have a point. I guess I could offer her some therapy sessions, considering that's the reason she came to see me in the first place. I could try to work out what makes her tick. And then I could persuade her to un-tick off my dick."

Hunter nods, looking awfully pleased with himself. "My thoughts exactly. And don't say I never do anything for you."

I rub my chin in thought because this might work. The only downfall would be that I would have to get inside her head, a place I would rather not be. Not to mention, I have a feeling a lot of sessions would be needed to figure out what the fuck is wrong with this messed-up woman. All of this equates to too much alone time with her.

Finch sees my dilemma and states, "Just be honest, Dix. The right thing to do is to tell Madison the truth."

I down my scotch the moment it's placed in front of me. Finch is right, but I know if I do tell her the truth and nothing but the truth, I'll lose her forever.

My pocket vibrates, indicating I have a text. Reaching in, I hold my breath, hoping it's not Juliet. I let out the breath when it's Madison.

I figured out something fun to do on Sat.

To say I'm relieved she's talking to me is an understatement.
Oh yeah?

Yup. I wanna go dancing.

Dancing? Like ballroom ;)

LOL! No, you old fart. Let's go to Cherry Pop.

Memories of when I saw her there last flood my brain, and I instantly type out an **Okay, sounds good.**

Mary wants to tag along. Is that okay?

Of course. I look at Hunter and grin. **I'll bring Hunter.**

We're in for an interesting night

We sure are.

"So," I say, looking at Hunter as I place my cell back into my pocket. "Are you back on the 'women are all evil' wagon?"

He takes a long sip of beer before replying. "I never got off."

I raise an eyebrow, and he smirks. "Oh no, I've gotten off, but for the life of me, I can't remember their names or faces."

There was a time when he was preaching to the choir.

"Great. In that case, you can continue with the hating on Saturday."

"What's Saturday?" he inquires, appearing suspicious.

Motioning to the bartender for another scotch, I reply, "We're going to Cherry Pop."

He pulls a puzzled face. "And why would you want to go there? I'd have thought you'd much prefer getting kicked in the balls…repeatedly…over going there again."

"Seeing Maddy on that dance floor is worth the pain," I reveal. Images of her hot, sweaty body have me reaching down and adjusting the dancing currently going on in my pants.

And just like that, Hunter ruins my fantasy. "And where do I fit in with all of this? You want to see me bust a move on the dance floor, too?"

"No, you idiot. Her friend is coming, so I thought you could keep her entertained."

He rubs his hands together wickedly. "Is her friend hot?"

I laugh when thinking about the fiery redhead. "Yeah, she's hot in a crazy, kind of psychotic way."

Hunter looks like he's just won the horny male's version of Lotto. "Sounds like my kind of woman."

Unable to hide my grin, I reply, "Good luck with that."

"Challenge accepted, Dr. Mathews."

He has no idea what he's in for.

"Now back to the issue at hand. What are you going to do about the harlot?"

I groan. What a way to ruin my mood. "I don't know." When Finch shakes his head, I add, "I know what I should do, but I'm—"

"A pussy," Hunter finishes for me.

Seeing no point in denying it, I nod. "Yeah, man. That's exactly what I am."

Talking to these guys has just affirmed what I know I have to do. I know the consequences won't be pretty, but I have to be a man and tell them both.

"I'll tell Juliet Saturday," I reveal, meaning every single word.

Hunter chokes on his drink. "She's coming Saturday? Don't you think that'll be a little awkward?"

"Yes, Hunter, that would be a lot awkward. I've agreed to meet Juliet Saturday morning," I clarify, still puzzled about why she's requested this meeting.

"Why?" both Finch and Hunter bark.

"I have no idea why. But you're right." I look over at Hunter, who widens both eyes.

"Can I get that in writing also?"

Ignoring him, I firmly proclaim, "It's time I tell that cunt to fuck off and die." I raise my glass and throw back my scotch, the celebratory burn tasting of victory. A taste I've so missed.

Four

Dixon

I feel like a complete impostor hidden behind my dark shades, torn jeans, and Yankees sweater. But I blend in with every tourist in New York, which is exactly what I want.

I still have no idea what I'm doing here, which is a dangerous thing when it comes to Juliet. I've learned the hard way to expect the unexpected, so it's safe to say my guards are in place and I'm not in any mood to put up with her bullshit a second longer. I meant what I said. This little game of hers stops, and it stops today.

"Good morning, Dr. Mathews." Her voice makes me shrink away in aversion.

"There is nothing good about this morning. What do you want, Juliet?" I turn around to face her.

She has the gall to smirk. "You know, there was a time when our mornings were very good."

"That was a long time ago."

"Not that long ago," she rebukes, thankfully keeping her distance.

"What are we doing here?" I ask, choosing to ignore her trip down misery lane.

"You'll see." She turns on her heels and saunters down the street, expecting me to follow.

I'm faced with two options. I can turn the other way and tell her to shove it, or I can follow. The masochist in me chooses the latter.

Keeping my distance, I stroll behind with my head dropped low, as I'm afraid of whom I might see. I don't know what it is, but she has a true, regal bearing about her and even the rudest of New Yorkers step aside to make room for her. It could be most of them are checking out her fuller tits thanks to the seed of evil fermenting in her stomach. Whatever it is, they all need their heads checked—mine included.

"Here we are," she declares, stopping in front of a shoe store.

I look up and scowl. "I draw the line at being your foot model."

She laughs softly. "No, silly." Before I have a chance to step away, she turns my cheek to the left. This time, I fucking scowl when I read the store name.

Babylicious.

"I am *not* going in there," I spit out, removing her hand from my face.

She looks genuinely hurt by my refusal. "Why not? I thought you'd want to be a part of this."

"Well, you thought wrong. Very wrong," I add, shaking my head animatedly. She wanted to meet up so we could go shopping for *baby clothes*? Is she fucking nuts? Looking at my current predicament, I know the answer is hell yes.

If this isn't mixed signals, then I don't know what is. First, she claims she only wants me to fuck her. And now, she wants me to play Daddy to her child? I have no idea what she wants.

"Dixon, this baby *is* your child." She cups her tiny bump while I feel bile rising.

"How do I know that?" I question, feeling my cool slowly eroding away. "Quite frankly, I have my doubts that you even know who the father is."

She steps back, appearing hurt by my claims. "Regardless of what you think of me, I *was* faithful to you. Unlike you, I never cheated."

I scoff, as now I've heard it all. "Cheated would imply we were in a relationship. We never were. We were fucking. That's all." I don't know how many times or ways I can tell her this before it sinks in because it obviously hasn't worked thus far.

"Keep telling yourself that," she smugly replies, folding her arms across her chest. "Yes, I've been seeing Dylan on and off—" Just the mention of his name has me gnashing my teeth in rage. "But the entire time I was with you, I was with *you*, and you only. You can deny it all you want, but it is your baby whether you like it or not."

"Or not."

Her little speech has not softened me in the slightest, but I can't deny that a small part of me believes her. This is the first time since this ordeal started that I actually believe she's telling me the truth.

Well…fuck.

I've never given much thought to being a father. I mean, how could I? What kind of role model would I be?

"You need to abort this abomination immediately," I declare, realizing this is the only humane future I could ever offer this child.

"What?" Her hands flutter over her stomach protectively. "But it's our child."

"It's a monster!" I rebuke angrily, not bothering to camouflage my tone. The best thing about New York is that New Yorkers don't care what's happening around them. "Why the fuck are you doing this? What do you want from me?"

"I want *you*. I always have," she replies, taking a step toward me. Appearing the sincerest that I've ever seen her, she confesses, "Is it such a crime that I...love you? I want to be normal. And I want that normalcy with you."

I actually choke on her admission.

She loves me? Since when? She doesn't know the first thing about love, and quite frankly, I call bullshit. This is just her way of manipulating me into doing what she wants. She wants every male in her life begging at her feet, worshiping the ground she walks on. To get my, Dylan's, her father's, and God knows who else's affection makes her feel like she's in total control. We're all just pawns in her narcissist game, fueling her need to be loved, and to be loved by all.

Slipping off my sunglasses, I glare at her. "I think I've made my feelings for you perfectly clear."

Her genuine mask slips and in its place, lies the real Juliet Harte I know. "Have you forgotten I could break you?" Her face contorts evilly.

I snicker, powerless to hold back my spite. "And that right there proves that you don't love me. A person who's supposed to love someone doesn't blackmail them. I'm done."

49

"You're what?" she asks, her tone heated.

"I won't do this, Juliet. I don't care what secrets of mine you hold, I refuse to be blackmailed this way. Whatever choice I make I lose, but at least my loss will be by my own hand, and not yours."

I've caught her completely off guard and, just as I did with hers, she reads my words as complete truth. "You'd really jeopardize everything—your career, your reputation, your precious Maddy?"

I smirk with conviction. "Yes." Closing the gap between us, I snarl, "I'd rather fuck up my life...than fuck you." Her mouth hinges open—a sight I'll forever celebrate.

"I *hate* her. She has taken *everything* from me," she maliciously professes a second later.

So I was right. This entire situation has got to do with power, but power over Madison rather than me. I'm just a means to an end. How...interesting.

Juliet's comment comes back to haunt me. "*I'm always second best,*" I remember her saying the night of her bogus engagement party. "*I'm never good enough for anyone, and I'm sick of being runner-up. I'm especially sick of being runner-up to her.*"

What did Maddy ever do to her?

Hunter's words suddenly come to mind. I could offer her therapy, putting an end to this nightmare. But what will I lose in the process? A piece of my soul, no doubt.

I need to get out of here.

Slipping my shades back on, I turn to leave.

"I'll tell her everything."

Juliet's desperation is apparent, but quite frankly, I'm done caring. She can go to hell. "Not if I tell her first."

Five

Madison

"What's wrong with it?" I ask, tugging at the short hem of my black dress.

Mary kicks her legs in the air as she flips through *Cosmo*. Glancing up briefly, she shrugs. "You look like you should be charging by the hour."

"Lamb!" I almost choke on her honesty.

"What? You asked." She continues flipping through the magazine, not at all bothered that her mouth filter is nonexistent today.

Turning toward my cupboard, I sigh at what's left standing, or hanging. The selection is measly and doesn't scream "devour me," which is what I want.

For the past two weeks, Dixon hasn't been himself. Although I don't know what's wrong, I do know *who's* wrong.

Beth.

Ever since they met, Dixon has been distant, distracted,

and detached. He tells me nothing is wrong, but I don't believe him. I know Beth is the cause of whatever is troubling him, but I just don't know why.

"Would you stop obsessing over this? He's stupidly crazy about you, Maddy," Mary wisely says, obviously reading my internal dilemma.

"I can't help it. I've got this sinking feeling in the pit of my stomach." I rub my hand over my somersaulting belly.

"That's called hormones."

I spin around, grinning. "Not funny."

She innocently shrugs. "I wasn't trying to be funny."

She's part right. I never thought I'd feel this way, but I actually miss the physical connection between Dixon and I. It's like being cut off after having a first taste—a very addictive taste.

My insecurities are once again plaguing my sanity and I can't help but conjure up reasons Dixon won't touch me. At the forefront is, now that he's met Beth, does he feel like he's dating the wrong sister?

I'll never be like her. I'll never have her confidence. Or her sexual prowess. And I'm afraid now that he's met her, he wants that and not me. That's what has me stepping out of my comfort zone and attempting to look like someone other than myself.

"So tonight should be fun, right?"

Mary's comment snaps me from my thoughts and I smile. "It'll be great." Grateful for the derailment, I tease, "I can't wait for you to meet Debbie. I mean Hunter." I can't help but smile at his porn inspired nickname.

She rolls her eyes, not at all excited. "With a name like Hunter, he's bound to be a dumbass."

I bite my lip to stifle my laugh. "This night needs tequila and tequila."

She happily shoots up and heads for the kitchen, and for once, I don't stop her.

I texted Dixon and told him Mary and I would meet him at Cherry Pop as I wanted to have a few cocktails before I met him in *this* outfit.

Regardless of Mary calling me a hooker, I decided to wear my little black dress, which is more little than dress. But I wanted to show Dixon that I too can be a little bad. Not Beth bad, but bad enough to hopefully have him touching me again.

I remember when I saw Dixon here after our three-month separation. His feral look of possession and longing is one I'm hoping to elicit from him tonight.

"Drink!" I shout over Beyoncé, before bringing the shot to my lips and throwing it back before Mary has a chance to tell me to slow down.

I know that I should as I'm way past drunk, but each hit gives me the confidence I so need.

Slamming the shot glass down onto the bar, I wipe my mouth with the back of my hand, probably smearing my red lipstick in the process.

"Maddy, how about we get you some water?" Mary flags down the bartender.

I have other ideas, however. "How about we get you some water and me another tequila?" I suggest, pointing at the three blurry Marys.

"I've forgotten how adorable you are when you're drunk. It's not a sight I see often."

"Me either," I say, hiccupping. I slap my hand over my mouth while Mary giggles.

"Oh my God! It's my song," I scream when 'Telephone' by Lady Gaga comes blaring over the speakers.

Latching onto Mary's wrist, I drag her to the dance floor and push aside anyone who stands in our way. When we find our own little dancing oasis, we both let the music take over and begin moving to the upbeat tempo. Closing my eyes, I get lost in the lyrics and feel a sisterhood to the verse of leaving my head and my heart on the dance floor.

I dance like no one is watching but Dixon. Every sashay of the hips, flick of my hair, and wriggle of my butt is for him. Continuing my risky moves, I don't sense someone brush up near me until I feel foreign fingers wrap around my waist. My eyes snap open and I instantly dance out of his hold because his closeness brings on a bout of panic. Mary is dancing with some Latino Swayze a few feet away, so I can't flag her down.

I can only handle this type of closeness from Dixon because I know he'll never hurt me, but the feral look in this stranger's eyes reveals he's jacked up on way too much booze and probably party favors to think straight.

When he makes an attempt to grab me once again, my demons, ones I have tried so hard to control through therapy, come roaring to the surface and I feel myself shutting down. I squeeze my eyes shut. It's my fault. What did I expect from wearing this dress and dancing so suggestively? Mary was right. No wonder my brother did…it's my fault.

Just as the walls start closing in, my lifeline, my savior

comes to the rescue and makes everything all right again.

"Madison!"

Focusing on my light, my eyes pop open, and I run into the safety of Dixon's arms. "Are you okay?" The fear, anger, and relief are reflected in his deep voice.

Too shaken up to reply, I nod, burying my face in the crook of his neck.

The loud music drowns out most of his exchange with the man I'm presume is my groper, but the words "If you fucking touch her again, I'll skin you alive and feed you to my dog," can be clearly heard.

When he begins moving, guiding me off the dance floor, I follow, trusting him completely. His rigidity reveals he's livid. I know the only thing restraining him from going back out there and beating the guy to a bloody pulp is me. He knows I'll break without him.

He's become my world, and that scares the living hell out of me.

"Are you sure you're okay?" Dixon asks, stopping abruptly and pulling me away at arm's length.

Now that I'm not blinded by fear, I appreciate how epic he looks in dark, fitted blue jeans, a chic, high-collared, button-down navy sweater vest, which he's pulled the sleeves up on, exposing his taut forearms. Underneath, he sports a light gray, soft woven T-shirt with the top button undone, and on his feet are black boots.

"Yes, I'm fine," I affirm when I can speak without drooling.

He narrows those beautiful blue eyes and runs a hand through his tousled hair.

"I promise," I add, stepping forward and snuggling back

into his warm embrace. I'm thankful when he cuddles me back, and I feel his shoulders drop—an inch.

"Where are Mary and Hunter?" I ask after calming down my racing pulse.

His chest rumbles as he replies, "I asked Hunter to take her to the bar as she was seconds away from murdering that punk. And that motherfucker was mine."

Pulling out of his arms, I latch onto his muscled forearm as I'm afraid he'll go back out there and give him more than an earful.

"I'm sorry. I shouldn't have drunk so much. It's my fault." Feelings of shame overwhelm me, and I lower my gaze to the floor, embarrassed.

"Hey." He places his finger under my chin, coaxing me to look at him. "Some asshole pawing you against your will isn't your fault."

I nod, mewling when he strokes his thumb over my lower lip.

"But while we're on the subject of drinking, did something happen? I mean, you hardly drink. Is everything okay?" His intelligent gaze scans every plane of my face; it appears he's trying to decode a secret I'm not privy to.

"Yes, everything is okay." *Well, apart from my vivid imagination dreaming up every possible scenario to explain your detachment*, I silently add.

"Okay. As long as you're sure." He seems relieved by my response.

He guides me into a booth, making sure to keep his arm around me. As I'm looking around for Mary, Dixon randomly asks, "So you didn't talk to anyone today, did you?"

I raise a confused brow as I turn to look at him.

"You know. Your mom? Or maybe Juliet?" he clarifies. Her name passing through his lips is like a sharp dagger piercing my side.

Why is he asking about her? And more importantly, why would it matter if I had spoken to her? "No, I haven't spoken to either. Why?"

His shoulders instantly depress. "No reason."

When I continue staring at him, he explains, "I just know how much you loathe her, and I wondered if she was the cause of your need to drink, dance, and dress"—his eyes blaze as he scans down my body—"so boldly."

His heated gaze pushes thoughts of Beth aside. He has me feeling even more exposed than I already feel. "Do you like my dress?" I ask, hoping my nerves don't betray me.

When he tilts his head to the side and slowly traces his upper lip with his tongue, my nerves are swiftly replaced with the need to kiss him until I can no longer breathe. Sadly, all daydreams are put on hold.

"Do you realize how stupid you sound when you open your mouth?" snaps Mary as she charges into the booth.

I look up to see Hunter trailing behind, a mischievous smile on his face. "You could always open your mouth then. I've got just the thing to fill it with wisdom."

Dixon raises his eyes to the ceiling while Mary scoffs, "Not in this lifetime, you disgusting pig."

The corner of Dixon's mouth curves in humor when he hears her response. "Good to see you two getting along so famously," he teases, while I can't help but smile.

"Don't be so quick to tease, Doc. I should be chewing your

ass out, seeing as you left me alone with this pervert," Mary warns, her tone revealing he's next in line for her wrath.

I burst out laughing when Dixon quickly cups his privates.

"Oookay, how about we get something to drink?" I suggest, still chuckling as I loop my arm around Mary's shoulder.

Mary nods eagerly. "Anything to erase the past five minutes of my life sounds good to me." She launches out of the booth and stomps in the direction of the bar. In the process, she nudges a smirking Hunter out of the way.

With nothing but worship in his eyes, he declares, "I think she likes me." He then looks over his shoulder, playfully biting his knuckle.

I can't help but grin at his humor.

"I think you're sorely mistaken, my friend," Dixon rebukes, shaking his head as we exit the booth.

We all head for the bar, and I'm surprised to see Hunter dart ahead, desperate to catch up to Mary.

"I think he likes her," Dixon says into my ear as he wraps an arm low on my waist, guiding me through the crowd.

My senses are titillated by the contact. "Well, I know for a fact she doesn't like him," I reply, shivering harder when he chuckles into my ear.

Hunter squeezes between people and smiles victoriously when he stands by Mary's side in line.

He turns over his shoulder and motions to Dixon if he wants a drink. He nods in response. When Hunter glances at me, I wave a no. I've had enough alcohol for the night.

We move and stand off to the side. "The answer to your question is yes." His breath is warm on my neck as he leans in close.

"W-what question?" I stutter, forgetting everything but the way he makes me feel.

"The one you asked me earlier. I do like your dress. I like it a lot," he adds, his hand slipping low and coming to rest lightly on my behind.

I take three deep, calming breaths before replying. "Oh. That question. Thank you."

"No, thank you. Although, you know you could wear anything, and you'd still look like a goddess." His husky voice is heavy with desire.

When he begins to slowly palm my right butt cheek, the fire within begins raging out of control. "I wanted to look different," I confess, deciding to address the issue plaguing me for the past couple of weeks.

"Why? You're the perfect the way you are."

But that's the problem. I don't want to be perfect. I don't want him to treat me like I'll break. I want him to devour and destroy me until I'm begging for more.

"I just…I thought maybe if I looked different, if I looked a little more provocative like…I dunno, like Juliet…" I finally find my lady balls and say it "…that you'd want to maybe…" And just like that, my lady balls shrivel up and go into hiding.

"Maybe what?" he asks, his hand stilling.

I raise my shoulders, focusing on my stilettos. "That you'd maybe…want me more."

"*What?*" The shock is apparent in his tone as he draws out the W. "Why would you think that, Madison?"

I shrug once again, suddenly feeling incredibly stupid for the overshare.

He swiftly spins me by the shoulders to face him. "Look at

me," he demands.

I do.

"You are the only person I want. Juliet..." When he grimaces painfully, I begin to doubt my theory. "Is most definitely *not* the person I want. I want nothing to do with her, and for you to think that you need to look more like her to gain my affections..." he pauses, looking away briefly before angrily concluding "...is ludicrous. She is the epitome of who I do *not* want. Ever. But you..." He tenderly cups my cheek. "You are exactly who I want. Who I choose to be with."

His words are what I needed to hear, but it's *her*, it's Beth and her fascination with Dixon that troubles me. "I think she likes you, Dixon," I confess, feeling my lower lip tremble.

He pulls away, disgusted and infuriated. "There isn't enough scotch in this world to help process that appalling accusation." He works his mouth open and shut as if tasting something bad.

"I know her and, like I once told you, she's toxic. I don't trust her and I especially don't trust her around you."

Pinning me with his stare, he declares, "You have absolutely nothing to worry about. I don't plan on being around her ever again." I believe him, but I can't help but dwell on his strange behavior. If it's not Beth, then...is it me? Is my past too much?

With whatever courage I have left, I press, "But you've been so distant. You've hardly touched me." I avert my gaze, embarrassed to be sharing my fears. "I thought..." But he doesn't let me finish.

His grip is unyielding as he wraps his long fingers around my wrist and drags me through the sea of people. I can barely keep up with him and protest by securing my fingers over his to signal him to stop, but he doesn't.

He hauls me down a long, dark hallway. The farther we descend, the seedier it becomes. It's filled with amorous couples groping each other passionately while using the walls as their makeshift pleasure posts. I attempt to turn away, but just as I twist to the left, I get another eyeful of way too much skin and tongue.

"Dixon, where are we going?" I object, but it's useless as the loud music drowns out my complaint.

Just as I'm about to protest once again, he opens the last door on the right and shoves me inside. As I gather my bearings, I pull out of his hold while my eyes adjust to the dim lighting. Looking around, I see that we're in a small, private function room. Red velvet couches are scattered along the wall, and a circular bar sits in the corner of the room. I get the vibe that this room is used for private dances of the lap kind.

"What…" But my question is drowned out by the door slamming shut behind me and the unmistakable sound of a lock clicking into place.

I spin around and see Dixon pressed against the door, watching me with a look I've so missed. "Tell me what you want," he demands, not bothering to mask his dominance.

"I-I…" I fumble, suddenly lost for words.

"Now is not the time to be bashful. Tell me." He pushes off the door, a look of untamed possession in his eyes.

I back away, afraid of what I've started.

"What do you want, *angelo*? Tell me," he presses, making it clear he won't stop until I enlighten him.

Stepping up to the plate, I shyly confess, "I won't break, Dixon. I want you to touch me. I want you to forget my past and touch me the way I know you want to."

My words appear to have slapped him. "Your past has nothing to do with this."

I stop backing away and stand my ground. "Then what? If it's not Juliet or my past, why won't you touch me?"

He grits his teeth together. "I want to touch you. So bad." His clenched fists support his claim.

"Then why? I don't understand."

He stops stalking toward me and heatedly runs a hand through his hair. "I don't want to push you if you're not ready."

He's right. I'm not ready for sex, but the other stuff, I'm ready for. I was ready the first time I felt him worship me in a way no one has ever done before. My cheeks heat at the memory and the feral growl which erupts from Dixon reveals he remembers, too.

Without a word, he saunters over to a red settee and takes a seat, his legs spread wide. After a painful few moments of silence, he beckons me with a menacing finger. I don't hesitate. I walk toward him, my heels clicking loudly, reflecting my pounding heart. I only stop when I'm standing inches away, not bothering to mask my rapid breathing because my heaving chest betrays my aroused state.

"Are you wearing anything underneath that little dress of yours?" Dixon asks, casually leaning back and resting his arms across of the top of the settee.

"Just my underwear," I reply timidly.

He coolly nods. "Take them off."

"W-what?"

The corner of his mouth pulls up into a smug grin. "You heard me. This is what you wanted, right?"

He's right. I did ask for this and I would look like a total hypocrite if I backed out now.

Before I can chicken out, I reach underneath my dress as discreetly as I can without flashing him and shimmy my black lace thong down my legs. I step out of it and secure it in my trembling hand.

Dixon extends his palm and I place it into it.

I look on a little mortified, but mostly a lot turned on as he draws them up to his nose. "You smell delicious, Madison. I want a taste."

Before I can voice my approval, he slips the thong into his back pocket and adjusts himself so he's lying down. He places his head on the armrest. I swallow when I see the huge bulge tenting the front of his jeans. "Get on."

"What?" I ask, not understanding.

Our gazes tango in a dance orchestrated for us alone when he slowly turns his head to look at me. "You heard me. Get that sweet pussy on my face."

I gulp. His words are exactly what I want.

"But if you don't want to…" he playfully says when he sees me hesitate.

"No, I do," I interject quickly when he attempts to sit back up. "I just don't know how." I feel foolish, but I don't know how I'll stay on without falling off.

"I've got you, *angelo*," he affirms assertively. His confidence overrides my fear, so I step out of my heels before walking over.

"That's it." He settles back down and extends his hand out, which I gingerly take. He guides me onto him, but encourages me to slide up farther until I'm hovering above his face, my knees on either side of his head.

He hums as he looks up, getting a full-frontal view. "I

could look at this view all day." With a leisurely slow speed, he slides up the short hem of my dress until it bunches up just underneath my belly button.

I'm totally bare, and I'm wicked because I like it.

With both hands, he scores his short fingernails up and down the outside of my thighs. "Lean forward and hold the wall," he instructs.

I do as he says.

My hips are still suspended above his face, as I'm afraid I'll suffocate him if I lower myself onto him.

But Dixon won't allow my fears to overshadow this moment. "C'mon, Maddy." He slides his hands up and secures a firm hold around my waist. "Don't tease me." His warm breath bathes my swollen center, and I finally cave, unable to take it any longer.

With shaky legs, I lower myself slowly, but Dixon unexpectedly tightens his hold around me and forces my hips down. With no other choice, I slam onto his face. A loud gust of wind escapes him, and I instantly try to wiggle off, afraid I've hurt him. But he fastens his hold and fixes me even tighter around him. With encouraging fingers, he then guides me to move my hips. And I do.

My movements are cautious and paced at first, but unable to fight against Dixon coaxing me to move faster and faster, I give in. I rock my body while slamming my palms onto the brick wall to anchor myself, all while Dixon licks, sucks, and…fucks me with that skillful, wicked tongue. The deeper he delves, the faster I move, and before long, I'm riding and bouncing on his face, desperately galloping to the finish line.

His longish whiskers add to the pleasure, and a bittersweet pain begins building in my core. The room is soaked with animalistic groans, and the raw smell of desire leaves me panting and wanting more...more...more. My eyes are squeezed shut, and being blind, relying on my other senses, is an unbelievable aphrodisiac. The feeling of trusting another person this primitively has me letting loose and crying out in need and relief.

I want to slow down, afraid I'm grinding too hard, but Dixon's fingers clasp my flesh so firmly, directing the speed and friction of my movement, I can't stop.

"Ahhh!" I whimper, my insides beginning to unravel. My unrefined sounds seem to spur Dixon on, and he continues lapping at me, sucking me dry.

The impassioned sounds coming from him are music to my ears, but I want so badly to reach around and give him the same pleasure he's giving me. I push a hand off the wall and attempt to reach behind me, but Dixon's palm snaps out and secures my wrist. His simple action has just told me that this right here is all for me. When he lets go and devours me with such intense ferocity, I'm powerless to do anything but ride this moment out, so I do.

Dixon's hot mouth sears my flesh, and as he secures my ass cheeks in a tight hold, spreading me wide, I scream in utter bliss. He takes advantage of my generous exposure and buries his face even further into me. Suddenly I lift my hips, feeling like a total vixen as I tease him and pull out of his reach. Looking down, I see his lips are coated with my arousal, which complements the feral, possessive look in his eyes.

"Get back on," he commands. But when I hesitate, he unexpectedly brings his palm down, spanking me firmly on the behind.

I yelp in shock, but that shock soon turns to brazen lust. "Don't make me repeat myself, Maddy," he warns, attempting to force me back down. I use my core muscles to resist.

"And what if I don't?" I have no idea where this burst of confidence came from, but I roll with it and reach down to lightly rub over my aching clit. His hungry eyes follow the movement and the look electrifies me beyond belief.

Just as I'm about to dig in deeper, his hand comes down, and he slaps me harder. This time on the other ass cheek. "Mine," he growls before arching his neck and looping his arms around my shaky upper thighs. When he sucks on my cleft in one long, hard passionate pull, I know he's won, and I slam back down on his face.

He eats me out so vigorously that it brings tears to my eyes. He slaps his tongue against my core, akin to how he spanked my ass. The memory has me shouting uncontrollably and letting go of all my reservations. With no other choice, I chase out my impending release loudly. Nothing has ever felt sweeter.

This is what I've craved. What I've needed. No one can make me feel this way. No one.

It feels like I'm floating, sated and content for minutes, but when I remember where I am, I raise my hips, mortified that I've smothered Dixon to death.

When I look down, I'm greeted with a satisfied grin. "We need to do that again."

I redden and look away, suddenly embarrassed that I'm straddling his face. However, I'm beyond mortified when I see his satisfied grin is now slathered thickly with my arousal.

"You really do blush pink all over," Dixon coolly says while I feel my face set alight.

Thankfully, he shuffles down and sits, allowing my tender knees the reprieve of moving as I attempt to gracefully get down from my perch. I pull down my dress before falling back against the cushions, attempting to catch my breath.

"You're beautiful."

I turn to look at Dixon and smile. "Thank you."

His hair is a tangled mess, and I have the urge to run my fingers through the soft strands. So I do.

His eyes slip shut, and a low hum rumbles from his throat. The look of absolute bliss on his face reveals what an idiot I've been. To question Dixon's feelings for me was just my insecurity, my fear clouding what I know to be true. I know that he cares for me, and I also know my past doesn't make a difference to him. Maybe he really has been stressed at work, and I've been reading things into it that aren't there.

Things like Beth.

"I'm sorry."

"Sorry?" he asks, his eyes popping open. "Whatever for?"

"For being a crybaby," I reply, toying with his locks.

He leans down and kisses my forehead. "Shall we go home?"

Nodding, I unexpectedly feel the excessive alcohol rattle my brain.

Dixon must be able to read my sudden queasiness because he chuckles. "I say we go for a run tomorrow morning."

I groan, burying myself into the sofa. "I say no."

"It's not optional. And besides, you'll thank me in the morning." He rises with a smile.

"How?"

"Wouldn't you rather run off your hangover than throw it up?"

I blanch because he's right. "Fine, you win."

He leans in, imprisoning me as he rests his hands on either side of my head. "You should know by now that I always win." His eyes rake down my body, lingering on my heaving chest.

"Not always." I swallow hard.

He licks his top lip. "I win where it's important." Leaning in even closer, he adds, "The underwear currently sitting in my back pocket is a confirmation of that."

My tongue weighs a thousand pounds, so I simply nod.

His husky laughter has my pulse speeding up to an unhealthy staccato. What is this man doing to me?

As he slowly closes the distance between us and kisses me tenderly, I know what. And that *what* scares me half to death.

Six

Dixon

L ooking down at my upright cock, I sigh, cursing the infernal thing.

"Fuck you, man. Fuck you and the day I allowed you to control my life."

My teeth chatter as I attempt to freeze out my hard-on in my ritualistic morning ice-cold shower. Today is worse than ever, seeing as Madison is lying in my bed with nothing but my Einstein T-shirt on.

Every time she got too close and attempted to wrap that hot, supple body around me, I subtly shifted away until I was practically lying on the edge of the mattress. I was afraid I didn't have the strength to stop myself from giving in to my desperate desire of fucking her senseless. And I refuse to do that because she deserves better. She deserves flowers and candles and all of that romantic shit. But truth be told, I can't take away something so pure without telling her of my sins.

The thought of my sins has my dick retreating and leaving me with a serious case of blue balls, which is the story of my life lately.

I finish up showering and dress in my running gear. I don't bother shaving and run my fingers through my sleep-mussed hair. As I make my way into my bedroom, my eyes feast on Madison's bare legs, which are twisted around the sheets. My shirt lies just underneath her ass, and if she moves, it'll ride up, exposing pure perfection.

Realizing I'm gaping at her like a complete pervert, I clear my throat loudly, hoping she'll wake of her own accord. I don't want to go anywhere near her in my aroused state. Thankfully, her sleepy groan reveals that she's awake.

I hunt for my sneakers while she comes to. "Ugh, what time is it?" she croaks. I can't help but smile at her adorability.

"It's time for you to get up." I sit on the edge of the bed, slipping on my shoes, still avoiding looking at her because all that exposed flesh and wild bed hair will not help the predicament in my pants.

"I can't believe you were serious about going running."

"I never joke about fitness," I conclude, finally gathering the balls and turning around to face her.

I was right. She looks so innocent and pure wrapped in my white sheets. However, when I think of her riding my face not so innocently last night, I realize that underneath that purity lazes a need that only I can fill. That fact has me feeling like the luckiest son of a bitch alive.

"C'mon, Sleeping Beauty. I'll make coffee while you get ready." I playfully pinch her big toe while she squirms and giggles. I leave her to shower and get dressed while I head into the kitchen.

As the coffee machine permeates the air with caffeine goodness, I can't help but ponder on the fact that I still haven't told Maddy about Juliet. Last night wasn't really the right time, but hearing her confess that she knows something is up, and that something has got to do with Juliet, has me beyond nervous to tell her. She near tore my heart out when she confessed her fears. How wrong, yet right she was.

I don't want to tell her, but what else am I supposed to do? Honestly, I'm surprised Juliet hasn't called Madison to rub her face in the mess I've made.

Pouring myself a cup of coffee, I drink it without really tasting it, as my mind is plagued with so many thoughts. How do I tell her, and where do I start? I know it doesn't matter because no matter what I say, I'm fucked. I need a plan B because plan A sucks.

"Coffee smells good."

Masking my inner turmoil, I turn around with a staged smile. However, when I see her wearing a navy bra and tight running shorts, all my worries disappear. "Where's the rest of your top?" I inquire, unable to tear my gaze off her toned, slender midriff.

She laughs, which does mindboggling things to her chest. "It's called a crop top. People run in them all the time."

It should be called a cock tease, I silently reply.

"Yes, but I bet none of them look as good as you do." How does she expect me to focus on anything other than all her scantily clad good bits?

"Dixon?"

"Hmm?" I distractedly reply, undressing her with my eyes.

"You're staring."

"You would, too."

Her suddenly flushed flesh reminds me of last night, and I can't resist her any longer. Placing my mug on the counter, I reach her in two huge strides. Before she has time to react, I pull her into my arms and smash my lips on hers. She's stunned, her mouth slack underneath mine, but as I nudge it open with my tongue, she explodes around me.

I want to fucking eat her alive, so I devour her like she's my last meal—and in a way, she is. I know, once the day is done, I'll be starved of her love.

I've never been more forceful with her, but her tiny whimpers and desperate touches reveal she likes my domination. I kiss her madly, fisting my hand into her loose hair, holding her prisoner as I consume her mouth. Her succulent perfume assaults my senses, and my need to overthrow her assails me, so I lift her, planting her ass onto the counter. She opens her legs, welcoming me home.

Our mouths never miss a beat as we kiss, robbing each other of air. But who needs air when Madison is my life source?

My impatient dick demands to break free from its confines, so I drive my hips forward, pressing my hard-on into her center. However, when she gasps and stills, I scold myself for being so aggressive with her.

"I'm s—" But the words die in my throat when she slowly reaches between us and strokes over my cock.

Her hands on me are exactly what I crave, and although I don't deserve it, I need it so, so badly. She watches me with curious eyes as she fondles my arousal and appears to be gauging the feel of my cock as she works up and down my length unhurriedly. Meanwhile, her jerky, unsure movements are sending my brain into overdrive, and if I don't pull away now, I will, like a pubescent teen, come in my pants. That would be embarrassing.

"Madison..." I attempt to pull my hips away, but she surprises me by holding on tight.

"I want to...to go down on you," she confesses, biting her lip a second later.

My dick is standing in salute, so ready to get this show on the road. But my conscience is punching me in the guts, telling me that I cannot take that from her until I tell her the truth. If she knew where my dick had been before her, I'm sure she wouldn't be so eager to pleasure me with that chaste mouth. And just like that, my cock flips me off and retreats.

"You don't want me to?" she asks with a small frown.

With regretful fingers, I gently remove her hand from my crotch. "Of course I do. The proof is in my pants."

"But?" she prompts.

"But..." I'm a lying, undeserving bastard. "But not now," I settle for instead.

She appears disappointed but doesn't press. When she hides behind her hair, I know I've hurt her feelings. By trying to protect her and her decency, I've inadvertently made her feel unwanted.

Fucking great.

"Maddy..."

"You ready to go?" she interrupts, trying to appear unaffected.

I could give her the whole, "it's not you, it's me" speech, but I've been on the receiving end of that little sermon, and quite frankly, it blows. No matter the truth, the entire concept is belittling, and I would rather say nothing than deliver her such an excuse.

So I nod.

When she jumps down from the counter, excusing herself as she needs to finish getting ready, I know I'm screwed.

As we begin our run around Central Park, I know Madison is angry with me.

Her clipped responses are a sure sign she's thinking of ways to tell me to take a hike in the opposite direction. Not that I can blame her. I am telling myself the same thing. But this is the push I needed. I've put it off for long enough. She needs to know.

I'm winded, and it's not because I'm running. For the first time in my life, I am absolutely petrified. I know there is no way to soften the blow of what I'm about to reveal. Hunter's advice plays over in my head, and although it's the worst piece of advice to follow, I decide to put my spin on it and hope it works.

I plan to declare my feelings for her before I tell her what a lowlife scumbag I really am. Here's hoping she'll focus on the positives rather than the negatives. But I realize this is all wishful thinking. Once I'm done telling her the truth, she'll want nothing more to do with me.

"So this is nice." Not the lead-in I wanted to start with, but it'll have to do.

Maddy turns to look at me and nods, waiting for me to

elaborate. I don't. She huffs and kicks up her speed, darting ahead of me. Normally, I would check out her ass, but today the sight is too depressing as it's a sight I'm unlikely to see again.

I catch up to her, but she continues to focus ahead as she runs with determination.

"Maddy, about this morning…"

"Don't worry about it," she breathlessly says, avoiding eye contact.

"No, I am worrying about it. I need to tell you something."

That has her sharp focus wavering as she turns. "What do you need to tell me?"

My voice catches in my throat, and my heart begins hammering. "I need to tell you the truth."

"The truth about what, Dixon?" She slows down her strides and watches me, silently begging me to explain.

I too slow down, as I'm afraid I'll fall over my feet once I tell her who I really am. "I…remember when you asked if I knew Juliet?"

The moment I say her stepsister's name, she stops running and spins around to face me. She slowly nods. Her eyes reveal she's scared, anxious, and confused, and the sight, no matter how painful, goads me to go on.

Threading both hands through my hair, I come to a halt and sigh. We're standing face-to-face, and I've got nowhere to hide. "Well…I lied."

She takes a step backward, her chest rising and falling so quickly I'm afraid she's about to pass out. "You…w-what?"

They say the truth will set you free. I can only hope that's true. "I lied, Maddy. I do know her."

She blinks.

75

"I do know Juliet," I clarify in case she's misunderstood me.

"You—how?" she manages to choke out, her face turning a ghastly shade of white.

Watching the world explode before me, I confess, "I know her...because I...fuck—" I pause, placing my hands on my hips and taking a deep breath. This is just like a Band-Aid—do it quick. "I know her because I, she was—"

"Sunny?"

That one simple word, which would usually convey light and warmth, shrouds Madison's face with nothing but darkness. I don't need to turn around to see who stands behind me because only one vile human being calls Madison that. It's been his nickname for her ever since they were kids.

Instinctively, I reach for Maddy, who has solidified into stone. Her entire body is taut, and her heavy breathing has turned into tiny exhalations filled with pain. Her eyes are stretched wide, and she blinks once, appearing to disbelieve who stands in front of her. But when her brain processes that her asshole brother stands before her, she begins to break down.

Her body begins to tremble so fiercely, I'm actually afraid she'll faint. As I scoop her up in my arms, I observe that her previous shade of white looked like a rainbow compared to the color she is now. I've never seen her so afraid.

"It is you," the motherfucker has the gall to say. I want to cut out his tongue as Maddy whimpers and buries herself into my chest.

"Maddy, let's go," I whisper, looking down at the zombie in my arms.

Her unresponsiveness has me beginning to worry. Sadly, I have another worry to add to the mix.

"Dr. Mathews. What a pleasant surprise." This surprise is so far from pleasant, and Juliet's mocking tone reveals she loves the ugliness.

"We were just leaving," I say, securing my hold around Maddy's trembling shoulders as I turn around to face the Antichrist and her right-hand man.

"Oh, really? That's a shame. I suppose we'll have plenty of time to catch up soon." Juliet purses her lips, her haughty gaze never wavering from mine.

I've never hated anyone more than I do her right now. I know what she's implying, and it's all my fault.

"That's not going to happen," I firmly state, my nostrils flaring in rage.

Maddy finally speaks, her voice nothing but a mere whisper. "W-What?" she questions, breaking from my hold and bravely facing the malevolent duo.

My fists itch as I want to slam them into Dylan's face when he stares at Madison indecently.

Juliet's cruel eyes flick her way, dissecting her. "Oh, Rachel didn't tell you?"

"Tell me what?"

Juliet snuggles into Dylan's side, which breaks his trance-like stare. He looks down at her like she's a disease. She either doesn't see his repulsion or she just doesn't care. "Dylan is moving in with me. We'll be neighbors," she happily declares, revealing Madison's and my worst nightmare.

"When?" is all Madison can say as she sags against me.

"This week," Dylan replies, smiling. "That means I can visit you any time I want, Sunny. Isn't that great?" His entire sentence is dripping with a disgusting undertone, and I gnash my teeth together, seconds away from ripping off his fucking head.

I don't care who sees. I'm going to kill him. I'll kill them both with my bare hands.

Just as I lunge forward, Madison grabs my forearm, stopping my attack. I twist around to look at her, but she gives nothing away. "Let's go, Dixon."

Go? Has she gone mad? There is no way I'm leaving without her brother's head in tow.

But when she tugs on my arm, her desperate need to escape clear on her frightened face, I push aside my fury and put her safety first. She leaps into my arms as we turn to leave this clusterfuck behind.

"Toodles. Let's do coffee next week," Juliet says in a singsong, her voice displaying nothing but victory.

I ignore her and tear down the walkway before I act on impulse and end them both. When we're a safe distance away, Madison suddenly stops and rushes over to a flowering shrub, hand over mouth.

"Maddy?"

"I'm going to be sick." With that pained admission, she bends forward and throws up the entire contents of her stomach.

"Oh fuck." I run to her aid, but she reaches out her palm behind her, indicating I'm to stay put.

She's sick for what seems like minutes, but I respect her wishes and wait off to the side, feeling completely helpless as I pace the concrete anxiously. This is my doing. She's sick because of me. And her brother moving into her building is because of me, too. I have brought this girl nothing but misery, and I don't know how to make it stop.

"Madison?" I ask, flinching when I see her hunched-over

form shudder. "Are you all right?"

She doesn't reply.

How can I fix this? How can I make this all go away? The only way I know how was just prohibited by Madison.

Why?

"Maddy, why did you stop me? That asshole deserves to be put down like the dog that he is!" My anger erupts as I continue pacing the sidewalk like a caged tiger.

She slowly stands to full height, wiping her mouth with the back of her hand as she turns. She looks lost, scared, and utterly defeated. "You can't! My mom will find out what happened if you fight him."

I pull back, confused. "Who cares? She should know! She should know what that animal did to you!" If Rachel knew, then this entire shitstorm would be over with. Madison may never forgive me for lying to her, but at least I'd know she'd be safe. She'd have her mother to protect her from the monsters. And those monsters include me.

Maddy turns her face, hiding her shame. "I don't want her to know, Dixon. It'll kill her. I can't do that to her."

Without warning, my wrath ignites, and I slam my fist into a tree mid-stride, a frustrated scream following. "Are you shitting me? By keeping quiet, you're protecting that motherfucker!" My hand burns. I'm quite certain I've just sprained it. But I couldn't care less. The pain feels divine.

She jolts, surprised by my reaction. "Dixon, don't." She looks around at the slow-forming crowd surrounding us, pleading that I don't make a scene, but it's too late.

I throw my hands up in defeat. "Don't what? Fight for your freedom? Aren't you sick and tired of being scared all the time?

I know I am!" I want her to fight. I want her to prove me wrong, to prove that this won't break her like I foresaw because if she succumbs to her fears, then I will have no other choice—I'll be driven to sin. I'll be driven to sin to keep her safe.

Tears well in her eyes as she chews on her bottom lip. "I'm sorry. I-I can't do this right now."

"Can't do what?" I yell, latching onto her bicep as she attempts to run—run away from me. "You can't keep running away, Madison."

This situation is spiraling out of control, yet I can't stop.

"Ouch, you're hurting me." She attempts to pull out of my grip, but I hold on tight, afraid to let her go.

"Hey bro, let her go," some Good Samaritan says, trying to intervene. But when I turn to glare at him, he stops, hands raised in surrender.

"Let me go!" Maddy cries, struggling madly to break free. But I can't let her go. I know that if I do, she'll be gone forever. I can't let the only thing I've ever cared for walk away from me because I know she won't look back.

"No, not until you stand up for yourself, Madison. Stop letting him control you!" Stop letting them control *me*.

Her loud sobbing suddenly kicks me in the balls, and the fact I am manhandling the woman I supposedly care for hits home. What the *fuck* am I doing?

Quickly releasing her, my gaze drops to her tiny arm, the tiny arm which is red raw from my meaty hands pawing her. I gasp. What have I done? Looking at my outstretched palms in disgust, I realize I am no better than her brother.

Stepping forward, I beg, "Maddy, I'm so sorry. Please forgive me."

"Don't," she wails, placing a hand in front of her to stop my advance. Her eyes are swimming in tears, and each one stabs at my weeping heart.

"I'm sorry. I didn't mean to hurt you. I'm a fucking idiot. I just, I hate that he has this effect on you. I hate that he still controls you." My trembling voice is filled with desperation, but I will fucking beg on hands and knees for forgiveness.

She sniffles and lets out a bitter laugh. "So you thought you'd do one better and control me instead?"

"What? No, I would never," I gasp, clenching my palms into fists by my side. "That was never my intention. I'm sorry. I fucked up. Please, just come back to my place so we can talk about this."

I want to step forward, but I don't.

When she doesn't reply and simply looks at her sneakers, unable to bear the sight of me, I crumble. "Please, I'm sorry. I truly am." If I've ever felt this afraid, then I don't remember when it was.

The air is weighed down with a miserable silence, and I know her response before she even says it.

"I can't do this right now. Goodbye, Dixon." Those concluding words break the final piece of my heart.

I swallow hard. "Goodbye? Maddy, wait! Please!" I lunge for her desperately, but she steps out of reach, shaking her head.

"No!"

This is not the end. No, not like this. "Please, let me explain." I'm ready to tell her everything. That option is far better than her thinking. I thought she was a coward for not sticking up for herself. "There's a reason—"

She cuts me off, angrily retreating farther and farther away.

"I said no! Just leave me alone. I need time to think."

"Think about what?"

"About everything. About my brother…" She leaves the sentence unfinished, a fresh set of tears spilling down her cheeks.

Her withdrawal kills me. I plead, "Maddy, no. Don't do this. Please, *angelo*. I'm sorry."

But my apology is not enough. "Yeah, so am I." With that, she turns, and just like I predicted, she doesn't look back.

Seven

Dixon

"Hi, it's me…again." Pause. "I…I'm sorry…again. I know there aren't enough ways for me to say sorry because what I did…" Pause again. "What I did was unforgivable. I hate myself for putting my hands on you that way, and I would happily cut them off if it meant you would at least acknowledge me—" The loud beeping in my ear and the patronizing voice alerting me that Madison's voicemail is full just cements the fact that she will never talk to me ever again. Honestly, I don't blame her.

I fucked up.

There is simply no other way to phrase it. I fucked this entire thing up, and I didn't even tell her my most vilest secret. By trying to save us, I pushed her away, and now, after day three, her silence says it all.

I've tried emailing, calling, texting, driving by her home on the off chance she'll walk by. I've even resorted to camping out at her place of work, hoping I'd catch her there, while ignoring the glares of her best friend, but nothing. It's like she's dropped off the face of this earth, which worries me.

I know she'd never do anything silly, but this disappearing act just confirms she's making herself scarce because she doesn't want to be found. She doesn't want to be found by me.

I can't let it end this way. The next option would be to contact Rachel, but I can't guarantee I'd be able to keep my mouth shut as to why we argued in the first place. Groaning, I rub a hand down my face, my long whiskers prickling my hand.

A knock on my door reminds me that I'm at work. I need to pull it together. "Dr. Mathews?"

"Come in, Ms. Vale." Ever since this debacle started, Susanna has been hovering. Usually, I would find this annoying, and if it were anyone but her, I'd fire them, but I know she has my best interests at heart.

"What can I do for you?" I ask when she enters but doesn't fully step inside.

"Dr. Turner will be here soon, and I just wanted to ensure…"

My brow furrows when she pauses and looks away. "Wanted to ensure that I hadn't forgotten? Or that I'm wearing pants?" I finish for her, as these are all plausible concerns.

She smiles, stepping in. "Well"—she tugs at her pearl earring nervously—"yes."

"All is well, Ms. Vale. See?" I stand to reveal I'm properly clad.

She quickly shakes her head, appearing apologetic for hinting at such a thing. "I'm sorry, Dr. Mathews. I didn't mean to imply you are…" She uneasily pauses once again.

"Losing it?" I offer with a grin as I take my seat.

"May I be frank?" She steps forward, her wise eyes zeroing in on me.

"Well, I think Susanna is a lovely name, but if you wish to be called by another, I'd gladly comply," I tease, attempting to hide behind my humor.

She ignores my quip. "Since you've taken up with Ms. Roberts, I've noticed a change in you. A change for the better. I know this is highly inappropriate, with you being my employer and all, but she brings out a side of you I've not seen. She makes you a better..." Today seems to be the day for noncommittal sentences. When I lounge back in my seat, she suddenly appears guilty for saying too much.

I put her out of her misery a moment later. "Man?" I suggest. When she casts her eyes downwards, I know that's exactly what she intended to say.

"Excuse me, Dr. Mathews, for speaking out of line."

"Nonsense. You speak the truth. You're right. Before Madison, I was a selfish bastard with no respect for anyone, not even myself. But she's made me see the error of my ways. She's the strongest person I know. I just wish she saw that." I sigh, feeling the weight return to my belly.

"So what do you intend to do?" she presses gently.

"I'm moments away from setting up camp outside her door. The police can haul me away, but I need her to know I'm sorry," I confess, feeling utterly helpless.

"Have you thought that maybe you're going about it the wrong way?"

My head snaps up. "What do you mean?"

"Maybe the reason she isn't listening is because she doesn't want to hear you say sorry, but rather, she wants to see it," she ambiguously reveals, like I'm supposed to know what that means.

"How?"

Her lips tip up into a small smile. "I don't know, Doctor. You're a smart man. I'm sure you'll figure it out."

I'm glad she has faith in me because I have no idea what she means. But I'll be damned if I can figure it out.

As I'm pondering her statement, Ms. Vale softly says, "Seeing as we're ignoring the rules of social etiquette…your mother would have been proud of you, Dixon. I know she'd also love Madison."

The mention of my mother and Madison in the same sentence is really too much, and like a pussy, I quickly wipe my eyes. "I think you're right. My mother would have loved her. It's too bad she isn't…here," I add a moment later. The wheels suddenly begin turning.

I've got it. Ms. Vale was right. The problem is I've been approaching this the wrong way. Words mean nothing if they're not backed by actions of the heart.

Rising hastily, I rush over to Susanna and smile. "This is highly inappropriate, with you being my employee and all, but I'm afraid words cannot express this." Catching her completely unaware, I step forward and enfold her in a hug.

She stands stunned, but moments later, she hugs me back.

"Thank you, Susanna."

"My pleasure, Dixon."

We break apart before it gets too weird, and she smiles. "I'll see to getting your coffee before Dr. Turner arrives. Did you want soy milk, too?"

"Too? Chad wants soy milk?" I ask, pulling a repulsed face.

When did he turn into a tree-hugging hippie?

She nods. "Yes. Apparently, he's watching his waistline."

No doubt this new craze was inspired by the harpy Rebecca. "He should be more concerned with watching his wallet."

Susanna bites down on her bottom lip to hide her smirk. "I'll page you once he arrives."

When she leaves, I return to my desk, hunting through my drawers for a loose piece of paper. Reaching for my ballpoint, I start doing something neither millions of Americans nor I have done in a long time—I write a letter.

> *Dearest Madison,*
>
> *Words cannot express how sorry I am. I understand you're mad at me. You have every right to be.*
>
> *If you can find it in your heart to give me another chance, please meet me at this address this Sunday at 2 p.m.: 678 Easton Ave, New Brunswick, New Jersey. It's time I show you how I felt, rather than tell you.*
>
> *I hope to see you there.*
>
> *Dixon x*

Just as I sign it, Susanna pages me, alerting me to Chad's arrival. I place the letter in my drawer just as the door opens.

"Dixon."

Chad Turner is a busy man, as he's on the Psychiatry and Behavioral Sciences board. He's usually not one for social visits, so I can't help but wonder why he's here.

Standing, I extend my hand. "Nice to see you, Chad. You're looking well." I can't help but mock.

He proudly pulls up his pants. "Rebecca has me on some

vegan diet. The food may be hideous, but I've never felt better. I've never had more energy." When he concludes his sentence with an insinuating wink, I swallow my distaste with a strained smile.

I don't have the energy to make small talk when it comes to that piranha. "So what can I do for you?" I ask, taking a seat while gesturing to the chair in front of me.

"That's what I like about you, Dixon; you're not one for small talk."

Susanna knocks before entering with our coffees. Placing them on my desk, she's out the door a moment later.

As Chad reaches for his, he says, "I presume you've heard the unfortunate news about Dr. Rubin Gold?"

"No, I have not." That lucky bastard was the winner of this year's Gerald Harriet's Award. He should be celebrating with cheap wine and cheaper women.

Chad looks awfully uncomfortable as he reveals, "Well, he was caught in a…compromising position in Mexico a few days after the awards ceremony."

"Oh?" My interest is piqued.

"Yes. His blatant use of illicit drugs, providing alcohol to a minor, and inappropriate dealings with a…goat has given us no other choice but to strip him of the award and title."

I raise a brow. A goat? And I thought I had issues. "So what now?"

"The medical board has decided, to save face, we will pretend the first event never took place. We're organizing a redo."

How typical.

"And besides, who doesn't like dressing up and having a

drink or two with colleagues?"

Indeed.

I still have no idea why he's telling me this, so I play along. "Well, that's great news. If I can be of any assistance, please let me know."

Sipping his dishwater, he replies, "Actually, you can. That's why I'm here."

I lean forward, indicating I'm listening.

"I would like to nominate you as a candidate for the award."

"Really?" I conceal my excitement because surely there's a catch.

He nods, his jaw firm. "Yes. I find your methods quite ingenious. You remind me of me at your age. I really think you're in with a good chance of winning. Your research has been unlike any of its kind. I was going to nominate you for next year's award; however, with this opportunity arising, I couldn't resist. You'll be up against five other doctors."

I stay silent, unsure of what to say. I can't detect a hidden undertone, and Chad looks rather sincere. This is un-fucking-believable.

When Chad initially came to me with the suggestion of possibly nominating me for next year's award, I was beyond appreciative, but now, I'm ecstatic. This is everything I've ever wanted and more. I feel no sympathy for Dr. Gold because his lewdness has just scored me my golden ticket.

"Thank you, Chad."

"The pleasure is all mine, Dixon. I'll be in touch once a date has been set. In the meantime, please keep your nose clean. Our industry doesn't need any more bad press."

I try to mask my tension. "Clean as a whistle," I reply, hoping he doesn't read my bullshit. Yes, my personal dealings don't involve goats, but they do involve a bitch. If anyone got wind of my immoral actions, I'd be ruined. My thoughts wander to how imperative it is now to keep Juliet's silence.

Chad's cell ringing gives me the breathing space I need. He apologizes before answering it. "Oh, darling, I'm just with Dixon. Can I call you back?"

It's like the universe is taunting me with what can be taken away from me in a blink of an eye because his "darling" is just another nail in my coffin.

He wraps up the conversation and stands. "I'd best be off. I'll speak to you soon."

Shaking hands, I try to remain composed. "Most certainly. Thank you again, Chad. This is truly an honor."

"Not a problem. We should catch up for drinks one evening. I'm sure Rebecca would love to see your lovely other half again."

Yes, I'm sure she would. "Sounds delightful. I'll check my schedule and get back to you."

"Splendid." With that, he exits my office, and I let out a pent-up breath of relief.

This is the best news a doctor could ever receive. The things winning this award could do for my career are mindboggling, but with my dirty little secrets looming over my head, winning this award could also ruin my career. Or more accurately, *Juliet* could ruin my career. I can pretend all I want that her spilling the beans about my immorality to the board means nothing to me, but being presented this life-changing option just cements that it does.

Opening my desk drawer, I pull out the letter to Madison. This is the first step to claiming back my life. As I address the

envelope to her, I realize the second step has my hand wavering. The step which was inevitable from the day I met Ms. Juliet Harte.

Eight

Dixon

Giving my letter of hope one last look, I place it in the mailbox. My fate is now in Madison's hands. However, the huge apartment block looming behind me reminds me that my fate is also in somebody else's hands.

Earlier today, I did something I thought I'd never do again—I texted Juliet. The message was simple enough.

We need to talk.

Her response, **Come over at 7.**

Looking down at my watch, I see that it's now 7:05. Time to face the music.

The elevator ride is as comfortable as one can imagine seeing a scorned ex to be. What makes matters worse, however, is that that ex lives in the same building as your newest ex. This entire situation is grating on my already raw nerves.

I knock on Juliet's door, half expecting her to answer it nude. Thankfully, she doesn't. "Hello, Dixon. Please, won't you come in?" She steps aside, welcoming me into the lair of doom.

I enter, swallowing down the revolting memories of all the nasties I did to her on that wall, that couch, that coffee table, that Persian rug, and God forbid, that antique ornament.

"Can I offer you a drink?"

The door closing behind me feels like a death sentence, but I push down my disgust and nod. "Scotch if you've got it."

"Of course. Please, take a seat." She gestures to the leather sofa. I blanch, hoping she's had it reupholstered.

As she's busying herself in the kitchen, I unfasten my tie because it's hard enough to breathe as it is. I remind myself I'm doing this for the greater good. I can only hope that good doesn't lead me to sin.

"Here you go." She steps into the room, two drinks in hand. I gratefully accept mine, ensuring our fingers don't touch.

"So what can I do for you, Dixon? You being here is quite a surprise. I'm intrigued." She's keeping her distance as she sits on the sofa opposite me. She crosses her legs, giving me her full attention.

"Dr. Chad Turner paid me a visit today. I believe you met his fiancée in Boston?" I watch her closely over the rim of my glass.

She nods, a secretive smile pulling at her ruby lips.

"Well, it seems my profession is filled with many fucked-up individuals, but hey, thanks to one disturbed doctor's fondness toward farm animals, I'm now the top nominee to win the Gerald Harriet's Award."

Juliet's eyes widen, and she appears...happy for me. "That's great news. Congratulations. No one deserves it more than you do."

"Thank you. It really is an honor, and I won't lie, I want to win." Taking a sip of scotch, I begin to put into practice why I'm really here. "However, you have the power to break me, Juliet, and I don't like it. You've shown you're not going to back down, so I've come here asking for your exact terms. If I agree to them, then you must swear to never divulge what went on between us to anyone. And by anyone, I also mean Madison."

When she sits up tall, I know I have her attention. "You know what I want."

I shake my head, feeling my confidence spike. "No, I don't. Apart from some ambiguous clues, I have no idea what exactly you propose. You haven't told anyone about us, which has me wondering what exactly it is you want. You claim you just want me around for a fuck, but then you take me shopping for baby clothes? What are you playing at?

"The fact you're still engaged to that lowlife motherfucker reveals you're happy to play along with the pretense that the baby is his. But I'm assuming his cock doesn't satisfy your ravenous appetite. I mean, what other reason are you blackmailing me for?"

Juliet's breathing begins to increase. The low neckline of her peach dress displays her swelling breasts, betraying her excitement. Just like I knew they would.

"I-I..." She falters, licking her dry lips quickly.

"C'mon, Juliet. I know what that venomous mouth is capable of. Tell me." Coolly placing my glass onto the coffee table, I rise and walk over to her. As she bows back into the cushions, watching me from underneath those long lashes, I make no attempt to sit. I stand, domineering over her, just the way I know she likes it.

"I want to fuck you," she finally reveals, but her voice is small and shaky.

Folding my arms across my chest, I pin her with my stare. "That's not going to happen."

"Then we have no deal," she's quick to reply, shooting upright angrily.

"Shh," I condescendingly hush her. Leaning forward, I encage her with my arms as I place them on either side of her head. She falls back against the leather, her harsh breathing fanning my cheeks. "But...I didn't say I won't fuck you."

A pink hue overtakes her features, and for once, it's a sight I'm pleased to see.

"Stand up," I command, leveling my eyes with hers. I slowly release her and coolly sit on the sofa beside her.

For a moment, she looks lost and unsure; if I didn't know better, I would feel sorry for her. But I know what lies beneath the surface of this conniving, scheming bitch.

There is *no* way in hell that I will touch this woman the way she wants me to. But I'm afraid I'll have to get my hands a little dirty if I want her to succumb to what I have planned.

I did some soul-searching today, and after much thought, I realized that to win this game, I'll be forced to take a page out of Juliet's book and lie, cheat, and steal. It's the only way I can get what I want. It's the only way she'll leave me alone. And it's the only way I can keep Madison in my life because in this circumstance, the truth will not set me free. I've made my decision, and there's no turning back.

This is my plan B.

"This innocent act is growing old, Juliet," I say, lounging back into the sofa as I turn to look at her. "We both know you don't have an innocent bone in that hot little body of yours." I actually feel nauseous as the lie passes my lips, but I press on, knowing what I'll gain once this is done.

My words have the exact effect I was hoping for. "Not anymore. I'm fat. This baby weight is turning me into a whale." She pouts, and the look is not at all attractive.

But I fake horror. "Don't be absurd. You still look good enough to"—I lick my upper lip—"eat. Speaking of…don't make me repeat myself." I try to keep my voice low and seductive, hoping my allure will work.

It does.

She slowly rises, nervously running her hands down her dress as she stands before me. This is the first time I've ever seen Juliet appear bashful and not jump at the opportunity to get nude. But that's about to change.

"Strip." I casually cross my ankle over my knee as I lean back to get comfortable.

Her trembling fingers reveal she's tense, but she does as I command. Lifting the loose-fitting garment over her head, she drops it to the floor. It lands with a soft thud by her painted toes. Gathering my wits, I start my dance with the devil.

Raking my gaze up her body, I ensure I take my time. However, I'm not savoring the sight but encouraging myself to go on. Even though I know this is for the greater good, I still want to pluck my eyeballs out because I feel like I'm betraying Maddy by looking at someone who isn't her.

When I arrive at the junction of her thighs, I press down

the heavy memories of when that was my favorite place in the world. She shuffles under my watch when my gaze falls to her small belly. Seeing it in the flesh makes this all real, but I can't stop, not now. Her fingers suddenly flutter over her stomach, drawing my attention to the fact she doesn't like to be bare.

"See? I told you. I'm hideous. My body isn't how you remember it. That's why you like *her*, isn't it? She's young and thin with perfect skin, not a bloated, blotchy pregnant buffalo like me. I'm losing my looks. This was a bad idea." Just as she bends down to pick up her dress, I jump up to stop her.

"Nonsense." She looks up, watching me with uncertainty in her eyes. "You're still incredibly beautiful, Juliet. Your body has just filled out, and that's not a bad thing." I approach her slowly, steadying my racing nerves. Pausing in front of her, I force myself to touch her voluntarily without vomiting.

Stroking her cheek, I smile. "Surely Dylan"—I try my best to keep smiling—"tells you that every day?"

This idea came to me thanks to Dylan's transparent aversion toward Juliet. At least one good thing came from that day.

She leans into my touch. "No, he doesn't. He rarely touches me now. He says he doesn't want to hurt the baby, but I know he's lying. I know it's because I'm fat."

Oh, you superficial, blind twit. He doesn't want to touch you because he clearly wants to touch someone else.

That thought spurs me on.

"Well, you know what?" I thumb her pouty bottom lip. "That's his loss. I think those curves accentuate all your good bits." I deliberately drop my gaze to her enormous tits.

"You think?" she hesitantly asks, the hope clear in her tone.

Taking a deep breath, I lie through my teeth. "Yes, I do.

97

You are so beautiful. A goddess. You always have been. I have been a fool to deny you." Unable to look at her a second longer, I walk behind her. I can deal with her back better than I can her front. Standing inches away from her, I will my fingers to move and begin a slow descent over her shoulders and down her arms. Her skin instantly prickles with the contact while my gut contracts at what I'm being driven to do.

"That feels good," she hums, her words caked in pleasure.

I'm glad someone is having a good time. But I press on. "How does it make you feel?"

"Happy."

"Why?"

"Because it's nice to feel wanted."

"And you feel unwanted?"

"Yes."

"Why do you think that is?"

This is a dangerous game I'm playing, but it's the only way I can win. By setting up the illusion that she's won, she'll inadvertently let her guard down, and just like Hunter said, I'll be able to use my psychobabble bullshit to break her down.

Hunter's advice has proven to be most valuable. The more I thought about it, the more I realized he was right. I'm going to do something I've not yet done where Juliet is concerned. I'm going to use the head on my shoulders, rather than the head between my legs to dig my way out of the mess I've made. I'm going to break down the lioness and turn her into a helpless little kitten. I plan on pulling back the layers of who she really is—something I should have done the first moment I met her. And when I do...then, I'll break her.

"Because everyone puts her first," she hisses angrily.

"Who?" I whisper.

"You know who." She groans when I trace over the racing pulse in her neck. I need to reel her back in.

"Why do you think that is?"

"Because she's fucking perfect," she spits while I refrain from strangling her. "She's taken my father, my fiancé, and now you away from me."

I can feel I'm losing her, so with no other choice, I close my eyes, swallow down my disgust, and draw the warm flesh at the side of her neck into my mouth. I gag on her taste and smell, but I breathe through it, remembering why I'm here.

It's a soft tug, but it's enough. I pull away, discreetly wiping my mouth with the back of my hand. "I'm here, aren't I?" I present while she sleepily nods.

"Yeah, you are."

Holding back my sigh of relief, I go on with my scheme. "So can we come to an agreement then? Will you promise to keep our secret? You know what will happen if you tell anyone, don't you?"

She nods again.

"What will happen?" I ask, ensuring my plan has worked.

"You'll get into trouble."

"And?" I prompt, breathing warm air onto her arched neck.

"And this will stop between us."

I've completely manipulated her, and it's worked. Telling someone something they need to hear can influence them into doing anything. And for someone as superficial as Juliet, making her feel wanted and needed is the key to her surrender.

"And you don't want that, do you?"

When she remains silent, I bite down on my tongue before

leaning forward and capturing her earlobe between my teeth.

She groans and tosses her head back. "No."

"Good girl. You always knew how to please me."

As inconspicuously as I can, I slip my hand into my inner jacket pocket and pull out a piece of paper and pen. "You must understand that I need something more than just your word. I mean, you did say on numerous occasions you'd destroy me. All I need is just your signature here." I run my fingertips up and down her arm while slyly placing the ballpoint between her slack fingers. Holding the paper in my other hand, I wrap my fingers around her wrist, coaxing her to sign.

"What is it?" she asks, her head moving slightly to look at what I'm holding.

"Just something to make me feel better. And you want me to feel good, right? Otherwise, I can't make you feel good." I sense her retreat, so I act fast. With one regretful movement, I drive my hips forward, rubbing myself into her ass.

It works.

She moans and quickly signs my…NDA. The non-disclosure agreement my attorney drew up that states if she tells anyone about us, I'll have the power to ruin her. I'm surprised she signed without reading it first. I guess my air of seduction worked. Or more to the point, playing on her weaknesses worked like a charm.

Getting what I wanted, I slowly pull away, not wanting to draw attention to my desperate withdrawal. I may have the legal side covered, but I still don't have the emotional side down pat. I know regardless of what my NDA says, if I don't break her down, she'll go after Maddy until she cracks.

When we first consummated our sin, I remember thinking

she's worn the proverbial pants ever since. She's always been in control. But now, it's time to put that bitch back in her place. It's time I get my balls back. It's time she knows who's boss.

I'm done being fucked over. It's time I do the fucking.

"I better go," I whisper into her ear. Just as she's about to protest, I say, "I know I'm leaving you high and dry, but I want you to go to bed and think of me as you fuck that wet cunt of yours. Picture my fingers dipping into your warmth and brushing over your gorgeous tits as you make yourself come. Can you do that for me?" I bite the flesh between her neck and shoulder as encouragement.

"Yes," she moans loudly. "Yes, Dr. Mathews. I can do that." Her breath is choppy, and I can hear her rubbing her thighs together.

And just like that, I know I've won.

We all have a trigger, a button one can push. And in Juliet's case, her trigger is sex. I've just made the undesirable feel desired, and in turn, I'm now in control.

They don't call me New York's finest shrink for nothing.

"Okay, good, Ms. Harte," I say, addressing her as I would if we were in a session. "Don't touch yourself until I leave," I instruct, not at all interested in seeing her get off. Reaching for my tie, I slowly make my way to the door, watching Juliet's trembling form.

"Goodbye, Ms. Harte."

"Goodbye, Dr. Mathews."

As I close the door behind me, I scrub my mouth with the back of my hand. Dashing to the elevators, I pray I don't see Madison on the way out.

Thankfully, I don't.

Driving home, I look at my reflection in the rearview mirror. Do I feel guilty for manipulating someone who had no qualms about manipulating me?

Absolutely not.

Deep down, I knew it would always come to this. This entire time, I was looking for "some other way." And this option, this *is* my other way. I'll do what I have to in order to survive.

Losing a piece of my soul is worth it for the girl who makes my entire existence worthwhile. And besides, I never said I was the hero of this story or even the good guy. However, who wants to be good when it feels so *good* being *bad*?

Nine

Dixon

It's Friday night, and although I'm overjoyed I haven't heard from Juliet, I'm feeling quite the opposite regarding Madison's radio silence.

I don't know what I expected. An acknowledgment that she'd received my letter would have been nice. I guess I'll just have to hope she shows up on Sunday. Otherwise, I don't know what to do.

Finch is down for the count with the flu, so it's just Hunter and me, which usually means trouble. I've been in enough trouble this week, so I suggested we have pizza and beer at my place as this limits the possible danger we can get into.

"Where's the pizza? I'm starving," says Hunter as he barges through my front door.

"Please, come in," I sarcastically reply, looking up at him from the sofa. I must remember to lock my door.

He ignores my mockery and slumps down onto the cushion

next to me. "How's your week been?"

I shrug and sip my beer. "Apart from Maddy giving me the cold shoulder, it's been good."

He pulls back, appearing stunned. "Good? I thought I'd come over, and you'd be listening to Michael Bolton while curled in the fetal position."

"Gee, thanks for the vote of confidence."

"Hey, I just know how hung up you are about her, that's all. So why are you good?"

The joys of knowing someone your entire life is they know you better than you know yourself. Seeing no point in denying it, I confess, "I saw Juliet the other night."

"What? By choice?" The disgust in his tone is clear.

"Yes, by choice. Ironically, I had no other choice."

Just as I raise my beer to my lips, Hunter snags it from me. "I have a feeling I'll be needing this."

I don't argue.

"Dr. Chad Turner visited me this week and, to cut a long, fucked-up story short, I'm now in the running to win the Gerald Harriet's Award."

"Fuck me, that's awesome. Congrats!" Hunter's silence reveals he's piecing together why I needed to see Juliet. "What did you do, Dix?"

Although I'm not proud of what I did, I lean forward and snatch the NDA off the coffee table. I pass it to Hunter, who reads it over, his eyes widening. "How the hell did you get her to sign this?"

When I look away, he groans. I'm brought back to earth when my neck jars forward, thanks to a slap to the back of the head. "You stupid motherfucker. So help me God, I will cut off your dick if you tell me you fucked her."

I shift away, afraid for my dick's and my safety. "Again, thanks for the vote of confidence."

"I'm sorry, but there is no way that dirty she-devil would sign this without—" When he pauses midsentence, I see the light bulb. "I take it back. You smart motherfucker. You totally used your smarts on her, didn't you?"

I nod. "Just like she did, I used sex—well, the illusion of sex—to get what I want."

"Holy shit." He whistles, appearing genuinely impressed with my mastermind plan. "I guess they don't call you Dr. Love for nothing."

I chuckle, rolling my eyes. "No one calls me that. I've got the legal side covered, but I still have to ensure she won't tell Maddy."

Hunter sips his beer, deep in thought. "So you're totally ignoring Finch's advice, then?"

Feeling like a total ass, I confess, "Yes and no. This is the only way I can tell Madison the truth, Hunt. I can't lose her, and I know that'll happen if I tell her everything. There are some things people can't forgive someone for, and this is one of those things. And even if she does accept it, it'll change everything between us. She'll never look at me the same way again. Especially if that baby is mine."

Hunter shudders. "You think Juliet's really knocked up with your kid?"

I raise my shoulders in defeat. "I think there's a good chance that it's mine."

"Fuck."

"My thoughts exactly. Can you now see why I'm doing

this?"

Hunter nods, although he looks a touch disappointed. "I get it, man, I do. But Finch was right. How can you trust Juliet? What are you prepared to do to keep your secret under lock and key?"

"I don't have a PhD in psychology for nothing."

He blows out a deep breath. "So you're going to take my advice and use your psychobabble bullshit?"

Running a hand through my hair, I reply, "Yeah, man, I am. There's no other way. The truth will fuck me over. This is the *only* way." I look at him intently, hoping he agrees with me. Hoping he tells me that I'm not as messed up as I feel.

"And you think she'll fall for it?" he asks, narrowing his eyes.

"She already has," I declare, rubbing the back of my neck.

"Well, fuck me with a cherry on top. This plan of yours, although completely and utterly unethical, just might work. You're totally playing on her weaknesses to break her down. It's quite an ingenious plan."

His comment makes me feel like Dr. Evil, so I feel the need to clarify. "I'm not a total bastard. I do intend on getting to the root of her issues. How I deal with them, well, that's still undecided." I know I'm abusing my knowledge, but what other choice do I have? Telling Maddy the truth is no longer an option. It never was. So at this stage, this is the only plan I've got.

Hunter brings forward a question I've desperately been trying to avoid. "That's great and all, but you need to ask yourself if you can really do this. You may get away with it, and Madison may never find out, but *you* will know the truth. You will know what you've done. For the rest of your life, you'll know you lied to the one person who has never lied to you. Can you live with that on your conscience?"

Sighing, I run a hand down my face. "It's a small price to pay. I'd rather that than lose her forever. I was kidding myself, Hunt."

Hunter raises an eyebrow.

"I tried to tell her the truth, but it was like some higher powers from above stopped me," I openly explain. "And besides, telling her is the right and honorable thing to do, but I never said I was honorable." There, I said it. Do I feel better about it?

No.

"It's your call, Dix," he replies with a shrug. "I can see why you're doing it, as I tend to agree with you. I don't think Madison will forgive you for what you've done, but you just need to think about what this will do to *you*. Sooner or later, you won't know the truth from the lies you've told. Just be careful, dude."

I want to tell him to lighten up, but I can't. His concerns are the same ones that have plagued me all week. But there's no other way. In this circumstance, there is no gray matter—only black and white.

If I tell Maddy the truth, I lose her. If I lie to Maddy, I lose myself. I know which option I would rather.

A knock on the door gives me the pardon I need. "Must be the pizza."

Hunter casually nods and turns up the TV when baseball comes on. And just like that, this conversation is over.

Reaching into my back pocket, I pull out my wallet and open the front door. However, my neighbor, Mr. Amos, stands before me. Unless he's now delivering pizzas, I have no idea why he's here.

"Evening, Mr. Amos."

"Good evening, Dr. Mathews. I'm sorry to intrude, but I seem to have your mail by mistake," he replies, producing a wad of letters.

I raise an eyebrow, my heart beginning to pick up the pace. "Thank you for bringing them over. I really appreciate it."

"It's not a problem at all. We must have a new mailman. George would never make such an error," he says, each word drawn out. I'm convinced that the older people get, time no longer exists to them.

"Yes, you just may be correct." I'm practically bouncing on the spot, waiting for him to get the hint and leave. Thankfully, he does.

"Well, good night. Don't do anything I wouldn't do." He winks, and I let out a strained laugh and a quick goodbye before shutting the door in his face.

Extremely rude, I know, but I'll make it up to him when I don't possibly have a letter from Madison in my hands. I throw letter after letter over my shoulder, as most are bills.

"C'mon," I mumble under my breath.

The commotion has Hunter turning to look at me while I litter my home with insignificant junk. "Where's the pizza?" I ignore him and continue hunting through the stack of letters. It has to be in here.

As I near the bottom of the pile, my optimistic heart begins a slow decline into despair until I see a white envelope with my name written in a beautiful script. "Yes! Motherfucking yes!" I exclaim, tearing into the envelope with eager fingers.

Taking a deep breath, I open the seal but halt when I see a coaster inside. "What in the hell?" I mutter, my brow crinkling in confusion.

Tipping the envelope upside down, the coaster slips into my palm. Thanks to my outburst, Hunter is now standing by my side, also looking down in confusion.

"I don't get it," he says, tipping his head to the side.

"I don't either." Why would Madison send me a Bud Light coaster? Is this a hint that she's been resorting to alcohol to deal with our fight? Or that I'm to drown my sorrows because she's not coming?

"Who's it from?" he asks, reaching for the envelope and turning it over. His action gives me an idea and I do the same thing with the coaster.

What I see has a string of profanities leaving me.

I'll be there...

Holy shit! She's coming.

Hunter looks down and lets out a sigh in understanding.

This is beyond words. And the fact she's written it on the back of something readily available to her at work proves that I've been on her mind.

"This," I say, holding up the coaster in front of his face, "makes everything worth it, my friend. *She* makes everything worth it." Unable to hold back my excitement, I cup Hunter's cheeks and plant a big kiss on his lips. It's not a kiss per se, more like a slamming of lips for a millisecond.

"Eww, get the fuck off me! Save your kisses for your girl," he states, pushing me away with a grin while wiping his mouth.

"This is fucking amazing!" I say, ignoring his staged disgust. "This calls for a drink."

"This calls for ten drinks. I need to clean the doctor from my palate."

"Ah, c'mon, you know you liked it," I tease, walking to the kitchen. My bad mood instantly evaporates, and just like that, I'm me again.

I may feel like an ass for choosing the road that I have, but knowing a reconciliation with Madison may be on the horizon makes me forget my sins and focus on why I chose the coward's way out.

As I open my fridge, Hunter's humor dissolves my last trace of worry. "I now see why the chicks dig you, Dix. Five more seconds and *I* would be blackmailing you to have sex with me."

And just like that, weirdly enough, everything is where it should be.

Ten

Madison

I have no idea what I'm doing here, but the masochist in me has me locking my car door and walking toward the address Dixon gave me.

His letter sits in my pocket, as it has since the moment I received it. Who would have thought a simple thing like a letter could be life-changing? But that's exactly what this letter is.

Having my first real fight with Dixon cemented that he has the ability to break my heart. And he did. I went home numb, unsure of what came next. I switched off from humanity and slept my pain away. I awoke the next day to an abundant amount of missed calls and text messages, but while I was originally hurt, my pain was overtaken by anger.

He said that I was to stop allowing Dylan to control my life, but honestly, I felt like he was doing the same. He apologized for having his hands on me, but the worst thing was that it felt like he was trying to step into my brother's shoes. That fact overshadowed the faint bruising on my arm because the unseen bruising hurt more.

But Dixon is persistent, and it seemed the more I ignored him, the more unrelenting he became. I wasn't ignoring him to gain attention. I needed to sort myself out. When he's close by, he clouds my judgment.

So for the past week, I've done some soul-searching and spoken to my doctor about what I should do next. The fact Dylan will be living in the same building as me has really stirred up a lot of memories, ones I thought I was slowly overcoming. Once again, I feel like a prisoner in my own skin.

The only thing keeping my mind from going stir-crazy is school. However, when I stumbled on questions along the way, all I could think was that I needed my personal tutor to show me the way. Nursing internships are steadily approaching, and the possibility of being miles away from New York seems all the more appealing.

So I'm here because, honestly, I don't know what else to do. This past week has been awful, and no matter how much I try to ignore Dixon, he simply won't go away. Not just physically but also emotionally. He's embedded firmly in my heart, and I feel lost without him. And I hate it.

Today, I will listen to what he has to say because ignoring him is no longer an option. I'm curious to know why I'm here, and I also want answers to how he knows Beth.

So many emotions are running through me right now; if I escape this day unscathed, it'll be nothing short of a miracle.

My palms begin to sweat the moment I amble up the driveway and am faced with the broad back of Dr. Dixon Mathews. His head is lowered, and his defeated exterior reflects my current feeling. I press on, anxious to know what happens next.

The invisible pull evident between us from the beginning sizzles, and with a slow, steady turn, Dixon spins to look at me. My choppy breath gets caught in my throat because no matter how confused I am, I'm ecstatic to see him. Instead, I squash down my glee and remind myself I'm here for answers. I will my legs to move until I am standing a few feet away.

We stand staring at one another silently, so many unspoken words passing between us. How I'm going to get through the day without it ending in tears is beyond me.

"Hello, Madison."

His voice breaks my daze, and I nod, not trusting myself to speak.

"Thank you for coming. Shall we go in?"

I can feel him watching me intently underneath his sunglasses, waiting for my reply. Is he afraid I'll say no? Or can it be he's afraid I'll say yes?

I have no idea why we're standing at the bottom of the steps of Sunnyfields Hospital, but I have an inkling it's got to do with his dad. Dixon has gone into little to no detail about his father, but since he's shared that his father had a breakdown after his mom passed away, I figured he was in a rest home. The security guard manning the well-enforced glass doors tells me otherwise, however.

Looking up at Dixon, I nod once again, still too afraid to speak.

With a sigh, Dixon turns and climbs the steps, his pace slow and poignant. I can see he doesn't want to go in here, but he does anyway. He stands at the top of the stairs, holding the door open for me. I enter quietly and am instantly hit with the smell of despair. Looking around, I see soft pastel colors everywhere, which conceal the loneliness inhabiting these walls.

"Hello, how may I help you?" asks a young nurse behind a glass alcove.

Dixon removes his glasses, his blue eyes appearing crystal under the fluorescent lights. "My name is Dixon Mathews. I'm here to see Pino Di Matteo."

"Are you family?"

Dixon clears his throat. "Yes. I am his son."

I remain motionless while the blonde nurse smiles, slipping a sign-in book through the panel under the window. "Will you please both sign in, and I'll get you visitor's badges."

Dixon scribbles his name and moves to the side so I can do the same. I can feel the heat radiating off him, but I tell myself to focus because I'm intrigued about why we're here. The nurse hands us our passes and gives us directions to his room.

Dixon's hands are dug deep into the pockets of his jeans as we silently make our way down the hall. The cleanliness is harsh and sterile, and the farther we descend, the more obvious it becomes that the name of this place is indeed deceptive. People sit, staring into vast nothingness as we walk past them, not appearing to even register where they are or that most are sitting in pajamas at two in the afternoon.

As we reach a doorway, a guard presses a computerized panel and lets us into a section that thankfully isn't as bad as the one we just walked through. The doors in this ward aren't locked, and the atmosphere isn't as barren. Arts and crafts are scattered along the walls, but some of the works look to have been made by young children. Where are we?

Stopping outside of room fifty-nine, Dixon takes a deep breath. He doesn't hide his uneasiness, and I suddenly understand why we're here. In this circumstance, Dixon's actions amount to a thousand words. He's allowing me access to his most vulnerable reality, opening up a piece of himself that I know he hasn't revealed to anyone else. I've shared my secrets, and now, it's time for him to do the same.

I want to reach for his hand, but I don't. I, better than anyone, know that something like this needs to be done with both feet firmly cemented to the ground. His heavy breathing and transfixed stare reveal he almost certainly hasn't seen his father since the day he left him here.

A small part of me weeps for the man who isn't as invincible as he wants the world to think.

He hesitates one final time before he steps forward and walks into his father's bedroom. I follow but give him some breathing room, not wanting to smother him. The room is modestly decorated with a single bed, bedside table, and a small table and chair. I can't help but feel this space is bare, not because there is no room but rather the simple man sitting in a tattered brown lounge chair in front of the bay window doesn't have the need for such fancy riches. He's content with a good view and the silence.

"*Ciao, Papà.*"

The already stagnant silence becomes deathly still, and I can suddenly hear the beating of a heart—but it's not mine, it's Dixon's.

Dixon's father doesn't stir. He continues gazing out the window, not appearing to even register his son's presence.

Dixon runs a hand through his hair, fisting the longer locks

115

tightly. "*Papà, sono io.* Your son."

The desperation and the plea to be acknowledged are obvious in his voice, but sadly the plea falls on deaf ears. Dixon turns to look at me, appearing mortified by his father's blatant disregard. Impulsively, I extend my hand. He peers down at it, surprised by the offering, but after a few seconds, he takes it loosely and smiles. I'm providing him with the strength he so often gives me.

He squeezes my fingers lightly before letting go. "Well, you said you wanted to meet my dad…" He sweeps his hand toward his motionless father, looking defeated. "Here he is."

I realize I still haven't said a word. But what can I say? Nothing I say will make any of this go away. So I say nothing at all.

Dixon slumps onto the small bed, cradling his face in his hands. I can only imagine how hard this is for him, so I give him some space.

I walk over to a small shelf, looking at the dusty photo frames sitting along the ledge. When I see the intelligent eyes of a young Pino Di Matteo staring back at me, I understand where Dixon got his brains from. However, when I move onto the next picture, I can see where Dixon got his looks from. Not that his father is unattractive, but his mother was a true beauty, and if I didn't know better, I'd say she was Sophia Loren's sister. With long black hair, sultry blue eyes, and a pinup model's figure, she would have turned the heads of all the boys. But it was Pino Di Matteo who caught her eye. Not that it surprises me because his son has done the same to me. I continue gazing down the shelf, surprised not to see any pictures of Dixon. However, when a downturned frame catches my eye, I know whose picture sits in the wooden frame.

The gesture is symbolic in so many ways and that symbolism is not lost on Dixon. "I deserve that," he says, cutting through the stillness of the room. "I left him here to rot."

I turn over my shoulder to look at him. Wishing my first words had a little more meaning, I offer, "Maybe it fell over?" But we both know that's not true.

Without thinking, I reach for the frame, unable to stomach the sad look on Dixon's face a moment longer. However, I suddenly stop when, from the corner of my eye, I see Pino's head shift. My hands are still mid-reach, but I can't move. I'm totally entranced by Pino as he turns slowly and locks those blue, soulful eyes with mine.

Pino is still a handsome man with a full head of thick gray hair and strong features akin to Dixon. "H-Hello, Mr. Di Matteo." I turn to face him completely. "My name is Madison Roberts. I'm…I'm Dixon's—" I look at Dixon, who lowers his eyes. "I'm Dixon's girlfriend," I declare softly. Dixon's head snaps up, and just like that, his vulnerability is replaced with joy.

Yes, I may be quick to forgive, but this is exactly what I needed. I needed this from Dixon. I needed him to stop being so damn invincible and let me be the one who comforts him for a change.

"It's nice to meet you," I conclude before walking to Pino. I feel incredibly rude standing over him, so I bend down and give his smooth cheek a light kiss. I hope I haven't crossed any lines, but he's Italian, and I figure this is standard practice when saying hello.

His eyes are still pinned to mine when I pull away, but the look doesn't make me feel uncomfortable. It's as if he's studying every inch of my face.

"Your wife was very beautiful. What was her name?" I ask, hoping to make a connection.

He remains mute, however, and turns to look back out the window.

"Her name was Angela," Dixon replies in place of his father. "And you're right, she was very beautiful—inside and out."

I nod.

The stony quiet returns, so I too look out the window, wondering what Pino's view is like. His room overlooks a small veggie patch and greenhouse. With all the greenness and fertility, I can see why he's so intrigued by the view.

"We used to have the most amazing veggie patch at home." I jump, startled that Dixon is behind me, as I didn't hear him move. "It was my father's pride and joy. He'd spend hours out there, tending to his garden. Wouldn't you, *Papà*?"

Silence.

I know Dixon is trying, but his father appears to be as stubborn and headstrong as his son. Whatever issues they have, his father won't easily forgive him.

By Dixon's heavy sigh, he knows it too. "I'm sorry, *Papà*. I truly am. I messed up. I didn't know what to do after *Mamma* died. It's no excuse, but I'm here now. I want to make amends for the mistakes I've made." With one final breath, he confesses, "I'll keep trying until you forgive me."

I bite my lip, his words reflecting our situation also.

But his father merely peers out the window. He could cuss him out, tell him what a disappointment of a son he is, but his silence speaks volumes. There is no greater punishment than silence.

Dixon doesn't back down, however. He rounds his father's chair and crouches down in front of him. "You can ignore me all you want, but I don't give up on the people I love." He meets my eyes briefly while my cheeks heat. "I learned that from you. *Ciao, Papà.* I'll see you next week." He slowly rises and bends forward to kiss his unmoved father on the brow. He brushes past me and exits without a word.

I'm left standing, incredibly touched by what I just witnessed. With Dixon's words ringing loudly in my ears, I bid Pino farewell also. "Goodbye, Mr. Di Matteo. It was lovely meeting you." I turn to leave but abruptly stop, as I'm unable to depart without letting him know how I feel. "Your son…he's a good man. I hope you can see that again," I whisper, totally out of line.

Just as I'm about to apologize for speaking on matters I have no right to be speaking about, I notice something which has me blinking twice. At first, I think the bright sunshine has distorted my vision, but as I take a closer look, I see that what I'm witnessing is really there.

A single tear falls from Pino's eye—a tear of hope.

Without making a commotion, I quietly walk to the shelf. With trembling fingers, I gently flip over the frame and rub my palm over the dusty glass. What I see brings tears to my own eyes. This snapshot into the Di Matteo family is a happy one—one that will never be relived. It's a photo of two proud, loving parents holding their newborn baby boy.

Silently placing the frame upright, I exit, determined to make everything whole again.

Eleven

Dixon

Well, if Madison didn't think I was a complete asshole already, she sure as shit does now.

I brought her here because I wanted to share this part of me with her. A part I've never shared with anyone before. I wanted to show her how much she means to me because words are not enough. Instead, I've shown her the weak, selfish, cowardly bastard that I am by leaving my father in here to rot.

Taking a drag of my cigarette, I don't hear Maddy until she rounds the corner of the small garden shed I'm hiding behind. Pathetic. I can't even face her. She stands a few feet away, watching me closely—waiting for me to explain.

Exhaling deeply, I confess, "Madison, I'm so sorry. For everything. This is who I am." I thump my chest forcefully. "I'm weak, I'm selfish, and I'm a coward. I deserve every bullshit thing that has happened to me because I'm not a good man. This was a mistake. I'm sorry."

I flick my cigarette into the dirt, ready to hightail it back to Manhattan and drown my miseries in a bottle of scotch, but stop when Maddy takes a step forward. I watch, confused. Why is she blocking my exit? Does she not want me to leave?

"Madison...?" She continues staring at me, her emerald eyes wide. "Is everything—" But I don't have a chance to finish. She suddenly springs at me, catching me completely off guard. I catch her, desperately searching her face for answers.

She makes her intentions clear a second later when she seals her lips to mine. I can't keep up with the frantic rhythm of her kisses, but I don't care. I let her dominate me because it's what we both want.

She pushes me backward, my back crashing against the rough wooden door, the prickles adding to the heightened sensation of Maddy fucking my mouth with hers. I don't know what's come over her, but I don't question it. It's what I've been dreaming about and craving since she left my side.

She claws at me, crazed to close the already diminutive distance between us, and I comply. I frantically scoop her up into my arms, and she wraps her legs around my waist. My cock has been starved, and it demands to be fed. Maddy groans low when she feels me pressing against her quivering hot center. She wants this as much as I do.

Blindly searching for the door handle, I celebrate when it turns with a creaky whine. I lead us into the shed, spinning around quickly so it's now her turn to be imprisoned as I slam her up against the door. We're kissing madly, and the longer I kiss her, the harder I become. The throb is almost unbearable; I know this time around, it's not going anywhere until I come.

She's pressed flat against my chest, her frenzied heartbeat in song with mine. I'm certain nothing has ever felt this good. But when she slips a hand between us and strokes my hard-on, the thought dies in my pants, and I'm proven wrong.

Like a typical male, I can't do two things at once. My kisses become slow and sluggish; all I can focus on is her small hands on my cock.

"Oh, fuck, Maddy."

My heated curse encourages her, and she rubs even harder. I haven't seen her newfound confidence often, but I like it—a lot.

I pull back, needing to look into her eyes and read what's going through her mind.

"Does this feel okay?" she breathlessly pants against my lips.

"Yes."

That single word spurs her on, and she continues stroking me wickedly.

I've never been a fan of hand jobs. I mean, there are so many other jobs I would prefer. But that was before I felt Maddy's tiny hand wrap around my dick.

"Dixon," she whispers, while I almost come when she squeezes me hard. "Can I go down on you?"

Those six words, in that particular order, are now my most favorite words. But the fact we're in a garden shed no bigger than a closet makes my sexually charged mind realize that I can't allow this *angelo* to give her first blow job in a room filled with sharp garden tools and manure.

"Not here."

She sighs, and just like that, I watch her confidence wash away.

"I just don't want you on your knees in this filth," I quickly explain, not wanting to spoil the moment.

"Stop it."

I arch a brow. "Stop what?"

"Stop wrapping me in cotton wool." She slides down my body, placing her feet steadily on the ground.

"You're angry with me for being concerned about your personal hygiene?"

Her mouth twitches. "Stop putting me on a pedestal. I'm not fragile. And I'm not perfect. Nobody is." Is this her way of saying she forgives me? "So shut up, Dr. Mathews. This is happening."

Well, who am I to argue with that?

"C'mon then, Ms. Roberts." Leaning forward, I whisper, "It's time for you to put your money where your mouth will be."

She blushes a lovely pink, and the sight gets me even more wound up than I already am.

She's nervous, so I will try to respect her wishes and allow her to take control. But when her pink tongue dances out to wet her bottom lip, I lose all restraint and take hold of the reins. I bend down slowly, watching her mounting breaths push out her gorgeous tits. I stop advancing forward only when we're inches apart. Her harsh exhalations fan my face, and when I close the distance, her breaths intensify to a quicker pace.

I cup her beautiful face with my palm and nuzzle her nose with mine. "You smell divine."

She fumbles when unfastening the button on my jeans. But her inexperience, strangely enough, is a heady rush of pleasure. She kisses me lightly while unzipping my fly. Her gasp reveals she's found me standing at full salute. I didn't bother with underwear, as my junk has been confined enough as it is.

"Can I touch you?"

"You don't have to ask me. I'm yours. Touch me because you want to touch me, not because you asked."

My surrender provokes her inner vixen, and she timidly slips a hand inside my pants. The moment she makes contact with my raging hard-on, I hum low, the feeling absolute fucking bliss. She wraps her fingers around me and strokes up and down my shaft. Her stilted, jolted movements have me pushing my hips forward, encouraging her to take control.

"I'm sorry. I'm not very good at this," she confesses in a small voice.

"Don't be silly. It feels…incredible." I sigh, closing my eyes.

"I just—you're so big. I feel like I'm not doing it properly."

Those words are what every hot-blooded American male wants his girl to say when her hands are wrapped around his cock.

Keeping my ragged breathing under control, I suggest, "Try making a looser fist and relax your wrist."

"Like this?" she asks, doing as I instructed.

"Yes, exactly like that."

She slackens her grip and begins moving up and down my dick, her confidence spiking. The friction is kind of rough, but I'm not going to stop her because I can feel her finding her rhythm.

"You're a good teacher, Dr. Mathews," she breathlessly says, her strokes getting quicker and quicker.

"It's because you're a good student, Ms. Roberts." I swallow hard when she runs her thumb over my sensitive head.

As great as this feels, if she wants to act on her request,

she'd better do so soon because I'm seconds away from coming. Thankfully, she reads my desperation and stills. Before I can protest, she slips my jeans down, and I spring to full attention.

Opening my eyes, I watch as she swallows nervously. "Wow."

I would usually be filled with crude comments, but with Madison, I simply smile. Brushing my fingers through her hair, I give her an encouraging nod. She bites her lip and gulps before dropping to her knees in front of me. This sight is one I'll cherish for the rest of my life.

Her harsh breathing bathes my dick because she's inches from taking me into her mouth. I can't stand the wait any longer. I subtly shift my hips, begging her to put me out of my misery. She does. She looks up at me from under those long lashes and licks her lips before brushing back her hair and lowering her mouth onto me.

I let out a low, animalistic groan when I feel her lips wrap around my throbbing head. I have been waiting for this to happen for so long, but my imagination pales compared to the real thing.

She goes in too quick, too fast, and ends up gagging. She pulls back and leaves a quarter of me in her mouth and begins sucking slowly. She's a fast learner.

I bunch my hands into fists by my side, not wanting to force her into taking more of me than she's ready to take. But she must be able to read my sexual anguish because the clever girl raises her hand and covers what she can't take in her mouth with her palm.

That's the death of me and I throw my head back while pumping my hips forward. When I feel her choke on my eager cock, I instantly draw my hips back.

"Sorry." My words are a jumbled mess.

She surprises me by loosening her grip around my base and bobbing her head up and down, taking me in gradually. "Relax your throat," I command, my voice hoarse. She does as I order. "That's it."

When I slip in deep, the pleasure ripples through me, and my cock pulsates in her mouth, about ready to come. However, I'm not ready to blow—not yet.

She picks up the speed and finds her rhythm, her mouth working in sync with her hand. I've been blown countless times before, but there is something about this that makes me feel like it's the first time. When she cups and squeezes my balls, I moan and quickly attempt to push her away. But she fastens her mouth on me and strokes my shaft faster.

"Maddy...stop." It's a plea, one I'm seconds away from blowing—literally.

But she doesn't stop. She buries her head further, and when I look down and see her head bobbing up and down and working my cock like it's a lollipop, I can't stop myself and come with a loud, sated roar. She surprises me because she doesn't pull back. She continues sucking and swallowing, not pulling away until I'm sucked dry.

I want to say so many things, but the only thing I can say is, "Holy fucking shit!" Not exactly poetic, but hey, that's the best I can muster after blowing such a load.

When my dick slips from her lips, I look down, admiring her flushed cheeks and swollen wet lips. She looks fucking beautiful. I offer her my hand, which she accepts while shyly brushing back her matted hair as she stands.

This would usually be when I zip up my pants and make up some excuse as to why I have to go. But now, all I want to do is hug Maddy and ask her to do that again.

Tucking myself into my pants, I try to collect my breath, but it's useless. I'm a fucking mess. I'm completely embarrassed because now that I'm not squirming and whimpering like a baby, I realize I just came in thirty seconds. Talk about shortcomings. Maddy probably thinks I'm some two-pump chump.

"What's the matter? Did I do something wrong?"

I look at her, beyond horrified she would think my shortcomings are her fault. "Wrong? Are you kidding me? That was fucking incredible."

She blushes and wipes her lips. "That was…fun."

Oh, sweet baby Jesus. Fun and blow job in the same sentence is a marriage made in heaven. But before I go planning their wedding, I need to clarify something.

Brushing my pointer down her cheek, I ask, "So we're okay?" I pin her with my stare, searching her eyes for any clues.

Turning into my touch, she nods. "Yes, we're okay. I just needed time."

Nothing has ever sounded sweeter, and I can't wipe the smile from my face. Everything is where it should be. However, when I take in Maddy's flushed complexion and jagged breathing, I know one thing is out of place.

"C'mon here," I command, my eyes landing on her lips.

"W-Why?" she asks, stepping closer.

Pushing her up against the door and kissing her neck, I whisper, "Because now…it's my turn."

"Your turn for what?" She whimpers when I bite over her speeding pulse.

"My turn to make *you* scream."

Twelve

Dixon

I feel ridiculous, but after my second phenomenal blow job from Maddy, I'm her fucking slave. I had no idea what to get, so I ordered one of everything. But as I look down at the assortment of breakfast choices, I know she'll probably only want coffee.

I don't know how it happened, but somehow, my plan has worked. By showing Maddy my weakness, she's seen my strength, and those simple words— "we're okay"—have made me forget the smidge of guilt I feel for what I've done. But I've done what I had to in order to survive. I won't let Juliet win. My hands are tied, and I'm playing by her rules. I just have to keep reminding myself of that fact.

"Morning."

That voice has me spinning around, forgetting everything but her. "Good morning. I got you breakfast."

"I can see that." She giggles as she spots my overloaded

kitchen counter.

I smirk and go about pouring her a cup of coffee.

"So did you cook this?" she asks, stealing a slice of bacon as she hops onto a stool.

"I can't take credit for anything but the coffee." I place a mug in front of her, the coffee steam wafting through the air.

She laughs. "I don't know what I did to deserve this, but thank you." The moment the words leave her lips, she blushes and quickly reaches for the cup.

"You know exactly what you did." When her ears turn pink, I put her out of her misery. "Amazing blow job aside, I'm talking about the fact you're sitting here in my kitchen, drinking my coffee when I never thought you'd do so again. I really missed you."

She smiles. "I really missed you, too." But when her smile slowly disappears, and she lowers her eyes, I know what she's thinking. "Dixon…" She scratches her fingernail over the handle of the mug. "I…how do you know Beth? I mean, Juliet."

And there it is, the question I've been dreading.

When I remain quiet, she presses, "You said you—"

But I interrupt her. "I know what I said." Reminding myself of why I'm doing this, I begin to spin my web of deceit. "She was my patient."

"W-What?" Maddy gasps, her mouth hanging open.

"She came to my office, seeking therapy for a problem she has."

"What problem?"

"I shouldn't be telling you this due to doctor–patient confidentially, but well…" I massage the back of my neck. "She's a sex addict."

Maddy's mouth drops open even farther. "A what?"

"A sex addict. Juliet is addicted to sex." Amongst other things.

I can see Maddy's processing everything I just said, trying to think back to any signs that might have clued her in to her condition. "I don't know what to say."

"I know it's a shock, but I only saw her twice before I referred her to another doctor."

"Why?"

Keep it together, Dixon. "Because she made it quite clear she was interested in more than just my skills as a doctor."

Maddy's jaw clenches. "That *bitch*."

"You must understand this was before I even knew you existed. So you can imagine my surprise when I discovered you were connected."

"Why didn't you tell me?" Her tone is accusing. If only she knew the whole truth.

"Why do you think I didn't tell you?" I interlace my fingers on the countertop.

"Well, apart from the fact I'd lose my shit, I know it's because you're a good doctor and respected the confidentiality code."

If only she knew how I disrespected the code over and over again, but I nod. "That's correct. I'm sorry I didn't tell you, but it was for the greater good."

When she frowns, I lean forward and stroke her cheek. "Everything I do, I do for you. I do to protect you." This entire story may be total bullshit, but that's the God's honest truth. I'm lying to protect her.

She nods slowly. "It shouldn't surprise me. I always knew she was sick."

She really does wear her heart on her sleeve. "Why do you say that?"

When she shuffles in her seat and looks anywhere but at me, I know something is very wrong. "Maddy? Hey, look at me," I press. Have I slipped up? Can she see through my lies?

When she finally meets my gaze and tears sting her eyes, I begin to panic. My plan was foolproof, but I should have known Madison is no fool.

"Dixon, seeing as you're being honest, it's my turn to be honest, too."

"Okay," I say apprehensively, my heart rate beginning to rise.

She takes a sip of coffee. "As you know, Beth and I aren't exactly on friendly terms. There's a reason for that."

I can feel it. I know that whatever awful secret she's about to divulge will make me hate Juliet even more than I already do.

"Do you remember when I told you…" She blows out a shaky breath. "When I told you about the night Dylan r-r-raped me?"

That word is so, so ugly. But I nod.

She sniffs, her hands twisting in her lap. "I told you someone saw what he was doing to me and didn't stop it."

I feel bile rising. I think I'm going to be sick.

She gulps in a mouthful of air. "Well, that someone was… Juliet."

No, please, no. This can't be. But as I watch the tears rolling down her cheeks, I know that it's true. This god-awful nightmare is true. I really *was* fucking the devil.

"I think she knew all along. But that night, it confirmed that she indeed knew everything, yet she didn't help me. The next day, she acted like she didn't see a thing. I was dying inside, and she didn't care. She was the only person I could talk to about this. Then, in return, she gets engaged to my brother. How messed up is that?" She laughs bitterly, the tears continuing to fall.

I'm shaking. My entire body is trembling in anger.

I. Am. Going. To. Kill. Her.

My brain is convulsing, unable to digest what she's just shared. As I pull it together, however, I realize this entire time, Juliet hated Madison because, in her sick, twisted mind, she saw Dylan's act of violence as an act of *love*. As a sign that he loved and cared for Madison more than he loved her. That narcissistic, psychotic…cunt.

"Say something, please," she begs when I remain mute.

Her desperation pulls me out from a very dark place. "You are…the strongest, bravest person I know."

"I don't feel brave." She sniffs, wiping her nose with a napkin.

"Well, you are. To survive this, you are a remarkable human being. You are the reason I go on."

More tears sting her eyes, but I'm happy to see they're of the happy kind. "So now you know it all. Now you know why I can't tell my mom because not only will it kill her, it'll also kill Sebastian. I tell anyone this secret, it'll destroy my entire family. And I can't live with that. This pain…" She presses her fist to her heart. "I can live with it. I have for over ten years. But I can't break my mother and father's hearts. Better I suffer than them."

I can't stop myself. I need to touch her, to hold her, to tell her how much I…love her? *Do* I love her? Right now, at this moment, I know that I do. I think I always have. I've just been

Wicked**DIX**

too blinded to see it. I round the counter and enfold her in my arms. She cries softly, but they seem to be tears of relief. She's finally been able to share her secrets with someone, and in return, I fucking lie to her.

I hold her, allowing her to grieve for a lost childhood. For the Madison Roberts she might have been.

After a few moments, her sobbing ceases, and she pulls away, embarrassed. "Sorry. I just…I haven't told anyone that. Not even my shrink."

"Thank you for trusting me." I kiss the top of her head, hoping to disguise the fury bubbling inside me. "What are you up to today? Have you got class?"

"No. Not today. I was going to study. Internships are coming up, and I want to get into a good hospital."

"I can always refer you. I know people," I tease, wiping away her tears with my thumb.

"Thank you, but I want to do this on my own." I nod in complete understanding. "Besides, all the hospitals are good. Even the ones in Colorado."

I pull back, horrified. "You're not considering going there, are you?" I feel a lump form in my throat.

"I was," she confesses. "But not anymore."

I breathe a sigh of relief. "I've got to get ready for work, but do you want to study here? You'll have the house to yourself."

She looks almost relieved. Just as I wonder why, I clue on to the obvious when she says, "Home doesn't really feel like home these days."

I grind down on my jawbone. "You can stay here as long as you like. Do you need me to fetch any of your books or clothes?"

"No, I'm okay. I've been staying with Mary, so I have most

of my stuff in my car." That explains why I didn't catch her at home this past week.

"Wonderful. In that case, make yourself at home." I kiss her nose, suddenly struck with an idea.

"What? You're not going to eat any of this?" She gestures to the mountain of food in front of her.

"No. It's all for you. I'm late for work anyhow, so I better get moving."

"Oh well, more for me." She bites into a waffle while I kiss her cheek quickly.

"Don't ruin your appetite. We're going out to dinner to celebrate."

"Celebrate what?" she asks around a mouthful of food.

"I've been nominated for the Gerald Harriet's Award."

She pulls back, confused. "What? I don't understand."

I look up at the clock, time slowly ticking away. "I'll explain everything tonight. But let's just say I have a goat to thank."

She pulls a grossed-out face while I bend down to kiss her syrupy lips. Just as she slips in her tongue, I pull away. "Save your kisses for tonight."

Before she can tempt me further, I kiss her cheek once more before heading down the hallway to my room. Shutting the door behind me, I listen to ensure Madison isn't following. When the coast is clear, I reach for my cell and dial.

"Good morning, Dr. Mathews."

"Good morning, Ms. Vale. Can you please reschedule my morning appointments?"

"Of course. Is everything okay?"

Looking into the mirror, I reply, "Yes, everything is fine. I have a rodent problem I need to deal with."

"Oh, dear."

"It's okay. I've got it under control. Once I'm finished, they'll all be gone."

Deep down, I always knew it was Juliet who saw what happened to Madison. But now that my suspicions have been confirmed, I don't feel relieved—I feel fucking worse.

When I made the decision to venture down this path, it was about protection. But now, it's about revenge. This isn't about right or wrong anymore—my scruples are long gone. They vanished the moment Madison told me the ugly truth.

I'm going to take great pleasure in seeing Juliet burn for what she did to Maddy, and I won't stop until there's nothing left. That's the reason I'm knocking on Juliet's door at eight thirty on a Monday morning.

The door opens a second later, and I try not to retch when I see Juliet standing before me. "Dixon? What are you doing here?" By her hushed tone and the slice of doorway she's peering through, I dare say she's not alone.

This reminds me of the time she turned up at my door unannounced and masturbated on my doorstep while Maddy slept innocently inside. I, unlike her, have the decency to prove my point without having to whip out my dick. "I'm sorry for not calling first. Are you alone?"

"No, Dylan is here. He's still asleep."

I can't believe she'd willingly share her bed with that monster—but who am I kidding? She's a monster herself.

"Oh, really?" I look over her shoulder, not bothering to

135

mute my voice.

"Yes. What do you want?" She's nervous, and because she's not in control of the situation, she wants me gone.

This will only take a moment.

"I want to fuck."-*ing kill you*, I silently add.

"Oh?" She licks her lips nervously.

I nod, laying on the charm. "But I'll leave you be, seeing as you're currently indisposed." I turn to leave but grin when she stops me.

"Wait!" She flings open the door. "It's just…now isn't a good time. Can you come back later?"

I adjust a cuff link coolly. "No can do. I'm working all day, then have dinner plans. It's okay. I'm sure Dylan can keep you company."

She looks over her shoulder and frowns. "Not likely."

I sigh and lean against the doorframe casually as I look down at her plaid pajama bottoms. "Is he still holding out?"

She nods unhappily.

I tsk. "I have no idea what's the matter with him. I remember a time when your bed was solely for the purpose of fucking and nothing more."

Her frown grows deeper. "The only fucking it's seen is when I'm in it alone."

"Like last week?"

She actually blushes. "Yes."

"Good. From now on, when you slip in under the covers, I want you to think of me."

"Why?" Her breathing begins to climb.

"Because you know I'm the only person who can make you come, and come hard," I cockily reply. "It doesn't seem your fiancé is taking his role too seriously. Shame that."

She pales as I plant the seed of doubt. Plant the seed and watch it grow. "He's just tired from work," she defends, unable to accept that her life with Dylan is anything but perfect.

I shrug. "So was I, but I still recall delivering where it counted."

She stews over my words and glumly confesses, "You're right."

This is really too easy.

By rocking an already unstable boat, I hope that Juliet will doubt Dylan's feelings for her more than she already does. Deep down, she knows he wants someone other than her, and in the past, she's used sex as her card to win him over. But now that that isn't working, I want her to doubt the entire foundation their "relationship" is built on. Doubt it so much that she'll believe the grass is greener on the other side. And that other side is me. I'm going to take away everything that matters to her, and I plan on starting with her relationship.

My aim is not to have her end things with him, seeing as she's the only person keeping Dylan away from Madison. I just want her to keep him on a tighter leash. He'll partake in the façade because he's using her as a front for what, for *whom*, he really wants. If he can't have Madison, then Juliet will do. I want her to be aware of that fact every time she looks at him. I want her to know she's always going to be second best.

"I must go. Remember; think of me whenever your pussy is involved." Another psychological seed is planted. She can't come unless she thinks of me. Have fun fucking your fiancé now.

Leaning in close, she purrs, "I sometimes do."

Great, I'm already halfway there.

I smirk, also leaning in so we're inches apart. "Sometimes isn't going to cut it. Make it all the time."

"Okay, Dr. Mathews." Her breaths are small and winded.

"Excellent. Good day, Ms. Harte." I push off the doorframe.

"Dr. Mathews?"

"Yes."

She pulls at the hem of her baggy tee. "Do you really think Dylan isn't taking us seriously?"

I squash down my smile. "How do you define fiancé?"

She mulls over my question before replying, "Someone who loves, cares, and worships his fiancée."

"And is that how Dylan makes you feel?"

She frowns but doesn't reply.

Putting forward my last play for the day, I pin her with an overconfident stare. "I know if I were your fiancé, you wouldn't be out here talking to another man, unsatisfied, and wearing those hideous pajamas. If I were your fiancé, you'd be too busy sucking my dick to talk to another man, totally satisfied, and not wearing anything at all."

She whimpers and bites down on her bottom lip.

I shrug arrogantly. "But that's just me. See you soon. And hopefully, see you in something a little more…you." I don't wait for her reply. I turn my back, unable to wipe the smile clean. Step one was a complete success. Juliet will be torturing herself with everything I've just said.

If I told Juliet she were a green bucket, she would scoff at the idea, as she knows she's neither green nor a bucket. But because I've told her something she has been questioning herself about, she'll begin to doubt everything. Food for thought, you bitch. I hope you fucking choke.

I think in her own twisted mind, she really loves Dylan. She always has. But things are not what she thought them to be. I know she'll never leave him, so I plan on bringing the dysfunctionality of their relationship to her attention regularly. I believe he's the only person who can hurt her, and I plan on using this to my advantage.

As I drive to work, I begin orchestrating my next plan of attack. I've dissected her relationship, so it's now time to start working on something she loves almost as much—her vanity.

Thirteen

Madison

It's Saturday afternoon, and Dixon and I are playing my new favorite game—strip studying. The rules are simple. For every right answer, Dixon removes an item of clothing. For every wrong one, an item of clothing goes back on.

At the moment, he's down to one sock, jeans, and a navy tee.

He flicks through the monster textbook and smiles. "Idiopathic thrombocytopenic purpura is?"

I think over the question before replying, "A bleeding disorder characterized by too few platelets."

He looks impressed. "Well done." When he reaches down and slips off his other sock, I try to hide my disappointment that he didn't reach for his shirt instead.

Thankfully, he doesn't address my frustration that he's still dressed. "Which of the following joints normally has three-hundred-and-sixty-degree circumflexion? The knee. The shoulder. The elbow. Or the fingertips."

I know this answer, but I'm too distracted by Dixon's hotness to concentrate. "Um, the knee?" I respond dreamily.

"The knee? That would be awfully painful."

Painful? The only thing painful is the fact he's still clothed. "Huh?" I ask, finally coming to and meeting his amused eyes.

When he raises a brow, I so know I'm busted. I try my best to appear innocent, but I can't help but grin.

"Now Madison…" His voice is laced with promise. "If you wanted to see me naked, all you had to do was ask." He places the textbook onto the coffee table while I lean back and gulp.

He stands slowly, grips the hem of his tee, and yanks it up over his head. The moment his defined chest is bare, I press my legs together and stifle my moan. Somehow, I've ended up spending every night in Dixon's bed this past week. At first, it was because I was too afraid to go home, but now, it's because I don't want to leave his side. Not only do I feel safe around him but I also feel myself beginning to open up in ways I never thought possible. We've fooled around some, but when he stopped because we were getting a little heated, I found myself wanting more.

Just like right now.

He's absolutely gorgeous. I never tire of his slightly rugged facial hair, which sets off the blue in his eyes. Nor do I ever tire of his muscled chest, rebellious tattoo which poetically says 'We are never so defenseless against suffering as when we love,' or that hardened V muscle, which is accentuated with a painting of dark scruff leading into his low-slung jeans.

"You keep looking at me that way and I won't be held accountable for my actions."

His comment doesn't sway me in the slightest as I continue eye-fucking him. "Duly noted."

A growl rumbles from his chest before he bends forward and pushes me back onto the sofa. I fall willingly, welcoming his weight against me. He locks my lips to his and kisses me with such ferocity he takes my breath away. I can't keep up with his speed, so I surrender, allowing him total control. He presses into me even farther and wraps his hand behind my neck, fisting my hair in a tight hold. The pressure increases as I duel my tongue with his.

A small knot begins to build in my belly, my body hinting at what it wants. I scissor my legs, the need to feel him pressed against me almost too much. His heated skin sets my flesh alight. Without thinking, I reach for the bottom of my tank and draw it up my body. Dixon stops kissing me and rises up, resting his weight on his palms.

Looking down at me, he smirks. "You take that off, and we've got a problem."

Without a second thought, I sit up and lightly push him so he falls backward. He's watching me carefully. I see his chest rising and falling as I shyly slip the tank over my head. I'm sitting before him in nothing but my black strapless bra and jeans.

Under his intense stare, I feel like a goddess, so I don't cover my almost nudity like I usually would. I like that I can provoke that look in his eye because it shows me he feels the same way as I do about him.

I'm forming some crazy-strong feelings for Dixon, and if I were to scratch at the surface, I know those feelings would translate into love. I think I've always loved him, but now those feelings have deepened, and I can't imagine my life without him.

Sitting up, he leans forward and draws me into his lap. When his erection presses against me, I can't suppress the moan which escapes me. Every part of my body feels like lava, and I'm seconds away from erupting. Dixon senses my need and rewards me with his trademark mischievous grin as he reaches around and unsnaps my bra. The lacy material falls away, and a second later, I'm bare. He doesn't break eye contact, however. He continues gazing at me hungrily.

I shift away, a touch self-conscious, but he stops me from moving by wrapping his palm around my waist. "Your body is unbelievable, Madison. Don't ever feel uncomfortable around me. I fucking worship you. Inside and out."

His passionate words only stoke my fire, and I feel my skin break out into tiny goose bumps. He runs a finger up my arm, his eyes focusing on each one. When I watch him glide his pointer over my shoulder, along my collarbone, and then down to my chest, my breathing begins to mount, pushing my breasts out dangerously close to his mouth.

He smirks before he bends forward and takes a needy nipple between his warm lips. I can't help but cry out as the sensation sends sparks all the way to my toes. He tastes me, sucking and kneading in a way only he knows how. With the other hand, he massages my other breast, pulling and tugging at my nipple until I'm left panting and whimpering in need.

I arch my back, granting him greater access as I need more. And I know that *more* will only be doused by reaching into my pants and extinguishing the inferno between my legs.

"More," I shamelessly beg as I begin rocking, his length pressing against me in just the right way.

"You want me to get you off?" he hoarsely questions around my breast.

"Fuck yes." I can't help the profanity, but desperate times call for desperate measures, and there is no greater desperation than right now.

Dixon chuckles before reaching between us. With deft fingers, he unsnaps the top button of my jeans. He takes my nipple back into his mouth as he slips his hand into my pants. He bypasses my underwear and goes straight in for the kill. We both hiss the moment he touches me in the flesh.

"You're always so ready for me. You know what a fucking turn-on that is." It's not really a question, but rather a statement, a statement filled with pure ownership—ownership of my body. And it's true. I belong to him. I always have.

I grunt in response, focusing on the way his fingers and mouth work in sync with one another as they bring me closer to the edge. He bites my nipple softly while inserting a finger into my starved body. He works his way in slow, but tonight, slow is not enough.

"More. Please."

Dixon growls and slowly works in another, filling me so deliciously full I never want him to leave. He begins stroking me gently while I work my hips, his fingers moving deep within me. He's skating around my center, teasing me because he knows the moment he touches me, I'll explode. He wants to ride out my pleasure as long as he can.

He delves in deeper and deeper, so deep he takes my breath away. I gasp, feeling that sinister knot tightening and tightening.

"I want these." He goes from one breast to the other, sucking, nipping, and licking madly. "I want this." He twirls his fingers inside me while circling his thumb over my cleft.

I scream and squeeze my eyes shut. The feeling of being worked over this way sends my senses into overdrive. But he's stalling and teasing me, as I know he's holding out and waiting for the grand finale. "Please, Dixon."

"Please what?"

"Please, finish me off. I'm so close."

"I know," he smugly replies, coiling his tongue around my nipple.

"If you d-don't, then I will." I impulsively reach down and nudge his hand out of the way as I slip a finger into myself. It's a poor substitute, and my body instantly demands Dixon's return.

"Holy shit. That is so fucking hot." His hand cups mine, guiding me to insert another finger, so I do.

I'm totally touching myself in front of another person, and I don't care. All I care about is my release.

"C'mon, chase it out. Touch yourself and feel what I feel every time I touch you."

I throw my head back as I continue touching myself quickly with Dixon's hand still locked over mine. He's directing the speed and how deep I go, and when he flicks over my core, it's almost my undoing. I'm so close. I'm speeding toward the finish line…but when Dixon withdraws his hand and slips his fingers, the ones which were inside me moments ago, into my mouth and orders me to suck, I lose all control and come so violently that I see stars. I ride out my release, my fingers not stilling until the last tremor wracks my sated body.

When I collapse in a heap, Dixon hums. "That was by far the hottest thing I have ever witnessed in my entire life." I grunt in response, my head resting lazily against his shoulder.

I'm not sure how long I stay this way, and only Dixon's cell chiming has me moving an inch so he can reach around me to snatch it off the coffee table. "Hey, Finch. Oh, man, that's awesome," he says, pressing the phone to his ear as he runs his fingers down my back.

My skin instantly reacts to his touch.

"Maddy is over. I'm, er, helping her study."

I can't help but laugh.

"Sure. Let me ask her."

Pulling back slowly, I brush my matted hair from my eyes. When I see Dixon, I instantly flush as it hits home that I just masturbated on his lap.

He smirks, totally reading my thoughts. "Finch and Heidi have invited us over for dinner. Gabriella just started walking, and they want to celebrate. Do you want to go?"

I nod animatedly as I've yet to meet Finch. "I would love to. Tell him thank you."

He uncovers the phone and smiles. "Did you hear that?" They go on talking with me perched on Dixon's lap as he touches me instinctively.

It's so nice to feel this comfortable with another person, especially knowing that all our secrets are out in the open. He knows my secrets, and I now know his. I know he's ashamed for leaving his father in care. I also know that my gut instinct was right about Beth. Just the thought of her attempting to seduce him has my high slowly fading. But all of that is in the past. I understand why he didn't tell me. It's not a big deal. I mean, it's not like they were involved or anything. The thought has me wondering what if they were. Could I ever get over it and be with Dixon anyway? Running my hand over his whiskers, I know that I could. If he were honest, then I could get over anything.

So no more lies. He's accepted my horrible past, and it feels like he cherishes me more. A secret that I thought would hinder my future relationships has done the opposite because I've never felt closer to anyone in my life. I've forgotten about our fight because none of that matters now. The truth really does set one free.

"What are you smiling about?" he asks as he ends the call.

"Just how nice this is."

When he raises a smug eyebrow, I playfully hit his arm. "Not that. I meant it's nice that we can be honest with one another about everything. There are no more secrets between us."

I notice a tic under his eye but write it off as me probably saying too much. I have to learn to control my feelings before I go and say something stupid like I love you.

"We should get ready," he says with a slight strain to his voice.

Just as I wonder what's wrong, I feel that he's still hard. "Oh, sorry." I quickly climb off his lap, realizing I'm probably not helping the situation in his pants.

He smiles and rises, kissing me on the forehead. "I'll take a quick shower."

I nod as I slip on my bra. I'm waiting for him to playfully suggest I join him as he's done in the past. But he doesn't. He sighs, appearing to want to tell me something, but at the last minute, he changes his mind.

When he walks down the hallway, I tell my overactive imagination to quit it with the conspiracy theories. Everything is where it should be, and I couldn't be happier.

Fourteen

Dixon

And just like that, my guilty conscience rears its ugly head. This week has been wonderful, and not once have I regretted my decision not to tell Madison the truth. But her statement earlier tonight reminded me of what a lying asshole I am.

"Is everything okay?" Madison asks as we walk to Finch's front door.

I raise my head, realizing my eyes have been glued to the floor. I need to get a grip. "Yes, fine. I can't wait for you to meet Finch."

"Me either," she says, smiling. "Will Debbie be here?"

Before I have a chance to press the doorbell, the door opens wide. "S'up, bitches!"

I look over at Maddy, who hides a smile behind her hand. "Sadly, yes."

"Give me a hug, you sexy thang." I step aside, presuming

he's addressing Maddy, but I'm caught off guard when he wraps his meaty arms around me. "Your turn next, Cherry Pie," he promises over my shoulder while Maddy giggles.

"Get off me, you ape." I push him away while Hunter chuckles. "And I'd appreciate you not calling my girlfriend a bitch."

"Oh, girlfriend. My little boy is growing up," he quips, wiping his eye.

Reaching for Madison's hand, I flick him in the nuts as I walk past. "Too bad you haven't." I laugh as he clutches his junk and breathes heavily through his nose.

"Speaking of girlfriends, is your little redheaded friend attending this evening?" he asks, still clutching his balls as he closes the door.

Madison shakes her head as she looks up at me, confused. "No. I didn't know she was invited."

Hunter scoffs. "Of course, she is. Call her right now."

He pulls out his cell, offering it to Maddy. She tentatively reaches for it, but I slap his hand away. "Nice try."

Maddy appears completely baffled, but of course she is. She's not devious like Hunter, and has no idea he's playing her.

"You dial her on his phone," I explain. "She'll be subjected to heavy breathing, drunk dials, and dick pics from this pervert." I know Hunter's tricks. Hell, I taught him his tricks once upon a time.

Maddy screws up her face while Hunter slaps a hand over his wounded heart. "I'll have you know I'm not into drunk dials." However, he doesn't dispute the other claims.

"Hey, guys. Welcome. You must be Madison," Finch says as he rounds the corner, a dishcloth thrown over his shoulder.

"I am. And you must be Finch." She steps forward and automatically gives him a kiss on the cheek.

His enormous grin reveals he likes her. "My wife, Heidi, is just feeding our daughter, Gabriella. She won't be too long."

"Oh, that's okay. I can't wait to meet them both."

Finch looks as smitten by her as Hunter and I are. Not that I can blame them. She's perfect.

We follow Finch into the living room. A bottle of white wine and a cheese platter sit on the coffee table. "Please, sit. Dinner is almost ready." He heads back into the kitchen while we take a seat on the sofa.

"Wine?" I ask Maddy, reaching for the bottle.

"Yes, please." I don't even bother asking Hunter, as I know his answer.

"So Cherry Pie, how've you been?" I casually peer over at Hunter as I pour the wine. What's he up to?

"Never been better," she innocently replies.

"That's awesome. I'm happy you guys worked out your shit. The doctor was one sorry sad sack," he reveals, lounging back in his seat.

I pass Maddy her glass, ensuring my hands don't shake. This secret is turning me into a paranoid mess.

"Were you?" she asks softly, sipping the wine.

"Of course I was," I reply without delay, not at all ashamed.

"It's good to see you shaved. And showered," Hunter teases while I smirk. "But honestly, it's good to see you happy, Dix."

I look over at him, surprised to catch him with his serious face on. "Thanks, man."

He reaches for the wine. "You know what would make *me* happy?" We both look at him. "If you'd call Mary."

And just like that, his serious face is promptly replaced with his horny one. I can't help but laugh. "I'll give you points for trying."

"But?"

"But I know you'll do something to piss her off, and I value my nuts where they are, as I'll be guilty by association."

Maddy almost spits up her wine while Hunter chuckles roughly.

"I'm so sorry to keep you waiting." Heidi enters the room with a sleepy Gabriella in her arms. "She wouldn't go to sleep until she saw Uncle Dixon."

"Is that right?" I place my glass on the table and stand. "Hello, little *bambola*." Gabriella extends her chubby little arms as I walk toward her. "You're getting heavy," I say as Heidi passes her over to me.

She replies with a bunch of gibberish before giggling and pulling at my nose. If only my life was that simple.

"Gabby, I want you to meet someone." Turning her around, I say, "See that pretty lady over there?" Gabby babbles on happily as I point at Maddy. "Well, that's Madison." I lightly grip her tiny wrist and wave at a smiling Maddy, who waves back.

"Hi, Gabriella. You're just beautiful."

Gabby cackles loudly when I tickle under her chin. "She just adores you, Dixon," Heidi reveals, looking lovingly at her daughter.

"Well, I simply adore her, too." I tap her on the nose.

"You're going to make a great dad one day," she innocently states while I try not to blanch.

I smile weakly, hoping no one can read my instant retreat because all I can think is one day too soon.

"I think I'll be way cooler," Hunter composedly says. In true Hunter fashion, he's eased an uncomfortable situation by cracking a joke. I must remember to thank him.

Both Heidi and Maddy laugh, none the wiser that I'm squirming where I stand.

"How rude of me. I'm Heidi. I was too mesmerized by how good my daughter looks in your man's arms," she says, walking over to Maddy, who stands.

"Me too," she dreamily replies, still looking my way.

The girls hug and talk amongst themselves while I look over at Hunter, who raises his eyebrows and blows out a silent breath of relief for the both of us.

Dinner has been wonderful. Everyone loves Madison—not that I ever doubted they would.

Conversation and food have flowed freely, and not a minute has been filled with uncomfortable silences. I don't remember it being this way with Lily, but that's because Lily was an antisocial bitch who thought she was too good for any of my friends, bar Leo, of course.

But she's a distant memory, thanks to Madison.

"Are you sure it's okay if she comes over?" Maddy's sweet voice brings me back to the now.

"Of course it's okay. Tell her, Finch," Hunter says, speaking on behalf of the hosts as he nods animatedly.

"Of course," Finch replies with a grin.

Hunter beams and attempts to fist-bump with Finch, but he looks down at his fist, confused.

I actually think he's got a thing for the fiery redhead. "I haven't seen you this excited since you discovered RedTube," I state, sipping my wine.

The entire table bursts into laughter, including Hunter, who doesn't deny my claims.

"Okay. As long as you're sure. I'll call her now." When Maddy stands to fetch her bag, I too stand, as I need a cigarette.

"I'm just going out for a smoke." As I make my way to the balcony doors, I look over my shoulder, surprised to see Hunter and Finch following.

"We'll keep you company." Thanks to Finch's nonexistent poker face, I know I'm about to be grilled. The moment the glass door slides shut behind me, I brace myself for what's about to come.

"Spit it out," I demand, placing the Marlboro between my lips and lighting up. I don't even bother to turn around.

"Madison is a sweet, kind girl, Dix."

I nod. "I know."

"I just…we think you should tell her."

Blowing out a smoke ring, I watch it evaporate before I reply. "Thank you for your concern, Finch, but no. This is for the best."

"Oh, cut the crap. Stop dicking around with Juliet and tell Madison the truth." I turn around and lean against the railing as I look at Hunter.

"I am *not* dicking around with Juliet. That's the whole point of this. My dick is clean," I explain for the hundredth time.

"Yeah, but your-your soul isn't," he refutes, nodding smugly, challenging me to contest his ridiculous claim.

Pulling back, I can't help but laugh. "My *soul*? Are you

fucking kidding me right now?"

"Look man, I'm only saying this because I love your ugly ass, but how long can you live this double life before one of them finds out?"

"I've done well so far. Neither will ever find out," I reply arrogantly.

Hunter shakes his head. "That's not the point."

I spread my arms out wide. "Then what is?"

However, when Finch lowers his eyes, I look his way to answer my question. "It's wrong."

I point toward the balcony doors, pinning them both with my stare. "So is breaking Madison's heart. And that's exactly what'll happen if I tell her."

Finch runs a hand over his beard, appearing troubled. "I don't agree. Give her some credit, Dix. I really think she'll understand. You can come back from telling the truth. But lying to her this way—you can't."

"That's a risk I'm willing to take."

Both Finch and Hunter sigh, appearing angered by my stubbornness, but I'm not budging on this as I've made my bed, and I'm prepared to lie in it.

"Thank you for your concern, but drop it."

"You're such a stubborn asshole," Hunter declares, his tone revealing he's given up.

I flip him off. "Thank you."

The phone vibrating in my pocket is a godsend. As I pull it out, I see I've received a text from Juliet.

Are you busy?

Yes. Why?

I wanted to talk.

About what?

About us.

"It's her, isn't it?" Hunter asks, attempting to look at my screen.

I ignore him and turn around. **What about us?**

I want to know where we stand.

My stomach drops. Is she clueing on to my plan? **You stand with your fiancé.**

I've come to realize it's not the place I want to be. Are you still seeing Maddy?

Shit. Idle hands are the devil's plaything. Juliet must be home alone, thinking over everything I've said.

Yes. I decide to be honest to gauge her response.

So what am I to you?

I think the better question is, what am I to you? I'm not the one who's

engaged.

Are you with her now?

"Dixon, seriously. You need to stop this."

But what Finch and Hunter don't understand is that I can't. I've invested far too much to stop now.

Yes.

Choose.

And there it is. Juliet is back and badder than ever. I knew breaking her would take time, but I need to step it up.

Hating myself more than ever, I reply. **I'll be there in 20.**

"I have to go," I state, slipping my phone into my back pocket.

"Dix!" Hunter scolds. "Do not go to her."

Ignoring him, I butt out my smoke and turn to look at Finch. "Thanks for having me, Finch."

"You're really going? We haven't even had dessert yet. And what about Maddy? What are you going to tell her?"

"Don't worry about it. It's under control."

Hunter angrily states, "No, it's not under control. What does she want from you? I mean, you say you're not sleeping with her. So why are you going over there? I doubt it's to play a game of Yahtzee!"

I run my hands down my face. "She wants to win."

"Win what?"

"Me!" I heatedly spit, poking myself in the chest. "Don't you get it? This has never been about sex. It's always been about control. And power. And now that she's lost that, she wants it back. She can't stand that I'm happy when she's not. I have to allow her to believe that she's winning. That she's in control, as it's the only way I can get out of this. It's the only way I can keep Madison safe! If you only knew what she did to Madison, you wouldn't be so quick to disapprove. She deserves this. Every single thing I plan on doing to her, she fucking deserves."

Hunter's face drops when he reads my frustration loud and clear. "Dix—" But he stops when the balcony door opens.

We all turn our attention to Maddy, who is standing before us. By her slightly narrowed gaze, she knows something is up, but she chooses to ignore it. "So Mary will be here in around forty-five minutes. She's just finished work, so she'll shower and come straight over. I hope that's okay." Her gaze bounces between us. I bottle my anger because I need to get a grip.

"That's fine," Finch nervously replies.

I hate that I've put him in this position, but I can deal with my guilt tomorrow. "Actually, I've got to go," I reveal, thankful I sound composed.

"Go? Go where?" Madison asks, her brows furrowing in confusion.

"There's been an emergency at work that I have to deal with."

"Oh? But it's Saturday."

"I know. But my patients don't care what day it is. I'm sorry." I walk over to her, giving her a gentle smile. "But you stay."

She sighs, looking disappointed. "It's okay. You can just

drop me off at home on the way."

That's the first time she's suggested going back there. But that won't happen. It can't. Seeing as that's my stop, too.

I shake my head. "No. Stay. I won't be long. And besides, I think Hunter just may cry if he doesn't get to see his girlfriend." I turn to look at Hunter, who smiles half-heartedly. He's so not impressed with me right now.

As she works her lip, she finally agrees. "Okay." But I can see the hint of doubt behind her eyes.

Needing to erase that look, I reach into my pocket and pull out my wallet. Searching inside, I pull out my spare key. "Just in case you want to go, and I'm not back in time. Get Hunter to drive you back to my place, and I'll meet you there." I open up her hand and place my key into her palm.

"Okay. Thanks. I'll give it back to you."

Brushing my knuckle down her cheek, I shake my head. "Keep it. It's yours."

Her eyes widen. "W-What?"

I can't help but smile at her response. "You heard me. Keep it."

She holds up the key, waving it in my face. "This is a key. To your home," she states, appearing stunned that I would give this to her.

"I know what it is," I reply calmly.

"And you're giving it to me? To keep?" she clarifies, still watching me closely.

I nod with a grin. "But if you don't want it…" I reach for it teasingly.

She quickly snatches her hand away. "I never said I didn't want it. I just meant, are you sure?"

"Yes." And I mean it. I've never been more certain of anything before in my life.

This is a big step in our relationship, but it's one I'm taking without any doubts. Giving her the key to my home seems so natural, considering she already holds the key to my heart.

"Thank you." She looks up at me, her smile filled with nothing but delight.

"Welcome home," I whisper, kissing the tip of her nose. Wishing I could stay, I sigh and gently kiss her lips. "I'll give you a call once I'm done."

"Okay."

"Have fun. Don't let Hunter corrupt you while I'm gone."

She smirks. "I'm sure he'll be too busy trying to corrupt Lamb."

I turn over my shoulder to look at Hunter, who clutches his chest over his heart. "Lamb? It's meant to be. Hunter and the lamb."

"Yeah, but in this circumstance, you're the lamb."

Madison laughs while Hunter shrugs. "I'm okay with that."

The mood has lightened, which makes leaving a little easier. "On that note, I better get going. I'll see you later."

"Hurry back. I miss you already," Madison whispers, crushing my resolve.

God only knows I don't want to go, but with no other choice, I kiss her lips briefly. I nibble on her bottom lip before pulling away. She whimpers low, her eyes slowly opening. "I'll see you soon," I affirm, kissing her forehead, not wanting to let her go. But I have to.

"Okay. Bye."

Saying goodbye shouldn't be this hard, but it is. And that's because a small part of me knows that what I'm doing is wrong. I can make all the excuses I want, but I'm leaving Madison to go see Juliet. Go see Juliet do only God knows what.

Pushing aside my guilt, I grow a pair and turn around to face Hunter. "Look after my girl." He nods, understanding the double meaning.

I walk out the door, unsure of what I'm walking into.

Thump.
Thump.
Thump.

My short, sharp knocks reflect my mood.

"Why, hello." Juliet smiles as she opens the door. I don't even bother replying and stroll past her, my hands dug deep in my pockets.

When the door closes behind me, I put on my game face and swallow down my disgust at being here. "So I've chosen. What do you want?"

I keep my back turned because the sheer slip she's wearing answers the question for me. "Well, I'm home alone. I'd hate to waste this opportunity."

I close my eyes in distaste when I feel her fingernail run down the side of my neck. "Indeed," I reply when I trust my voice not to betray my abhorrence.

"I've missed this between us, Dixon. I've been thinking a lot about what you said about Dylan. It's true. Things are not what I thought they would be. He used to fuck me with such vigor, and now he can barely get it up. He's not a real man like you are." She

presses into my back as she slides her hand to my front.

I remain still, keeping my breathing under control. As she glides her fingers lower and lower, I feel my humanity evaporating with every touch. And when she reaches my crotch and begins massaging, my brain and body become two separate entities. But this is exactly what I had hoped for. Groping aside, I wanted to break down her person, chip away her confidence until she was mine to control.

I haven't figured out what I'll do once I've achieved total domination because, honestly, I wasn't sure if it would work. But it has. She's played into my palms—but sadly, her palms are the ones doing the playing.

My dick has absolutely no interest in coming out to play, and my apathy gives me an idea. Stilling her hand with mine, I draw it away from me. Turning around with an unhurried, calculated speed, I stop to face her.

She licks her lips nervously, watching and anticipating my every move. I take one step toward her, and then another. A raspy breath hitches in her throat when I gather up the hem of her slip. I make my intentions clear when I place her fingers over her pussy.

With our eyes still locked, I command, "Touch yourself."

"Here?" she questions, raising a brow. "Wouldn't you rather we take it into the bedroom?"

"No. Right here will do." I remove my hand from hers and take a step backward, thankful for the breathing space.

She looks at me while I return her gaze, refusing to look anywhere past her neck. "Take a seat," she purrs, pushing me backward. "And enjoy the show."

Slumping down into the armchair, I lounge back and steeple

my fingers in front of my mouth in hopes of hiding my scowl. Juliet doesn't seem to notice my disgust as she grins and slips a hand back underneath her gown. I swallow hard and hope my plan works.

She begins rubbing over her cunt, moaning lightly while I force myself to look. She's not totally exposed, as the slip gives her a shred of coverage, but the small glimpse I'm getting is more than enough. Her wetness glistens, and when she begins rubbing over her clit with two fingers, I see her flushed skin come alive. I, on the other hand, feel utterly lifeless.

Her pert nipples push through the thin material and she cups one breast while speeding up the dance of her fingers. "Oh, God," she pants, her eyes slipping shut as she throws back her head.

There is completely zero movement within my pants, and if possible, the act in front of me has my cock retreating, not at all interested in seeing the depraved show. I feel appalling, sitting here, watching this, but I knew things would have to get a little dirty if I wanted to be rid of Juliet for good.

By now, the old me would have had my pants around my ankles and dick in hand. But that person is somebody I used to know. The new me, the *real* me, finds this display sickening and needs to get the hell outta Dodge.

Juliet must sense my detachment because her eyes pop open and drop to my very unenthused lap. Her hand stills from fondling herself. "Is everything okay?"

I scratch the side of my head. "Sorry. I'm just not into it."

"What do you mean?"

"You're not doing it for me," I bluntly reply.

Her hand falls out from under her slip. "Why? You never

162

had a problem getting hard before."

Shrugging, I casually cross my ankle over my knee. "I know, but that was before…" I pause on purpose.

"Before what?"

I remain silent, allowing her to fill in the blanks. "Before I got fat and resembled a beached whale?"

I look away, not because her words hold any truth but because she's played into my trap perfectly. I couldn't care less that she's put on weight. She's not doing it for me because she's not who I want. She doesn't stimulate me emotionally, and my emotions are now the ruler of my dick.

Just like I knew she would, she's jumped to the conclusion that her looks are what have left me with a flaccid cock. She would never presume that I can't get a hard-on because she's a blackmailing, lying bitch. I never once said her pregnancy is the reason for my impotence—she did.

At this moment, a small, tiny, stupid part of me actually feels sorry for her. To live her life like this must be so…tiresome. She'll never understand that true beauty is found within.

Just like with her relationship, I've planted a seed, and now I'll watch it grow. "I'm revolting." She self-consciously tugs at the hem of her slip. "No one wants me anymore."

"And that bothers you?"

"Of course it does."

"Why?"

"Because there was a time when people were begging to have sex with me. Now I'm the one who's begging. I'm begging for sex," she scoffs.

"How does that make you feel?" I lean forward, implying I'm listening.

She slumps onto the sofa across from me. "It makes me feel like a fucking leper, Doctor. Going from being wanted to unwanted in a blink of an eye is a slap to a girl's ego."

"Maybe it's time you work on that then." I'm slowly deconstructing her. There has to be more to her than just sex. She can't be all bad, can she? But I know the answer is yes, she is. What she did to Madison reveals what kind of a person she is.

"How? I'm not even halfway through my pregnancy. I'm only going to get fatter," she reveals, totally missing the point.

"I know you're creative. Think of another way."

She purses her lips, appearing to be deep in thought. "The only way is if she disappeared."

I count to three before I speak. "You can't wish all your enemies to disappear to solve your problems, Juliet. You need to take responsibility for your actions."

"I don't understand."

"Do you think you hide behind sex? That you use it to gain control?"

She laughs incredulously, but when her lips pull into a thin line, I know I'm on to something. "And now that sex isn't working, you feel helpless and powerless?"

She shrugs. "For argument's sake, if what you're saying is true, what do I do about it?"

"Well, for starters, you could stop hiding behind your pussy and start working on yourself."

She pulls back, appearing hurt. "So now you're saying I'm ugly on the inside as well as the outside?"

If possible, she's even uglier within. "I never said that," I reply, omitting my true thoughts.

She folds her arms over her chest. "You may as well have."

"Why do you think that?"

She appears overcome as she looks away.

Her defeat has me pressing. "Juliet, are you happy?" I intend to keep asking her this until she cracks. I need to discover her weaknesses, which is the key to breaking her.

"As of this moment, no, I'm not. I'm unhappy because I'm sexually frustrated," she replies, hiding behind sex once again.

I shake my head. "Take the sex out of it. Are. You. Happy?" I repeat slowly.

She blinks once, then twice. "Yes. Very."

"I think you're lying," I state with poise.

"Well, I'm not," she replies defensively.

"You're only lying to yourself. I think you're extremely unhappy, and you have been for a very long time. As they say, misery loves company, and I think you're the most miserable of the bunch."

Tears prick her eyes.

Her vulnerability gives me an idea. "Have you ever thought your misery was a consequence of your actions? They do say karma is only a bitch if you are." She pulls back like I've slapped her. "Maybe this is your karma catching up to you?"

"Nobody's perfect." She sniffs, wiping her nose.

"You're right. But some people are just born bad. And those people are the ones who end up alone."

Juliet blanches, her worst fears expressed out loud.

I'm tearing her down both physically and mentally, and when a tear runs down her cheek, a sense of wrongdoing passes over me. Breaking Juliet will be easier than I thought it would be, and suddenly, I feel like the villain in this story.

I quickly stand before I lose my cool and fuck up everything I've put into motion. I'm here for a reason. I must never forget that.

"Where are you going?" She jumps up, wiping her eyes, embarrassed.

"Home."

"I want you to stay. We don't have to do anything. Maybe you could...hold me?"

Hold her? Even when we were involved, not once did I hold her. But I squash down that response. By tonight's short evaluation, I've diagnosed Juliet as being a vulnerable narcissist with a borderline personality disorder. I still believe she has a deep-seated sense of shame that emerged during early childhood. Could it be she secretly feels guilty for what she saw? Or was her mother's passing the one event that totally fucked her up?

In her own way, Juliet has a fragile self-esteem. The fact I haven't succumbed to her spell has left her feeling disempowered. She also feels inadequate. When I walk out that door, she'll be preoccupied with fears of rejection and abandonment because her charm no longer works. She can no longer control those she wants with the lure of her golden cooch. And to a narcissist, that is their worst fear.

She actually *cares* what Dylan and I think of her. That's what distinguishes her from being a total sociopath.

The problem is, now that I know what's "wrong" with her, what do I plan on doing with that information? I could really crush her, but do I want to? By playing this game with her, I'm lowering myself to her level. I'm totally manipulating someone who could use my help. I suddenly feel like I'm kicking a defenseless puppy.

But when I think about Madison and how Juliet could have saved her, my emotions overthrow my conscience, and I know what has to be done. I must remind myself that a narcissist is always playing to win. And by *not* playing, but rather by playing her back, is how I win.

"Maybe next time," I reply without emotion.

I need to leave her wanting and craving more because she's too damn proud to beg. She replies as I know she would. "Okay."

I stroll toward the door, going over my Psychology 101. Compliments are like food to starving narcissists. "By the way," I say over my shoulder, "I'm still as intrigued by you as I was the day I met you." This is true. But just not in the way she thinks I mean it.

Her cheeks flush, and she appears sated…for now.

She doesn't reply and allows me to leave. I've stoked her self-importance. Therefore, she thinks she's won. But she has no idea who she's playing against.

She never did.

Fifteen

Dixon

One month later

"**N**ow remember what I told you?"

"Yes."

"Say it out loud." I adjust the volume on my Bluetooth to ensure I hear her properly.

"You'll be gone for ten days, and you will be unreachable because you'll be stuck in meetings all day."

"Good girl."

This past month has been trying, but in the words of a great woman, Maya Angelou, "All great achievements require time." And there is no greater achievement than seeing Juliet become putty in my hands.

I've molded and manipulated her into whom and what I want her to be, and that person is somehow keeping Dylan away from Madison. She's also no longer threatening to tell Madison about us because she's under the pretense that she's in control.

To achieve this power over her, I've had to continue lying to Maddy and see Juliet behind her back. Yes, I feel guilty, but that guilt has slowly been replaced with victory. I've finally won the game Juliet was so sure she'd win.

I haven't done anything too deplorable, and not once have I touched her to get what I want. I have encouraged her to touch herself, but only when I'm gone, as I'm not interested in seeing that sight ever again.

From the time spent with Juliet, I have discovered that her addiction stems back to one person: Dylan Roberts. She is completely and totally infatuated with him, and has been since the day they met. Too bad his obsession lies with someone other than her. Juliet knows who that person is, and it haunts her every day. Because of that, she despises Madison. She always has. Madison has what Juliet wants—Dylan's unconditional love.

It's safe to assume that I was right, and she saw Dylan's act of violence as an act of love. She didn't tell anyone about what she saw because she was jealous, so from that day forward, she used sex to reel Dylan in. When that didn't work because she still didn't have Dylan's complete affection, she used sex to control other men and women because the one person she wanted didn't want her back. And like a complete and utter moron, I fell into her trap.

But not anymore.

She's now filled with self-doubt over everything, self-doubt I planted.

Clearing my throat and squashing down my feelings of shame, I say, "Okay, I'm just heading to the airport now. I better run."

"I wish I could come too. I've always wanted to go to Switzerland."

I indicate to make a right-hand turn. "Maybe next time. Do you have anything planned for this evening?"

Her unimpressed sigh answers my question. "No. Dylan has to work late."

"Check your emails," I command, zipping in and out of traffic because I'm running late.

"What? Right now?"

"Yes."

I hear her phone beeping away and then a gasp. "Dixon, this is amazing. Thank you."

"The pleasure is all mine. You deserve some R&R, and what better place for that to happen than the Hamptons?" I state, referring to the spa and hotel package I purchased for her.

"The ticket is valid for two people," she says, reading over the details.

"Yes. I thought you may want to take Rachel along," I reply, knowing damn well she won't take her stepmother.

She pauses before asking, "Would you mind if I took Dylan instead?"

I fake sigh. "I suppose not. Do whatever makes you happy."

"Thank you, Dixon. This is exactly what we need. Seven days away from Manhattan and everybody who lives in it."

"You're welcome." Little does she know, this is exactly what *I* need.

It's Madison's birthday in three days, and I meant it when I said I was taking her to Rome. However, I didn't want Juliet to know. I have been playing off my relationship with Madison as just a casual thing, but taking her to Italy for her birthday doesn't really support that claim, so I needed Juliet busy, and the only way I can do that is by sending her away to some retreat and occupying her time with foot massages, yoga, and whatever else they do at those places.

I also needed Dylan to be gone, as I have no doubt he's secretly been watching Maddy's door, hoping to catch a glimpse of her. Although the majority of her time has been spent with me, she still drops by her apartment every couple of days to pack clean clothes. If he didn't see her, he'd start asking questions, questions that Rachel knows the answers to. I can't risk him accidentally spilling the beans to Juliet. I know I'm being extra cautious, but I won't have anything ruining my time away with Maddy.

As much as I hate to admit it, this double life is growing old, just like Hunter and Finch said it would. But I have a plan.

I can see a change in Madison. It may be small, but it's a change nonetheless. She never divulges what she discusses at therapy, but I know that sooner or later, she'll be ready to tell Rachel and Sebastian her secret. And when she does, I'll be free.

I'll no longer have to continue with this charade, as I have no doubt Dylan will want to get as far away from Rachel and Sebastian as he can get. So will Juliet. She's just as guilty as he is, and I know he'll take the coward's way out and run. I also know Juliet will go with him. She'll move heaven and hell to be with him, so I'm hoping he runs far, far away and never comes back.

This is the only thing keeping me going, and as much as I want this reality to be now, I won't push Madison in any way because this is something she can't rush.

"I just got to the airport. Enjoy your time away," I say,

pulling up at the curb.

"Thank you. You too. I'll speak to you when you get back."

I can't help but smirk. "Yes, you will."

I end the call and wave to an excited Madison who is waiting for me in front of her workplace. She runs over to the car and yanks the door open. "Please tell me you remembered to bring my luggage?" she says as she jumps into the passenger seat.

I look over my shoulder to answer her question—my back seat and trunk are filled with suitcases.

She chuckles and leans across the seat to give my cheek a quick kiss. "Well, that's what happens when you don't tell a girl where you're taking her. We could be going to Alaska for all I know. I needed to pack for all seasons," she explains while I playfully shake my head.

"So you're really not telling me where we're going?" she asks as I pull into traffic.

"Nope. It's a surprise. But I can assure you, it's not Alaska."

She slumps low in her seat and dramatically crosses her arms over her chest. "Okay, I suppose I've waited this long. A few more minutes won't hurt…too much," she adds with a smile.

Her excitement is palpable, and honestly, so is mine. I can't wait to spend ten whole days with her. And ten whole days without the she-devil. I'm quite certain Madison has no idea, and a small part of me is concerned that I'm getting better at lying to her. But being away from Manhattan allows me to forget all about that and focus on what's important—her.

"How was work?" I ask, taking the turn for JFK. Maddy couldn't get out of her morning shift but was able to leave at ten thirty so we could catch our one thirty flight.

"It was boring. I was able to cram in a ton of homework, though. Hey, are we going to the airport?" she questions, sitting up tall and practically pressing her nose against the windshield.

"Maybe," I reply, unable to hide my smile.

"Oh my God! I thought we were going on a road trip."

"We still might be."

"Ugh." She falls back into her seat. "You are too good at keeping secrets."

I know her comment is harmless, but I still feel a heavy weight form in the pit of my stomach. Ignoring that sinking feeling, I focus on Maddy as she talks about internships. She really wants the gig at Mount Sinai Hospital, and her chances are looking good.

The drive into JFK is thankfully short and as I park my car into the long-term parking lot, Maddy raises an eyebrow.

"Can you please tell me where we're going?" She interlaces her fingers into praying hands.

"No," I reply, kissing the tip of her nose.

We jump onto the shuttle and ride it until we reach the international terminals. I unload Maddy's three suitcases while she bounces on the spot excitedly.

"Dixon, you're killing me!" she whines behind me as I steer our cart through the glass doors.

She really is too adorable, and I can't wait until she finds out where we're going. As we make our way through the crowd, I can't stop thinking about what lies ahead. Our own private villa allows us complete seclusion, and truthfully, I don't know how I'm going to keep my hands to myself.

"Oh my effing God! No? No way!" Madison's almost curse alerts me to the fact that she's guessed where we're going.

I come to a halt and smirk. "See, now wasn't that worth the wait?"

Looking down at her, I realize that this secret, all my secrets, have been worthwhile because nothing can ever compare to her throwing herself in my arms while crying happily. "You're really taking me to Rome? I thought you were kidding!" she says, sniffing back her tears.

"No, I think I took a wrong turn," I tease, hugging her tight.

She chuckles and sobs in the same breath, but then suddenly pulls out of my embrace, looking troubled. "I didn't pack my passport!"

"Looks like you can't come then." I sigh, but quickly grin when she looks like she's about to start crying again.

"Oh, you're so mean, Dixon Mathews." She pokes her tongue out at me playfully.

I lower her to her feet and reach into my jacket pocket, producing her passport. "Lucky your mom did."

She raises an eyebrow. "My mom was in on this?" When I smirk, she snatches the passport from my hand. "Don't answer that." As we check in at the first-class counter, Madison's eyes grow wide. "I've never flown first class before."

"There's a first time for everything," I reply without thinking, as my comment might make her feel uncomfortable.

But when her cheeks flush, and she nervously tugs at her bracelets, I know it's had the opposite effect. "I can't wait."

I stifle my desperate growl and slip my fingers through hers as we make our way through the security checkpoints.

We have a little while before our flight leaves, so we decide to chill out and sit in the lounge. As I scroll through my emails, I can feel Madison watching me closely. I unhurriedly look up from my screen and catch her staring at me openly. Usually, she would look away, embarrassed to be caught, but this time she doesn't.

I match her stare, wondering what she's thinking. She makes her thoughts clear when she slowly stands and walks over to me. Without a word, she perches on my lap, wraps her arms around my neck, and rests her ear against my chest. The gesture is so trusting that I can't help but smile.

"Thank you, Dixon," she whispers.

"You're welcome. Happy Birthday, Madison," I reply, cocooning her into my arms.

When her breathing becomes deeper and heavier, I wonder what's wrong. "Best birthday present ever," she finally says. "I love…it."

I don't reply or make a big deal about it. I simply hold her tighter than I ever have before because if I didn't know any better, I'd say she was going to say something crazy like…I love you.

Sixteen

Madison

"Wow," I gasp for the hundredth time as I look at the magical, moonlit scenery in front of me.

I know it's not exactly poetic, but it's all I can muster because I am literally speechless. And that's probably not a bad thing, considering I almost told Dixon I loved him. I was so wrapped up in the moment, and it was nearly out before I could stop myself. I'm certain he knew what I meant to say but, funnily enough, I don't care.

Bringing me here to Rome for my birthday is kind of a big deal. I mean, I've only ever traveled as far as Boston. But here I am, sitting in a fancy Mercedes in Rome, faced with yet another surprise.

We've ventured out of the city and are traveling farther and farther into the countryside. I've had to sit on my hands to stop my fidgeting because I am so damn excited. Ten whole days with just Dixon in Rome—it's a dream come true.

My eyes widen when I see where we're headed. "We're staying here?" I ask, lunging forward to look out the windshield.

"Maybe." Dixon gives a vague response. He's so enjoying watching me explode in anticipation.

The gravel driveway takes us up to a beautiful two-story terracotta home set on a hillside. When Dixon turns off the car, I spin around to look at him. "Our own private villa? You've got to be shitting me!"

"Welcome home, honey," he says with a dimpled grin.

I can't stop my feet as I wrench open the door and dash up the steps of the house. It's simply enchanting. The rustic building is surrounded by olive tree groves and beautiful views of the surrounding hills. The air out here is so fresh and clear, I can't help but take in a big lungful. As I turn in a circle, I see that there is absolutely no one around us. We have this entire paradise to ourselves.

"So it's safe to assume you like it?" Dixon asks over my shoulder.

Without tearing my eyes away from the serene sight in front of me, I nod. "You assume correctly, Dr. Mathews. Thank you. This is perfect."

Turning around, I thank him the only way I can. I catch him completely off guard when I throw my arms around his neck and kiss him passionately. It only takes a second or two before he catches up.

Something is changing in me. I can feel it. Every time I kiss or touch Dixon, a small piece of my past slips away, and before long, I think it'll disappear. It'll no longer rule me because I am no longer afraid. And that's thanks to the man I'm falling deeper and deeper in love with.

I put all my love and affection into my actions, kissing him tenderly and tugging at the strands of hair curling at his nape. He returns the response by matching me kiss for kiss. Before long, I can't keep up and allow him total control. He dominates my mouth and body, leaving me panting and desperately clinging on tight as I can't get enough. The constant burn gets stronger and more painful, and I know the only thing that'll douse those flames is him.

When Dixon slows down and steadily pulls away, I know he feels it too. "We better get inside. It's getting late," he says, his beautiful eyes appearing translucent under the bright moonlight.

I nod, not trusting my voice.

We gather our luggage and make our way up the concrete stairs to the front door. The moment I step foot inside, the reality of where I am and who I'm with sinks in, and tears sting my eyes. I can't ever remember being this happy.

As the door closes behind me, I quickly wipe my eyes, not wanting Dixon to see me cry. "Wow."

Dixon chuckles and gently brushes past me as I continue gaping around in awe. The rural feel continues inside, where the walls are painted in a dark beige, and the roof is supported by long wooden beams. As I step through the archway and into the spacious living room, I see an antique-looking chandelier hanging in the middle of the room. It complements the lavish oriental rug beautifully. The plush, cream furniture looks suitable for royalty, and I resist the urge to see if it feels as silky as it looks.

I'm lost in the beauty of my surroundings and don't hear

Dixon's entrance until he wraps his arms around my waist and whispers, "I've put your bags upstairs."

I'm barely able to contain my shiver. "And what about your bags?"

"They're sitting upstairs next to yours. Is that okay? There's a guest bedroom if you—"

I quickly cut him off. "You're not staying in the guest bedroom. Of course it's okay."

He kisses the side of my neck. "Good because I was actually going to suggest *you* could stay in the guest bedroom." I burst out laughing. "Would you like some wine? It's from a local vineyard."

"Sure, that'll be nice." Realizing I'm still in my work clothes, I say, "I might take a shower."

"Of course. I'll bring it upstairs. We can sit on the balcony for a while if you like."

"That sounds wonderful." I turn around and kiss him quickly before dashing up the carpeted stairs.

I try not to gape at the stunning artworks strewn along the walls for too long and find the main bedroom is the last room on the left. When I open the door, a swarm of butterflies takes flight in my belly. The room, which is decorated in shades of brown, beige, and champagne, seems designed to highlight the Victorian-style four-poster bed. A gorgeous gold canopy drapes down over the dark wooden posts, shrouding the bed in elegant luxury.

I ignore my sudden nerves and sit on the floor to hunt through my suitcase. Unzipping my bag, I pull out my toiletries and reach for my flannel pajamas. However, as I look up at the majestic bed, I boldly run my fingers over my satin slip instead.

I've never owned anything like this before, but when Dixon said he was taking me away for my birthday, I used the Victoria's Secret gift card my mom gave me and splurged. The butterflies unexpectedly return, but I don't know why. I've slept beside Dixon countless times before, but for some reason, this feels different.

As I sneak another quick peek at the humongous bed in front of me, I know the reason. Being here, away from everyone and everything, has left me feeling like a normal woman on vacation with her normal boyfriend. All my troubles and worries have somehow been left in New York, and I feel like I can finally breathe. With that thought in mind, I gather my toiletries and new slip, and make my way into the extravagant en suite.

Twenty minutes later, I'm feeling incredibly relaxed after my scalding shower. Now that I've somewhat got over my shock of being here in Rome, I realize it's almost dawn. Sadly, my exhausted body is still functioning on New York time, and I'm ready for bed.

Determined to stay awake for at least one glass of wine, I run my fingers through my hair and make my way into the bedroom. The wooden double balcony doors are open, suggesting that Dixon is outside. I wander out in bare feet, the cool stone floor feeling divine under my warmed skin.

Dixon is lounging on a seat, appearing deep in thought as he looks out into the vast openness. The sky has a light pink hue, but the darkness still governs the heavens.

"Hey."

"Hey yourself," he replies, not turning around.

A half bottle of wine and a glass sits on the small circular table, so I reach for the goblet and take a seat next to Dixon. As I peer over the solid stone balcony, I gasp. The crest of dawn is on the horizon, spreading a sheet of warm radiance over the picture-perfect landscape.

"It's so beautiful," I say, unable to hide my awe.

"It is." When he slowly turns to look at me, his sultry gaze scans down my body. "However, I've just seen something more beautiful."

"T-Thank you." I'm always so nervous when he looks at me this way. I can barely breathe. His lopsided smirk reveals he knows it, too.

"Are you tired?"

"A little," I confess. "I might call it a night or morning soon. How about you?"

He gazes out over the balcony. "I think I might stay up and watch the sunrise. It's not too far off." His calming, gentle tone has me stifling an unexpected yawn behind my hand. "Go to bed. I won't be too far behind."

Looking down at my untouched wine, I know if I take one sip of the fruity nectar, I'll be out for the count in seconds. "Okay." I stand and stretch, taking one last look at the spectacular countryside before me.

Dixon glances up and rewards me with a soft smile. "Good night, *angelo*."

Just like it does every time he uses that pet name for me, my entire body melts and I have to smother my moan. He doesn't realize how much it means to me because this term of endearment erases out any others, others that I never wanted.

With that thought in mind, I place my glass on the table and surprise Dixon as I lower myself into his lap. He opens his arms, and I nestle low, turning my head to look at the sight in front of us. "I think I'd like to watch the sunrise, too." He tightens his arms around me but doesn't say a word. We're both silent, neither of us needing to speak.

As my eyes slip shut, I can't help but think that this right here, right now, is everything I could ever wish for and more.

I wake to the smell of coffee.

My foggy brain plays catch-up, and as I feel the satin sheets underneath my fingertips, I realize I'm cocooned in our glorious bed. I don't remember getting here, and that's because I was sound asleep when Dixon put me in here. I recall seeing about five seconds of the sun mounting over the hills, but then I'm pretty sure I blacked out and was out like a light.

Looking at the bedside clock beside me, I see that it's almost 1 p.m. As I stretch out my lax muscles, I decide to go in search of that delightful smell. I slip on my robe and attempt to tame my snarled hair, but I give up when another smell, one of a sugary, syrupy sweetness kind, wafts up the stairs. I practically leap down them and run into the kitchen, not bothering to hide my excitement.

However, I stop dead in my tracks when I'm confronted with Dixon's muscled bare back as he flips pancakes on the stovetop. His blue jeans sit low on his narrow waist, revealing two perfect butt dimples above his firm ass. As he turns to the side to reach for a plate, the sunlight streaming in from the window highlights his tattoo. He really is a sight for sore eyes.

"Good morning," he says, not bothering to turn around.

I jolt, his husky voice snapping me from my very depraved thoughts. My heavy breathing must have given me away. Clearing my throat, I walk over to the kitchen counter and take a seat. "Morning."

He throws me a wink over his shoulder. "I hope you're hungry because I've made enough food to feed a small starving nation."

Giggling, I sit up tall to look over his shoulder. He's right. The enormous stack of pancakes sitting on the counter beside him resembles the Leaning Tower of Pisa. "One can never have too many pancakes," I say, wanting to show my appreciation.

He laughs and serves us a small feast while I look at every topping, filling, and condiment sitting in front of me. Reaching for the syrup and berries, I lick my lips when Dixon places my breakfast in front of me. I tuck my hair behind my ears as I lean forward and take a big sniff. It smells…interesting.

"I hope it tastes okay." I look up to see him watching me nervously.

"It'll taste amazing," I confirm, pouring a decent helping of syrup over my mountain of food.

Dixon pours us a cup of coffee while I scatter some mixed berries onto my plate. Reaching for my silverware, I cut into the gluey, uncooked dough and try not to giggle when it sticks to my fork. As I take a bite, I try not to blanch because Dixon is gauging my response closely.

"It's bad, right?" he says, placing the cup of coffee in front of me.

"No, it's great," I lie around a mouthful of food. I eye the coffee, very tempted to pour it over my meal to balance out the sweetness. When I take another bite, I fear my teeth might

183

disintegrate in my mouth. "Yum."

"Okay, stop." Dixon grins and swipes my plate out from under me.

"Hey, don't. It's good." I attempt to snatch it back, but he draws it away from me and steals my fork.

As he cuts into it and takes a bite, I quickly reach for my black coffee and gulp it down, not caring that it burns my throat. I watch with amusement over the rim of my cup as he pulls a sickened face and grips onto the edge of the counter.

"Don't they taste yummy?" I ask, nodding in encouragement.

Dixon looks at me like I've gone crazy. "I'm pretty certain I just became a diabetic," he replies, scraping the contents of my plate into the trash.

I watch, trying not to laugh, but I can't help but smirk. It's so incredibly sweet he attempted to make me breakfast when it's apparent he's probably never made pancakes before.

"They weren't *that* bad," I counter, defending his efforts. He halts from trashing the rest of his pancakes and turns to me, raising an eyebrow in complete dispute.

"Okay, they were a little sweet, but I loved that you tried…"

"To put you in a sugary coma?" he finishes for me. I bite my lip to contain my chuckles. "How about we get dressed and go out for some real food?"

I nod, my stomach rumbling in agreement. "What are we doing today? Besides eating?"

He runs a hand through his disheveled hair. "I thought we could take a drive. I have a few things planned over the next few days, so I don't want to wear you out too quickly." As soon as the words leave his lips, he appears to regret using that particular phrase. I noticed he wore the same look at the airport. But what he doesn't realize is that I don't mind.

Standing up, I finish my coffee and rinse my cup out in the sink. Dixon sneaks up behind me and wraps his hands around my waist. "You want to take a shower first?"

I nod and lean backward into his embrace. "I won't be too long." However, when he tightens his grip around me and lays a soft kiss over my shoulder, all thoughts of showering are gone.

Dixon reads my surrender and continues his kisses along the slope of my neck. I tilt my head to the side, allowing him complete access to my heated skin. When he takes my earlobe into his mouth, I whimper and feel my knees buckle beneath me. He slides a hand up my torso, only coming to a stop when he cups my left breast. I can't help the tremor that passes through me.

"You better go take that shower," he says, his fingers squeezing and fondling me. "Otherwise, you're about to get very dirty."

"Cleanliness is overrated," I breathlessly reply, my heart pounding faster and faster.

Dixon spins me around and smashes his lips to mine. He fists my hair and holds me captive as he devours my mouth whole. We kiss like we're starved—not for food but for each other. I get lost in the feel of his mouth and the hungry strokes of his tongue, and before long, I'm reaching between us to rub over the hard bulge pressing against me. He moans into my mouth, his erection getting harder and harder.

I want him like I've never wanted him before. So with quick fingers, I unsnap the top button of his jeans and drive my hand down his pants. We both grunt when I make contact with his flesh. He pumps his hips forward, encouraging me to move, so

I do.

I remember him detailing what he likes, and I follow those precise instructions as I grip him in a firm hold and begin stroking up and down his hardened length. He throws his head back, small, aroused growls coming from his parted lips. His approval urges me on, and I increase the speed of my hand.

Literally having the power in my palm is a heady feeling, and my hormones suddenly take over as I drop to my knees and yank down his pants in one fluid motion. When I'm greeted with his arousal, I lick my lips, hardly believing how desperately I want to go down on him. How desperately I want to feel him inside me.

Just as I'm about to take my first taste, I hear the front door open and a female voice calling out to us. "*Ciao. C'è qualcuno in casa? Sono la cameriera.*"

I shriek and jump up, mortifed that whoever this is will walk in and find me on my knees about to go down on my very naked boyfriend.

"*Sarò fuori in un minuto. Attendere prego,*" Dixon shouts, quickly tucking himself into his jeans.

"Who is it?" I whisper, running to hide behind him.

He sighs, running a hand through his hair. "It's housekeeping."

"Housekeeping? We don't need housekeeping," I state softly, still hiding.

"I know. I told the real estate agent that. Sorry, Madison." He turns around to look at me and brushes his knuckle across my cheek. "I'll get rid of her because her timing completely blows."

I slip around to his front and cheekily whisper, "Unlike

you."

He looks like he's about to choke on my sexually fueled comment. I don't know where this show of confidence has come from, but I like it. He's still staring at me like I have two heads when I say, "I'll go take a shower then."

He simply nods while I slip past him, loving the new me.

After a day of sightseeing around Tivoli, Dixon has taken me to a little restaurant in the hills. The venue is very intimate, and the small candles burning brightly on the tabletops and sweet Italian melody playing over the speakers add to the cozy vibe.

We're about forty-five minutes out of Rome, which I quite like. We're close enough to do all the touristy things but far enough away that we aren't swarmed by sightseers.

"Is there anything special you wanted to do for your birthday?" Dixon asks as he pours me a glass of wine.

"No. Being here with you is special enough," I reply sincerely. He nods, his smile revealing he's as happy as I feel.

Looking over the menu, I try to decode what it all means. "I'll have whatever you're having," I finally decide as I can't read a lick of Italian.

Dixon laughs and passes me my wine. The moment I take a sip, my cheeks heat, and the alcohol goes straight to my head. "Wow, that's strong."

"It's locally made. I guess the farmers don't really worry about the alcohol content," he teases, reading over the label.

A pretty brunette server saunters over to our table to

take our order. The moment her eyes land on Dixon, a surge of jealousy passes over me. She doesn't bother to conceal her blatant flirting when she bats her eyelashes and smiles. "*Buonasera. Sono Julia. Avete bisogno di aiuto con il menu?*"

I have no idea what she just said, but I hate her regardless.

"Hello, Julia. I think we're ready to order," Dixon replies, thankfully in English.

But *Julia* gives him a cutesy, sheepish smile and shakes her head. "*Io non parla inglese, signore.*"

Dixon looks at me and pulls an apologetic face. "She doesn't speak English," he explains. How convenient. But I nod, waving off his apology.

He switches to Italian and orders our meal. I only know this because Julia writes down whatever he's saying on her notepad. Once she's done, she reaches for our menus, her eyes never wavering from Dixon. Just when I think we're Julia-free, she strikes up a conversation with him, speaking a million miles a minute. Dixon laughs at something she says while she uses her hands to explain God knows whatever they're talking about. I suddenly feel like the third, uneducated wheel.

Reaching for my wine, I take a big sip, needing to do something with my hands and throat before I yell at Julia to stop looking at my boyfriend while strangling her with her long beautiful hair. Dixon picks up on my jealousy and thankfully wraps up the conversation quickly.

Julia gives him a playful wink before heading off to the kitchen. When Dixon smirks smugly at me from across the small table, I ignore him and continue gulping down my wine. I refuse to allow that Italian beauty to spoil our night.

"So what did you order?" I ask, needing to fill the silence.

"I was going to order the chicken, but Julia suggested we try the fish as it's their specialty."

"Did she now?" It's out before I can stop myself, and that smug smirk returns to Dixon's face.

"It does sound delicious," he replies, leaning back in his seat, watching me closely.

"I hate fish," I childishly reply, which is a total lie, and Dixon knows it.

"Since when?"

"Since *Julia* suggested it." I slap my hand over my mouth, mortified that I said my thoughts out loud.

Dixon rocks back in his chair, his mouth tipped up in a permanent grin. "Are you…jealous?" he asks, pausing for effect.

I scoff, but I can't deny that I am. I hate that he seems to be the object of every woman's affection because he's mine. It seems his hotness knows no international boundaries because, wherever we go, he's got a line of willing females lagging behind. That thought has me reaching for the bottle and filling up my empty glass.

"How about you wait until you've had something to eat?" Dixon suggests, still watching me carefully. I ignore his request and take a big sip. The room is spinning by the time I place the half-empty glass back on the table.

This is not like me. I've never ever been jealous over anyone or anything before. But as I see Julia wiggle her butt as she walks past our table, that sheet of jealousy washes over me once again. I don't know whether it's the wine or, as the saying goes, "when in Rome," but words fly out of my mouth before I can stop them. "How many women have you slept with?"

Dixon chokes on his wine in response.

Probably not the best place to ask such a question, but now that I've said it, I want to know. I fold my arms across my chest, waiting and watching. Dixon looks at the table to his left, giving them a polite smile as he wipes down his stained shirt.

"You really want to do this here?" he asks, circling his finger around the room.

"Sure, why not? No one will understand, seeing as no one speaks English." The corner of Dixon's mouth tugs.

"Why do you want to know?"

"I'm just curious. So how many?" I press, leaning in close. He shrugs, and for the first time in forever, I think I've caught Dr. Mathews off guard. "Like ten?" I ask, starting the count. He drums his fingers on the tabletop, avoiding all possible eye contact. His action just fuels my curiosity. "Twenty?"

"Madison, let's change the subject." He goes to reach for my hand, but I pull it away.

"No. I like this subject. Fifty?" When he uneasily reaches for his wine, I know I'm not even close. "Holy shit. What, you're telling me it's over fifty?"

Silence.

"Oh my God, a…hundred? Dixon, are you telling me you've slept with over *one* hundred women?"

He takes a big breath before fixing me with his intense stare. "Maddy, I don't know the number because…I've lost count."

My mouth pops open because I know he's telling me the truth. Wow. I don't even know how to react. I can count all my partners on one hand, well, no hands because the total amount is zero. What happened with Dylan doesn't count because he… it was…I quickly reach for my wine and down the entire glass.

I can't believe he's lost count. I mean, I get that some men are more promiscuous than some women, but holy shit, over one hundred partners equates to…I gulp. I don't even want to know how many that totals a month, or worse still, a week. I'm certain he was faithful when engaged to Lily, so are these one hundred partners before or after her? I have nothing to offer him sexually because he's seen it all before.

That thought doesn't help my unsettled stomach, and I suddenly feel like I'm going to be sick. Covering my mouth, I shoot up and make a mad dash for the front door, which is closer than the bathroom out back. Once outside, I round the corner and brace my hands on my knees as I bend over. The cool air is exactly what I need, and after three calming breaths, I swallow down my nausea.

"Madison?"

Dixon's concerned, panicked voice alerts me to how embarrassed I am. And also, what an idiot I've been. I've turned a lovely evening into a disaster because I couldn't keep my mouth shut. What is the matter with me?

"Go away, Dixon. I'm fine." I wave him off blindly.

"Like hell you are." He walks over and gently runs a hand down my back. "Are you all right? I'm so sorry if I upset you. I'm an asshole. I shouldn't have said anything."

He's the one who's apologizing? Is he serious? I'm the one who should be apologizing for my stupid behavior. "Dixon, *I'm* the one who's sorry. I shouldn't have asked. I don't know what's wrong with me."

"Maddy, please stand up. Look at me."

I don't want to look at him, but I feel light-headed, so I gradually stand tall and turn around. I keep my eyes glued to the floor, but Dixon coaxes me to look at him as he places two fingers under my chin. His tender eyes reveal nothing but care.

"There is nothing wrong with you."

"I highly doubt that. Why can't I just be normal?" I attempt to avert my gaze, but Dixon gently seizes my jaw.

"Don't get hung up on what's normal and what's not. You're you, Madison. And I wouldn't change a thing."

"Then why can't I have a regular conversation about…sex?" I ask, needing the doctor in him to tell me I'm not a complete freak.

"Do you want to know what I think?"

I nod.

He strokes over my jawline, his thumb brushing over my lower lip. "I think that it's because you're normal that you can't talk about sex freely."

"That makes no sense," I reply, sighing.

"Madison, with what happened to you, no one expects you to be comfortable talking about something you're only just coming to grips with. It's going to take some time. And that's normal. That's what living is all about. So stop beating yourself up over it, okay?" He levels my eyes with his. "Okay?"

"Okay," I softly reply.

His heartfelt speech has me wanting to clarify something I'm quite certain he already knows, but I want to make it clear anyway. "I don't care how many women you've been with." When he goes to speak, I press my finger over his lips. "I don't care because we can't take back our past. We can only move forward, and I want to move forward…with you."

Taking a deep breath, I go on. "As you know, I'm not very experienced at sex. I'm sorry." The moonlight reflects the pools of sadness in his eyes. "That night, with Dylan. He…r-raped me, but he didn't…not there." I'm falling over my words, but I press on. "What I'm trying to say is that I'm still a virgin."

When he stares at me wordlessly, I'm hoping he understands what I'm trying to say. But my customary feelings of shame overwhelm me, and I instantly regret my decision to share. "I'm sorry. I know that's probably not what you wanted to hear. I understand if you need some time…" But the air whooshes from my lungs when Dixon wraps me into his arms, cutting off any further discussion.

Tears fall freely as yet another part of me soars free.

"It's more than fifty, but less than one hundred. I think," he reveals a second later, the disgust evident in his tone. "I'm the one who should be apologizing for not being able to offer you something more…wholesome. If I could take back every single one of those women, I would."

I sniff back my tears, not caring about the number anymore. "Maybe our tainted pasts can wipe our future slates clean?"

"Maybe." That is his saddened response.

Wanting to put all my cards on the table, I confess, "I *was* jealous."

He sighs, rubbing his hands up and down my back. "That's good. Jealousy shows me that you care."

"I—"

But he doesn't let me finish. "Shh. Let me just hold you, Maddy. No more talking. Not tonight." I don't know what that means, but I comply. And besides, I think I've done enough talking for the night.

As we stand hugging for minutes, I bite down on my tongue before I reveal how much I really do care.

Seventeen

Dixon

"This would be a lot easier if we had a selfie stick."

I keep smiling until Madison snaps our picture in front of the Colosseum. Once the happy snap is taken, I turn to her with my eyebrow cocked. "What in God's name is a selfie stick?"

"You seriously don't know what a selfie stick is?" she asks, biting her top lip in an attempt to conceal her grin.

"No, I seriously do not. From the name alone, it could be misconstrued as being a number of things."

She bursts out laughing, covering her mouth to mute her giggles. "Oh my God, you really *are* old." She continues snickering at my expense while I resist the urge to Google what the hell this thing is.

Her comment, however, does raise an interesting point. I've never thought twice about the nine-year age gap between us. Has she? As if on cue, a young man close to Maddy's age

194

strolls past us, his ridiculous baggy jeans sitting halfway down his ass, exposing his cheap-looking boxer shorts. I highly doubt an intelligent, beautiful young woman like Madison would find this wankster attractive. But I sure as shit know he finds someone like her attractive as he's completely checking out her gorgeous rack.

My jealousy rivals hers, so I tug on her hand and steer her in the opposite direction.

"Hey! I wanted to look at the tunnels that lead underground," she gripes, looking at her tour map while I drag her away.

"We can do that later. Let's go this way first," I suggest, turning over my shoulder to glare at the disappointed youth.

"Okay, fine. What are you looking at?" she asks, looking behind her. Thankfully, she doesn't notice my territorial pissing.

As we go on to visit the dungeons, Maddy walks ahead with her eyes wide in awe as she takes in the sights around her. It's nice to see her so happy, especially after last night. I feared she was seconds away from telling me that she wanted nothing to do with my whore ass after I revealed how many women I've been with. I know her jealousy over the server sparked her questions, and most men would be flattered, but I'm not. I'm ashamed that I don't actually know the precise number. And I'm ashamed that that unknown number of women includes her stepsister.

Juliet has thankfully not contacted me. Here's hoping that trend will continue when I return home, but I know I'm not that lucky.

Pushing thoughts of the she-devil aside, I turn the corner and see a young woman holding a gigantic stick with her iPhone attached on the end. Smiling, she pushes a button and her photo is instantly taken. Looks like I just discovered what a selfie stick is.

Maddy turns to me, her lips tipped up into a knowing grin. "Now can you guess what a selfie stick is, you old fart?"

I reply by lunging forward and capturing her in a bear hug. She squeals as I lift her off the ground. "Put me down, you barbarian!"

Her tiny hands playfully slap at my back, but this only encourages me to squeeze her tighter and call out like a caveman. "Considering our surroundings, I'll take that as a compliment."

I love this easiness between us, and every day, I feel like Madison is finally opening up and becoming more and more comfortable with herself and her past. After she confirmed what I knew to be true about her brother, my worship for her grew to immeasurable bounds. The fact she wants to move forward with me, both physically and emotionally, makes me the luckiest son of a bitch alive. But funnily enough, I'm in no hurry to push the physical side of our relationship because I'm enjoying the emotional side so much. I never thought I would *ever* say that, but with Madison, I'm a different man.

"Are you all right?" she asks, looking down at me closely.

She must be able to read my pensive thoughts. Deciding to be honest, just as she was with me, I ask, "So you think I'm old?"

The humor on her face disappears. "What? No, I was just kidding. Why? Do you think I'm too young?" When I don't reply and lower her to the ground, she nudges me in the ribs. "Do you?"

"Too young for what?" I tease, watching her cheeks flush.

However, she doesn't let my evasive question deter her from getting an answer. "Too young for you."

I take two slow steps forward while she takes two quick steps back. When she bumps into the wall behind her, I cage her by placing both hands on either side of her head. "I suppose there *is* almost a decade between us. I'm not sure if my ancient mind can keep up with your youthful spirit. You may have to teach me a thing or two."

When her chest begins rising and falling quickly, I don't conceal the fact that I'm admiring the way her amazing tits are inflating with each raspy breath she takes. "There are only eight years between us. I do turn twenty-four in a few hours. And I-I think we can teach one another a thing or two."

Dear God, what is this woman doing to me?

Ensuring I don't sound like a slobbering fool, I nod, hoping I appear calmer than I feel. "It's your birthday? I'd totally forgotten."

She grins but pulls at her lip nervously. "So you don't think I'm too young?"

Her lip pops free when I run my thumb along the seam of her mouth. "No, Madison, you're perfect. I think I'm the one who should be beating off your young admirers with my walking stick."

"Admirers? What admirers?"

She really has no idea how beautiful she is.

"Just trust me on this." Just the thought of these men has me grinding down on my jawbone.

She places her tiny palm on my cheek, cupping my face gently. "Well, I haven't noticed because I've been too busy giving all of your admirers the stink eye."

"They can all go to hell," I honestly counter while Madison laughs.

"We really are just as bad as the other, aren't we?"

I nod. "Yes, and I'm not ashamed to admit it."

"Me neither."

Her honesty has me growing some balls, and I suddenly want to tell her how I feel. "I'm irrevocably and willingly under your spell, Madison Roberts. No other woman exists but you. So feel free to stink eye anyone you like. Odds are I won't see it because I'm too busy looking at you."

I sound like a complete and utter pussy, but this is the only way I can tell her how I feel without freaking her out and telling her that I love her—because I do. I fucking love her. There wasn't a precise time when I fell in love with her because I've been in love with her all along. And when the time is right, I'll tell her.

But now is not that time because I currently have a dozen pairs of eyes on me as a group of school kids pass us by, giggling. Giving Maddy some breathing room, I uncage her from my arms. "Shall we continue with the tour?" She nods and loops her arm through mine.

I don't fail to notice the slight tremor in her body as we continue the rough path. Could it be that Madison is irrevocably and willingly under my spell also?

There's only one way to find out.

While Madison is taking a bath, I hunt through my suitcase, desperately trying to find her birthday gift. I know I packed it because it was the first thing I grabbed. Gripping my

case in frustration, I tip it upside down and litter the carpeted floor with its contents. When the small blue velvet box catches my eye, I reach for it, cursing in celebration. I quickly throw everything back into the suitcase and shove the box into my pocket, not wanting Maddy to see her gift until after dinner.

She has no idea what I have planned, and that's part of the surprise—one I hope won't backfire on me. Instead of going out for dinner, I hired a local catering group to set up while we were out for the day in the city. They've prepared a superb five-course meal, and left instructions for me so I don't burn down the house re-heating it all.

I've placed the antipasto platter, which consists of olives, cured meats, cheeses, and different grilled vegetables, in the center of the table on the balcony. The night is too charming to waste, so I thought we could eat outdoors and enjoy the countryside that Maddy and I are growing to love.

Just as I finish pouring the wine, Maddy comes out barefoot, wearing a blue summer dress with a floral print. Her hair is left hanging naturally, and she has no makeup on. She looks absolutely beautiful. She gasps when she sees the sight in front of her.

Reaching for the lighter in my pocket, I light the two taper candles and smile. "Happy Birthday."

"Thank you." She takes a step closer and runs her hand over the linen tablecloth. "My birthday isn't for a couple of hours. And besides, when it's twelve a.m. here, it's still six p.m. in New York."

"That just means we can exploit your birthday celebrations for even longer," I reply with a grin.

She smiles and takes a seat when I pull out a chair for her.

When she reaches for the wine, I notice her trembling slightly. Is she cold? As I brush the backs of my fingers along the slope of her neck, I feel her skin is heated. She must be nervous. Maybe she too can feel that the usual static bouncing between us has just been amped up to five billion watts. I cool it and take a seat across from her.

"Help yourself. I promise you won't pass out from a sugar overdose this time."

She giggles and goes about serving up a small amount of everything. The moment she bites into the cheese, she closes her eyes in bliss. "That is so good."

"It's all locally made," I reveal, taking a sip of my wine.

"That wine is amazing too," she says, reaching for her glass after eating a piece of salami.

"It's Frascati. It's a traditional Italian wine. When in Rome," I say, raising my glass, proposing a toast.

She raises hers, waiting for me to speak.

"May this birthday be the start of a year that brings you the answers you seek, the love that you want, and the happiness you deserve because every day spent with you is the happiest day of my life. I wish all great things for you, Madison. Happy Birthday."

Even though the candlelight and moonlight are our only light sources, I can clearly see the tears prick her eyes. She doesn't bother wiping them away as she clicks glasses with me. "Thank you, Dixon. This birthday is the best one yet because I get to spend it with you."

"I'll drink to that."

As we both watch one another closely over the rims of our glasses, I know something big is about to happen. I don't know what, but as before any natural phenomenon, I can feel the earth rumbling in anticipation.

Ignoring this unexpected forewarning, I laugh when Maddy piles more food onto her plate.

"What?" she asks, stopping mid-fork load.

"We have another four courses to go," I explain, not wanting her to fill up early.

"Four?"

I nod.

She puts down her fork, but eyes the artichoke heart on her plate.

"Go on then," I say, shaking my head in amusement.

She happily reaches for it, sucking the juices from her fingers as she places it into her mouth. "You spoil me, Dr. Mathews."

Ignoring what the image of her blissfully suckling her fingers is doing to my cock, I reply, "The best is yet to come."

"I told you the best is yet to come."

"I know, but you could have warned me the best came in the shape of a humongous tiramisu. I think I'm going to be sick." Madison places her hands on her belly and falls back into her seat.

The food has been delicious, but although I thoroughly enjoyed it, I have enjoyed watching Maddy devour each course more.

"Please take it away from me," she groans, eyeing her half-eaten dessert. I reach for her plate, but she shoots up and takes one final bite. "Okay, now I'm really done," she says, her lips painted with the sweetened cake.

Laughing, I stand and take the temptation inside. It's a great ploy to fetch the impromptu birthday gift I purchased for her today. As I step back outside, I see that Maddy is standing by the balcony, looking out at the view.

When she turns to look at me over her shoulder, I present her with the black plastic bag. "Happy Birthday."

Her eyes widen, and she shakes her head. "Dixon, you didn't have to get me anything. I mean, taking me to Rome is more than enough."

"Too late." I place the gift into her hand.

She gives me a playful, disapproving look before opening the bag. The moment she sees what's inside, she bursts into fits of laughter. "You shouldn't have," she says, pulling out the selfie stick.

"Now there are no excuses not to take perfect pictures. And now you can't call me old. I've been assured that's the best selfie stick out there," I reply, thankful I was able to find this thing while Maddy was in the bathroom.

"I love it. Thank you so much." She wraps her arms around me and gives me a big hug. As I hug her back, I wonder if I should give her her second present, the one which means so much more than an insignificant gadget.

Deciding to go with my gut, I let her go and slowly reach into the pocket of my jeans. As my fingers brush over the box, my hesitation disappears. "Happy Birthday."

Madison looks down at my hand and gulps when I produce the small velvet box. "I-I don't understand. You've already given me so much. I can't accept anything else. You've already spent too much money."

"This didn't cost me a thing. Please, I want you to have it." I extend the box her way, indicating I won't take it back.

"Dixon…"

But I press. "Madison, just open it. If you don't like it, I can take it back."

"That's not the point. Whatever you give me, I'm going to love. It's just that…this is too much."

"You don't even know what's inside. I could have a hot tamale in there." She smirks and sighs when I nudge the box into her palm.

I can't bear to watch her open it as I'm terrified she'll hate it. I'm terrified that this was a bad idea. I walk over to the balcony and turn my back, unable to stomach the thought that she might hate something so important to me.

When the box hinges whine open, I take a deep breath and look out into the star-filled sky. There is no noise, only the sound of my harsh breathing. Do I regret giving Madison this?

No.

"Dixon…I don't know what to say other than it's beautiful. Thank you so much." Her bewildered voice reveals she means every word.

"It was my mother's," I explain. "She was a devout Catholic and wore that medallion every day. It's Saint Christopher, he's known as the patron saint of travel. That was given to her by her aunt the day she left Italy. I know traditionally he's meant to protect travelers, but I figure he'll protect you from the emotional journey you're currently on.

"Protect us on our travels, wherever we may roam; keep us safe and guide us, always safely home," I say, reciting the prayer my mother used to say every day. But now, it holds more significance than I ever knew it would. "I want you to know that I will always be your home. No matter how far you roam, I'll always be here, waiting for you to come home."

I know my mother would have wanted Madison to have this. I also know she would have loved Madison as much I do. Whether she decides to wear it or not, that's entirely up to her. I just wanted to give her something special, something personal, to show her how much she means to me.

"Will you help me put it on?" Maddy asks.

"Nothing would please me more." I turn around and smile when I see Madison standing before me. She hands me the silver necklace and brushes her hair to one side. I walk behind her and place the chain around her neck, fastening it gently. I can't help but run my fingers along her neckline.

She spins around slowly, fingering the charm as she peers down at it. The tears running down her cheeks reveal she likes it. Unable to see her cry, I wipe them away with my thumbs. More just fall in their place.

"What's the matter? Are you unhappy?" I ask suddenly, watching her lower lip tremble uncontrollably.

She shakes her head.

"Then what is it?"

"Dixon…" Her voice is hoarse, and I can hear the terror in her tone. "I love this." She grasps the charm, her eyes never wavering from mine. "And…I love…you."

"What?" I jar backward, not believing the words I just heard. Surely, I'm mistaken. There's no way she said what I thought she just did.

Taking an agonizingly slow breath, she steps back and shyly reaches for the hem of her dress. I'm watching in complete and utter fascination when she draws the garment up and over her head. It drops to her feet a second later and then she's standing before me, completely naked.

I am rendered speechless. The fact she came out here totally naked underneath her dress is a fucking turn-on.

Under the moonlight, she appears godly and ethereal. I've seen her naked before, just not her entire body at the one time. There are simply no words to describe what I'm seeing.

"Make love to me."

And again, there are simply no words to describe what I'm feeling.

But as she stands watching me nervously, I know I have to pull it together and be the man she deserves. "Are you sure, Madison? There's no hurry."

She nods. "I know I'm being greedy, seeing as you've already given me so much. But this is my way of giving something back."

"You don't have to give…" She steps forward, placing her finger over my lips.

"I want to. I want you."

No man could ever turn down such a request.

"I want you, too."

"Then make love to me," she repeats with nothing but conviction in her eyes.

Running my finger along the length of her face, I nod, utterly mesmerized by the beauty in front of me. Not about to take her virginity out here in the open, I scoop her up and carry her into the bedroom.

She watches me with wide, frightened eyes as I lower her onto the mattress. I stand at the foot of the bed as I take off my T-shirt. Her gaze drops to my flank. She admires my tattoo as her tongue darts out to wet her pink bottom lip.

Reaching into my pocket, I open my wallet and pull out a condom. I then slip out of my jeans. I'm miraculously wearing boxer briefs, and decide to leave them on for now.

"Will it hurt?" she asks, nervously shuffling up the bed to rest on the pillows.

"Not the way I do it," I reply with poise, hoping I help her feel at ease.

"O-Okay."

I place one knee onto the mattress and then the other, and commence my climb up toward her. She lies flat, her chest rising and falling so quickly her gorgeous breasts inflate with every breath she takes. Now that I have her naked beneath me, I don't know where to start. This experience is solely about her, so I decide to ask her.

"What do you want?" I place the condom on the side dresser.

She leans up on one elbow. "I-I don't know. Is there a certain position you want me in?" Her breaths come out faster and harder, and I can feel her heart thrashing about in her rib cage as I press my chest to hers.

I smile. "No, I meant is there anything you've liked that I've done in the past."

"Oh." Her mouth forms into a perfect O. The moment it does, my dick twitches.

"I like it when you touch me."

"Yeah?"

She nods.

"Where?"

"I like it when you touch my…breasts," she whispers,

looking away, appearing timid for confessing her desires aloud.

"And what else?"

"I like it when you touch them and go…down…on me." Her cheeks flush and she appears mortified, but little does she know, this is exactly what I want to hear.

"Your wish is my command. Lie back, *angelo*."

She does, licking her lips nervously.

I don't waste another minute and move up her body, keeping my full weight off her as I kiss her tenderly. I kiss her deliberately slowly, while she tries to speed up the pace by thrusting her tongue into my mouth. I don't take the bait and suck on it in one long, hard pull. She whimpers, her legs scissoring impatiently beneath me—which is exactly what I want.

I'm going to try my best to make this as comfortable for her as I can, and to do that, I need to get her so worked up that when I slip inside, she'll be ready and waiting. I need her to push past the pain and only focus on the pleasure.

I pull away and work my way down her body, sucking on the tender spot over her carotid pulse. Her whimpers intensify as she tosses her head back. I suck and softly bite, only letting go when I leave a red, inflamed, love-stained hickey.

I continue with my journey, only stopping when I reach her pebbled left nipple. Without delay, I take it into my mouth and suck leisurely, flicking it occasionally with my tongue.

"Ahhh!" she groans, the sheets bunched in her tight fists.

I make my way over to her other breast and give this nipple the same treatment as the first. Being buried in her chest this way is one of my most favorite things in the world. But my need to be buried someplace else has me walking my fingers over her flat stomach and stopping only when I reach the junction of her thighs.

Continuing to suckle and fondle her breasts, I run my finger along the seam of her pussy, happy to feel how hot and wet she already is. She needs no further preparation, so I insert a finger, moaning around her breast as she clenches and pulls me into the hot cavern of her sex.

I may be patient, but I'm not a damn saint. So I push in another finger. Maddy cries while her body trembles, alerting me to the fact that she needs more. And goddamn it, so do I.

Her breast pops free as I slide down her body. I twirl my tongue in her bellybutton before kissing my way down to her clit. Her body stiffens at the slight intrusion, but as I settle between her thighs and open up her legs, her body is mine to do as I please.

And all I want to do is please her.

I spread her pink glistening lips with my fingers, licking her entrance in one long, slow lick. Her cleft is so swollen and needy, I know it wouldn't take me long to make her come. But I'm going to hold off her orgasm for as long as I can.

Circling my tongue, I bury it as deep as I can go. Her hips buck upward and she fucks my face as I fuck her with my tongue. I reach up and begin tugging at her erect nipple. Her flesh feels like it's burning underneath me and with that thought in mind, I bury my face deeper into her pussy and fondle her breasts hungrily.

"Oh, God," she whimpers, her body undulating wildly.

I've never seen her so riled up before. The sight has my cock pushing at the cotton barrier of my briefs, desperately trying to escape. When it does, I know it'll be explosive.

I'm fervently eating out Maddy, not giving her a moment to catch her breath. I'm relentless and I'm also ruthless, as I'm not giving her what she wants. "Dixon, please," she begs, choking on her gasps.

"Please what?" I mumble against her folds.

"Please get me off."

Those passion-filled words are almost my undoing, but I don't give in. She's not ready. Not yet.

"Soon," I reply, pumping two fingers in and out her body, almost blowing when imagining my dick will soon replace those digits.

"Now," she impatiently counters, gripping my hair and shoving my face back into her pussy.

She raises her hips, silently pleading to give her what she wants. I slap my tongue over her clit gently, not enough to make her come, but enough to leave her a quivering mess. I need her to be so unbelievably wet that I'll slide right in. I devour her—licking, sucking, biting, and consuming until she screams out in frustration, ready to explode.

Now she's ready.

I quickly pull away but insert two fingers as I reach for the condom from the nightstand. Her eyes widen when she sees me tear the wrapper open with my teeth. Her greedy muscles clench around me as I try to pull down my boxers with one hand.

"Are you sure?" I ask one final time. Her response is to lean up and help me undress. My briefs are on the floor a second later.

As I'm slipping on the condom, she swallows fearfully while staring at my cock. "We can stop at any time," would be the gentlemanly thing to say. But once I'm sheathed inside her, I know I won't be able to stop.

So I say the only thing I can to show her that this will change us both. "I love you, too."

She appears stunned by my revelation but, as tears well in her eyes, I know that shock has turned to joy. Unable to wait a second longer, I grip my dick and rub her wetness over her entrance. She's going to be impossibly tight, so I'll go in slow.

I press the tip of my cock into her, hissing the moment she opens up and allows me in deeper. I keep my eyes glued to her the entire time, watching for any signs of discomfort. But she nods. I gently push into her, and as I feel something resisting, I know this is the part that'll probably hurt the most.

"You okay?" I croak. She nods once again.

Bending low, I take her nipple into my mouth while massaging over her clit in a slow circling motion. She groans low while squeezing her eyes shut. I push and then pull out, getting her used to the sensation. When I feel her body soften, I drive forward in one fluid movement, breaking through the thin veil of her virginity. Her mouth parts, and she cries out in a passionate mewl.

Her nipple pops free as I smile because she's now mine. My alpha howls in possession.

"Almost there," I reassure her. "Are you still okay?"

Her cheeks are flushed and her hair is a wild, tangled mess, and if that isn't the prettiest thing I've ever seen, then I don't know what is. "Yes."

That's all the encouragement I need and I propel my hips forward, filling her full. She cries out, her face scrunching up in pain. I attempt to quickly pull out, but she surprises me by wrapping her arms around my lower back, stopping me from moving an inch.

"Keep going. It feels good," she confesses.

"Okay. I'll go slow." I pull out and then plunge back in, her wetness providing all the lubrication I need.

I rock into her with measured, deliberate strokes, allowing her muscles to accept me. When she relaxes, I pick up the tempo and hook her leg around my waist to sink in at a deeper angle. I'm unable to tear my eyes off the way my cock is pumping in and out of her.

She feels fucking incredible and from this moment forward, I know I want no other pussy but hers. It's not just the feeling of being inside her, it's the feeling of being connected to her—it's just how sex, how making love should be. *This* is what I've been missing. Not the sex, but the emotion. She is the reason they call it making love.

As I increase my strokes, Maddy thrashes her head from side to side, her body beginning to learn this unfamiliar dance. Each time she clenches around me, I feel it all the way to my balls, and I'm embarrassingly close to coming. But I'll be damned if I blow before she does.

"Faster," she whispers, licking her lips as she presses the heel of her foot into my ass.

I don't want to hurt her, but the moment I hear *faster*, my hips begin pumping furiously. I reach down and hold her waist, helping her find her rhythm so she can work her way up and down my cock freely. She milks my dick, squeezing and throbbing around me.

"I love you!" she cries, the sound like music to my starved ears. I don't care that she's said it in the throes of passion because

I know she means every word.

"I love you too, *angelo*. So much."

I can feel the friction is still a little rough, so I decide to give her some verbal encouragement. "Your pussy feels incredible."

A strangled groan gets caught in her throat as she moves in sync with my faster pace.

"Does it still feel good?"

She nods, trapping her lower lip between her teeth. "More."

I know she can take it, so I thrust my hips, pistoning into her over and over again before she screams out loudly. "Oh my fucking God! Faster."

I comply, wanting nothing more than to please her.

As I rub my fingers over her cleft in a wide circle, I can feel she's close and desperate to come. So I pull out quickly, while she looks up, confused by what I'm doing.

"Trust me," I gently reassure her.

Still on her back, I turn her slightly to the right. I kneel while straddling her right leg and curling her left leg around my left flank. This opens up her pussy and I drive in, the angle allowing deeper penetration for us both. This position also allows us close eye contact, and I want that. I want to assure her that it's okay to let go.

As I thrust into her over and over and over again, I insert two fingers into her mouth, which she suckles and tongues hungrily. Pulling them out, I rub the moisture over her erect nipples, while she screams out, throwing her head back violently.

"I love you," she moans. "I fucking love you!"

Her body suddenly convulses around me, squeezing and sucking me into her warmth and wetness in one heady explosion. The intense feeling has me blowing in seconds, and we ride our release out together. I collapse on top of her in a very ungraceful manner, unable to hold up my own weight. I've come a thousand times before, but never like this.

"Are you all right?" I ask when I'm able to catch my breath.

"Yes," she whispers, her entire body trembling from head to toe.

Lifting my head, I peer down at her, unable to believe how lucky I am. Kissing her quickly, I untangle our limbs and roll off her and make my way into the en suite to dispose of the condom.

If this was anyone but Maddy, I would be thinking of any excuse to hightail it out of here, but all I can think of is going back out there and holding her until we both fall asleep. And then I want to wake up beside her and do it all again.

I walk back out into the bedroom to see Maddy sound asleep on top of the tangled sheets. Taking a moment, I appreciate her entire being. This beautiful creature is mine, and I'll do everything in my power to never let her go.

Eighteen

Dixon

I wake to one of the best feelings in the world. I wake beside Madison. I also wake beside Madison while she's giving me a gentle hand job.

Last night exceeded all my expectations. She gave me her virginity, and now she's giving me a hand job. I love having a girlfriend.

"Good morning," she huskily whispers when she realizes I'm awake.

"It most certainly is."

"I hope you don't mind," she says, palming my shaft.

"Not at all. In fact, I insist." When I open my eyes and witness her beauty for the first time today, my insides turn to mush. "How are you feeling?"

"Good," she shyly replies.

"Good," I counter, unsure if she wants to talk about last night.

"You were right."

"About?" I grit my teeth as she begins stroking faster and faster.

"About it not hurting the way you do it. It felt good. Real good." She emphasizes her point by rubbing her finger over my sensitive head.

"Well, I'm glad it was good for you because it was fan-fucking-tastic for me." I falter over my words because all I can focus on is her hand on my cock.

"This amazing part of you seems to make a potty mouth out of us both." She tugs harder and harder.

"I've always been a fuck…potty mouth." She is killing me. "If I recall correctly, you didn't mind my potty mouth all over your pretty lips last night."

"Well, that is true. Looks like I found a nickname for your—" She blushes, unable to finish her sentence.

"Hey! Why does my cock get a nickname, and I don't?"

She leans in close and whispers, "Because when I'm around him, all I want to do is say fuck."

As if on cue, my dick pulsates, happy to lay claim to that title. "I can live with that."

"Dixon?"

I grunt in response as words have finally escaped me.

"I really…can we…do you have any condoms left?" she finally spits out.

I nod with a grin. "I just happen to have two more left."

When her face falls, I don't understand why. She explains her response a second later. "Would it be okay if we visited a drugstore this afternoon then?"

My cheeky, cheeky vixen. "Yes, ma'am."

Talk of condoms and nicknames for my dick has me gently pushing her hand away and jumping up to hunt through my wallet for my golden ticket. As I roll it onto my shaft, I see Maddy watching closely. "You want to do the next one?"

She blushes but nods and then quickly looks away.

When I'm suited up, I attempt to go down on her, but she stops me by placing her hand on my shoulder. "I'm already wet," she confesses.

I growl low, those words like gospel to my rampant brain. As I insert a finger, I feel that her words are in fact true. It doesn't take long until she's squirming beneath me, begging. She pulls a pained face when I slowly work my way into her.

"You sore?"

She nods.

I automatically draw my hips back, attempting to pull out. But she stops me. "Don't you dare. Just go slow." I smile, as it seems she's just as addicted as I am.

When I'm sheathed all the way in, I compare the feeling to total utopia. "Maddy…" I grunt, beginning the dance I'm predicting we'll dance many times to come.

"Hmm?" she hums, her mouth parting as she draws in passion-filled breaths.

"Happy…birthday." I thrust into her so hard the force drives her up the bed.

She whimpers but surprises me as she grins while hooking her leg around my waist. As she raises her hips, I begin to move. "Best *fucking* birthday ever."

I smirk. Looks like my nickname is an appropriate one after all.

I'm checking over my emails while Maddy is on the phone to Mary. I'm trying not to eavesdrop, but it's hard not to when I'm the topic of conversation.

"Yes, Lamb, I used protection. Uh-huh. I don't know. Like twice."

Twice? What was twice? If she's talking about orgasms, then what about the time I went down on her twenty minutes ago?

Deciding to put myself out of my misery, I slip in my earbuds and listen to some jazz while concentrating on my emails. Most are notes from Susanna keeping me up to date. However, there are two messages which catch my eye.

One is from Chad, forwarding me the details for the Gerald Harriet's Fellowship Awards night which will be held early December. The other is from Sunnyfields Hospital, inviting me to a family fun day which will take place in a couple of weeks.

Although I have been visiting my father once a week, he still hates my guts. The only time I get a glimmer of a response is when Maddy is with me. It almost looks like he's listening a quarter of the time. But when it's just him and me, I may as well be invisible.

I jolt up when I feel a hand on my shoulder. "Sorry," Maddy apologizes as I slip out my earbuds.

"It's okay. How was Mary?" I ask, spinning my chair around to face her. When her cheeks flush, I decide I don't want to know.

She looks at my laptop and smiles. "That looks like fun. Are you going?"

I turn back around to look at the invite. "I don't know. It would feel kind of weird going, considering my father wishes I were dead."

"Don't say that. No, he doesn't. I've seen small improvements. You just have to keep trying," she encourages.

I sigh, running a hand through my hair. "He's a stubborn old fool."

"Look who's talking." She giggles when I turn over my shoulder and raise an eyebrow.

"So would you like to come with me?"

"To the family day?"

I nod and swivel my chair around.

"Um…"

When she hesitates, I quickly backtrack. "If you don't want to, I understand."

She quickly shakes her head. "No, it's not that."

"Then what is it?"

"It's just…" She pulls her sleeves over her hands. "It's a family day."

"And?"

"And I'm not technically family."

Unable to help myself, I lunge forward and draw her onto my lap. I brush back her hair so I can look into her eyes. "You're my family, therefore you're also my father's. If you'd like to attend, then the invitation stands. If it's too weird, then I totally understand."

"Do you think they'll have those mini pigs in blankets like they did the last time we visited?" is her reply.

I smile. "I'll make sure of it."

She nestles into my arms, sighing contentedly when I slip my hands over her ass. "So did you want to go get something to eat? It's your birthday. We can't waste it indoors when it's such a nice day out."

She seems to weigh up my question. "Maybe we could take some of the leftover food and a bottle of Frankcati..."

I laugh and correct her. "It's Frascati. I think it's time I taught you some Italian."

She pulls out of my hold and rolls her eyes. "Anyway, Mr. Smarty Pants, like I was saying, maybe we could take the leftover food and have a picnic. I saw some gorgeous spots on our drive yesterday."

"Sounds like a plan." I playfully smack her ass as she jumps up. "How about you put something together while I finish up in here?"

She nods. Her happiness is contagious, and I can't help but smile as she skips off to the kitchen.

However, I look up from my laptop when she comes into the room a moment later. "Maybe you could teach me something easy in Italian? Just to start me off." As she swallows nervously, I wonder why.

"Sure." I slip off my glasses. "What would you like to know?"

She toes the carpet before replying, "I love you. How do I say I love you?"

I remain calm, understanding her sudden nerves. "*Ti amo.*"

She nods and mimes the words as if trying to get her tongue around them. With a deep breath, she locks her eyes with mine. "*Ti amo. Ti amo, Dixon.*"

The phrase has never sounded sweeter.

Standing, I walk over to her. "*E ti amo, Madison.*"

219

I've never seen her happier than right now. "Maybe you could teach me another?"

"Of course. What would you like to know?" I ask, brushing back her hair.

When she toys with her bottom lip, I know what she's thinking. "Where's the nearest drugstore?"

With a smirk, I reply the only way I can. "*Non abbastanza vicino.*"

Not close enough.

Nineteen

Madison

It's our last night in Rome. Although I'm sad to leave, thinking back over my time here, I don't regret a thing.

This trip has been one of many indulgences—food, wine, sights, and sex. I never in a million years thought I could add sex to that list, but thanks to Dixon, I can.

The night we made love was unlike anything I've ever experienced before. An act I had been so afraid of ended up feeling entirely heartfelt and pure. I'll never forget what Dylan did to me. It's a part of who I am. But every time I feel Dixon inside me, the ugliness and fear is replaced with nothing but love.

The last couple of days, however, I've noticed Dixon has been a little off. Every time his phone chirps, I watch him hold his breath, only letting it out once he checks who's on the other end. I'm guessing he's anxious to go back to work, as I know he'll be busy preparing for the awards ceremony. Or maybe he just doesn't want to leave this paradise behind either.

Whatever the reason, I'm going to make our last night here as memorable as possible.

We've decided to eat in and call it an early night as we have a 10 a.m. flight tomorrow morning. Taking yet another photo of the Italian countryside I so love, I quickly post it on my Facebook page, as Mary has been living vicariously through me.

We've done everything I could have ever asked for and then some. We've visited every church, ruin, and museum there is to see in Rome because Dixon didn't want me to miss a thing. My favorite experience of all, however, was taking one special photo in front of the Trevi Fountain. My profile picture is currently that photograph, and it's of Dixon kissing me tenderly, his hand cupping my cheek.

I have so many incredible photos to look back on and remind me of a time I'll never forget. But now, it's time to make new memories.

I straighten out my red dress and fasten my hair into a high ponytail. After applying a light shade of lipstick and adjusting my beautiful pendant, I'm ready to go. I bounce down the stairs and find Dixon in the living room watching TV. He looks up and smiles when he sees me.

"You look beautiful."

"Thank you." I lounge down on the sofa next to him, curling my feet underneath me. "What are you watching?" I ask, looking at some movie flickering on the screen.

"Nothing really," he replies, passing me the remote.

That heavy feeling is back, and I don't know why. "Is everything all right? You look…sad?" I settle for, as I can't pinpoint what's wrong. I just know something isn't right.

Dixon sighs, confirming my suspicions. "I suppose I am a little sad. I've had such a wonderful time. I really don't want to leave."

"I know, but we have to."

"Do we?" he unexpectedly asks, turning to look at me.

I smile, thinking he's joking around. But when he continues staring at me seriously, I know he's not kidding. "You really want to stay? What about work? Your home? Your friends?"

He shrugs, gently reaching out to touch my cheek. "They're all things that can be found here."

"You're serious?" I ask incredulously.

He nods.

"What's keeping you in New York? Besides your mom and Sebastian?"

"School," I reply. "Internships are coming up soon, and I have a good shot at getting into a really good hospital. And what about Mary? I promised we'd never be apart."

"Mary could always visit. And you could get a transfer. I could help get you into a really good hospital here," he counters, appearing to have thought this all through.

Why does he want to leave New York? What isn't he telling me?

"I can't leave. It's my home," I reply honestly. "I finally feel like I belong there."

My answer has disappointed him. "I understand, forget I said anything." He returns his gaze back to the TV, indicating this conversation is over. But I want to know what's sparked this suggestion.

"Why don't you want to go back to New York?"

I see the hair on his arms stand on end. "It's becoming tiresome. I think I need a change."

"And that change is moving halfway across the world?" I ask, beginning to panic. "If you need a change, find a new gym. Or get a haircut. What you're proposing isn't a small change. It's life-changing."

Dixon senses my mood shift and frowns. "I'm sorry if I upset you. Forget it."

I shake my head. "No, I can't. If you're unhappy, then I need to know. Have I done something?" I rack my brain for anything I've done to tick him off.

As I'm listing all the possible things in my head, Dixon pulls me into his lap. I look into his tender eyes and see nothing but despair. I'm sure that look wasn't there a week ago. What's going on?

"Dixon—" He cuts me off by pressing his lips to mine.

"Forget this conversation ever took place," he says around my mouth.

"No," I stubbornly retort, refusing to let his charm distract me. "Tell me what's wrong." When he tries to kiss me again, I pull away and stand my ground.

He sighs once again. "I'm afraid that once we're home, all of this"—he circles his finger around the room—"will just be a distant memory. I want this with you every day, but…"

"But what?" I prompt, waiting for him to finish.

He works his jaw angrily. "But New York is filled with… fuck! I don't know." He suddenly picks me up and lightly tosses me onto the sofa, my ass bouncing on the soft cushions. I watch as he stands up and walks out the front door, slamming it shut behind him.

What was that about?

New York is filled with what?

I should let him calm down, but I can't. I need to know what's wrong. Counting to ten, I stand and go outside to find him. I don't have to look far as he's standing a few feet away, having a smoke.

"Dixon?" My voice is a mere whisper out here in the open. His shoulders stiffen when he hears my voice. "Dixon, you need to talk to me. You're scaring me."

Silence.

Tears begin forming in my eyes, but I wipe them away because I'm no longer that girl who cries at the first sign of trouble. I walk toward him but give him some space. "If you're really serious about moving here, I could maybe think about it. But I can't make that decision—"

"Please, Maddy, forget I said anything," he says irritably, blowing out a cloud of smoke.

I sniff. "No, I will not. I've got this awful feeling in the pit of my stomach that you're not telling me something." I place my hands over my tummy, suddenly feeling sick. "If you're unhappy with our relationship, or me, I can change. Just tell me what it is." I know I sound incredibly desperate, but I will do anything to make this relationship work.

"Don't you get it?" he spits, spinning around to glare at me as he throws his cigarette to the ground. "It's me." He jabs his finger violently into his chest. "*I'm* the problem. You're perfect. I'm the messed-up bastard who doesn't deserve you."

"What are you talking about?"

I'm met with a wall of silence, which annoys me. "Dixon, please. Just tell me what's wrong!"

He abruptly charges toward me, gripping my upper arms and shaking me lightly. "I'm talking about the fact that when we get back to New York, I'm terrified you're going to see the real me! You're going to find out what I've done, and then you'll hate me."

"What?" I gasp, unable to hold back my tears a second longer. "No, I would never."

He shakes his head firmly. "Yes, you will, Madison. I hate myself for it! And when that time comes, I will have to let you go. I'm surviving on borrowed time as it is."

"Dixon—"

"I'm not who I say I am," he sadly confesses, before releasing me and turning away.

But I chase after him, refusing to let him walk away. "You don't get to say all those things and then just walk away!" I grip his bicep and spin him to face me. "Why would I hate you? What have you done that's so bad?"

"What haven't I done?" is his broken reply.

I don't know what to say. My paradise has just been shit on and I don't know why. I don't understand what's going on. When did this all go to hell?

"Madison, please don't cry. I can't stand to see you cry."

I'd hardly even realized that I'm crying. I'm too busy trying to decode everything he just shared with me. Although it was all a jumbled confession, it was a confession nonetheless.

What has he done?

Fingering the charm around my neck, the charm that meant so much to Dixon, I realize that whatever he's done, I don't care. The only thing I care about is losing him, and losing this feeling of being complete when by his side.

"I don't care," I state, digging my fingernails into his arms. "Whatever you've done, I don't care."

He turns his head like I've slapped him. "Don't use words you don't understand."

"Well, if you stop talking in fucking riddles, maybe I can understand what the hell is going on! What has happened from the time I was upstairs to now to have you behaving like a lunatic?"

He lowers his eyes and it's the first time I've ever seen him admit defeat. But I won't let him give up. Not on himself. Or on us. The thought of losing Dixon, of losing what we have punches a hole straight through my chest. I find it hard to breathe.

"Please don't leave me."

Dixon cups my cheeks roughly, his eyes frantically searching mine. "Don't you understand? *You'll* be the one leaving *me*."

No. Fucking *no*.

All of my emotions come roaring out of me and I act before I can think. I slap his hands off of me and watch him watch me in confusion for a split second, before I attack him. I slam my mouth onto his, knocking the breath from both our lungs. But the connection feels too good to worry about a trivial thing such as breathing.

We devour each other, the kiss frenzied, rushed and desperate, but it's everything I need to confirm that I'm alive.

I pull at his soft hair, fisting the strands in both my hands because I need to feel as much of him as I can.

The adrenalin of the past five minutes pumps harder and faster through my veins, animating me to bite down on his lip and suck it hungrily into my mouth.

I whimper when I feel his massive erection nudge me,

demanding entrance. I've never felt this crazed before. Never wanted him inside me more than I do right now. I need it. Nothing makes more sense than him being inside me.

Dixon must be able to read my desires because he tears his mouth away, leaving me gasping for air. I'm unable to catch my breath, however because he backs me up fiercely and slams me against the brick wall. He presses his chest to mine, trapping me with his stare as he avidly slides his hand underneath my dress and bunches my underwear into his fist. With one sharp tug, he tears them clean off me. I gasp, my heart pounding hysterically, the blood whooshing through my ears.

Looking down at his tenting jeans, I know what I have to do. With desperate fingers, I unsnap his button and yank down his fly, shoving my hand inside. The moment I feel his hard-on, we both groan, but it's not enough. I need more.

"Suck," he commands, thrusting two fingers into my mouth as he lifts up my skirt. I do as he demands, imagining it's his length I'm sucking. He groans in approval.

He pulls them out before circling my center and then inserting them both into me. I cry out, the sharp intrusion exactly what I need. He searches his pockets but curses. "Fuck! I don't have a condom."

But I don't care.

So I say something that I've not ever said before. "Fuck me anyway."

I've never referred to our love-making so crudely, but I know this act comes in all different shapes and sizes. And what we're about to do is going to be primeval.

Dixon growls, and without further delay, his jeans hit the dirt. He hooks my leg around his waist and thrusts into me passionately. I scream, but the pleasure overrides the pain, and I take it willingly as he slams into me over and over.

It feels so different with nothing between us, and I like it. It feels raw, and it feels real. Just like our love.

I buck my hips forward, moaning when he pushes into me so deep, I feel him in every single pore.

Wrapping my arms around his neck, I draw his face toward me and kiss him wildly. My climax is already building and I know I'm going to unravel in next to no time.

Dixon pulls his mouth away and sucks on my neck hungrily. I feel like he's devouring me from the inside out, and I love it. With hasty fingers, he undoes the top three buttons on my dress, freeing my breasts in seconds. The moment they spill free, he sucks them passionately, biting and pulling my nipples with just the right pressure to have me mewling in pleasure.

I need to touch him, but as I attempt to run my fingers through his hair, he grabs my arms and pins them above my head. He secures both wrists into his huge palm and holds me prisoner in every aspect of the word.

His strokes are fierce, almost punishing, and I crave it. He suckles at my breasts and drives into me hard while my arms are suspended above my head. His need for me is evident, and I can no longer hold on.

I whimper out my release, my body rippling and trembling with an orgasm so fierce, it brings tears to my eyes. A second later, Dixon yells and pulls out while I feel a warm sensation jet out against my inner thigh.

It feels like it takes minutes, but when I'm finally able to see clearly, I see regret and pain in Dixon's eyes. "Oh, Maddy. I'm so sorry. I'm a fucking animal. Did I hurt you?" He quickly lets my wrists go, kissing over the tender skin.

But I won't accept his apology. "Stop it. I'm fine. I'm more than fine. Just tell me you love me."

"What?" he asks, shaking his head in bewilderment.

"Just tell me you love me because if you do, we can overcome everything."

"Of course I love you. I've never loved, nor will ever love any woman more than I do you."

"Good." I breathlessly sigh, sagging against his chest.

I know it's naïve of me, but I don't want to face reality—not yet anyway.

Twenty

Dixon

We need to talk.

Nothing good has ever come from that phrase—especially when that phrase comes from Juliet.

Staring at the ominous text message over my morning coffee, I wonder what the hell she wants. The simple message shouldn't have ruined my holiday, but it did. And that's because I knew there was nothing simple about it.

Why was she texting me?

She was supposed to be lost in a spa-induced coma and not thinking about me. Or thinking about talking to me.

This text message sparked my insanity, and before I knew it, I was talking crazy. But a small part of me wonders what would have happened if Maddy had agreed. Would I really have left this life behind?

As I stare back down at the text, I know the answer is yes.

"Good morning," Maddy chirps as she gives me a kiss on the cheek before stealing my coffee.

I quickly place my cell into my pocket and smile. "You all set?" Maddy has internship interviews today, and I know she's incredibly nervous.

"Yup. Fingers crossed I get into Mount Sinai."

"You will."

When she cocks an eyebrow, I raise my hands. "Hey, I promised I wouldn't intervene, and I haven't. I just have faith in you, that's all."

She smiles. "Thank you. Oh, I'll have my phone off for most of the day. I have a study group in the library after interviews. We're going to do some serious cramming. So if you don't hear from me, don't worry." She sips her coffee before stealing my half-eaten bagel. "Shit. I'm late. See you tonight for dinner?"

I look down at where my food once sat. "It's a date. Seeing as you've eaten all my breakfast, God knows I'll be famished by then."

She giggles, swallowing the last of my bagel. "You talk funny. Have fun at work."

"That's unlikely. Good luck."

She pecks my lips before I slap her on the ass and send her out the door.

"And how does that make you feel, Mrs. Chan?"

"I feel inadequate. My husband's sexual desire to sleep with other women hurts."

I look up from my notepad and actually feel sorry for her

when I see that she's crying. We men are bastards. Plucking out two tissues from the box beside me, I pass them to her.

"Thank you, Doctor."

"Would you like a minute?"

She blows her nose and shakes her head. "No. I'm okay."

"In that case, how about you tell me…" But I'm unable to finish my sentence because in charges Satan with Susanna on her heels.

"Dr. Mathews, I am so sorry! She just barged in," Susanna explains breathlessly.

I narrow my eyes when I'm confronted with a pissed-off Juliet.

"Well, I wouldn't have to resort to such methods if Dr. Mathews replied to text messages," she reveals, glaring at me.

"This is completely unacceptable. You must leave immediately. Shall I call security, Dr. Mathews?"

I coolly place my pen onto my notepad. "It's fine, Ms. Vale. Mrs. Chan, will you please excuse me for just a moment? My apologies, but I need to deal with this."

She nods, looking at Juliet, no doubt wondering who the crazy bitch in my office is.

"Ms. Vale, will you please bring in a cup of coffee for Mrs. Chan?"

"Of course, Doctor." She eyeballs Juliet before turning to leave.

Standing slowly, I button up my suit jacket and brush past Juliet, not bothering to make eye contact. I hear her heels follow in hot pursuit as I walk into the meeting room. She smugly walks past me while I turn to look at an anxious Susanna, who is standing at her desk. I raise my palm, indicating if I'm not out in five minutes, she's to call security.

She nods.

I shut the door and turn to face the devil. "So you've got my attention. What do you want?"

"How was your trip?" she asks, crossing her arms over her chest.

I don't like her tone but reply calmly. "It was fine."

"Just fine? So you worked the entire time? You didn't do anything special?"

"Juliet, if there is a point to this story, please get to it," I coolly declare, adjusting my tie.

Her lips pull into a thin line before she snarls, "You're a fucking liar, Dr. Mathews."

I shrug, placing my hands into my pockets. "Well, you're hardly a saint."

"No, I may not be, but I've never lied about my feelings for you." She has the audacity to sniff.

I have no idea where this has come from because I've lied about so many things, but my nonexistent patience suddenly snaps. "You have *no* feelings, you narcissistic bitch."

She jerks backward, my honesty wounding her, but she pulls it together a second later. "I know you didn't go to Switzerland on business. You took Madison to Rome for her birthday, just like you said you were going to!"

Well, shit.

I don't confirm or deny it.

"Are you just going to stand there? Aren't you even going to defend yourself?" she spits after I yawn, bored by her melodramatics.

"Why would I bother? You seem to have made your mind

up." There's no need to panic until I have to. However, when she huffs, I know now would probably be a good time to start.

"Fine. You want to play that game." She hunts through her bag, producing her cell phone.

I watch, keeping my calm. She has no proof. Until I'm caught red-handed, I'm in the clear.

"Explain this," she sneers, flipping her screen around. I instantly see a picture of Madison and me, kissing in front of the Trevi Fountain.

It really is a beautiful photo, and I can't help but smile.

"Well?" she barks, ruining the moment.

"That was taken months ago," I reply with a flippant wave of my hand.

"Don't lie to me!" She frantically opens up the Facebook app. She scrawls through some sidebar gadget thing and scowls when she finds whatever she is looking for. "Read the caption and date," she demands, throwing the phone at my head. Thankfully, I catch it.

When I see she's found Madison's Facebook page and her rather large selection of holiday snaps, which are all dated, I internally groan.

Best birthday present ever. Not only has my amazing boyfriend taken me to Rome for my birthday, but he's crawled into the 21st century and discovered what a selfie stick is :P

Damn you, Zuckerberg, you geeky, nerdy, techno-savvy dweeb.

"So care to tell me the truth?" Juliet demands, snatching the cell from my hand.

"You seem to know it all. How about you tell me what you think?" This is my way of finding out what she thinks she knows.

She steps forward angrily. "I think you've been lying to me this entire time. I think you sent me to the Hamptons so I wouldn't catch on to what you were doing. I think Madison means more to you than you've let on. I think you love her, and I think you've been playing me this entire time! That's what I think, Dr. Mathews."

Abort! Abort! Abort!

But I stand tall, ignoring the urge to flee. "And what if what you're saying is true? What now?"

She clenches her jaw. "Now, I ruin you. I don't like being played for a fool. And that's *exactly* what you've done."

Thinking on my feet, I casually take a seat, drumming my fingers on the table. "How do you propose you'll 'ruin' me?" I ask a moment later, using air quotes to belittle her.

She smirks wickedly. "I'll show the world what a lying, unethical doctor you really are."

"Go ahead." I sweep my hand out. "You do, and I'll sue your ass for defamation."

"How?" she scoffs, not believing a word.

"You remember that little waiver you signed?" Her face drops at the mere mention of it. "Well, it was an NDA. If you weren't so busy thinking with your pussy, you'd know that if you say a word to anyone about what transpired between us, *I'll* be the one ruining *you*. We both know you're the breadwinner in your family. Do you think Dylan will really stick around if you're a broke, expectant mother of a bastard child who isn't even his?" Raising a smug eyebrow, I watch as she processes everything I just said.

"You're lying," she gasps.

"No, I can assure you I'm not. I'll have my attorney email you a copy if you like."

She shakes her head, smiling in disbelief. "You asshole."

"I've learned from the best."

"I'll tell Maddy," she threatens.

But I call her bluff. "If you were going to tell her, you would have done so by now." Clenching my jaw, I decide to inform her that I know everything. Her ruse is up. "I know why you hate her, Juliet. I know what you saw. You won't tell her because you know if you do, Maddy will tell your dad everything. He'll find out what a fucked-up little bitch his daughter really is."

I don't know why I didn't think of this sooner. By telling Maddy my sins, Juliet now knows she will also inadvertently blow the lid on a few sins of her own. Once it's out, it's out, and Juliet knows Madison will tell Rachel and Sebastian everything.

Leaning forward, I glare at her, not bothering to conceal my pure hatred for her. "You make me sick. You are pathetic. You use what's between your legs to get what you want, but let me tell you, I've had better."

Tears sting her eyes. "Fine." She snatches her phone off the table, her fingers trembling as she dials. I match her stare as I lounge back in my seat. It goes straight to Maddy's voicemail. The moment I hear her sweet voice, I know what I have to do.

Juliet scowls at me. "Hi, Madison, it's Juliet. We need to talk. Call me as soon as you get this." She ends the call furiously. "I'll tell her this time. I swear it."

No, she won't. By doing that, she's implicating herself. But I play along. "Good. You'll do me a favor."

"You mean it?" she says, reading my resolve.

I nod. "I'm done playing this game." And this time, I actually mean it. I can't lie to Maddy a second longer. I'll tell her tonight.

I thought lying to Maddy and playing this game with Juliet was the easy way out. But it wasn't. Telling Maddy the truth from the very beginning would have been the easy and honest thing to do. Instead, I let my arrogance lead me to a decision I'll never be able to take back.

Juliet suddenly bursts into tears as she realizes she's lost for good this time. "I know you have feelings for me," she pathetically claims, sobbing.

Her sniffles don't move me in any way, shape, or form. "No, I really don't," I candidly reply.

"Dixon—" Before I can fend her off, she swoops forward and kisses me. Her mouth is like a damn vacuum cleaner, and I grip her biceps firmly to pry her away.

"Get off me!" My first instinct is to shove her away, but I can't. As much as I hate that she's pregnant, I won't hurt an innocent child.

"You're serious?" she says as she stumbles backward.

"Yes. Very." I wipe my mouth vigorously with the back of my hand. But no matter how hard I scrub, I can never erase my sins.

"You tricked me. And like an idiot, I fell for your lies. You psychologically brain-fucked me. You're a cruel man, Dr. Mathews." She clutches her arms around her belly, her eyes filling with tears.

But her tears will never measure up to the ones Madison has shed thanks to Juliet's maliciousness. "Anyone will believe anything they want to hear," I counter with a shrug. "Manipulating you was easy because you're weak and shallow."

Her lower lip trembles. "Meet me tonight."

I pull back, disgusted. "Whatever for?"

She sniffs. "I want you to give up all rights to this baby."

I can't believe my ears. "You don't even know if it's mine."

Her cold eyes focus on mine as she explains. "Either way, I want you to have nothing to do with it. You've got your NDA. Now I want mine."

It takes me a millisecond to realize why she's doing this. "You don't want Dylan to know that that baby might not be his, do you?"

She lowers her eyes, confirming my theory.

"Juliet, I feel sorry for you. How can you love a monster?" I ask, genuinely interested, as I'm unable to understand her love and loyalty to him.

She looks up sadly. "I loved you, didn't I?"

I clear my throat, not expecting that reply. "*You* created this monster."

She snickers. "Maybe you're the one who needs to see a doctor. We both know you're addicted to sin just as much as I am."

I ignore her lies. "What time tonight?"

"I don't know. Let me organize everything, and I'll text you. Because I'm not cruel like you, I'll let you tell Maddy the truth. It's going to hurt her and you a lot more if you tell her than if I do. But if you don't tell her by tonight, then I will."

Her blackmailing won't stick. I'm done. "Get out of my office," I snarl, my nostrils flaring.

"I'm serious."

"So...am..." I stand, bracing my palms on the desk, my exasperated breaths coming out in loud, labored exhalations. "I," I conclude, leaning forward and fastening her with my

239

anger.

She knows she has five seconds to leave of her own accord, before I act on instinct and throw her out. "Goodbye, Dr. Mathews. I'd say it was a pleasure, but that's a complete lie." She adjusts the strap on her bag, standing tall.

"Good day, Ms. Harte." I too stand tall, folding my arms across my chest. She has three seconds left.

Two…and…

"Oh, and go fuck yourself," I add as she yanks open the door. She glares at me over her shoulder before storming from the room.

"Get out of my way, you old hag!" Juliet yells. Susanna has no doubt been standing guard. As she stomps off, I can't help but smirk as her frenzied footsteps reflect her rage.

Susanna ducks her head around the door a second later. "Is everything all right, Dr. Mathews?"

"It is now, Ms. Vale."

She walks into the room, appearing mortified. "I am so sorry. She just barged right past me. I tried to stop her."

I place my hands on her upper arms softly. "It's fine. I know how assertive Ms. Harte can be. But if that ever happens again, you have my permission to call security."

She tilts her head in doubt. "Surely she won't be back after such a display?"

Sighing, I reply, "I wouldn't be so sure."

"Madison, this is message number seven. I hope you're okay. Anyhow, I'll be a little late tonight. I have something I have to take care of. You go ahead and order wherever you like for dinner, and I'll eat when I get home. I love you." I end the call, frustrated that Maddy has been MIA all day.

I know she said she'd be inaccessible, but I can't help thinking the worst.

Looking at the text message Juliet sent me earlier, I can't believe she's chosen to meet at the worst possible motel in Queens, of all places. But I suppose she wants to be as inconspicuous as possible seeing as our dealings are rather shady after all.

Turning off my computer, I slip into my jacket and grab my leather briefcase. Looking around my office, I know that when I return tomorrow, I'll be a different man. I'll most likely be a broken one because once I sign those papers, I'll tell Madison the truth. I'll tell her all of it, just like I should have from the very beginning.

As I lock my office door, I'm surprised to see Susanna is still sitting at her desk. "Ms. Vale? Why are you still here? You should have left hours ago." I look down at my watch and see that it's now 7:45 p.m.

When I notice her handbag is perched in her lap, I query, "Is everything all right? Did something happen to Leroy?"

She shakes her head and looks up with a smile. "No, he's fine."

"Then what is it?"

"I just wanted to make sure you went home at a reasonable hour."

"And?"

Her fingers grip the top of her bag. "And I wanted to make sure that *woman* didn't come back."

I am absolutely touched that my sixty-two-year-old assistant wants to be my bodyguard. "When I said I give you permission to call security, I didn't mean you had to take on the role personally."

She muffles a laugh behind her hand.

"Is Leroy picking you up?"

She stands and turns off her computer. "No. I'm taking the subway."

"Don't be silly. I'll drive you home." I pull out my car keys from my jacket pocket.

"Oh, I don't want to put you out," she says, slipping into her coat.

"Nonsense. It's the least I can do for my head of security."

She smiles. "Thank you, Dr. Mathews."

We make our way into the elevator and ride it downstairs to the parking garage. Once we're buckled up in my BMW and I zip into traffic, I notice she shuffles in her seat and sighs.

I look over and ask, "What's the matter?"

My question seems to jolt her from whatever is plaguing her thoughts. "The matter?"

"Yes. I've known you long enough to know that something is wrong." I steal a quick glance her way. "And besides, it's my job to know these things."

She clears her throat a few moments later. "Excuse me for being so blunt, but what did that woman want?"

I can't believe she's still thinking about Juliet. Looks like she made quite the impression—the wrong impression, but an impression nonetheless. "She's an old patient," I explain.

"Yes, I know that. But why is she still wishing to speak to you?"

I could tell her to mind her own business, but I decide to try honesty on for size. "Ms. Harte is an old patient of mine. She's also my ex…lover."

I peer out of the corner of my eye, waiting for shock, disgust, horror, but all I get is, "You still haven't answered my question."

My mouth drops open.

"Don't look so surprised, Dr. Mathews. There were many times the radio was turned up high whenever that tramp was in your office."

My mouth drops open even farther. "Ms. Vale!"

She suddenly appears guilty and nervously tugs at her pearls. "Forgive me, I've said too much."

I shake my head, unable to pry the smile from my face. "On the contrary. I was going to say that comment was worth a pay raise."

She laughs. "So what did she want?"

I sigh, gripping the steering wheel tight. "She wants to make my life hell, Ms. Vale. She has from the moment I met her."

"Why don't you tell her to hit the road?"

"Because I am a damn fool."

"Well, it's not too late," she encourages.

"I hope not. This all ends tonight. I just hope Madison can find it in her heart to forgive me," I reveal, wishing it didn't have to come to this.

"What has Madison got to do with this?"

My confession is bound to give Susanna a heart attack. "Ms. Harte is Madison's stepsister."

She shakes her head, frowning. "Oh, dear. And the child? Is it yours?"

Nothing passes her by. "Quite possibly."

She shuffles in her seat. "This is quite the predicament you find yourself in."

I snort. "Tell me about it. Any advice before I sign my own death warrant?"

"If I've learned anything in my forty-one years of marriage, it's to just be honest."

And there's that word again. "Where were you six weeks ago?"

"If anyone deserves a second chance it's you, Dixon," she kindly says, but she's wrong.

"Maybe you could talk to Madison on my behalf?" I tease, ignoring the ping of emotion I feel for her constant loyalty toward me.

"No one can do that but you."

We're silent for a few moments, the sounds of New York our background noise. "If you were her, would you forgive me?"

She turns and looks at me closely. "Love makes you do stupid things."

I nod, taking what she's just said on board. But I can't figure out if she's calling me stupid or not. We ride the rest of the way in silence.

When I pull up to her modest brownstone home in Brooklyn, I ask, "Would you like me to walk you in?"

She unbuckles her seat belt with a mischievous smile. "I wouldn't want the neighbors to talk."

I smirk at her spunk.

"See you tomorrow, Dr. Mathews."

"Yes you will, Ms. Vale." She waves me good night and closes the door behind her.

I idle by the sidewalk, procrastinating as long as I can. I

don't want to do this, but it's the end of the line. Blowing out a frustrated breath of air, I know it's time to face the music.

The drive to Queens should take roughly forty minutes. It takes me over an hour. However, it's not that I'm nervous about facing Juliet, more that I'm putting off going home to see Madison. I've used this drive to figure out what I'll tell her, but nothing can prepare me for such a talk. It's all or nothing. I'm ready to give her my all.

Pulling up at the dump motel, I get out of the car and set the alarm. I'll be very surprised if it'll still be here when I return. I pass a guy on the corner who not so inconspicuously asks if I want a blowjob for fifteen bucks. I thank him for his kind offer, but grab my nuts as I pass him to find room 205.

The empty swimming pool is now home to an assortment of unwanted furniture and a family of raccoons. This place should have been closed down months ago, but as I look around and see most of the lights are on in the rooms, I can't help but wonder if they're here by choice, or if most are conducting unpleasant business just like me.

Room 205 is up a flight of stairs which is missing half its railing. I manage to get up them without breaking a leg. The walk down the passageway is akin to a death match, but I block out the wails of screaming babies, drunken fights, and impassioned moans and focus on the issue at hand—getting Juliet out of my life for good. Once this is done, I'll be free.

When I get to the room, I see the faded maroon door is slightly ajar. This is so incredibly dangerous, considering where we are. I quickly enter and shut the door behind me. There's a dim light streaming out from under the bathroom doorway.

"Juliet?" I call out. "I'm here."

I scan my surroundings in disgust. The ghastly floral bedspread, the vomit-colored carpet, and the stained yellow walls confirm that this place is just as ugly on the inside as it is on the outside—a bit like Juliet.

I really wish she would hurry the hell up. I feel like I'm catching a disease just by breathing in the sordid air. "Juliet!" I bark, taking a step toward the bathroom door.

But as the door slowly opens, nothing could ever prepare me for what I'm about to see.

"How could you?" gasps the girl, whose heart I've just shattered into smithereens.

"I can explain." But I can't. There is no explanation worthy enough to excuse why I'm here.

"Well?" The single, slow-falling tear which traces a path down her porcelain cheek highlights what a true bastard I really am.

"I-I…" Fuck! What am I even trying to say? Where do I start? When was the exact moment this all turned to shit?

"Just like I thought." She spins on her heel and scampers toward the door.

"Madison, wait! Please hear me out."

"Why, Dixon? To hear more of your lies!"

"Maddy, please," I plead, reaching out and latching onto her arm like the desperate man I am.

"No!" she shrieks, recoiling, my touch appearing to repulse her.

"Don't do this. Please don't do this."

My feeble voice betrays my fear. But I don't care. The only good, decent thing in my life is about to walk out that door, and I wouldn't blame her if she never came back. I'll grovel, beg at her feet if I need to, but a small part of me knows it was bound to come to this.

"Don't do what?" she cries, her fingers unsteady as she brushes back her long hair.

I deserve this.

I'm a man-whore.

And I'm a coward.

I don't deserve this beautiful *angelo*'s love. I never did. But I wanted it so badly I thought consequences be damned. But now, now I've gone and fucked it all up.

"I'm sorry. It's not what you think." But it is.

I *was* meeting up in this fleabag motel to conspire with her sister—a sister who truly represents sin.

"I hope it's not what I think because if it is, then I don't know who you are."

Words have never hurt more than those just spoken.

"I'm the same man I was this morning. I'm the same man who loves you more than life itself. That hasn't changed. That'll never change," I press, stepping forward, needing to touch her. But she steps away, nothing but disgust in her eyes.

"Just tell me one thing…what are you doing here?"

I could lie. I mean, that's all I've been doing. But when you can no longer distinguish between the lies you've told and the truth, it's time to come clean.

My silence is cementing my guilt.

"Tell me this isn't what I think it is, and I'll forget I ever saw you here."

Everything at this moment is heightened—the clock on the discolored wall sounds in time with my lashing heart, my heavy breathing is in sync with the wild wind thrashing about outside, but most of all the torrent of tears streaming down Madison's cheeks are in concert with my drowning soul.

"Dixon?" Her lower lip trembles as she waits for me to remedy this situation.

Every inch of my body is telling me to lie, but I can't. I do the only decent thing I've ever done in my entire life.

I say nothing at all.

"I thought so," she whispers brokenly after a minute of silence.

Her beautiful green eyes reveal nothing but betrayal as she yanks open the door. "Goodbye, Dr. Mathews. Thank you for being the biggest regret of my life," she sobs, her voice stuck in her throat.

I want to say so many things, but I don't. I simply stand numbly and watch the best thing in my life walk out on me. And for once, I do the right thing.

I let her go.

Twenty-One

Dixon

Now...

I fucked up.

I've just made the biggest mistake of my life...I trusted Juliet.

But who am I kidding? The biggest mistake was the day I met Juliet Harte.

She fucked me. And she fucked me hard. I should have smelled a rat, seeing as I literally smelled one when she sent me to this shithole dump. I should have known it was too good to be true because Juliet would never let me off that easily, but I wanted to believe that this was finally over. Now I know it has only just begun.

I stand dumbfounded, not understanding why Madison was here instead of Juliet. It takes me all of two seconds to realize I was fucking set up. And like an idiot, I walked into this totally blind.

Juliet never had any intention of me signing any papers. She fabricated that lie so I'd meet her here. But in her place, she sent Maddy instead. God only knows the lies she's told her. Or worse still—what if she's told her the truth?

I have to make this right.

I run out the door, not caring who or what stands in my way. I charge down the stairs two at a time, almost tripping over a tricycle sitting at the bottom of the staircase. As I frantically search the poorly lit courtyard, I hope there's only one exit. There is. And Maddy just walked out of it.

I take off in a dead sprint, running faster than I ever have before. Nothing or no one else matters except getting to Maddy and telling her the truth. "Madison!" I roar, my desperation sounding off the washed-out walls.

But she doesn't stop.

The rusted gate whines as I yank it open so hard I almost rip it off its hinges. "Sir, there is no running on the premises," says someone from behind me as I bolt past reception, but the warning falls on deaf ears.

"Madison! Please! Stop!" I shout from across the parking lot as I see her run toward her car. Panic hits me hard because I know that once she gets into that car, she'll never turn back.

The gravel crunches underneath my shoes as I weave between the parked cars to reach her in seconds. I get to her just as she sounds the alarm on her car.

"Madison! Stop." I lunge out to stop her from getting into her car, but she jumps back three feet, not wanting me to touch her.

"No, Dixon! Leave me a-alone," she stutters, choking on her

torrent of tears.

"Please let me explain," I beg.

"I think you being here is pretty self-explanatory." She angrily wipes at her eyes, but the tears continue to fall.

"I know what it looks like, but I need to know what Juliet told you."

"Why? So you can lie?" Her question is filled with anger but mostly pain.

Her accusations stab at me deeply. "No. I'm done lying to you."

"So you admit that you've been lying to me this entire time?"

My heavy sigh speaks volumes. "I never lied about my feelings for you. It was *because* of my feelings for you that I lied."

She scoffs, turning her face away from me.

"Please." I step forward, my hands raised in front of me, pleading with her to let me explain. "Hear me out."

Thankfully, she turns back to face me. "You have one minute."

I better make it good.

I don't know what Juliet has told her, so I decide to divulge it all. "What I told you, about meeting Juliet at work, is true. She came to me seeking help. And I did refer her over to another doctor, as I knew she was interested in more than just a professional relationship."

"But?" She folds her arms across her chest.

"But then I slipped up," I confess, making sure to keep eye contact with her.

"What does that mean?"

"It means I was a fucking idiot and made the biggest mistake

251

of my life. The morning we bumped into one another in the foyer of your apartment—I was coming from Juliet's apartment. It was the first time we had sex."

She wraps her arms around her waist, hugging herself tight. "So she's the reason you just disappeared? You chose her over me? Is that it?"

I violently shake my head. "It's not that clear-cut."

"Then what is it?" she shouts.

"I was in a bad place, Maddy, and Juliet was who I thought I needed. But I was wrong. I didn't want to lead you astray because I knew from the minute I met you, you deserved better than me. You still do," I sincerely reveal, knowing that although it's the truth, it sounds like just an excuse. "I swear it; I never knew who she was until the night of her engagement." The night this entire disaster started.

She blinks back her tears. "You could have told me then. There were so many opportunities for you to tell me, Dixon!"

"I could have. But I'm a coward, Maddy. I'm not a good man." I hang my head in shame.

"You're not a good man? What else have you done?" she wisely says. "Beth wasn't your patient when you were dating her."

"We were never dating," I miserably amend.

"So what then? She was your…fuck buddy?"

I don't reply.

She inhales a sharp intake of breath.

I'm surprised Juliet hasn't revealed all the sins of my past. But of course she hasn't. She wanted to leave the honors to me.

Her gasp reveals she's worked it out. "But it wouldn't matter if she were, right? I mean, that didn't stop you in the past? Did it?"

Running a hand through my hair, I pull at the strands as I raise my eyes to look at her. "No."

"Oh my God," she cries, her lower lip quivering. "Dixon, how could you?"

"I don't know!" I yell, spreading my arms out wide. "It sickens me. If I could take it back, I would."

She will never understand how sorry I am for what I've done.

"How many?" she unexpectedly questions.

My lip curls in confusion. "How many what?"

"How many women, how many patients did you fuck?" She suddenly dives forward and shoves me in the chest. She shoves me over and over and over again.

But I stand my ground and happily take her beatings, as I deserve them. "Eleven. Maybe twelve," I confess, turning my head to the side as she continues pounding on my chest.

"*Maybe* twelve?" she hysterically asks. "You don't even know?"

I shake my head. "No, I don't."

"You asshole! You f-fucking p-pig! How c-could you d-do this to m-me?" She's sobbing uncontrollably, her tiny thumps getting softer and softer as her snivels begin to rob her of breath.

I reach out and gently secure her wrists, but she violently pulls out of my hold. "Don't touch me!" She jerks backward and wipes her nose with the back of her hand.

Raising my palms in surrender, I expose, "There's more."

She already hates me. I may as well unveil it all.

"More women?" she asks, her red-rimmed eyes widening.

"No. More to the story."

She blinks back her tears. "More?"

"The baby Juliet is carrying, well…it may be mine." I swallow down my revulsion.

"Oh my God," she wheezes, placing a hand over her mouth.

I resist the urge to comfort her because I need to get this all out into the open before I chicken out. "I don't know what she told you about why I was meeting her here, but it was because she tricked me into thinking I was meeting her to sign over all parental rights."

Her face suddenly contorts in fury. "To who? To Juliet and my *brother*?"

"Yes," I reply. "She doesn't want Dylan—" I'm unable to finish my sentence because my teeth rattle in my mouth when Madison smacks me so hard across the cheek, I almost fall backward from the force.

I stare, stunned, moving my jaw from side to side. Why the hell is she slapping me over *that*? If anything, I thought she'd be happy I didn't want anything to do with Juliet and her child.

"Have you forgotten what he did to me?" she screams. "He is the *last* person who should ever be a parent! I would never wish my childhood upon anyone. And now you're signing all rights over to two unfit parents?"

"It might not even be mine," I pathetically counter as I rub my stinging cheek.

"Either way, until you're sure, you have to take responsibility for your actions. That child is innocent, and it deserves the best chance at life. If it's around my brother, it'll never get that."

She's right.

I know there is a small crowd forming around us and frankly, I'm surprised they haven't called the cops. But the masses don't deter Maddy in the slightest.

"How did you keep this a secret for so long?"

And this is where the plot thickens.

"The night of her engagement," I confess, closing my eyes briefly. "She gave me an ultimatum," I conclude, watching her face drop.

"What was it?"

"If I slept with her, she'd keep all my secrets safe."

She bites her bottom lip. "And did you?"

I pull back, disgusted. "Of course I didn't!"

Her shoulders drop. "Then what did you do?"

"I fucked *with* her," I reveal.

She scrunches up her nose. "What? I don't understand what that means."

"I manipulated her. I made her believe what she wanted to believe. And when she did, I tricked her into signing an NDA so she couldn't tell anyone about us. But that wasn't enough. I wanted her to pay for what she did to you. So I made her my puppet."

She looks as horrified as I now feel. "Why didn't you tell me? Why go to all this trouble?"

I sigh, revealing why I decided to venture down this sinful, depraved path. "Because she was blackmailing me with the only person she knew I'd do anything for."

"Who?" she whispers.

It's eerily silent, so silent that when I speak, it sounds like my answer echoes loudly in the still night. "You."

"I don't understand," she says, shaking her head slowly.

Taking a small brave step toward her, I declare, "If I was to play by her rules, she'd keep your...brother away from you."

She pales.

"Don't you see, I had no other choice. I play her game, and you'd be safe," I say, almost pleading with her to believe me.

But she doesn't.

"Lying to me was keeping me safe?"

"It was a small price to pay. I'll do anything to protect you." When she shakes her head in incredulity, I press, "I did it to protect you."

"No, Dixon," she refutes, saddened. "You did it to protect yourself."

"I—" But I suddenly pause. Is she right? I thought I was doing the right thing, but deep down, I knew it was wrong. I always knew there was another way, but I was too chickenshit to face it.

"If you had just told me the truth, I may have been able to forgive you…"

Her words cement what I know, what I always knew to be true. "And now?"

"I just…I can't," she cries, a tear spilling down her cheek. "How can I ever trust you? You know how hard it was for me to open up."

"I know." I step forward, but she recoils. Her repulsion is like a dagger to my heart.

"Maddy, please."

"No," she says. "I don't know who you are."

"I'm me," I plead, placing a hand over my heart.

With nothing but sorrow in her tone, she confesses, "I don't even know who that is anymore."

I stand speechless, trying to figure out how to fix this.

"Were you seeing her behind my back?"

"When?" I ask.

"This entire time."

"Not how you think." I come clean, but it's not enough.

"Stop talking in riddles!" she shouts, advancing forward angrily.

"After you and I started talking again, yes, I was seeing her. But then I stopped soon after. I knew she wasn't the right one for me. I wanted you," I sincerely profess. "I ended it soon after the night we met at Cherry Pop."

"And in Boston?" she asks, piecing it all together. "Was she supposed to be your plus-one?"

"Yes."

She frowns, shaking her head, appalled. "Oh my God. I'm a fucking fool."

"But that was before I knew I'd ever see you again," I expose, knowing this truth has come a little too late.

She exhales slowly. "What about after the engagement? Have you seen her behind my back?"

I wish my response was different. "Yes," I reply, shame-facedly.

She appears hurt and angered all in the same breath. "I *was* right. I knew there was something more."

"No, not like that," I quickly defend my actions. "I had to play along until I figured out what I wanted to do."

"Why didn't you just tell me the truth? There were many times that you could have!"

I nod sadly because if I had just been honest from the beginning, none of this would have happened. "I know."

"But instead, you lied, which is so much worse." She looks at me with nothing but disgust in her eyes, and the sight of that hurts more than I ever thought possible. I need her to see why I did this. I need her to see this was all for her.

"I knew Dylan was your Achilles' heel. I couldn't stand him to hurt you ever again. Can't you see that?"

She nods, but her firm jaw reveals it's not enough. "I can, but what you've done is far worse than what he ever did to me."

My mouth drops open. Does she really mean that?

"I'm getting stronger, Dixon," she reveals, her voice filled with conviction. "I could have dealt with it. If only you'd have given me credit and told me the truth, none of this would have happened."

I can't...I need a minute to digest this.

"With you by my side, I felt like I could achieve anything."

Her use of past tense is the beginning of the end. "And now?"

"Now?" She lowers her gaze. "Now I feel sick. *You*...make me sick. Everything that we once shared is a lie."

I don't blame her. I make myself feel sick. As I process everything, I can't help but wonder what exactly Juliet told Madison. It appears she was blind to the entire sins of my ways. So what *did* Juliet tell her?

"What did Juliet tell you?"

"She told me that you propositioned her for sex," she reveals, pulling a sickened face.

"*What?*" I ask, matching her expression.

"And that you've been doing so the entire time we've been dating. She also said that you manipulated and preyed on her when she was weak. She confessed to having sex with you— twice."

I'm left standing speechless at the lies Juliet has told.

And sadly, the story doesn't end here. "She knows that she's sick, and she's sorry for not helping me with Dylan. She told me that's why she came to see you in the first place. To help her deal with her guilt over what she saw. And since then, you've been obsessed with her and stalking her. She's afraid of you, Dixon. And she said that I should be, too."

"That's bullshit!" I yell when I can finally find my voice. "I deal in addiction, not canoodling patients' guilty consciences away!"

That bitch. She set me up. She knew I'd think the worst and believe she had told Madison everything. Instead, that's what I did. All she had to do was plant the seed—just like I did with her.

She beat me at my own game. Again.

I can't just stand here while Juliet is paraded around as the victim. "Maddy, c'mon! This is Juliet you're talking about. You cannot possibly believe her and this fictional tale?"

She shrugs in defeat. "I don't want to believe it. But you're here now, aren't you?" she questions me. I can see the war raging behind her eyes. She doesn't want to believe, but I've betrayed her in the worst possible way.

I have to make this right. "I told you why."

"But how can I trust you?" she asks, shaking her head. "After everything you've just told me, I don't even know who you are."

Her confession breaks me, but I suck in a deep breath and continue to fight. "You know Juliet is no angel. Look at what she did to you!"

Juliet is confessing to this fabricated story so she looks like the victim and comes out of this unscathed. The NDA means jack shit because I believe she now couldn't care less about ruining my career. She has just gone one better—she's ruined my life. She would never drag her name through the tabloids because that would ruin the fantasy world she's worked so hard to build. She told Madison that we only slept together twice for appearance sake's only. If Dylan were to ever find out about her infidelity, he could certainly forgive her for the two slipups, but not for the countless ones she's really made.

And now that she's got an iota of Madison's sympathy, she's going to play on that and use it any way that she can. I look like the deviant while Juliet wipes her hands clean.

"Madison?" I urgently press.

"I don't know what to believe!" she shouts, cradling her head and massaging her temples.

"Believe me! Why would I make all this shit up? It most certainly is not in my favor to do so. I'm telling you the truth," I state while I hear one of the spectators hum in accord. "Juliet is a lying, manipulative, calculating piece of work. I want nothing to do with her. I haven't from the moment I ended things with her. She can't stand that I love you and not her. She can't stand that your brother loves—" I quickly stop when she waves a hand out in front of her and covers her mouth to stop herself from being sick.

"Please, Maddy. Believe me. I did this...I did all of this... for you. I wanted to tell you so many times. I was just so afraid you'd leave me. I couldn't risk losing you," I pathetically confess, searching her face for answers.

"You should have been honest." She lowers her gaze and looks at her sneakers.

"I know that. I'm sorry. Please forgive me." I take a small

step forward. My hands are desperate to touch her, my arms desperate to hold her.

But her broken reply reveals that I'll never hold or touch her ever again. "No," she whispers, her hair shrouding her face.

The wind gets knocked from my lungs. "No? What do you mean, no?"

She slowly meets my eyes, her lower lip trembling as she cries, "I'm…b-breaking up with you, Dixon. I n-never want to see you again."

My heart skips a beat, and I doubt it'll ever return to its normal rhythm ever again. "Madison? No. Please God, no."

She ignores me and continues to crush me. "I can't be with you. I don't trust you. And I don't think I ever will."

Thump…

Thump…

…Thump

"Please give me a second chance." I drop to my knees, surrendering everything I am to her. "I was going to tell you everything tonight."

She shakes her head, closing her eyes. "I just…I can't. How can I believe you?" As she opens them, I begin to commit to memory everything about her because I know it'll probably be the last time I ever see her. "Too much has happened. I could have gotten over the fact you slept with Beth. Maybe even the fact you've slept with your patients. But you lying to me for so long. You doing this to 'protect' me. I can't ever forgive."

"Madison, please." Normal, coherent words have escaped me. All I'm capable of is begging.

But she doesn't want to hear any more excuses. "Beth may be a bitch, but she's sick, and you totally exploited that. That's a cruel thing to do to someone who trusts you."

"How is she the victim here?" I ask, interlacing my hands over my brow.

"She's not." Clawing at her shirt, she says, "The only victim here is my heart. Goodbye, Dixon."

"Maddy, no." A single tear rolls down my cheek. "You said that whatever I had done, you wouldn't care. You lied, too. Maddy, you lied, too." I thump my fist into the ground, unable to process what is happening.

She bursts into tears, covering her face and wailing. "I s-should have l-listened to you…I shouldn't have used words I don't understand."

I reach out desperately, grasping onto any last hope that this is all a bad dream. But when she sobs hysterically and jumps into her car, I know this nightmare is really happening. She starts the engine, puts the car into gear, and she doesn't look back as she speeds off into the night.

I'm left on my knees, watching the taillights of her Fiesta get smaller and smaller. I stay this way for how long, I don't know. It's long enough for the crowd to disperse, and I'm left alone, staring into the night where Maddy's beautiful face once was.

She's left me, and I know it's for good. I always knew it would come to this. But knowing something doesn't make the reality any easier to digest. My lies have unraveled, and now I'm left with the consequences of the mess I've made.

Fisting the stones underneath my fingers, I dig them into my palms until I draw blood. The feeling is an instant relief, and I wonder what'll happen if I open up a bigger wound and bleed myself dry.

Instead, I pull it together. I tell myself to man up and deal. With nothing further to lose, I slowly stand tall as I know what I have to do.

Twenty-Two

Dixon

Nothing else matters anymore. I stopped caring the moment Madison said goodbye.

If this were a movie, the heroine would eventually forgive the asinine hero, and both characters would live happily ever after. But this isn't a movie, nor am I the hero. This is real life. This is *my* life. And I intend to start living it.

Carpe diem, motherfuckers.

This mindset has me pounding on Juliet's door, not caring if she's asleep or in the middle of something important. I can hear the TV humming softly in the background and two voices, one asking the other who might be knocking on their door.

"Pizza," I say, disguising my voice as I step aside, avoiding the scope of the peephole.

"Did you order pizza?" Juliet asks as her voice gets closer and closer to the door.

"No. You probably did and forgot," the cesspool of filth

replies.

"We didn't order any—" I don't let Juliet finish, however because I charge forward the moment she opens the door and shove her out of the way. I focus my fury on Dylan, who quickly stands as he sees me stampede through the living room.

"Dixon!" Juliet cries, running after me and latching onto my arm. She knows that the proverbial shit has hit the fan, and there is no stopping me now.

I shrug her off and continue my rampage toward the scum of the earth. "Hey, you're Sunny's boyfriend," he says in surprise. "What do you want?"

Just the mere mention of Madison has my already uncontrolled temper boiling over, and I know things are about to get ugly real soon. "I want you to catch necrotizing fasciitis and die a slow, painful death, but we can't have it all. So in that case, I'll settle for anything…just as long as you're dead."

I don't give him a chance to move, duck, or breathe because I swing out and punch the motherfucker right in the jaw. His head snaps back with a loud, satisfying thwack. The sound and sensation of hurting this bastard have me advancing forward and connecting with his nose in quick succession. He staggers backward, his hands flying up to protect his face, but this proves futile, so I raise my leg and knee him straight in the balls. He drops to the floor with a deafening thud, a pained, anguished wail following soon after as he cups his balls.

"Dixon! Stop!" Juliet screams, her tiny hands attempting to hold me back as she clasps my bicep.

But there is no stop in this equation. The only stop is when Dylan is dead.

I push her away, not even bothering or caring where

she ends up. All I can focus on is hitting Dylan some more. Dropping to one knee, I violently throw him onto his back and jab out my palm and connect with his shoulder joint to hold him down. He's squirming and attempting to fight back, but he doesn't stand a chance. I slam my fist into his face over and over and over again, feeling his lip, eye, and nose bust open with each strike I inflict.

During my possessed attack, Juliet attempts to restrain me by any means she can. She jumps on my back, screaming like a wailing banshee, but I fling her off, snarling, "So help me God, if you touch me again, I will tell him everything." My words have the exact effect I was hoping for, and she stays on the sidelines, sobbing and threatening to call the police.

I curl my bloodied fists in Dylan's shirt and yank him up, thrusting his limp body against the sofa. His face is a bleeding mess, and I'll celebrate that sight for the rest of my life. "Listen to me, you fucking son of a bitch," I spit, tightening my hold and shaking him brutally as I lean inches from his face. "I know what you did to Madison."

His right eye hasn't fully swollen over, and it widens. "You leave town tonight. You forget you have a sister, and you crawl back into whatever hole you came out from. And take your whore with you. If you go anywhere near her, I *will* kill you next time. This isn't a threat. It's a promise."

"Dixon, no!" Juliet screams, running over. She knows what's about to happen. Just like she did with me, I lied. I plan on divulging all her secrets.

"She liked it. She begged for it," Dylan slurs, his bloodied spittle running down his chin.

I gnash my teeth, resisting the urge to rip off his fucking

head. "Just like your fiancée begged for my cock."

I can see the moment Dylan processes what I've just said. He jumps forward, attempting to strike me, but I push him down, grinning sinisterly. "That's right. I doubt anyone was begging for your cock because if they were, your fiancée wouldn't be begging *me* to fuck her every chance she got. And I did. I fucked her, and she liked it."

"You motherfucker!" I'm actually stunned that he gives a shit, but I guess misery does love company.

"I would challenge you to a battle of wits, but I see you're unarmed," I sarcastically quip.

"It was only twice, Dylan. I swear it!" Juliet yells, trying to fight me off him.

I laugh malevolently. "C'mon now. You know it was more than twice. Off the record, Dylan, your fiancée has a mouth like a damn Hoover."

"Why?" Juliet sobs, pounding on my arms.

"Did you really think I wasn't going to say anything? Did you really think that you'd break me? All you did was push me into doing the right thing," I reply, pinning Dylan down harder while he's fighting like a caged dog.

"I can still ruin you," Juliet reveals, but there is no gravity behind her threat.

"No, you can't. I plan on telling everyone about what I did, just as I should have done from the very beginning. You'll have nothing over me. You...lose."

Juliet is delusional if she thought I wouldn't go down fighting. But that's why she fabricated the story of being the victim. That was her backup plan. What she didn't count on was no one believing her innocent act.

I know Dylan believes me. The fury in his messed-up face reveals he believes every single word. He once again attempts to lunge out and hit me, but he's trapped with his back to the sofa. I resist the urge to place my forearm across his windpipe and choke the life from this piece of shit because I have one final piece of information I wish to share with him.

"By the way, that baby is most likely mine. Or it could be half of Manhattan's, considering your beloved can't keep her legs shut. But believe you me, if it is mine—" I turn to stare at a bawling Juliet. "I will do everything in my power to make sure it has nothing to do with either of you."

Juliet slumps onto the floor, threading her hands through her hair as she yanks at the snarled strands. "The honeymoon is over, sweetheart," I smugly say, turning to look back at Dylan, who is pushing forward with all his might. "I know everything. And rest assured, so will your mom. And so will Sebastian." The moment I mention her father, Juliet howls. "*I* may not tell them, but Madison will. And when she does, you'll wish I had killed you."

I have no doubt that, ironically, this situation will make Madison stronger. It'll give her the strength to finally tell her mom the secret that has weighed her down for over ten years. She'll want every part of this tangled web to be exposed, and she'll also want to move forward. And to do that, she has to let go of her past.

Dylan pales, as I believe he too can see that I'm not joking. But that's all the pondering he deserves. I propel my head forward and headbutt the motherfucker straight in the nose. It squishes under impact, and I know it's broken.

The apartment is filled with anguished wails and screams

as I stand, fasten the buttons on my jacket, and coolly wipe down the blood from my lapels. I'm pretty certain I've broken my hand, but the bedlam I've left behind is well worth the pain.

I turn to look at a sniveling Juliet, who has curled in on herself. Walking over, I bend forward and brush a piece of matted blonde hair from her brow, leaving behind a smear of red. "You'll be hearing from my attorney."

"Why?" she weeps, tears running down her cheeks. "You don't even want this child."

"Why?" I question. She nods. "Because…payback's a bitch. Just like you." I may not want this child, but Maddy was right. It's time I dealt with the consequences of my actions.

"This wasn't supposed to end this way!"

Shaking my head, I snicker. "Yes, this is exactly how it was supposed to end. This is what we both deserve! Goodbye, Ms. Harte. I do hope you have the most miserable, most dissatisfied, loveless life you deserve. Oh," I add, holding up my finger. "Remember when I said I was sorry for destroying your life? No? Neither do I."

I rub my bloodied fingers on my jacket and smile as I leave behind the carnage I created. It's a sight I'll never forget.

Once out in the hallway, I take a minute to calm my ragged breathing and stop my racing heart from exploding out onto the carpeted floor. When I'm composed enough to walk, I press the call button and hope like hell no one is in the elevator because they'll think I've just slaughtered a family. Thankfully, the cart is empty, and I ride it to the seventeenth floor.

The moment it stops, I step out and march down the hallway with one final stop in mind. A door shouldn't hold any sentimental value, but it does, though it's what lies just beyond this door that has me leaning my forehead against the wood grain and bracing my palms above me.

I don't even alert Madison that I'm here. I simply close my eyes and imagine she's standing on the other side, listening to my confession. The confession which is the first step to living this new life.

"Madison," I croak, sounding weak and pitiable. "I'm so sorry, *angelo*. I know you've heard it all before, but I'm selfish, and I need to keep saying it just in case you can find it in your heart to forgive me. You once told me you were weak and afraid, but you're not. You're the strongest person I know. I know that you'll get over this, and that you'll move on. And…I want that for you. I want you to be happy. I wish that could be with me, but I know it can't. You go find yourself a good man, Madison. One who will treat you right. One who will treat you how you deserve. We'll always have Paris. Or, in our case, Rome," I say, wishing this was *Casablanca*. "Goodbye, *angelo*. Never forget to smile. The world is a brighter place because of it."

I can suddenly feel Madison. Her entire presence surrounds me, and before long, I'm drowning in the memories of what we once had. I can smell her sweet vanilla scent, hear her soft, shallow breaths, and taste her warm, tender kisses.

But my recollections of her will slowly fade, and eventually, I know that my memories will wither into blackness and she'll be gone. I'll question if what I'm remembering is actually true because the mind does amazing things to cope with grief.

But for now, I'll cherish every memory I have. It's the only thing that'll get me through this. It's the only thing that'll stop me from breaking down this door.

I stay pressed against the wood, knowing that when I pull

away, I'll never come back. I know that Madison is better off without me. Doing the one selfless thing I can, I push off the door and say goodbye to the love of my life for good.

On the drive home, I can't help but think that seizing the day isn't what it's cut out to be.

Twenty-Three

Madison

I don't know how many hours I've been sitting here, slumped against my front door. Four? Maybe five? It doesn't matter, however, because if I rise, I don't know what to do.

I can't believe tonight actually happened. I can't believe Dixon and I are actually over. I never thought I could hurt more than I have in the past, but tonight proved me wrong. Dixon's words tore through me, and I doubt I'll ever heal. Nothing could ever have prepared me for what he confessed because I would have never believed he was capable of such sin.

But he is.

When Beth called and spewed out her lies, I didn't want to believe her, but a part of me knew she was speaking the truth. I think I always knew there was more. But love really *is* blind, and I chose to believe that Dixon was the person he claimed to be. But I don't even know who that is anymore.

I don't know what I'm going to do. I feel betrayed and

deceived, but most of all, I feel numb. I fell for someone who *was* too good to be true because that person doesn't exist. I fell in love with a fraud.

Thinking of Dixon in this light turns my stomach, and I place my hand over my mouth to stop myself from being sick. My body is fighting me, and so is my mind, but I have no other choice. This is my reality. I can never forgive Dixon for what he's done.

How can I?

I can't trust him. And what's a relationship without trust?

I'm not totally naïve, and I don't buy Beth's innocent act for one second. Dixon may be a lying asshole, but he's right. What does he have to gain by telling me what he did? Every single disgusting detail he revealed I believe, but every word from Beth's mouth I do not. I know who she is. I have known from the moment she watched my brother rape me and did nothing.

I know I'm in no frame of mind to be making any decisions, but funnily enough, after tonight, I think I'm ready to tell my mom and Sebastian the truth. I need them to know who their son and daughter really are because my silence is protecting them.

Beth will never change. Lying to me to save her own ass shows that her telling me the "truth" was her way of pegging this entire mess on Dixon. She was hoping I'd fall for her lies, but I'm done being played for a fool.

Raising my weary body slowly, I feel as if my muscles have gone five rounds with Mike Tyson. My legs are like Jell-O as I try to stand without falling down. I place my arms out to the side, attempting to regain my balance. It takes a couple of minutes, but when I think I'm able to move, I take my first step and go in search of my phone.

My bag is on the other side of the room; I vaguely remember throwing it there in rage as I stormed through my home, not knowing what to do or where to go. So many emotions were and are still charging through me, but once the reality of what happened hit home, I fell into a sobbing hysterical mess and stayed that way until I heard, no, until I *felt* Dixon at my front door.

My traitorous body somersaulted in delight, so happy to hear his voice, so happy to have him near. I wanted him to tell me it was all a dream, but when I heard his solemn confession, I knew that nothing had been more real.

I crawled, dragging my body toward the front door, desperate to hear him one final time. But when I heard his broken voice, I knew that this really *was* the end. Dixon and I were no more.

His words were the sweetest he's ever spoken, regardless of the context because they were filled with nothing but sincerity. Not once did I doubt him, but it came too late.

Today was meant to be the happiest day of my life. If only I knew this morning what I know now, I would have pushed the pause button and lived happily in denial. I got offered two placements. One was the dream offer, and the other… the other was one that I confidently said no to. But now, that offer is my only hope of surviving this.

I scroll through my emails and type out a quick message to my teacher, hoping I'm not too late. I'll probably regret my decision in the morning, but for now, this is the only thing that feels right.

Looking around my home, I remember all the happy

memories, all the happy memories with Dixon. But now those memories are tainted with what he has done. They are plagued with doubt. Were any of those moments actually real? Did he really mean it when he told me he loved me while making love to me on the sofa? When he revealed that I was the only woman for him as we lay side by side in front of the fireplace, did he mean forever or did he mean at that moment?

Everything is tainted, and nothing seems real. My entire relationship with Dixon has been a sham. I don't want to believe that's true, but my heart can't deal with any more pain. I may not know what is fact and what is fiction, but I do know Dixon lied to me about Beth. He slept with her before and after me. I don't want to believe he cheated, but I don't want to be naïve, either. I also believe that poor, innocent child might be his.

His confession about sleeping with his patients makes me feel sick all over again. I blink back my tears; I can't believe the mess I find myself in. I know what I have to do. It's the first step to taking back my life.

My phone feels like a lead weight as I scroll through my contacts with shaky fingers. When I stop at the letter D, I allow a single tear to fall. Dixon's name stares back at me, a name which once brought me nothing but joy. Now it brings me nothing but sorrow.

I say goodbye to all my memories, all the happy times which now seem like such a waste of time. I say goodbye to all parts and aspects that make up Dixon Mathews. Thanks for the memories—memories which I wish had never been made.

With resolution, I promise myself this is the end. There is no looking back. Hitting delete and seeing Dixon's name disappear from my life should be liberating—even cleansing.

But it isn't. All it leaves me with is an empty place in my chest where my heart once beat for him.

To get through this, I have to focus on tomorrow, and to do that, I have to forget I ever met Dr. Dixon Mathews.

Carpe diem.

Twenty-Four

Dixon

Two weeks later

Y ou know you've hit rock bottom when you're lying in the same clothes, in the same position, in the same spot you were in two weeks ago, and using seven scotch bottles and an empty packet of Cheetos as your pillow.

Whoever said time heals all wounds is a fucking idiot. With time, my wounds have gotten worse. I can't remember a time when I wasn't weighed down with this heaviness, and as each day, each minute, each second passes, I doubt I'll ever be rid of this guilt.

Once I left Madison's apartment, I called Susanna and told her to reschedule my appointments for the next couple of weeks because I was in no frame of mind to be counseling anybody. I'm the one in desperate need of therapy, but I wouldn't even know where to start.

So this option of drowning my sorrows in a bottle of liquid gold and reminiscing about the good ole days is far better than dealing with my feelings. My feelings aren't going anywhere, so I can deal with them at a later date. A far, far later date.

My internal debate whether to visit my next-door neighbor to see if he has any booze I can buy off him is interrupted by a loud pounding on my door. I raise my stiff neck from my makeshift pillow, groaning the minute the light streaming in from the window hits my sensitive eyeballs.

I decide against answering it and toss the blanket over my head, hoping whoever is at my door will go away. They don't. The pounding continues for countless minutes, but then it suddenly stops. I breathe out a sigh of relief and return to my memories of the first time Madison and I made love.

Just as I'm getting to the good bit, the blanket is ripped from my head, and I'm doused with a torrent of freezing water.

"What the fuck?" I yell, wiping the water from my eyes.

"Oh, good. You're alive," replies Hunter, who is standing by my bedside looking relieved. He's holding a now empty water bottle.

"Of course I'm alive! Now get out," I gripe, attempting to throw the blanket back over my head. But Hunter reaches out and yanks it off the bed.

"Why in God's name are you clutching onto that pillow like it's your damn life raft?" he asks.

"Because it is," I reply, burying my nose in the cotton. "It's Madison's pillow," I clarify. "It smells like her."

Hunter pulls a repulsed face. "No, it smells like you. Therefore, it smells like shit. When was the last time you showered?" he asks, opening a window.

"Fuck off, Hunter." I'm in no mood for banter.

"Dude, I get it," he says, leaning against the dresser and folding his arms. "She broke your heart, and you've needed time to grieve or whatever, but c'mon, how long do you plan on staying cooped up? This is totally unhealthy, not to mention unsanitary."

"She didn't just break my heart. She destroyed me," I amend, clutching onto the pillow tighter.

"Yeah well, you've got no one to blame but yourself," he declares with no sympathy. I don't even bother fighting back because he's right. "I've been trying to call you all week. Why haven't you answered your phone?"

After a week of tormenting myself with should I or shouldn't I call Madison, I decided to put myself out of my misery. I look at the corner of the room where my cell lies in a thousand pieces.

Hunter follows my line of sight and shakes his head. "Now that's just wasteful."

"I don't care. It wouldn't stop ringing. It also wouldn't stop taunting me with the fact that I can no longer call Madison. So problem solved," I reveal, sitting up and running a hand through my snarled hair.

The moment I do, I flinch and remember my hand was the size of a balloon, thanks to the beating I gave Dylan. I tied a temporary bandage around it and didn't really do much else. The fact it's still stinging like a bitch confirms that I probably should have gone to the hospital to get it looked at. It's too late now. And besides, the hurt is worth it because I can only imagine the pain that son of a bitch is still in.

"Right, this is an intervention. Get the hell out of bed and go take a shower. We're going out," Hunter states firmly.

"No," I counter back.

"This isn't optional, Dix. If you don't get up from that bed, I'll light it on fire." To prove he's not messing around, he reaches for the lighter off my dresser and flicks it on.

I watch the flame flicker, not liking the resolve behind Hunter's eyes. "Fine, you win, you meddling asshole."

I throw my pillow at him as I slowly get up. The room spins, and I need a second to find my footing. Once I think I'm able to walk in a straight line, I stand and ignore my unused, protesting muscles. As I shuffle past Hunter, he places his hand underneath his nose and gags.

"You fucking stink. Are you sure you're alive?"

My response is to flip him off, but I don't disagree with him because I'm debating whether I'm actually alive or not.

"Dude, how about you give your liver the night off?"

"Dude, how about you fuck off?" I counter, flagging down the bartender. I agreed to come out, but I never agreed to be a social butterfly.

My best friends are trying their hardest to cheer me up. Finch even got permission to go out on a Saturday night. But it's not working. The more they try to pretend nothing is wrong, the worse I feel. I know they're walking on eggshells as they're afraid they'll say the wrong thing.

"Dix, you need to pull your shit together," Hunter bluntly says. It seems he's finally given up on the pretense that everything is all right. I look over at Finch, who shrugs. It appears they've both given up.

"I'm fucking peachy, now lay off." I ignore their concern and focus on getting my damn drink.

But Hunter won't hear of it. "No, screw you, you stubborn asshole. I will not lay off. I'm worried about you. After Lily, you licked your wounds for like a day, and then you were out fucking your sorrows away. But this time around, I actually didn't know what I'd find when I came to your apartment earlier tonight. Do you realize how fucking scary that is?"

I sigh as I run a hand over my full beard. The rare sign of concern behind Hunter's eyes alerts me to the fact that I am being a right royal bastard to the two people who have always had my back. I understand they say you hurt the ones you love, but that doesn't excuse my disrespect.

"Sorry," I say, lowering my head. "I'm a fucking mess, all right? I thought that by now I would at least be able to think about Madison without wanting to kill myself. But it's getting worse," I confess, feeling like a complete pussy.

"That's normal, Dix. You love her. Of course, you're feeling this way," Finch says kindly. "Maybe you could try calling her? She may have calmed down, and you may be able to save your relationship?"

I wish that were true, but I know Madison and I are over for good. "There's no point. I know there is no redo in this situation. I just have to accept the fact that I've lost her for good."

"How do you know that?" Hunter asks.

"I just do, man," I counter, remembering the hurt and betrayal in her eyes when she said goodbye. "And besides, she's better off without me. She was always too good for the likes of me. I won't be a selfish bastard and drag her down because I miss her. The radio silence is for the best."

"You remember what happened the last time you did what you thought was best for her?" Hunter rebukes, raising an eyebrow.

He's right, but a part of me can't handle the rejection. I know I've fucked things up beyond repair. But I stubbornly press, "We're done, Hunt. I just have to accept it."

He seems to want to say more but stops when Finch subtly shakes his head. The role of the social pariah sucks balls, so I toss back my scotch, hoping to become too intoxicated to notice the concerned stares of my friends.

We're all sitting in reflective silence—me thinking of ways I can slip away undetected—when a busty brunette sidles up next to me. I ignore her because I have absolutely zero interest in making small talk. Sadly, she reads my aloofness as playing hard to get.

"Hi, I'm Brea. Want to buy me a drink?"

Her huge tits are pushed up to the high heavens, and the sight, which would usually leave me a slobbering fool, has me inching closer toward Hunter instead. "Buy your own damn drink," I bark. Hunter's and Brea's mouths drop open while I calmly steal Hunter's beer.

Brea is persistent, however, and doesn't seem to want to take no for an answer. "How about you let me buy you a drink then?" she asks, smirking.

"I'm not thirsty," I reply, mid-sip.

She looks at my beer, raising an eyebrow.

I can't believe I am actually getting hit on, looking the way that I do.

"I promise I don't bite. Unless you want me to." She accents her sentence with a wink.

I shrink away, disgusted.

When she makes it clear she's not going anywhere, I do the only thing I can think of to get her the hell away from me.

Spinning around quickly, I smash my lips to Hunter's unsuspecting mouth and kiss him. The kiss is fucking awful, but I'd rather be kissing my best friend than this barfly. He pushes me off him, and I subtly chuckle when he wipes his mouth on the back of his hand, appearing absolutely disgusted.

I turn to face an uncomfortable Brea. "I'm so sorry. I've seen you here before with other women, and I thought you were straight."

"Nope, this is my life partner," I reply, attempting to reach for Hunter's hand. He stomps on my foot in protest.

"Sorry again," she quickly says and rushes off, mortified.

"Tell all your friends!" I yell out after her. Unsurprisingly, she doesn't turn around.

The moment she's gone, Hunter flicks me in the balls. I wheeze and almost drop like a sack of potatoes. "Oh, c'mon. You know you liked it," I tease between deep breaths as I clutch my junk.

"You motherfucker! Just because you're renouncing your sexuality doesn't mean I am. That chick is going to tell everyone she knows that I'm your"—he pales—"your life partner."

I pucker my lips and throw him a wink. He gags and downs his beer in one gulp.

Surprisingly, this ridiculous situation has made me feel slightly better. It's also given me a crazy idea.

"I'm over New York. This city is overrated. It should be renamed the city where dreams go to die." Finch looks at me, interested, while Hunter scrapes down his tongue with a cocktail napkin.

"What are you saying?" Finch asks, drumming his fingers on the bar.

"I'm saying I might go back to Jersey."

Finch pulls back, while Hunter stops mid-scrape. "Are you serious?" Finch says, shaking his head. He knows how hard I've worked to achieve all that I have, but what's the point of having riches if you have no one to share them with?

I nod. "Maybe. I need a change of scenery. I also need a clean slate. And I can't have that here because there is a line of Breas around every corner I turn."

Hunter suddenly rolls up his napkin into a tiny ball and throws it at my head. "Are you fucking insane?" I don't even bother replying because I don't know what my answer will be. "What are you supposed to do in Jersey? Have you forgotten how boring it is over there? Not to mention we moved to Manhattan to get *away* from there. Why would you move back?"

"Because I need boring, Hunt." The more I think about it, the more sense it makes.

"What about work? You've worked hard to establish your business."

"I can work anywhere. And besides, Manhattan isn't that far away. I'll work something out with my patients," I reason, thinking of all the ways I could actually make this happen.

But Hunter shakes his head. "No, fucking no. As your lifelong partner, I forbid you to go."

I laugh at his melodramatics. "You could come too."

He scrunches up his face like he's just smelled something bad. "Now I know you've really fucking lost the plot. What am

I supposed to do in Jersey?"

"Find a nice girl and settle down?" I suggest.

"There *are* no nice girls in Jersey. That's why we moved. And settle down to what? Settle down and become Captain Boring. No, thank you." He stubbornly folds his arms across his chest and juts out his chin.

I narrow my eyes, wondering why he's so worked up. Could it be my friend is scared of change? Or worse, is he afraid of growing up? But we've lived this bachelor life for far too long. I need a change in scenery.

Thoughts of going back to Jersey remind me of the date. Tomorrow is the family fun day at Sunnyfields. I'm not an idiot, and I know Maddy won't be there, but I won't let that stop me. If I'm really contemplating going back home, then I have to deal with the issue of my father and me. Avoiding him will be a lot harder with him being twenty minutes away as opposed to two hours. But the thought of reconciliation isn't as daunting as it once was.

Maybe moving isn't such a crazy idea after all. I mean, nothing is keeping me in Manhattan. I can count the reasons to stay on one hand. But I can't count the reasons to go because I'll run out of fingers.

I know I'm not in any frame of mind to be making any decisions, but this is the first time in weeks that things have looked a little clearer.

Sadly, Hunter doesn't agree. "Fuck you both. I'm getting a dog."

Both Finch and I chuckle.

Twenty-Five

Dixon

"Good afternoon, Dr. Mathews. We're so happy you could make it," says Pat as I sign in to see my father.

"Thanks for having me." I smile at the young nurse. "How's he doing today?" My father seems to be Pat's favorite patient. She constantly calls and gives me personal updates on his progress.

"He's doing really well. He's actually outside today."

I pause from signing in. "Outside? Are you sure it's not someone who looks like my father?" I tease while she stifles her smile behind her hand.

Once I'm done signing in, she passes me my visitor's badge and offers to show me where he is. We talk about my father's progress and how she's seen a vast improvement in his overall behavior since I've been visiting. I really want to believe her, but I have my doubts.

As we step outside, I whistle, impressed with what I see. The enormous green lawns are strewn with carnival rides, a small petting zoo, and colorful balloons and streamers hang off the white canopies. Long trestle tables provide the masses with an array of food and beverages. Everyone seems to be happily talking and eating, and enjoying the laid-back atmosphere.

"Your father is just over there," Pat says, pointing at a huge oak tree. I can see him sitting in his wheelchair with his back turned to the festivities.

"Thanks, Pat. I'll see if he wants to join in on the fun." She smiles and nods.

I make my way down the hill, wondering why my father has decided to sit down here and miss out on all the fun. As I round the tree, I almost trip over my feet, realizing why. "Madison?"

Her green eyes guiltily dart up to meet mine from where she's crouched at my father's feet. She quickly stands and replaces the knitted blanket over his legs. It appears she was doing up his shoelaces. She's taking care of him, but why?

"What are you doing here?" I abruptly ask, cringing when I realize how rude that sounded.

"I was just leaving," she bites back, leaning forward and kissing my father on the head. "*Ciao, Pino. Ci vediamo dopo.*"

My mouth drops open even farther. "You speak Italian now? Since when?" I shout. I need to quit yelling at her, but my emotions are running haywire, and I have no idea what's happening.

"Goodbye, Dixon." She attempts to shove past me, but I leap out and latch onto her arm. The moment we make contact, my body hums in familiarity. It never wants to let her go.

"Goodbye? I don't think so. You didn't answer my question,"

I press, tightening my hold.

She rips her arm from my grip and glares at me. "I was invited, remember? Or did you lie about that, too?"

I recoil, her words kicking me straight in the balls. I deserve them. "Of course, you were. I'm sorry. My mistake." She nods smugly and straightens out her red coat. But her self-righteousness disappears soon after, and she peers down at her boots.

This is so damn awkward. I never thought I would ever feel this way around Madison, but I do. I can't remember a time when I wanted to flee more than I do right now. So I stand mutely, rocking back on my heels and waiting for her to leave.

But she doesn't. Her gaze lingers on my bandaged hand. Does she know what happened to her brother? Either way, it doesn't matter anymore. She's no longer my concern. I remind myself I am doing this for her and continue to stand my ground.

Who am I kidding? Standing my ground is dreadful. I feel sick inside, and I think I'm seconds away from losing my lunch. I have never felt this way before, and I'm not afraid to admit it. "Madison…"

She looks up, tears welling in her eyes.

The sight kills me. But I persevere. "How have you been?"

She kicks at the dirt, biting her lip as she wipes her eyes. "I've been okay."

"That's good to hear," I lie. I want her to confess that she is as miserable as I am. "How's school?"

She shrugs. "It's fine. I got into Mount Sinai."

Thanks to the night where everything turned to shit, I never got a chance to ask Maddy how her interviews went. "That's fantastic. Congratulations. You must be over the moon."

But she appears anything but overjoyed. "I can't do this," she suddenly says, bursting into tears.

Telling my resolve to fuck off, I attempt to hug her, but she jumps backward and folds her arms around her slender torso.

"Can't do what?" I question, ignoring how I repulse her.

"I can't pretend everything is all right between us," she replies, reaching into her pocket and wiping her red nose with a handkerchief.

"I understand that, Maddy. I know things will never be the same, but I'd like it if we could still be friends."

She scoffs, shaking her head incredulously. "I believe it was you who said we were never just friends."

She's right. I did say that to her. But I just can't let her walk out of my life. Her being here means something, right? It's got to. "Why are you here?"

"I-I…" She falters.

"You what?" I ask, taking a step toward her.

"I wanted to see your father," she confesses.

"Why?"

"Because I missed him…I missed you," she softly reveals, meeting my concentrated stare.

My heart leaps at her admission, but I remain cool, not wanting to mess this up. "I missed you, too."

"But that fact doesn't change how I feel."

I blow out a frustrated breath, knowing this was too good to be true. She misses me, but she doesn't miss me enough to forgive me. So we're back to square one.

"I better go. I'm sorry for coming here and ruining your day," she apologizes softly.

I could try to comfort her, refute that she did anything of

the sort. But what would be the point? So I simply nod, feeling more disheartened than I felt the day she said goodbye.

She stands staring at me, appearing to want to say something more, but she doesn't. She pulls the lapels of her coat up toward her chin, indicating she's leaving. The action untucks her silver necklace from underneath her sweater. The moment my father sees it, he grunts because she's wearing my mother's necklace.

When she looks down at her chest, her cheeks flush. She appears embarrassed that she's been caught wearing it. She attempts to take it off, but my father and I lunge forward to stop her. She stops dead in her tracks, appearing just as stunned as I am.

Too many things are happening at once. My exhausted brain can't keep up with the fact that my father just showed a flicker of emotion, that Maddy is here, and that she's here confessing to missing me and wearing my mother's necklace.

"Keep it," I assert, finally finding my voice. My eyes are focused on my father, who has returned to being his catatonic self. Thankfully, she doesn't argue.

She too looks at my father because we both saw him move faster than we've ever seen him move before. "Pino?" she says, walking forward and crouching down in front of him. "*Mi senti?*"

I still can't wrap my head around the fact she's learned Italian. But that can wait because my father slowly raises his eyes, and…he fucking nods.

The air whooshes from my lungs. "*Papà?*" His eyes flick to mine, and I swallow hard. "Was he responsive before?" I ask frantically, dropping to a squat beside her.

Maddy shakes her head. "Not really. I didn't notice anything different. I haven't for the past couple of weeks." The moment the words are out, she bites down on her lip.

I pull back, baffled. "Past couple of weeks? This isn't the first time you've visited him?"

She guiltily shakes her head. If I wasn't in the middle of a major crisis, I would demand answers, but I have other pressing matters to deal with.

"*Papà? Sai chi sono?*" When I ask if he knows who I am, he fucking nods again.

"Holy shit!" I curse, placing both hands over my gaping mouth. "I need to call a nurse."

Springing up, I tear up the hill, thankful to see Pat close by. "Pat, my father—"

"What about him?" she asks, giving me her full attention as she places her plate onto the table.

"I think he's awake, or responsive, or fuck, I don't know," I ambiguously explain, and she scrunches up her nose. "Please come. Let me show you."

She nods and we quickly sprint down the hill, reaching my father's side in seconds. Madison is still crouched at his feet, but stands when she sees us arrive. Her eyes dart to Pat, who politely pushes past her.

"Pino, it's Pat. Can you hear me?" she asks, looking down at her watch as she places her fingers over my father's pulse.

I'm standing off to the side, watching anxiously and hoping I didn't imagine that the last two minutes actually happened. As she reaches into her pocket and produces a penlight, she moves the ray of light side to side and gasps when my father's eyes seem to follow the movement.

"What's going on?" I ask, diving forward.

She turns around and smiles. "I think your father is showing signs of awareness. This is great news, Dr. Mathews. I'll have to call the doctor to confirm, though."

"Yes, please do." I can't stand still, so I begin pacing the grass with both hands atop my head. I listen to Pat put in a call to the doctor, who says he's on his way. Maddy looks like she wants to comfort me, but she doesn't. And honestly, I can only deal with one drama at a time.

Pat senses my tension and walks over to me. "He's going to be just fine, Dr. Mathews." She places her hand on my forearm and smiles kindly. "He's in good hands."

Her reassurance makes me feel better, and without thinking, I place my hand over hers. "Thank you, Pat." She nods and goes back to checking on my father.

When I turn to look at Maddy, I see that her face is pulled into a tight scowl. I have no idea what's wrong, and as I open my mouth, about to ask if she's okay, she barks, "I better go."

"Go?" I ask, frowning. "You don't have to. The doctor will be here in just a minute."

She shakes her head. "I'm sure you've got all the help you need." When she glares at Pat, I suddenly understand what's wrong. She's jealous.

"Madison," I chide, not hiding the fact that I know what's bugging her.

But she doesn't want to hear it. "I hope your dad is okay. I'll check in tomorrow." She rushes off, but I follow in hot pursuit.

"Madison, you're being ridiculous! Absolutely nothing is going on with Pat and me. She's my father's nurse, that's all," I whisper, not wanting Pat to overhear. "Please stop."

Madison does stop, but she spins around angrily. "I wish

I could believe you, but I can't! And I hate that I feel this way. Before all of this happened, I wouldn't have thought twice about it. But now, all I can think is do you find her attractive, or have you had sex with her!"

I sigh, pressing a hand to my brow. "I can assure you having sex with anybody right now is the furthest thought from my mind!"

She flinches, taking a step back as I don't mask my annoyance. After a few seconds, she frowns. "I'm sorry, Dixon. I've made this about me, and I shouldn't have. This is about your father. Go be with him."

I want to say so many things, but she's right. This isn't about her. It isn't about me, either. It's about my dad. And I won't allow my selfishness to get in the way of his well-being any longer. I don't want to do this, but I have no other choice.

"I'm sorry you can't stick around, but you're right. This is about him. It was nice seeing you, but I think it's best…if we cut all ties. I can't keep living in this state of uncertainty any longer. It hurts too much. You can still visit my father. I will just ensure I'm not here when you do."

Her face drops, and she blinks back her tears, but she takes it in stride and nods. "Okay."

Every inch of my body is clamoring not to turn around. I shove down my better judgment and take one last look at the love of my life before doing what's right. The doctor comes rushing down the hill, and I follow him, focusing on nothing but my father.

I look on eagerly, observing every single thing he does. I breathe out a sigh of relief when my father responds with a slight nod or a forced blink to the doctor's questions. After a couple of minutes, the doctor turns to me and smiles.

"It appears your father has woken up." I have no idea what that means, but it's far better than him being asleep.

When my father's eyes suddenly meet mine, my entire body breaks out into a cold sweat. This is the first time I've actually seen him alert, and it scares the living hell out of me.

"*Papà?*" I say, stepping closer, not knowing what to expect. But he didn't raise me to be a coward. "*Papà? Sono io, tuo figlio.*"

He watches me closely, his breathing short and shallow. I walk closer and closer until I am standing inches away. I wait, not knowing what else to do. Just as I'm about to give up hope, he opens his mouth slowly.

"Pino? What is it?" Pat says, leaning in close.

But his eyes never waver from mine as he lets out two breathless gasps of air before uttering, "*Fottuto idiota.*"

The doctor turns to me, hands raised in confusion. "What did he just say?"

I don't know whether to laugh or cry. The first words to come out of my father's mouth are words I was so not expecting to hear. Either way, I'm just happy he spoke.

Laughing maniacally, I reply, "He just called me…a fucking idiot."

Twenty-Six

Dixon

Five weeks later

"Dr. Mathews, I cannot," admonishes Susanna as I travel down the highway.

"Yes, you can. I give you my permission," I counter, increasing the volume on my Bluetooth.

"No matter, I simply cannot walk up to Mr. Blackburn and…kick him in the genitals. He's your patient." Regardless of the fact he's my patient, he's still a major pain in my ass.

I slap my hand on the steering wheel, cackling in humor. "No, I suppose you can't," I rejoin, wiping the tears from my eyes. "But it would be a rather hilarious sight, don't you agree?"

Susanna clucks her tongue at me, but I can sense she's biting back her smile.

"I'll be back in Manhattan on Monday afternoon. Please call if I'm needed," I say, putting my serious face on.

"All will be fine, Dr. Mathews. You just focus on winning that award," she replies, referring to the Gerald Harriet's Awards ceremony, which will take place tomorrow night.

"I'll try my best, but I'm up against some solid contenders."

"There is no one better than you," she says kindly.

I smile, touched by her loyalty.

If it weren't for Susanna, I dare say I would be unemployed. She saved my ass and my practice after I went into hibernation with no intention of ever resurfacing. But the day my father woke was the day I pulled my shit together and realized that if he can do it, then so can I.

Things with Dad are going well. Although the doctors think he'll never fully "recover," he's so much better than the unresponsive man he was months ago. Our conversations are short, and sometimes we don't converse at all. But it's nice to have him listen and to actually acknowledge that I'm there.

I know he misses Madison. Every time he hears a female voice, his eyes dart to the door, excitedly awaiting her arrival. But she never appears. He's not the only one; I miss her so incredibly much that it hurts to think of her name. But I've stuck to my word, and no matter how hard it's been, I haven't given in to temptation and called her. I've left her alone—hence my father calling me a fucking idiot.

I really do believe she's better off without me. Me, on the other hand, I'm still a fucking mess. But I go on. I take each day as it comes because that's the only way I know how to survive.

Returning to the here and now, I reply to Susanna's comment. "Thank you, Ms. Vale. You are biased, however." She chuckles and wishes me good luck before ending the call.

I'm almost in Boston, and I'm glad I left Manhattan early to miss the standard horrendous Friday afternoon traffic.

Chad Turner has touched base with me over the course of the week, pretty much hinting at the fact that I've won the award. However, he'll most likely change his tune once he finds out what I have planned. I intend to reveal to my colleagues what a complete and utter fraud I am.

I wasn't lying when I told Juliet I would tell everyone about the sins of my past. Although these past five weeks have been Juliet-free, I'm not an idiot. I know she'll be back. So to remove her from my life for good, I need to destroy any leverage she may have over me, which is my sordid affair with her and my patients.

I know it won't be pleasant, but neither is living in fear that Juliet is lurking in the shadows, waiting to strike.

I pull up at the Marriott, leaving my car in the capable hands of the valet as I grab my backpack and garment bag. Once I'm checked in, I round the corner to ride the elevator to my floor. However, I'm surprised when I bump into Dr. Maxwell Wellington and someone I presume is his lovely wife.

Dr. Wellington is my old college professor. And as chance would have it, he's Madison's *current* college professor. Yeah, screw you, irony.

"Dr. Wellington?" I query, as I hadn't realized he would be in attendance. "What a pleasant surprise."

"Dixon, hello. And I thought I told you to call me Max," he responds, smiling happily. "I hear congratulations are in order."

I smirk. "Thank you, although I haven't won yet. But honestly, to be nominated is an honor in itself."

"If these judges have any sense, they'll see you're the best man for the job." He winks while I attempt to hide my shame as

I wish that were true.

There is a short silence before Max introduces the stunning woman by his side. "Dixon, this is my beautiful, angelic wife, Aiko."

"Always the charmer," Aiko teases playfully while shaking my hand.

It's obvious that these two are still very much in love with one another. I remember Max revealing in his inspirational speech at the Gerald Harriet's Fellowship Award night that they had been married for fifty years, which is quite an accomplishment in this day and age. Their devotion has me instantly yearning for Madison, and it must show on my face.

"Will Ms. Roberts be joining you this weekend?" Max asks, none the wiser to my fuckup.

"No. Sadly, Madison and I broke up," I reveal, unable to hide my regret.

Max's mouth dips into a frown. "I'm sorry to hear that. You two were quite fetching together. She appeared to be the yin to your yang."

"Thank you, Max. And yes, she was." All talk of Madison has me desperate to venture upstairs to drown my sorrows in scotch and baseball. "I'd best unpack. I'll see you tomorrow."

"You're not attending the cocktail party?" Max asks, and I shake my head. "The guest of honor not attending his own party? Whatever will the big wheels say?"

I laugh, loving Max's spunk. "Honestly, I couldn't give a damn," I reveal behind my hand.

Aiko and Max chuckle. Max steps forward and places his hand on my shoulder. "If you change your mind, I'd love to have a brandy with you. If not, I shall see you tomorrow."

"Okay, Max. Either way, we will catch up," I affirm. "It was lovely meeting you, Aiko. I hope to see you again soon." She smiles, and we part ways after we wave goodbye.

As I ride the elevator to my floor, I can't help but remember how Madison and I cemented our relationship under this very roof. If I'd known then what I know now, I would have confessed everything then and there. With hindsight, I would have done so many things differently. But that's the fucked-up thing about hindsight. It's useless.

As I enter the lavish room, I get hit with a serious case of nostalgia, as this room is a replication of the one I shared with Madison. As I walk to the bedroom, I can't help but wonder if this feeling will ever go away. Will I ever be able to walk into a room, smell a certain fragrance, or eat a certain food without thinking about Madison, or relating it to her somehow? When my eyes fall to the king-size bed, I know that the answer is probably no.

I hang up my suit and then go on to arrange my toiletries in the bathroom. The counter looks so bare without Madison's entire makeup collection crowding the surface space. And so does the glass, where my toothbrush sits by its lonesome.

Needing a distraction, I decide to pour myself a drink and watch some TV, but when an ad comes on detailing that Madison Avenue is the best place to shop, I quickly change channels and groan. When will this stop?

Leaning my head back against the sofa, I stare up at the ceiling, wondering if this is what the rest of my life will be like. If so, it's going to be one long, painful ride.

Deciding to take Max up on his offer, I quickly get up and leave behind my boulevard of broken dreams.

The ballroom is in full swing. I, however, am not. I've been here for roughly fifteen minutes, and already I can feel my cheeks start to ache from all the fake smiling.

I seem to be everyone's golden boy because as soon as I finish talking to one person, another takes their place. The majority of the conversations have been dull and drab, but I smile and nod, hoping I catch a break and someone pulls the fire alarm soon.

As I'm talking to Dr. Frenk about his experiences after winning the Gerald Harriet's Award, I can't help but look longingly at the bar; I need a scotch to deal with the boring content of his speech. How different my attitude is from what it was when I was last here. Of course I would be thrilled to win the award, but it doesn't seem as important as it once was.

With that thought in mind, I politely excuse myself and make a beeline for the bar. Max and Aiko are talking to Dr. Felding, looking as excited as I feel. I decide to have one drink with Max before calling it a night.

"Two scotches, please." The bartender nods and goes about pouring my drinks.

As I'm waiting, the hair on the back of my neck suddenly stands on end, and every part of my body tells me to keep my eyes in front. But it doesn't matter where I look because Rebecca, Chad's fiancée, will ensure she's all up in my face, demanding my complete attention.

"Hi, handsome. Aren't you a sight for sore eyes?" I

unconsciously shift away, hoping she gets the hint and leaves. She doesn't. "If possible, you're looking even hotter than when I saw you last. I like the scruff." As she attempts to run her fingers through my full beard, I pull away, almost bumping into the woman next to me.

I apologize quickly and rejoice when the bartender places the scotches in front of me. "Good evening, Rebecca," I dismissively say, grabbing my drinks and attempting to leave.

"Do you like my dress?" she randomly blurts out, running a hand down her torso. She looks like a Christmas ham in her laced ensemble, but I nod, not at all interested in what she has to say. "Well, you should see what I'm wearing—or *not* wearing—underneath."

Holding back my vomit, I step forward, but she moves to the side, blocking my path. "What do you want?" I snap, my patience wearing thin. I haven't forgotten what she did to Madison. Whatever awful, venomous words she spewed to Maddy the night of the Gerald Harriet's Fellowship Award ceremony brought on an episode that almost destroyed Madison's fragile mind.

I have no intention of pretending to stand the sight of her.

She pathetically pouts while I glance around the room to ensure no one is watching this painful encounter. "Where's your little girlfriend?"

Just the mere mention of Madison has me seeing red. "That's none of your concern." I step forward, not bothering to mask my anger. "Rebecca, consider this your first warning. This is strike one."

Her cheeks flush, and she licks her upper lip slowly. "What happens at strike two? Or better yet, strike three?"

Unable to put a lid on my emotions, I get into her face and snarl, "Don't test me, Rebecca. Unlike last time, I've got nothing to lose." A small breath catches in her throat, and she exhales heavily.

Great, my words have had the complete opposite effect, and now she's totally turned on. This time, however, I don't have Maddy to save me. I do, however, have Chad.

"There you are."

Rebecca leaps in the air, totally busted. "D-darling," she fumbles, brushing a hand through her hair. "Look who I found on my way to the bathroom."

Chad looks between us, and I see it—a hint of suspicion. But he smiles and shakes my hand. "Good of you to join us, Doctor. Attending your own festivities fashionably late, I see."

Thankfully, the air has cleared, and I don't have to enlighten him about what a harlot his fiancée is. "Ah, you know me. I like to drink alone. Speaking of." I hold up my drinks, indicating I was on my way out.

Chad reads me loud and clear but says, "I'm not one to stand in the way of a man and his scotch, but join me tomorrow morning? A few friends and I are going sailing."

Though donating my kidney would be more enjoyable, I nod. I just want to get away from Rebecca and all the bad memories she represents. "That sounds wonderful. Text me the details, and I'll meet you there."

I bid him farewell, not even bothering to acknowledge the shrew. With both drinks in hand, I search the room for Max. When I find him standing a few feet away, I stop dead in my tracks because I know that he knows. He so saw my exchange with Rebecca. The question is, what will he do?

Unable to stomach the wait, I raise one glass, indicating the drink is for him. He shakes his head and points at me, implying that I need it more than him.

I'll drink to that.

Twenty-Seven

Dixon

Why I agreed to go sailing is beyond me.

Not only do I hate the water but I also had to spend hundreds on "acceptable" boating attire. In other words, I feel and look like a total tool.

But I suppose it's a small price to pay to be sitting amongst the best of the best. I'm sailing with three of America's top doctors, who seem to really have taken a liking to me. We've bonded over khakis, the Red Sox, and Long Island iced teas. These docs can't handle their booze, however, and Dr. Lieberman has let slip that I have almost positively won the award.

Chad is thankfully not as intoxicated as these two other clowns, and as we sail through calm waters, he turns to me and smiles. "How do you feel about winning the award, Dixon?"

I shrug, not really knowing how I feel. "Fine, I guess."

He cocks his head to the side. "You guess? You're not excited?"

I realize I should probably show a little more excitement and gratitude. "I am. Very excited. I just won't count my chickens before they've hatched."

Chad smirks, my answer appearing to appease him. "Smart thinking, but let's just say your chickens *have* hatched, what do you plan on doing?"

I honestly haven't given it much thought. I know winning this award is life-changing. It'll open up many doors and opportunities for me, and as Chad once told me, I wouldn't solely have to practice because I could also teach.

But things with Madison have really had me questioning... everything. Do I want to stay in Manhattan? The more I think about it, the more the answer becomes clearer. My relationship with Manhattan has turned ugly, and I can't help but wonder if I was drunk the entire time I lived there because the thought of going back now turns my stomach.

I decide to answer Chad honestly. He is a doctor, after all. Maybe he can tell me I'm not as crazy as I feel. "I was thinking of getting out of Manhattan," I confess. "Maybe go back to Jersey."

He pulls back, not hiding his surprise. "You're serious?"

I nod. "I think it's time for a change." Although he knows nothing of my father's condition, I add, "I'd like to make the most of whatever time my father has left on this earth."

He's still wearing his shocked face when he replies, "I won't lie, Dixon, this comes as quite a surprise, but you have to follow your gut. You can practice wherever you like. So if Jersey feels like home, then go for it."

Coming from Chad, that advice is surprisingly reassuring. "So you don't think I'm taking a demotion by leaving the Big Smoke and moving on to greener pastures—literally?"

MONICA JAMES

Chad smirks as he sips his cocktail. "Not at all. Family is important." He looks over at Rebecca, who is sunbathing topless. Thankfully, she's on her stomach. "Don't let work shroud what's important in life. Having no one to celebrate your milestones with really puts everything into perspective."

I raise an eyebrow. Could it be Chad has finally realized that Rebecca is a gold-digging hussy? I don't say anything, though. He'll have to find out the hard way. Just like I did.

Chad clears his throat, appearing embarrassed to have shared too much. "I'd best check on those two fools." We both look over at Dr. Lieberman and Dr. Das, who are hanging over the edge of the boat, laughing hysterically at God knows what.

As Chad excuses himself, Rebecca cunningly rolls over so her tits are sitting sunny side up. She looks over at me and winks. I turn my head away, disgusted that this woman is in my line of sight. After Chad's confession, I actually feel sorry for him. Now that the novelty of Rebecca's cooch has worn off, he can almost certainly see that he should have stayed with his wife. But us men, we need to find out the hard way that all that glitters is not gold.

"Hi, Doctor."

Exhaling loudly, I turn to look at Rebecca. I'm thankful she's no longer topless. "Hi."

My insolent tone doesn't seem to deter her in the slightest. "So I was thinking, after tonight's proceedings, maybe we could meet up?"

"Whatever for?"

She tries to pull the innocent act when she toys with the drawstring of her bikini top and bites her bottom lip. "Maybe have a drink. I want to show you I'm not all bad. I think we got

306

off on the wrong foot." She's got a lot of gall.

She's come to realize coming on too strong hasn't worked, so she's now trying a different approach. It's still not working, however.

Leaning in close, I reply, "No, we didn't. I know your type, Rebecca. I'm not interested in having a drink with you. Nor am I interested in speaking to you. Please leave me alone." I turn around to look out over the railing.

Sadly, her malicious voice ruins my view. "Don't forget, I can blemish your little comradeship with Chad. One word, Dr. Mathews, that's all it'll take."

Strike two.

I am done with women blackmailing me. "No, you won't, Rebecca," I refute, not bothering to look at her. "You know that if you did, your cushy life with Chad will be over. He may have been blinded by what's between your legs, but believe me, it's beginning to leave a bitter aftertaste. Both literally and figuratively speaking." She stomps off a second later, thankfully not rebutting my claims.

Being around Rebecca has only reinforced how much I miss Madison. It has also cemented the fact that I *have* changed. I may have had to lose everything in the process, but you have to lose everything to appreciate what you have. Or, in Madison's case, had.

Feeling those familiar emotions of longing pass over me, I gulp down my cocktail and realize I'm one step closer in deciding my fate.

As I look at my reflection in the mirror, I know that something big is about to happen. I don't know how I know. I just do.

I adjust my navy tie, not feeling an iota of nerves because this has been a long time coming. I should have done this from the get-go. Madison's words about me dealing with the consequences of my mistakes can also be applied to this situation.

I can't believe how far off the path I've strayed. It's time to fix the error of my ways.

As I step out of the elevator, I can't believe how calm I feel. To onlookers, my arrogance might be mistaken for cockiness about my certainty that I've won the award, but winning the award is the furthest thing from my mind.

When I inform the staff member who I am, she smiles and leads me to table number one. Max, Aiko, Chad, Rebecca, and three other contenders and their partners are sitting at the large table. Bad luck for me, the seat between Rebecca and Max is the only one free. Not wanting to make a scene, I walk over and take it.

"Evening," I say, addressing the table.

"Hello, my friend," Chad replies, holding up his glass in salute. I nod and reach for the bottle of red.

The table continues quizzing Dr. Bora on his findings in abnormal psychology. As I'm listening to him speak, I can't help but compare him to a textbook. His findings are brilliant, but

I've heard most of them before. And if he uses air quotes around the word "abnormal" one more time, I'll have no hesitation about alerting him to the fact that we're not imbeciles.

Ten minutes in, Max leans over and whispers, "Can you believe this moron was actually nominated? A monkey smoking a cigar is more intelligent, not to mention more interesting than he is."

I can't hold back my laughter and mask it behind my hand. Thankfully, Dr. Bora is too busy in his egocentric world to notice the disruption. "I stick to my original theory of you being the only sensible choice to win."

As I subtly shift my leg away when Rebecca fondles my thigh, I can't help but think how wrong he is.

"I'll be right back. I just have to inform the emcee that we're ready for the proceedings to commence," Chad says as he stands, buttoning up his suit jacket. He looks at me and gives me a knowing smile.

Throughout the evening, Rebecca has been relatively tame, but now that Chad has gone, it's claws out, and I mean that literally. I move my leg away for the tenth time this hour, bored and angered by her tenacity. I don't know how many times I have to say no before she gets the hint and leaves me alone.

I'm quite certain my annoyance is showing because I haven't failed to notice Max looking at me with curiosity as I grind my teeth in frustration. Too bad Chad hasn't figured it out.

Rebecca leans close. "I'd have thought by now you'd realize I don't give up easily."

Unable to keep the anger from my tone, I reply, "Neither do I."

"I like a challenge," she counters huskily, not caring that we're in earshot of her fiancé's colleagues. I shake my head, feeling so unbelievably frustrated to find myself in this situation.

Max shifts beside me, and I know he can hear our conversation loud and clear. I bet he's rethinking his claims about me being the best contender for the award.

"You wouldn't have to do a thing. All you'd have to do is lie back and enjoy the ride," she states quickly because at that precise moment, we both see Chad walking back to our table, his eyes darting between our inappropriate closeness.

"No," I grind out between clenched teeth.

"Oh, for Christ's sake, anyone would think you've got something against blow jobs!" Her outburst is a little louder than she anticipated because as soon as the words leave her lips, she slaps a hand over her mouth. But it's too late.

The table grows quiet, appearing unsure if they actually heard what they thought they did. But sadly, they did.

"What are you two whispering about?" Chad asks suspiciously as he takes his seat. The entire table looks on with interest.

I could lie, but I know this is where it all begins.

Rebecca nervously brushes down her dress, while I lean in and whisper, "Strike three."

She twists to look at me, her eyes pleading that I don't, but she should have thought about that before cornering someone with nothing left to lose.

Calmly reaching for my wine, I take a sip before confessing, "We were discussing how your fiancée wants to deep-throat me and then fuck me into a boneless stupor."

The table gasps while Chad's mouth drops open and his face turns a ghastly shade of white. The truth hurts but better that than living a lie. "I'm sorry, Chad. I respect you immensely, but I cannot lie to you any longer. Your fiancée is a gold-digging whore." Chad's mouth drops even farther, while Rebecca spins to look at him, frantically claiming that it's all lies.

I look over at Aiko, embarrassed by my crudeness. "My apologies for being so vulgar." She waves it off, appearing comfortable with my honesty.

The emcee chooses this moment to announce that all nominees are to come up on stage. I stand and coolly button up my jacket. Chad's face has now turned a bright shade of red, and he too stands up, probably ready to knock me to the ground. I appeal to the rational man who lies deep within.

"A wise man once told me having no one to celebrate your milestones with really puts everything into perspective. And he was right."

Taking a great risk, I walk past Chad as the emcee calls out my name. Placing my hand on his shoulder, I give it a reassuring squeeze. "Get out now before it's too late. Believe me, I know."

I don't know what he's thinking, but I do know a small part of him must believe me. If not, he would have surely called me a lying son of a bitch and had me thrown out by now, but he's done neither.

Needing to apologize to the only other person at this table who I give a damn about, I look over at Max. "I'm sorry, Dr. Wellington. I'm afraid I'm not the person you believed me to be." I can't stand the look of disappointment any longer, so I commence my walk of shame up to the stage.

A million thoughts race around my head as I stand blankly in front of my peers, colleagues, and now, enemies. I'm barely listening to a word the emcee is saying as all I can focus on is the fact my prediction was right. This is it. All my secrets are about to be revealed. This isn't just big. This is fucking astronomical.

"And the winner is…" the emcee says, drawing out the anticipation.

Suddenly, my life, my entire existence, flashes before my eyes. Every important event, every important memory crashes so violently into me, I'm left standing breathlessly and rubbing the sweat from my palms. I close my eyes, trying to focus on one single memory because the internal roller coaster is making me sick.

It doesn't surprise me when my brain tracks back to the time Madison told me she loved me.

Nothing will ever compare to such a feeling because there is no other in the world that could ever make me so happy and feel so complete. Not even winning this stupid award.

"Dr. Dixon Mathews!"

My eyes snap open when the room erupts into deafening cheers. It takes a moment, but when I see a sea of people standing, clapping vigorously, I realize they're clapping for… me. I actually won.

I'm standing speechless, unsure of what to say or do. Thankfully, the emcee waves me over, holding the glass plate award in his hand. Looking out into the crowd, I see that Max and Chad are standing too, but unlike everyone else, they're not clapping. Rather, they look to be having heated words.

This vision is exactly what I needed to see, as it sets the wheels into motion.

Taking one step and then two, I accept the award from the relieved emcee, who appears thankful that I've returned to the land of the living. It takes a minute or so before the applause dies down and I'm faced with absolute silence.

I grip the wooden podium as I peer around the room. I don't really know where to start because it's not like I prepared a speech. However, as I look down at my name engraved into the glass, I know a good place to start is with the truth—to start with the reason I'm here.

I clear my throat. "Thank you." Now would be the time to say something witty and detail how it's been my dream to achieve such an accomplishment. But as I return my attention to Max, I know there is only one thing I can do.

Without further thought, I violently smash the plate onto the side of the podium. It shatters with a loud crash, splinters of glass littering the stage. The audience gasps and shouts, most springing up to avoid the projectiles of soaring debris. The emcee shrieks and ducks for cover.

I'm left holding a shard of glass and the sight has me breaking into the first genuine smile I've smiled all day. "I'm sorry for the dramatics, but this entire thing is a load of shit."

Ignoring the mortified faces of my audience, I bend down and pick up a few broken pieces of glass. "This," I state, holding up a shard which looks a little like Florida. "This is for Dr. Adler." Dr. Adler is a fellow nominee, and I enjoyed her detailing her studies in the psychology of gender.

She awkwardly looks around the room, but surprises me as she takes a step forward and accepts the slice I'm offering her. "Thank you." She smiles and walks back to her table.

Holding up another piece, I continue. "And this is for Dr.

Augustine." Dr. Augustine is another candidate. I found his humor refreshing, and he's also a fellow Yankees fan. He looks nervously around the room, but he too surprises me as he steps forward and accepts his makeshift award.

I go on and call up each nominee, giving them their small piece of reverence. Even the batshit boring Dr. Bora appears happy with his offering. After I'm done sharing, I take a deep breath and reveal the reason behind my madness. It's time for my redemption.

Holding up my sliver, I reveal, "I don't deserve this because…I'm a fraud."

I don't think the crowd can handle any more excitement, and the room erupts into pure bedlam. The pandemonium doesn't deter my confession, however. "I am probably the person least deserving of this award, as my recent unorthodox practices shit all over this honor and what it's meant to represent."

My confession soon hushes the room as they all eagerly wait for me to air my dirty laundry.

"I'm not proud of my actions, and it's time I pay for my wrongdoings. For the past…" I pause, as I don't even know how long it's been. As I'm calculating my sins, I see Chad unexpectedly run over to the stage. I figure he's finally grown a pair, and I'm about to get what's coming to me.

With that thought in mind, I quickly declare, "For God knows how long, I've been fuc—" But I don't get to finish. The air gets ripped from my lungs when Chad hip-and-shoulders me and yanks the microphone from my hand. I stumble, completely caught off guard, as I thought he was about to punch me, not bump me out of the way.

"What Dr. Mathews is trying to say is that for God knows

how long, he's been focusing on becoming a better doctor. Some of his research methods may be unorthodox, and at times, he's felt like a fraud because he's surrounded by so many intelligent and gifted colleagues who seem to be discovering the next big thing. He's a perfectionist, and he really is his own worst enemy. But in no way are you undeserving, Dr. Mathews." Chad turns to look at me. "What you just did shows everyone what sort of a doctor you really are. You shared your entitlement with your fellow nominees because you are selfless. And if that doesn't show this room what kind of a doctor you are, then I don't know what will."

This time, I'm the one whose mouth has just hit the floor. What the hell is going on? Why is Chad saving my ass? Did he not hear me when I called his fiancée a gold-digging whore?

"Three cheers for Dr. Dixon Mathews!" Chad exclaims, egging the stunned crowd on. By the third cheer, I can tell they've bought his bullshit spiel.

Before I have a chance to deny his kind but incorrect claims, some pop tune comes blaring over the speakers. I look over at the DJ and almost fall flat on my ass when I see Max over at the booth, looking at me knowingly.

What's going on?

"Dr. Mathews," Chad says from between clenched teeth. "Take a walk with me." I don't have time to get a word in edgewise because he stands behind me and practically shoves me down the stairs.

As I walk through the inquisitive crowd, I dodge hunks of glass, the sight outlining what a nightmare the past five minutes have been. We casually saunter out the balcony doors a few seconds later.

Fortunately, only a few people are out here. I gather the night's proceedings grew too spectacular for their tastes, so they snuck out for a much-needed cigarette. The thought has me reaching into my jacket pocket and diving for my own nicotine savior.

As I breathe in my Marlboro, I feel a touch better. "You care to explain to me what the hell is going on? Why on earth would you do that? I thought you'd be more than happy to watch me throw myself under a bus. Instead, you're up there making excuses for me. Why?"

Chad blows out a deep breath. "Can I trouble you for one?" he asks, looking down at my pack. I didn't know he smoked, but I offer him one without hesitation.

As he takes a long drag, his shoulders instantly drop, and he smiles. "That's the first cigarette I've had in over two years," he confesses.

"Oh?"

He nods and turns to look out over the balcony railing. "Yes. Rebecca says smoking is a filthy habit, and it was her excuse not to kiss me."

It takes all my willpower to keep hidden that offering to smoke a stranger's cock is an even filthier habit, but Chad must be able to read my thoughts loud and clear.

"But now I know that was only one excuse in a long list of many." I wasn't expecting that reply, so I continue smoking in silence. "The answer to your question is I won't allow a lying bitch to make a fool of us both."

I thump my chest as I choke on my intake of smoke. "Excuse me? Are you saying that you believe me?" I query, unable to believe my ears.

"Yes, I do," he confirms.

"How? I mean, I'm thankful that you do, but I just told you your entire relationship is a sham. Why would you believe me and not her?"

Chad sighs, appearing plagued and saddened by the truth. "Because deep down, I always knew. I'm not stupid, Dixon. I knew that Rebecca was more interested in my wallet than she was in being my wife. But I thought maybe one day she could grow to love me."

Us men, we are all closet sentimental fools. No matter how many people warn us, we have to find out the hard way.

"And Max told me," he adds.

"Max?" I question, pausing from taking another drag.

Chad nods and finally turns to look at me. "Yes. He told me he had seen you brushing off Rebecca's advances last night. He also confirmed that he heard her at the table."

I feel like a complete ass. "I'm sorry, Chad. I truly am. I should have pulled you aside and been a little more discreet about the entire thing."

He shakes his head. "No need for apologies. What's done is done."

I decide to leave out the fact that this wasn't the first time Rebecca waved her cooch in my face. I figure, why kick a man when he's down? "I suppose I owe you a thank-you."

"You owe me nothing. Just keep your nose clean. We can't afford any more bad press," he counters, butting out his cigarette. "We can make whatever you did go away. Just let me know if you ever need me."

I nod, grateful for the "get out of jail free" card. It's now official—Juliet has nothing over me any longer. You'd think I'd be happy or relieved. Instead, I feel numb.

I feel like I should offer some kind of condolences as I did kind of break up his relationship. But funnily enough, I'm not sorry. I'm sorry he's hurting, but I'm not sorry I helped him see that the Juliets and Rebeccas of this world are nothing but trouble.

"If you ever need to talk, I'm here or whatever," I say uncomfortably, feeling like a complete pussy.

Chad chuckles and slaps me on the shoulder. "Thank you, Dixon. Maybe I could do the same for you," he wisely says.

Although he saved me from major embarrassment and shame, he knows that whatever demons I have will never go away. Even if I confessed my sins, the disgrace and remorse would remain with me forever.

"Right, then." He clears his throat, probably as uncomfortable with the touchy-feely crap as I am. "I have some business to take care of. Thanks for the cigarette."

"Any time." And I mean it. He gives me a final nod before going back inside.

I need a moment to process everything because life doesn't get any more complicated than this. My minute is short-lived, however. "Dr. Mathews, may I join you?"

Max is standing behind me, waiting for my permission. "Of course, Dr. Wellington." He shuffles over while I butt out my smoke.

I have so many things I wish to say, but I don't know where to start. I'm utterly embarrassed that a man I highly respect and admire just witnessed my inexcusable outburst. Not to mention, he no doubt knows what went on behind closed doors.

But in true Maxwell Wellington style, he seems to overlook

the madness. "So I think the lamb was rather dry, don't you?"

I can't stop my laughter from bubbling out of me freely. After the past few weeks, it's nice to laugh and actually mean it. After I'm done cackling like a fool, I sigh. "Thank you, Max. You saved my ass tonight."

He shakes his head. "You would have done the same for me."

"Of course I would have, but I'd hope you'd have more sense than me," I counter, smiling.

There's a slight pause before Max grows serious. "We've all done things we're not proud of, Dixon. But that's what makes us human. To be unfeeling, that's what makes us inhuman. Whatever you've done, I can see you're sincerely sorry for it."

"That I am. I can't take back what I've done, but I sure as hell can learn from it." And I have. It's just unfortunate that to learn my lesson, I had to lose the best thing in my life.

"The world needs a hero, Dixon. And you're it," Max says, surprising me.

"I'm no hero, Max. I never was."

He stubbornly pulls in his lips. "Yes, you are. What you did in there took some balls. And in my eyes, I still believe no one is more deserving of that award."

I appreciate his vote of confidence, but I don't feel the same. "Thank you. Your faith in me means a lot."

"It's not only my faith. It's the faith of others as well." I watch with interest as he reaches into his pocket and produces a shard of glass.

I can't believe my eyes when I see my name staring back at me on the jagged piece. For this to survive is truly a miracle. And Max knows it, too.

"One must have chaos in oneself to be able to…"

"Give birth to a dancing star," I conclude, quoting Nietzsche.

Dr. Wellington is an incredibly smart man. He's also a man filled with hope and compassion. "I can only hope that I grow into the man you are," I sincerely confess.

He warmly reaches out to pat my shoulder. "Only hope to be you, Dixon. Be yourself because everyone else is already taken."

This exchange has somehow left me feeling…lighter. The heaviness is still there, but I don't feel like I'm drowning.

Just as I'm about to thank him, I see Max look over my shoulder and smile. I want to turn around to see what has him grinning so broadly, but he stops me. "Alas, fate has spoken once again."

I have no idea what that means, but I don't have the time to question him because he ambiguously instructs, "Count to ten."

"To ten? Why would I count to ten?" I question, curling my lip in confusion.

"Trust me, my friend." He pats my arm before walking off with an eloquent smirk.

I desperately want to turn around, but for some reason, I don't. I feel beyond ridiculous, but I've never had any reason to doubt Max in the past. So why should I start now?

"One…

"Two…

"Three…

"Four…

"Five…

"Six…

"Seven…

"Eight…

"Nine…"

But for some reason, I'm suddenly left speechless and can't go on.

Taking a moment to process why, I feel the air is charged with a familiar static—a static I haven't felt in weeks. A static that makes me feel alive. And there is only one person who can make me feel this way.

I can suddenly feel it. I can suddenly feel…*her*.

"Ten."

Twenty-Eight

Dixon

The moment I'm done counting, I turn around, my pace measured. Looks like Max was right. Alas, fate has spoken once again. And fate has never looked more beautiful.

"Madison?" I question. I'm beyond elated that she's here, but I don't understand why. "Please excuse my insolence, but why are you here?" She lowers her eyes and scuffs the tip of her boot across the ground.

It hurts that she feels so uneasy around me, especially since I finally broke down those walls. But I suck it up and wait for her response.

When she finally meets my gaze, I squash down my nostalgia and give her my full attention. "I saw what you did." Her soft voice brings back so many memories, but I nod calmly.

"Yes, well, it was time I came clean. I'm just sorry I didn't do it sooner."

Her face softens. "I know what you mean." But I have no

idea what *she* means.

As much as I love seeing her, I know this isn't a social visit. She's here for a reason, and I need to know why.

Madison senses my impatience. "Can we go somewhere a little more private? I need to tell you something."

"Of course," I reply a little too eagerly, so I tone it down. "Would you like to go to the bar?"

She surprises me when she shakes her head. "Can we go up to your room?"

Hell yes, we can! But I tell my premature excitement to cool it because we're going up there to talk. And only to talk. "Sure."

Her relief is obvious, and I wonder if she thought I'd refuse her. She should know by now, though, that I would never refuse her anything.

I can't stop staring at her. She looks incredible, and my hands twitch to touch her. Not trusting myself, I slip my palms into my pants pockets and lower my head as I walk past her. Her sweet fragrance hits me immediately, sending a pang of longing straight to my heart. I focus on passing through the masses without alerting anyone to my internal, raging war.

Thankfully, my colleagues are too busy gossiping about me to realize I'm feet away. We slip out of the room undetected in less than a minute. The elevator ride up to my room is incredibly painful. A cart has never felt so small, and Madison's rigid stance reveals just how uncomfortable she is finding this entire situation.

I dive out the doors the minute they open, not bothering to conceal the fact that I want this over with as soon as possible. I don't know what "this" is, but my cynical self knows it's not good.

Opening the door to my room, I step aside and let Madison in first. She graces me with a strained smile before slipping inside. I follow a second later, hating this doom and gloom.

"Can I get you a drink?" I offer, walking over to the kitchen counter where my half-empty bottle of scotch sits.

"Yes, please."

Reaching for two glasses, I pour us both a decent amount. I have a feeling we'll need it.

While waiting, she stands awkwardly in the middle of the living room, her face turned downward. Great, she can't even bear the sight of me. With that thought in mind, I toss back my drink and pour myself another.

I place her scotch on the coffee table before taking a seat on the sofa, indicating I'm listening. She reaches for the glass and guzzles it down in one gulp. Her repulsed face reveals the drink was simply for courage.

Leaning back, I cross my ankle over my knee, tapping my finger against the side of the glass, waiting for her to speak. The suspense is killing me, and I don't know how much longer I can last without exploding and demanding what she wants.

"I did it," she finally confesses in a mere whisper.

"Did what?"

"I told them," she replies, her long hair covering her downturned face.

She doesn't need to clarify who she's referring to. It appears both Madison and I needed the purge. "How'd it go?"

She shrugs, picking at her red nail polish. "Better than I thought it would."

I breathe out a sigh of relief. "I'm most pleased." I won't force her to tell me what happened. This isn't why she's here.

"I wanted to thank you for believing in me. If I had told them earlier, things might have been different between us."

I hate that she won't look at me. It's almost more than I can bear. But I understand her distance because confessing this to me is reopening up a part she has almost certainly tried to seal shut.

"It's okay, Madison. There's no need to thank me. I've always believed in you. I still do."

She sighs, her hands trembling as she brushes back her hair. I memorize her face because I know what she's about to do. "I finally feel…free. But one thing is still weighing me down. And I think it always will, but I have to try to let go because if I don't, I can't move on."

When she toys with my mother's pendant around her neck, I sit up tall, my heart thrashing about inside. Don't do this, *angelo*.

"Madison…"

But the words get caught in my throat when she looks up and meets my eyes. I can see it. It's finality. "There's one more thing I have to do to let go of the past."

Swallowing hard, I place my glass onto the table and stand with poise. "And what's that?" She blinks, her chest rising and falling in quick succession.

The air is soaked with a heavy current, but I don't move because this is her show. Her lips part as the sound of her breathy exhalations fills the air. Still, I remain motionless.

"Tell me," I demand, my gaze never wavering from hers. My dick begins to stir because I can smell it. I can smell *her*.

With shaky fingers, she lifts her sundress over her head, kicks off her boots, and stands before me in nothing but her underwear. "You," she finally reveals. When she reaches behind and unhooks her bra, I know she means that in every literal sense there is.

My body weeps when she drops the bra by her feet. She is magnificent. But when she attempts to shyly cover her breasts, I chastise her. If we're doing this, then there's no holding back.

"Don't deny me that. If you want this, you take all of me." She understands and drops her hands by her side.

I take a minute to appreciate her entirety. She really is the most beautiful woman I have ever seen. All women will pale in comparison to her and the way she makes me feel. But I can deal with my grief later because now, I just want to come.

I unfasten my tie, wrapping the length around my palm as I watch in longing as she presses her thighs together. The small triangular cloth between her legs is becoming an eyesore, and I point at it, indicating I want it off.

She flushes but hooks her thumbs into the waistband and draws the material down her legs. She kicks them to the side and then stands before me, totally bare. I need a minute.

Her pussy glistens, the circumstances already making her wet, and her perfect tits look flushed and heavy. My mouth waters, not knowing where to start.

"Dixon," she whimpers, and the delicious sound as she rubs her thighs encourages me further.

I don't speak; I simply saunter over, stopping only when we're inches apart. She opens her mouth, but I hush her as I push her lightly, and she falls onto the settee. She looks up at me, eyes innocent and mouth parted wide. The image gives me an idea.

With my tie still in hand, I gently brush the hair from her

brow while she mewls and leans into my touch. I'm thrilled she's still affected by my presence because the moment I feel her soft skin, my cock stands to attention, demanding out.

Gently securing her chin between my thumb and pointer, I draw down her plump bottom lip with my thumb. I'd give anything to kiss this mouth, and I will. But first, I have something else in mind.

I know I have no right, but I want her to know I would never hurt her. "Trust me."

Before she has time to object, I slip my tie over her head and fasten it securely over her eyes. She gasps, her hands darting up to her face. But I pull the ends, tightening it even further.

The image of her blindfolded and her naked, silky skin contrasting with the red velvet sofa is a sight I'll never forget. "You're extraordinary."

She sits silently, her heavy breaths mingling with mine. Her harsh exhalations push out her bountiful tits, and I can't wait a second longer. Running the backs of my fingers down her cheek, I trace down the slope of her neck and caress her sternum softly. I'm so happy she's still wearing my gift, and I toy with the pendant hanging between her breasts with pride. Her skin breaks out into tiny goose bumps, and her nipples instantly harden. I've missed this so much.

Bending forward, I capture a taut bud in my mouth and suck, tonguing the heavy weight of her breast leisurely. She leans back on her palms, thrusting more of herself into my mouth, whimpering and moaning loudly.

I begin to paw her other boob, flicking my thumb over her nipple and tracing around her areola. She moans and opens her legs wide. My gaze drops to her bare, pink pussy, and I almost come when I think about sheathing myself deep within.

She catches me by surprise when she reaches around with one hand and fumbles blindly over my belt buckle. Before I can protest, she flicks open the clasp and hastily unfastens my button and fly. With frantic fingers, she thrusts her hand down the front of my pants, feeling my feverish hard-on. I hum in unadulterated pleasure, my dick having missed her exquisite touch more than I thought possible.

"I want to—" She pants and cries out when I lash at her nipple with my tongue. "To go down on you," she breathlessly finishes.

She propels forward and pushes me away so she can pull down my pants and free my confined cock. With cautious hands, she searches for my erection, but she doesn't have far to go. The moment she wraps her hand around my shaft, I howl, unable to mask my pleasure.

Just as she lowers her head, however, I place my hand over hers, stilling her from moving an inch. She looks up at me, and even though she's blindfolded, I know she's silently asking why I stopped. To answer her question, I scoop her up, and we trade positions. She's left standing nervously, at my complete mercy, and if possible, my dick gets even harder. Unable to wait, I quickly undress.

I reach for her hand and thread my fingers through hers. "Get on," I command.

She licks her lips before stepping forward and attempting to climb on. But I squeeze her hand. "No, the other way." She appears confused, but a second later, her skin turns a lovely shade of pink.

I lie down, using the armrest as my cushion, and with our

fingers still entwined, I help guide her so she's straddling me backward. As I place my hand between her shoulder blades, she lowers her head while shuffling backward, giving me the best view in the world. Her perfect heart-shaped ass sits inches from my mouth, and as she positions herself, I raise my neck and take her burning pussy into my mouth.

She cries out and instantly drops down, deep-throating my cock in one steady motion. The sensation has me burying my face deeper into her folds as she rocks backward, fucking my face with a fierce momentum. Her head bobs up and down madly, and before long, we find a harmonious rhythm, a perfect tempo to match the other's pace.

I lock my hands to her hips, encouraging her to ride me faster as I thrust her backward over and over again. She screams out around me, the vibrations running all the way to my balls. I fuck her with my mouth and tongue, never giving her a second of reprieve. Her clit feels inflamed, and I know it won't be long until she's crying out her release.

With one hand, I reach underneath her body and toy with her bouncing tits, rolling her nipple between my fingers while thrashing my face from side to side. Her entire form constricts, and just as I predicted, she pulls away and screams out her orgasm in a howl of relief.

Her body convulses around my tongue, and I continue eating her out until she's squirming and begging me to stop. I do after a minute, my body missing her warmth the second she moves away. When she carefully climbs off, I try not to weep because that was over a lot faster than I had hoped. But when she attempts to slide the blindfold from her eyes, I jump up and stop her.

"W-What are you doing?" she pants, her body lax and supple. I squeeze her wrist gently, not wanting to confess my thoughts. "Tell me."

Nothing good ever came from hiding the truth, so I pitifully confess, "Leave it on. This way, you can pretend it's anyone but me."

Her face falls, and her lips dip into a tight frown. I don't understand her reaction. Isn't that what she wanted? Isn't that why she's here? To forget me? And what better way to do that than by leaving, blinded to what an asshole I am.

Nevertheless, she ignores me as she shrugs my hand away and slips the blindfold off. It takes a moment for her eyes to adjust to the lighting, but when they do, they fix onto my face. She smiles, but it's bittersweet. "That's the problem, Dixon. I don't want to pretend."

My expression mirrors hers. We're fucked.

I don't understand. She got what she wanted. I release her. I set her free. So why is she pushing me back down onto the sofa and climbing on top of me to straddle my waist?

I grunt out my pleasure when she grips my shaft and guides it to her pussy. When she rubs my cock along her entrance, we both moan, the feeling akin to nothing in this world. But when she lowers herself onto me, my dick sinking into her, I know that *this* is pure nirvana.

With our eyes locked, she lowers herself until she's filled full. Our connection is ecstasy, and I look down, loving how our bodies have become one. And with that, she begins rocking slowly, fucking me and taking control.

She plants her hands on my chest and leads a dance I've missed so much. My eyes roll into the back of my head. I've practically been neutered since she left me because my hands are a poor substitute for hers. But she reaches down and coaxes me to look at her. When I do, I see that tears have filled her eyes.

As she begins to move faster and faster, I don't know whether they're tears of happiness, pleasure, or pain. When she cries out, I know it's a combination of all three. For now, I will focus on the rightness of our union because I know I'll never feel this ever again.

Her confidence is a complete turn-on, and as she takes from me what she so desperately needs, I give her my all. She can milk me dry for all I care because, without her, I'm nothing. She raises her hips and then slams back down onto me, an impassioned moan whooshing from her lungs.

The sound of our bodies slapping against one another is a complete head rush, and I can't help but latch onto her hips to help pick up the pace. She whimpers and claws her fingernails into my pecs, bouncing up and down on my dick as we race toward the finish line.

If this is it, then I want her to know that I'll never stop loving her. "You're my everything. Never forget that, *angelo*." She groans low in her throat, tossing her head back and riding me wild. "I'm sorry for hurting you, but I'll never be sorry for loving you the way I do. I know you don't love me anymore, and that's okay. Knowing that you once did is enough. It's enough to get me through. It'll always be you, Madison. You'll always be my forever."

She begins to cry as she rocks faster and harder. Her muscles squeeze my cock, but I hold out a second longer. I need her to know one final thing.

I run my hand over her thumping heart, gently stroking

over her pendant. "*Il mio cuore è tuo. Ti amo sempre.*" I know she has no idea what I just said, and that's okay. I said it for me. I said it as the final goodbye.

She screams, and her body shudders wildly. The sight of her full tits, freshly fucked hair, and flushed skin is enough to send me over, and I attempt to pull out as I'm seconds away from coming. Madison swiftly clenches down and holds me prisoner, so with no other choice, I explode in a loud, sated growl.

I come so violently, I grip the sofa, afraid I'm about to launch off and not come back down. Soon after, Madison follows, but when she tumbles forward and sobs against my neck, "I love you. I fucking love you, too!" I freeze, not knowing what to do.

Did she understand me when I said my heart belongs to her and that I'll always love her?

I want to ask her, but I don't because it doesn't matter either way. Our fate has been decided. And that's the ironic thing. As she snuggles into me, wrapping her arms so tightly around me I can scarcely breathe, I know she loves me as much as I do her. But the problem is…she doesn't love me enough to stay.

I wake some time later, not knowing where I am.

It takes a second for my foggy brain to process that I'm lying on my hotel room floor, naked and alone. I knew this was bound to happen, but I was hoping, by some miracle, Madison would change her mind, and she'd stay. She'd forgive all the sins of my past, and we'd live happily ever after. But I should know by now that only happens to the good guys.

Raising my lethargic body, I head straight for the kitchen

to grab some much-needed water. However, when something shiny catches my eye, I know that I'll need something a lot stronger. Sitting on the counter are two things that seal my condemned fate. I won't shed any tears because this is what she wants. So for Madison's sake, I'll remind myself, every second of every day, that sometimes, moving on with the rest of your life starts with…goodbye.

Twenty-Nine

Madison

Then...

Dixon's soft exhalations reveal that he's asleep.

I don't want to, but I have to. I have no other choice. I remind myself of this fact as I quietly get dressed and pad through the hotel room, looking for a pen and paper. I came here for closure, and Dixon knew it the second I opened my mouth. So why does this feel so wrong?

Pushing those thoughts aside, I reach for the hotel stationery and take a seat at the small desk. A notepad and pen have never looked so daunting, and I suddenly have second thoughts.

These past few weeks have been the worst of my life. Finding out that everything you believed in was a lie really crushes a person and for a while there, I didn't know how I'd go on. But Dixon telling me to stay away was the best thing he could have done. He forced me to deal with my situation and stop being the victim.

I have so much I want to say, but I don't know where to start.

Taking a deep breath, I take hold of the pen and decide to start from the very beginning.

Dear Dixon,

I think I loved you, or at least knew I'd love you from the moment I met you.

You never thought twice about taking on the role of my protector, and from that day forward, you've never stopped. I know that you were the one who beat up Dylan, and honestly, I'm glad. He deserved everything he had coming, and in a weird way, your actions gave me the courage to deliver my own hand of justice as well.

I told my mom and Sebastian everything, and although it was the hardest thing I've ever done in my life, I felt relieved afterward. I was sick of secrets. Keeping secrets destroys people's lives. Look what it did to us. They, of course, needed time to get their heads around what I told them, but they believed me. They didn't look at me with shame or disgust in their eyes like I thought they would. And because of that, I could finally forgive Dylan, Beth, but most importantly, I could forgive myself for what happened.

In a way, telling my mom and Sebastian closed that chapter of my life. I'll never forget what happened but finally, for the first time in my life, I think I'll be okay.

It's no surprise that once Dylan was confronted, he left town in the dead of night, leaving Beth behind. No one knows where he's gone, and truthfully, no one but

Beth cares. The last I heard, she was packing her stuff and seeing out the end of her pregnancy with long-lost relatives in Oregon.

No matter what she did, she'll always be Sebastian's daughter, and he could never hate her. I'd never expect him to. But he asked her to leave, as he and my mother needed time to process everything. My mother blamed herself, just like I knew she would. I've tried my best to reassure her, but just like I did, she needs time to grieve. I don't think she'll ever be able to forgive Dylan or Beth. I've told her not to look back with regret but rather forward with hope. We'll wait and see.

A part of me has healed, and I thought that when that part mended, I would be whole. But I was so wrong.

I missed you every second, and I hated myself for it. How could I miss you? After everything you did, I should have hated you. But I didn't. I still don't.

I want you to know that I forgive you. And the reason is because I believe you, Dixon. It's still so hard to process, but I believe everything. I just needed time. I know you meant every "I love you" and that what we had was real. For that, I want to thank you for protecting me when I needed protecting. But I like to think that I protected you, too.

I still miss and love you with every fiber of my being. You're all I think about, but I can't this can't go on.

I know I told you I got offered an internship at Mount Sinai, and I did. But I also got offered a position at St. Peter's in Colorado. I took it.

I know moving a million miles away seems like I'm running

away, but it's not. I need to focus on my future, on who I want to become, and to do that, I need to move away from Manhattan. I need to move away from you.

I can't live in a city where you live. And I can't move on with you being so close by. You're too much of a temptation. I need to sever all ties, and this is the only way I know how. I'm not strong enough to resist you. If I don't go, I will just end up on your doorstep, and I don't want that. I don't want to ruin what we had because we can never get that back.

I don't know how long I'll be away because if all goes well, I've been offered a job. But I haven't thought that far ahead yet. For the moment, I'm happy taking each day as it comes.

I beg of you, please don't come after me. I want this. And I can assure you, I will also leave you be.

There are no words left other than thank you for believing in me. Thank you for taking a chance on someone who didn't think she was worth taking a chance on. But most of all, thank you for making me feel like the most loved, most cherished girl in this entire world. I will never forget our time together, and when things get tough, I'll return to the special place in my heart you'll always hold.

I love you, Dixon. I always will. But I have to love myself more.

Next to this letter, you'll find your mother's necklace. I don't feel right keeping it. I hope it can provide you with the comfort it's provided me. Maybe it's your turn to be protected on whatever journey you decide to take. Whatever your journey, I hope you find happiness because you deserve it.

    Yours forever,

    Madison x

    Protect us on our travels, wherever we may roam keep us safe and guide us, always safely home.

Thirty

Dixon

Nine months later

"Good morning, Ms. Vale."

"Oh, Dr. Mathews. Good morning." Susanna jumps up from her desk and passes me a cup of coffee. "How was traffic this morning?"

I gratefully accept, needing the strong caffeine to numb my pounding headache. "It was awful, as usual. I've forgotten how terrible Manhattan drivers are."

Her lips tip up into a small grin. "Already a convert?"

Draining my coffee, I nod. "Good Lord, yes. I only come back here because I couldn't bear to go a week without seeing you."

She snorts softly but quickly covers her mouth, embarrassed. "Always the charmer, Dr. Mathews."

Reaching over her desk and stealing a muffin, I honestly

reply, "Only with you, Ms. Vale." She appears to want to respond but changes her mind at the last minute. "Thanks." I hold up the chocolate muffin and make my way into my office.

The moment I turn on the lights, I groan as there is shit everywhere. This is one of the downsides of sharing an office with another psychiatrist who just happens to be a slob. I grumble to myself as I roll out my chair and notice stray granola bar wrappers under my desk. The trash can is inches away, so *how* she seems to keep missing it is a mystery to me.

But I've given up on understanding the mysteries of life a long time ago.

It's been nine months since the only woman I thought I understood walked out on me and left me for good. This time, however, there were no second or third chances, and although letting her go hurt more than I ever thought possible, I did it because it was the right thing to do.

The night Madison left me was the start of my new life. I wouldn't allow our relationship to be in vain, so once I returned from Boston with a broken heart and a little piece of award in hand, I turned over the proverbial new leaf.

First on the agenda was selling my shithole apartment. It was something I should have done months and months ago. But I suppose my house only really felt like a home once Madison set foot inside. When Lily left me, I had no qualms living within those four walls, holding on to the memory of what we once had. But when Madison left me, all I wanted to do was set it on fire and burn it to the ground.

Not keen on dabbling in arson, I contacted an old friend who was a real estate agent. He said he could make us a mint because my neighborhood was one of the most sought after in

Manhattan. But I wasn't interested in fortunes. I just wanted out.

It sold to a newlywed couple from Chicago within a week.

All of my possessions, well, the significant ones anyway, fit into one box. So with that box under my arm, I wished them luck and told them to burn some sage as I slammed the door shut behind me. I still wonder if they survived in the home which was my prison for years.

With no real place to go, seeing as I just upped and left the place that was my hometown for over ten years, I decided to go back to where it all began.

I went back to New Jersey.

There was no way I could work with my head the way it was, so I gave Susanna a much-deserved month off and referred my patients to other doctors. Once my work and home life were relatively sorted, I too took a much-deserved month off and figured out what the hell I wanted to do.

I rented a small two-bedroom home in the suburbs, and I just...slept. I was so tired. My body checked into its own personal rehab, and I detoxed from life.

I would have probably slept for another month, but of course Hunter wouldn't allow such a respite. When he banged on my door, demanding beer and a Jersey "hoagie," I knew that no matter where I lived, he'd always annoy the shit out of me.

He ended up staying two weeks as I hadn't even realized I'd missed Christmas, New Year's, and my thirty-third birthday. But honestly, I wasn't really in the mood to celebrate. I wasn't really in the mood for anything. The thought of going on without Maddy seemed so pointless, but I put on my big girl panties and decided to try this New Year's resolution fad on for size.

The first call of business was deciding what the hell I wanted to do with my life. Now that I was in Jersey, the thought of going back to Manhattan seemed like crazy talk. I missed the serenity, the simplicity of this beautiful state, so I decided to stay. It also gave me a chance to work on my strained relationship with my dad.

A few weeks later, I was the proud owner of a four-bedroom home in the 'burbs. I had no idea what I was supposed to do with four bedrooms, but considering the cost of living was ten times more affordable and comfortable here than in Manhattan, I figured what the hell.

It took some convincing, but about three months in, my dad finally agreed to come stay with me. Not live, but visit on weekends. At first, I regretted my decision and had to stop myself on numerous occasions from jumping into my car and fleeing back to Manhattan. But little by little, as my dad and I actually started communicating, I realized that things were going to be okay. Even though it was mainly me talking, spilling out my heart and soul, needing confirmation from the only person whose opinion I gave two fucks about, it helped me heal.

The doctors instructed me that my father would never return to how he once was. But one night, when I asked him if he thought I was a good man and he slowly reached for my hand, I knew that no matter his condition, this was enough. Two weeks later, he moved in with me permanently.

Now that my home life was under control, it was time to focus on my career.

I took a long leave of absence, handing my practice over to a well-respected doctor and associate, Dr. Caffey, aka the slob, temporarily. I didn't want to give up practicing in Manhattan entirely, but I knew I needed a change. And that's what led me to enroll in some night classes, and before I knew it, I was Dr. *and* Professor Mathews.

Chad was right. The award I had smashed into teeny tiny pieces opened up many opportunities for me, and I became a part-time lecturer at Princeton. I taught clinical psychology and cognitive and behavioral neuroscience.

It was fun teaching rich kids the way of the world, but before long, I found I wanted to steer them in the right direction and warn them off the path of sin. The path I lived on for too long.

I returned to practicing after a six-month-long, much-needed break, but due to my teaching responsibilities, I only worked three days a week. Dr. Caffey was pleased to welcome me back. I think she was seconds away from throttling my patients and my dear, harmless receptionist, Susanna.

Susanna expressed in not so many words that if she had to work for Dr. Taylor Caffey a second longer, she would have no qualms about poisoning her coffee. It's nice to know I'm missed.

So between work, teaching, and hanging out with my dad, I didn't have time for much else. And that suited me just fine. It still does.

Hunter and Finch have come to visit countless times, and I can see my father improve a touch each time.

The nights I'm in Manhattan, I've rented a cheap apartment in Midtown. So, all in all, Hunter's prediction that the distance would tear us three *amigos* apart has been wrong. If anything, it's brought us closer together.

You seem to take things for granted when they're sitting within your reach, but distance really does make the heart grow fonder. Especially distances as far away as Colorado.

But I can't even speak that word. It's like my Voldemort. It's a reminder that in it lives the woman who I still love with everything that I am.

I want to believe that what happened between us changed me—changed me into the better man I wanted to become. But a better man is still not on par with a good man. That's something I'm not sure I can ever be, thanks to my sins.

One of those sins is of course Ms. Juliet Harte.

I don't know what I did to be so lucky, but the night I left her a sobbing mess on her living room floor was the last night I ever saw or heard from her. For the first few months, I walked on eggshells, not believing this was finally over. But so far, she's kept away.

But that might change because by now, she will be the mother of a child who just may be mine. Madison's words still ring true because she's right. I have to take responsibility for what's mine. A month ago, my attorney sent Juliet a subpoena, requesting information to confirm or deny if the child is mine. I'm still waiting.

I wrote a letter to Rachel and Sebastian, detailing how sorry I was for hurting their daughter and letting them down. I never got a response, but I never expected one.

So yes, I've reached my breaking point. But I'm slowly climbing my way back up again. It's a long way to the top, but if I want to rock 'n' roll again, I have to endure the climb.

Looking at the wooden frame on my cluttered desk, I see a picture of Dr. Caffey and her partner, Alice, staring back at me. They look so happy. I can't help but wonder what their secret is. But it's not to put into practice; it's just out of curiosity. It's the doctor in me itching to know why they've lasted while Madison and I did not.

I meant it when I said my heart belongs to her and only her, as I haven't been able to look at another woman without wanting to dig my eyeballs out or run for the hills. I don't see that changing any time this century.

So once upon a time, I was Manhattan's biggest manwhore. But now, I'm just...me.

A soft knock on the door shakes me from my thoughts. I look up from my desk. "Come in."

Susanna comes in a second later, her hands filled with stacks of mail and another coffee. "I thought you'd need this"—she raises the coffee—"to deal with this." She then goes on to hold up the many envelopes and parcels.

"Great. One of the joys of working part-time."

"You could always come back full time?" Susanna suggests, hopeful I fire her archnemesis.

I can't help but laugh. "Miss me, Ms. Vale?"

She looks down at the untidy desk and sighs. "You have no idea."

Susanna had no interest in working for two psychiatrists, so she's organized her work days to coincide with mine. I'm pleased she's done so as she deserves the rest, but as she's told me many times, she'll rest when she's dead.

Even though their paths rarely cross, the tornado of Dr. Caffey and her personal assistant, Bianca, leaves enough debris in their wake to remind poor Susanna that we're no longer alone. "I miss the good old days," she confesses, trying to find a place on my desk to set down my mail and coffee.

"I don't," I counter, shaking my head.

She stops mid-tidying, looking awfully guilty for her comment. "I didn't mean—"

But I cut her off. "It's fine, Ms. Vale. I know what you mean."

She places my mail down in front of me. "So...how are you?"

I'm unable to conceal my smile because, since my return, this question seems to be her favorite one. I've lost count of how many times she's asked me, but I never grouch because I know she's just concerned.

"I'm feeling fine, Ms. Vale. Thank you for asking. I've written down the number of my shrink, just in case," I tease while she swats me on the arm.

"I'm glad you're back to your old self. I missed you." She turns serious, as do I.

"I did, too." It's just too bad I had to lose everything to find myself again.

The mood becomes too somber for my liking, so I reach for the top envelope, preferring to deal with bills than my regrets.

One of the many things I love about Susanna is that she knows when not to hover. This is one of those times. She places the cup of coffee to my left, and it's immediately back to business. "Your next appointment will be here in fifteen minutes. I'll page you once he's here."

As she makes her way to the door, I quickly thank her. "Thank you, Ms. Vale."

She turns over her shoulder and smiles, understanding that my gratitude extends far further than her just being the best secretary there is. She gently closes the door behind her while I exhale steadily.

Not interested in focusing on anything but work, I make

my way through the mountain of mail, most of which is bills or junk. However, when I see the signature label of my attorney on a white envelope, I quickly tear it open and frantically read over what the contents entail.

I read over the material twice, needing to ensure that what I'm reading is actually true.

Dear Dr. Mathews,
Congratulations...you are not the father.
I owe you a beer.
Sincerely,
Burt Keith.

I scan through the attached papers, which are the paternity tests displaying how my DNA doesn't match up to Duncan's. Who the hell is...oh, she had a boy? A boy who is clearly not mine. As I look over the results, I don't know whether I'm relieved or not, which is absurd. This is exactly the outcome I wanted. Or was it?

Of course I want nothing to do with Juliet, but in a morbid way, it would have been nice to have someone in my life I could have called my own. Someone who could have kept a small part of me alive once I'm gone. And someone who could write on my headstone that I was loved and a good man.

But that person isn't Duncan. It isn't anyone.

Wiping at my eye, I squash down such sentimental, silly thoughts as I realize Juliet wasn't faithful as she claimed she was. No surprises there. This letter is the final piece to close the chapter on what Juliet and I once had. It's *now* really over.

Tucking the letter into my desk drawer, I jot down a note

to email a thank-you to Burt. And to also detail which beer I prefer. Looks like I won our bet.

Looking at the clock on my mantel, I see that I have five minutes before my first appointment. I flick through the remaining letters, which are almost all the same except for the one which sits at the bottom of the pile. The moment I see it, I actually feel my heart rip into two.

In my hands I hold a stylish white envelope, but it's the handwriting and the imagery on the front that has me clenching my hand into a fist, the paper crinkling beneath my firm hold. This can't be happening. This is surely a dream. There is no way I'm holding what I think this is.

My rasping breaths leave me light-headed and anxious, but as I finger over the small image on the bottom right-hand corner, I know that this symbol is the reason I'm seconds away from losing my shit.

And that symbol is that of two entwined gold wedding bands.

Normally, this would be a harmless image, but nothing about it is harmless when the sender is the love of your life.

However, the love of my life is now the love of someone named Alex's life, and to celebrate their love, they've invited me to their fucking…wedding.

"You don't even know what's inside. It could be…"

"Could be what?" I question Finch as I look up at him. I'm currently using my folded arms as a pillow as I sprawl out across the bar.

"It could be an invitation to…the Olympic Games?"

Hunter spits out his beer, wiping his mouth with the back of his hand. "There'd be five rings—colored rings, I might add—if that were true. Not two gold, very suggestive ones." He holds up the envelope that has been taunting me all day. "This *is* what we all think it is. There's no denying it."

"And what's that?" I ask, a complete glutton for punishment as I eye the notorious envelope.

"This is what you need to get off your ass and fight for her." He slaps the envelope against the bar, emphasizing his point. "This is just a test."

But I groan. "No, I'm pretty sure that's an invitation to Madison's wedding, not a test." I blindly reach for my scotch, spilling most of it down the front of my shirt as I refuse to raise my head.

Finch pulls in his lips, appearing concerned as I lightly thump my head on the bar. "Well…fuck that…floozy. I never liked her anyway."

Hunter once again very ungracefully spits out his beer, while I can't help but smile. I know he's only trying to make me feel better. But just when I thought things were finally on the mend, Madison decides to rub my face in her happiness.

Hunter shakes his head. "This is your fault. If you'd just kept a lid on your pussyness and didn't tell her to go find herself a good man, none of this would have happened. You *are* the good man, Dix. But you have to go and put stupid ideas in her head, and now she's marrying some asshole who isn't you."

I wearily raise my head, ready to defend myself, but stop because I don't know what to say. Yes, I did tell her that, and I did mean every word. But now that it's actually happening, I regret every word.

The thought of anyone other than me touching her, kissing her, and fucking…but I stop, as that last thought is too much. The thought of her loving another man, wanting to marry another man, makes me feel sick. I reach for my shot of tequila.

"Why don't you open it?" Finch suggests.

"What would be the point? I know what's inside. I don't need to open it because I'm not going. Actually…" I snatch the envelope from Hunter's hand and place it in my pocket. "Let's talk about something else. How's Heidi?"

The mere mention of Heidi's name has Finch breaking out into a sickening, ecstatic smile. I drown my pessimism by stealing his beer.

"She's going really well. Actually, there's something I wanted to tell you guys."

Both Hunter and I stop mid-sip and turn to look at him. His ecstatic smile has just transformed into a euphoric smile.

"I don't get it," Hunter reveals, shrugging.

But I do. "Holy shit, man. Congratulations!" I slap Finch on the back while he gushes. Hunter, however, is still lost in translation. I decide to put him out of his misery. "Heidi is pregnant, you moron."

"She's actually pregnant with twins," Finch reveals, and my mouth falls open in surprise and happiness.

Hunter finally nods in understanding and elbows Finch in the ribs. "You sly dog. Your little swimmers are on fucking steroids."

A laugh rumbles from my chest as Finch shakes his head in disgust. I alert the bartender. "This calls for a celebration."

Finch caught an Uber back home to Brooklyn, but Hunter and I didn't feel like going home.

That's why we're riding the Staten Island ferry at one thirty in the morning.

We have no intention of getting off, but it's nice to cruise along in reflective silence and look out into the city, which can be kind to most but cruel to some.

That cruelness sits inside my suit jacket, a heavy weight against my heart. How could she think I would be okay going to her wedding? She may have been able to move on, but I haven't.

As selfish and as much of a bastard as this makes me, I'm not happy for her. How can I be? Nice people would wish them all the best, but I'm not nice. I want her relationship with "Alex" to fail. And I want her to realize I'm the one she wants to marry.

But that's not going to happen. Ever.

"Are you all right, Dix?"

Hunter's concern has me sighing loudly. "No, Hunt, I'm not." I see no point in denying it because, after Madison, I promised myself to tell nothing but the truth. "How can she think I'd even be remotely interested in attending her wedding?"

I look at Hunter leaning against the railing next to me. "I don't know, man. I've given up on understanding chicks."

Hunter tried his hand at "dating" a few months ago. He got bored within a week and is now single and over women just like me.

"How can it be two of Manhattan's biggest man-sluts are now single, desperate, and alone?" he asks, appearing genuinely baffled.

"The answer is within your sentence."

"I'm not following."

Looking back into the night sky, I explain. "The fact we are man-sluts, manwhores, or just plain bastards is the reason. Being a player doesn't live up to the hype, Hunt. It just leaves you old, alone, and thinking back to the heyday when we thought we had it all. There is always someone better-looking, or younger, or more charismatic ready to take your place. And honestly, I'd rather have bagged one chick than the hundred plus I have because I know that one chick would have stuck around. All the others have now moved on, probably found the love of their lives, while here we are, riding the Staten Island ferry at one thirty on a Thursday morning, pondering the what-ifs and where we went wrong."

It's a sad reality, but it's the truth. We thought we had it all. We thought we were living the high life by getting blown and fucked by half the population of Manhattan and its visitors. But we were only sealing our fate.

The damned envelope sitting in my pocket is a constant reminder of what could have been my life. It's a reminder that Madison and I will never, ever reconcile. And just like that, the small flicker of hope I've held on to dives to the bottom of the Hudson. And I mean that literally.

Before I second-guess myself, I reach into my pocket and pitch the envelope out into the open water with all my might. It stops for a millisecond before it catches on the cool breeze and sails away from me, taking my faith and dreams with it. I watch its descent as it spirals and twirls in the night sky before finally coming to rest in its watery grave.

I instantly feel better.

"You weren't curious to see what was inside?" Hunter says minutes later.

Staring at the waterway, I shake my head. "It wouldn't matter either way. It doesn't change the fact that Madison and I are really over."

The rest of our passage is traveled in silence, and as I clutch at the medal hanging underneath my shirt, I realize this "journey" fucking sucks.

Thirty-One

Dixon

It's Friday night, and I'm sitting with my dad watching the Yankees play the Rays. After two weeks of stewing in regret, this is the only think that makes me feel remotely better. I've decided the only way I can get through this is to drown my sorrows in beer, pizza, and baseball.

As a kid, watching baseball with my dad was one of my favorite things to do. Now that I'm an adult, not much has changed.

"Ah, c'mon! That was a strike!" I yell at the TV, standing up in protest. "What the fuck is the matter with this umpire?" My dad grunts in agreement from his wheelchair.

While it cuts to break, I decide to stock up on beer, as I need the booze to help deal with the stupidity of these blind officials. On the way to the kitchen, however, my cell chimes, vibrating loudly on the desk in my home office. I quickly make a detour to answer it.

"Hello?" I say without looking at the screen to see who the caller is.

"Good evening, Dixon. I haven't caught you at a bad time, have I?"

Pulling the phone away from my ear, I see that it is indeed Dr. Wellington on the other end. I wonder why he's calling. "No, not at all," I reply a second later. "I was just watching the Yankees get their asses whipped."

Max laughs. "In that case, I'll keep this brief. I was just wondering if you had received Madison's invitation."

Okay, that was so not what I was expecting. I'd have guessed he was calling to inform me he was an alien before I'd guess he was calling to see if I had received Madison's wedding invite. Why on earth would it matter to him if I had received it or not? Surely he knows how uncomfortable this is for me?

The drawn-out silence is becoming rather unbearable, so I clear my throat. "Yes, I did."

"Splendid. Are you attending?"

Am I attending? Is he fucking serious right now? "No, I wasn't planning on it."

"Oh?" He appears surprised. "I'd hoped you could have put your differences aside for the day. This means a lot to Madison, Dixon. I know she'd love for you to be there."

My mouth falls open as I cannot believe my ears.

He goes on, "Marriage is a very important thing. It signifies unity and commitment. I really hope you'll reconsider."

Yes, he's right. It signifies unity and commitment to the wrong person. If I didn't respect Max as much as I do, I would be telling him to shove it up his ass. But I swallow down my anger. "I'll see what I can do."

"Excellent." My answer seems to satisfy him. "You have all the details?"

"No, I um, seem to have misplaced the invitation. Can you please give them to me?" I quickly hunt around my desk for a pen and piece of paper.

"Of course. It's tomorrow at one p.m., down at Mist de L'Océan."

"Tomorrow?" I yell, my pen veering off the page as he reveals his bombshell. "And that's the venue in Westhampton Beach, is it not?"

"Yes, that's correct. Nothing is more romantic than a beach wedding, or so I've been told."

Indeed.

"Okay, Max. I will try my best to attend. No promises." My sharp tone conveys my anger.

"I understand, Dixon." He pauses. "Please excuse me for being so forward in calling you. Madison was not certain whether she should invite you because she was afraid you wouldn't come. But she decided to go with her gut. And I'm pleased that she did. Due to obvious reasons, I can understand why you might feel uncomfortable attending, but sometimes, you have to let go of the past. Otherwise, you'll never be able to move forward. Forgiveness doesn't change the past, but it does change the future. I really hope you can be there."

Screw Max and his words of wisdom. "Good night, Max." I hang up before he could lecture me further about why I should attend Madison's wedding.

I lean against the edge of my desk, trying to wrap my head around what just happened. What just happened is that Madison is getting married...tomorrow. And Max has turned rogue.

It'll be a cold day in hell before I attend this bullshit affair as I'm quite certain I would spear-tackle the groom, drown him in the ocean, and feed his body to the sharks. My mind is a million miles away, and it's not until I hear the wheels of my father's chair squeak over the floorboards that I come back to the here and now.

Looking up, I see he's watching me, eyes filled with concern. He looks down at the phone in my clenched fist and grunts.

"*Va bene, Papà.*" But he stubbornly shakes his head, calling bullshit. "Let's finish watching the game, okay?"

I push off the desk but slump back down onto it when he suddenly rushes forward and rams me in the ankles with his chair. "Ouch! What the hell? You're losing your mind, old man!"

My insult only spurs him on. He reverses a few paces before charging forward once again. I'm too slow, and he catches my leg as I attempt to duck out of his warpath. "Would you please stop trying to run me over?" I yell, hobbling to hide behind my desk.

He doesn't allow the huge oak desk to deter his tirade, however, and powers his chair to drive even faster.

"Stop!" I kick out my leg, using my foot as a wedge against his footrest. The motor whines in protest as he stubbornly maneuvers the joystick to keep advancing. "You're fucking crazy. *Aiuto!*"

My cry for help seems to stop his outburst, and the motor chugs out a sickening whirr as he takes his hand off the controls. "What is the matter with you?" I ask when I think it's safe to talk.

He doesn't reply and gestures with his head that he wants

the piece of paper and pen. I don't argue because I'm afraid he'll run me over if I do. I rub my sore shins as he slowly writes something down.

My father says the occasional word, but most times, he communicates through facial expressions, words, or writes things down. The doctors don't know why he chooses to correspond this way, but I'm happy he's communicating at all.

When he's done, he throws the piece of paper at my head. Bending down, I pick it up and see that in a shaky print, he's written the words, "*I didn't raise a coward. Go.*"

Unable to mask my smile, I flip the page around. "No, you didn't. You also didn't raise an idiot." He raises an eyebrow in contest. I ignore his quip. "She's marrying another man. It's too late. I know you liked Madison, but I blew it."

He shakes his head. He opens his mouth a couple of times, speaking voiceless words. I know this frustrates him, so I lean closer, placing my ear close to his lips. With a strained effort, he breathes out, "It's never...too...late...for love."

I pull back, stunned. My father doesn't speak often, but he always blows me away when he does.

"But..." I try to argue, but he reaches for my hand, clasping my cell, and shakes it. "I'm not calling Madison."

He growls in frustration as he jabs at his chest. "You want to call Madison?" I offer as an explanation for his sudden madness.

He rolls his eyes and snatches the phone from my hand. I'm stunned that he knows how to operate an iPhone as he swipes his shaky finger across my screen and scrolls through my contacts. He stops at Pat, the nurse who looked after him at Sunnyfields.

"Why am I calling Pat?" I inquire as he turns the screen

around so I can look at it.

"Go," is all he says.

It takes me a few seconds, but when I realize what he's asking, I run a hand over my beard, pensively. "You want me to call Pat so she can look after you?"

He nods, appearing relieved that I've finally gotten a clue.

Can I really do this?

As I think about Madison and the way she makes me feel, about how much I miss her, and about her marrying someone other than me, I know that fuck yes, I can. I was stupid not to do this sooner, but I wasn't ready then. Now, I am.

Bending forward, I quickly kiss my father on the brow. "*Grazie, Papà.*"

I quickly dial Pat, and within minutes, I've organized for her to stay over for the weekend. I offered her a ridiculous amount of money, and although she refused, I told her I wouldn't hear otherwise.

I don't know why, but I suddenly get a second wind and zip around my bedroom, packing the essentials. My father is watching me from the doorway, and when I stop to look at him and see the enormous smile plastered on his face, I know I'm doing the right thing.

As he wheels himself into my room, I jump to the side and use the bed as a barrier between us. He grins a lopsided smile. With my cell in hand, he extends it out to me. I have no idea what he's up to now, but I accept.

When I see Hunter's name on my screen, I laugh. "You want Hunter to look after you instead?" He snorts, exposing his abhorrence at that suggestion.

My father is an absolute inspiration. To convey what he has

in less than ten words is all the motivation I need. Most of us rely on speech to get us through the day, but I've just learned the most valuable lesson from actions of the heart.

I dial Hunter as I pull a black suit from my closet. He answers on the third ring. "I'm so bored. Please save me from my personal hell." I can hear the *Friends* theme song playing in the background.

"Pack a bag and suit," I demand, zipping up my bag.

"What? Why?"

"Because your dreams are about to come true."

"You're finally taking me to Disneyland?"

I chuckle. "No, you idiot. We're going to see if we can get to the Hamptons in less than an hour."

"An hour? That's impossible."

"Not if you're driving at a hundred and fifty miles the entire way."

"You're right, that is my dream, but what's the rush? What's in the Hamptons?"

Shouldering my bag and suit, I give my father a smile as I reply, "Something that's mine."

Thirty-Two

Dixon

"Can you please hurry up?" I gripe, watching Hunter eat his breakfast slower than a damn snail.

"Oh, calm down. You've waited nine months to see her. I'm sure you can wait a few more minutes. Let me finish my breakfast in peace." My words seem to have the opposite effect because if possible, he chews even slower than he has been for the past twenty minutes.

I pace the small dining room of the shitty hotel we checked into late last night—or was it early this morning? Either way, I just want to check out so I can stop Madison from making the biggest mistake of her life.

No, I don't know Alex, but I do know that he'll never love her the way I do. She belongs with me, and I'm going to do everything in my power to make her see that. She loved me once. I know she can love me again.

Unable to wait a second longer, I leap forward and steal

Hunter's half-eaten waffle off his plate. "Hey!"

Before he has time to protest further, I fold the rubbery, syrupy dough in half and stuff the entire thing into my mouth. I almost get lockjaw chewing furiously and gag a couple of times, but it's down my throat fifteen seconds later. I then gulp down his orange juice in one mouthful, thumping my chest to ensure it all goes down.

After I'm done, I wipe my mouth with the back of my hand. "There, now your breakfast is finished. Let's move."

Hunter stands up dramatically. "I could have taken it to go." *Now* he tells me.

Once we're checked out, I sprint toward my car with Hunter lagging behind. "We're kind of in a hurry," I state, throwing my bag into the back seat.

"Well, I'm kind of hungry, thanks to you, so I'm reserving my energy," he barks as he tosses his bag next to mine.

I jump into the driver's seat, reaching into my suit pocket for the keys. The moment I place the key into the ignition and turn it, I know someone has a voodoo doll of me and my car somewhere.

"Why isn't the car starting?" Hunter asks, drawing attention to the obvious as he buckles up.

"I have no clue." As I turn the key again, the engine simply clicks over but doesn't start. "No. No. No. Don't do this! Not now!" I bellow, thumping both palms against the steering wheel.

"I don't think that's going to help. You probably blew up the engine on the way here."

"I didn't hear you complaining. If I remember correctly, I had to wind up the window before your slobber coated my car," I say, referring to Hunter's impersonation of what a bulldog would look like driving down the highway at a hundred miles an hour with his tongue wagging out happily.

He shrugs, not denying my claims. "Pop the hood."

"What for?" I question, watching him as he unbuckles his belt.

"Could be a dead battery." He opens the door, appearing mighty proud of himself for solving our apparent problem.

But I roll my eyes. "The battery is in the trunk."

He ducks his head inside. "Oh. Good to know."

Great, between dumb and dumber, we're screwed. I'm not going to pretend I know anything about cars because I don't.

Reaching into my pocket, I pull out my cell. "I'll order an Uber."

"An Uber? Why don't you call Triple A?"

"Because they'll take too long," I reply, my patience about to snap. As I look at my screen, my dwindling patience goes up in flames. "Motherfucker! Have you got service?" I wave my phone from left to right, hoping to get a damn signal.

Hunter pulls out his cell, but when he too moves it above his head, looking at the screen in confusion, I know the answer is no. "How is that even possible? We live in America, for fuck's sake. There are no excuses for technology to fail us!"

I dance around the parking lot, flapping my arms above my head, hoping I get something, anything, but I don't. "Fuck this. I'll ask to use the phone in reception."

Angrily shoving my phone into my pocket, I storm toward the hotel, ignoring Hunter as he smugly says, "If we had just stayed at Westhampton Beach, none of this would be happening as we'd already be there by now."

I don't bother answering as my answer will be the same as

it was last night—we can't check into a five-star resort in the middle of the night/morning without a reservation. I know this for a fact since I tried to make a reservation at eleven thirty.

As I shoulder open the heavy door, my gaze lands on the young, pimply teen behind the counter.

"Can I use your phone?"

He looks up from reading his comic book, popping his gum, uninterested. "You'll have to wait until my manager comes back. She just went to the market."

I pinch the bridge of my nose. "How long will that be?"

He shrugs. "I dunno. Maybe an hour."

"An hour?" I shout, eyeing the phone on the counter. "Look, kid, I'll give you…" Opening up my wallet, I pull out a twenty-dollar bill. "I'll give you twenty bucks if you let me use the phone."

He leans forward, the cash speaking volumes. He drums his fingers on the heavy wood. "Fifty."

"You little shit," Hunter scoffs behind me. "Do not—"

But I wave him off. "Fine, fifty." I hunt through my wallet and toss the cash at him as he turns the phone around so I can dial.

I see a list of numbers by the phone, and thankfully, there is a number for a local cab service. I dial it quickly, impatiently tapping my foot as I wait for them to pick up. The moment they do, I bark out my address and where I need to go.

I breathe out a sigh of relief when they tell me no problem. But when they tell me, "The wait time is approximately three hours," my sigh of relief gets caught in my throat.

"Excuse me? Three hours? Why so long?" Is this a sign, a bad omen that I shouldn't go?

Hunter stands beside me, placing his hands out to the side, silently asking what's up. I cover the receiver and explain it'll be a three-hour wait.

The pimply teen decides now is a good time to intervene. "I could have told you that. There are like a dozen things going on down there this weekend. There's the Nutcracker Ballet, Senior Citizen Picnic, the eleventh Annual Great East End Community Picnic…" He goes on to detail each event on his fingers while I'm seconds away from using my fingers to strangle him.

"And you couldn't have told us this sooner? Maybe before you took the fifty bucks?" Hunter declares, leaning menacingly close while the kid slowly leans back.

He raises his shoulders, untroubled. "I suppose I could have."

Hunter immediately launches forward and grabs the kid by the scruff of his T-shirt. He drags him forward while I slam down the receiver and remove Hunter's hands from the terrified kid who yelps when I set him free. "How far away is the Mist de L'Océan from here?"

"Um…I…hmm…I dunno." When he hesitates, I take over the role of aggressor and dive over the counter like a wildman.

I fist his shirt as I demand, "Listen here, you little jerkoff, if you ever want to get laid, you'll think long and hard, as I am seconds away from ripping off your dick and using it as a doorstop!"

Hunter bursts out laughing, thumping the counter in delight while I shake the kid, demanding he speak. "It's like maybe a half-hour drive," he whines, trying to fight me off.

"Are you sure?"

When he falters, I drag him closer so we're eye to eye. Items strewed on the countertop spill onto the floor. "Yes, yes!" he shrieks. "Please, sir, don't rip off my dick. I'm a virgin!"

By this stage, Hunter is laughing so hard that he's choking on his raspy breaths. "Oh fuck. This is so worth the fifty bucks!"

I let the kid go, satisfied he's telling the truth. He quickly runs into the backroom and locks the door. I feel like a brute, but desperate times call for desperate measures. "Right, so he said half an hour drive, which is what, an hour walk?"

That shuts Hunter down immediately. "I am not walking for an hour. These shoes pinch my feet."

I look down at his black loafers and curl my lip. "Are you listening to yourself, you pussy?"

He folds his arms over his chest. "Fine, but you can carry me if my feet get sore."

"Fine, whatever, let's just go."

Snatching a visitor's map from a stand, I storm out of the office, hoping little Miss Twinkle Toes is following. Thankfully, he is, as I can hear him mumbling how he's the bitch in our relationship.

Unfolding the map, I look for any familiar landmarks to point us in the right direction. "According to this map, we need to go…" I turn the map upside down, to the side, and then back up again. "Shit, this is not to scale." I stop walking as I try to decipher which way to go.

"Fucking great. We're probably going to die of thirst and starvation."

"Oh, stop being so melodramatic. It's an hour. You've fucked for longer and somehow managed to survive."

My comment puts a skip in his step as he smiles. "Boom! Yes, I have."

We decide to turn right for no other reason than I think we drove in from the opposite direction. Ten minutes in, Hunter is complaining that the sea air is frizzing his hair.

"I've solved the puzzle of why you're single."

"Oh yeah? Why's that?" he queries. He's currently wearing his suit jacket like a cape over his skull, as the sun is apparently too harsh for his skin.

"Because you're a little bitch." He clutches his sides, pretending to laugh at my joke, while I actually do laugh 'cause it's funny.

However, I stop quickly when he smartly retorts, "*I'm* a little bitch? I didn't just drive over a hundred and fifty miles to crash the wedding of my ex-girlfriend, whom I have not spoken to since the day she left a Dear John letter over nine months ago."

He's right, so I stay silent because I've got nothing.

We walk in silence, Hunter's words churning around my head. I'm the first to acknowledge that I haven't thought this through at all, but I don't regret my decision in the slightest. I would have regretted sitting around doing nothing while Madison marries someone who isn't me.

This right here is what the saying *carpe diem* embodies. So I plan on seizing.

"So what happens if she actually loves the guy?" Hunter asks, obviously picking up on my pensive thoughts.

"I haven't thought that far ahead. At the moment, I'm more concerned about getting there in time."

"You really love her, hey?"

My heart hurts at the mere mention of her. "Yes, Hunt, I really do. I needed this time apart to realize just how much, so I can only hope she feels the same. However, seeing as she's marrying someone else, she probably doesn't. But I need to do this. Otherwise, I'll regret it for the rest of my life."

"Whatever happens, man, know that I'm proud of you for trying. It takes balls to do what you're doing."

I turn to look at him and smile. "Thanks. I wouldn't want to share this moment with anyone other than you."

When he unexpectedly stops walking, I turn over my shoulder to see why. As he begins to unzip his pants, I chuckle, afraid to ask what he's doing. He answers for me, mid-zip. "Are you going to suck my cock now? I mean, that was some sentimental shit back there. I thought you were giving off a 'I wanna suck your dick' vibe."

"You wish," I playfully counter, flipping him off. I suddenly hear a car coming up over the hill and groan when Hunter's pants are shimmying down his legs. "Zip your pants up, you creep. There's a car coming!"

Thankfully, he complies and is zipped up and tucked in by the time a little white van comes into view. "We're so hitching a ride in the Scooby Van," he excitedly states, clapping quickly.

We hook out our thumbs, hoping whoever is inside this vehicle stops and isn't a part of the Manson family. The van does indeed stop, and I'm quite certain the occupants are as far away from being serial killers as they come.

"Hello, boys," says the driver. "Where are you off to?"

Hunter shakes his head firmly, indicating there is no way he's getting inside the van. But this isn't optional. I need to get to Madison, and I need to get to her now. "We're headed into Westhampton Beach. Can we bum a ride?"

"Of course. We're headed that way. Get in."

Hunter is still shaking his head when I slide open the door and gesture with my chin for him to get inside. "No," he grits out between clenched teeth. But we've wasted enough time.

Walking behind him, I shove him into the van filled with about ten…little old ladies. I don't know why, but the silver foxes love Hunter. They always have. Sadly, he doesn't feel the same.

"For the love of God, please no, Dixon, stop!" As I push his torso in, he digs his feet into the pavement and turns over his shoulder, whispering loudly, "It smells like grandma vagina in here."

"What did he say?" a lady with purple hair shouts as she turns around.

"I think he said he's a handbag designer," the lady to her left replies just as loudly.

She nods, none the wiser. "Oh, how lovely."

Hunter is still fighting me, but with one hard thrust, he falls forward, supporting his weight on the back of a chair. One of the ladies turns around, smiling a denture grin, when she sees Hunter hanging off the back of her seat. "Hello."

He shudders.

I jump in behind him, pulling him up and dragging him to the back of the bus. His phobia needs to literally take a back seat because this is my ride to freedom.

"I'm Pearl. Where are you off to?" the lady in front of us asks, smiling at Hunter.

He hooks his thumb my way. "He's stopping the wedding of the woman he loves."

The entire van coos while I look down at my watch. I have time. I have over five hours to figure out what the hell I'm going to do.

"And what about you, young man? Anyone that you love?" Pearl questions.

Before Hunter can reply, I speak up for him. "No, he's single and looking, ladies." I wink at the raring-to-go women while Hunter stomps on my foot.

"You owe me," Hunter grumbles as we wave goodbye to the lovely residents of Shady Pines.

"Oh, come on. I think Pearl liked you." I reach out to clean the lipstick marks from his cheek.

He pulls away, wiping violently at his face. "We will never speak of this ever again." And he's right because now that I'm standing in front of the Mist de L'Océan, I know that playtime is over.

The driver, Bob, was lovely. However, he couldn't drive for shit. Thanks to his leisurely pace, it took us over an hour and a half to get here.

"So what's the plan?" Hunter asks as we race up the long, paved driveway. The lawns on either side look out of place, considering a sandy stretch of beach lies just over the hill.

"I thought we established there is no plan," I reply, feeling petulant as we approach the massive reception center.

Off to the right sits a lavish-looking hotel, a hotel which no doubt has a honeymoon suite, Jacuzzi, and heart-shaped bed. I grind my teeth and quicken my step.

Just as I'm about to kick open the door, Hunter latches onto my arm to stop me. "So what, you're just gonna ride in, gung-ho, and throw her over your shoulder, kicking and screaming?"

"Yee-haw! Now please let me go." I attempt to pull out of his clutches, but he tightens his hold.

"Be smart about this, Dix. If you go charging in there like a crazy person, odds are Madison will be glad she kicked your ass to the curb when she did. Be smart. I know you're angry, but this barbarian act isn't gonna stick. Not to mention, you'll probably get your ass hauled away by security. Take a deep breath and think about rainbows and unicorns, and naked chicks riding unicorns over rainbows."

His ridiculous pep talk has worked. I feel my heartbeat return to its normal pace, and the urge to murder Alex subsides a fraction.

"There you go. We need a plan, all right?"

I nod, and he lets me go. "You're right. What do you suggest?" For once, he seems to be the levelheaded one.

"Let's just play it cool. You were invited, after all. We're not crashing this wedding, per se. We're simply crashing the ceremony."

"And Alex's face," I spit out, glaring at the glass doors.

"And there you go again with the flaring nostrils and crazy eyes." He places his hands on my shoulders firmly. "You want Madison back? You gotta show her you've changed."

He's right, again. Taking three deep breaths, I nod. "I'm good. Now stop touching me."

He removes his hands and laughs. "Let's go get the girl."

"My girl," I correct, as I push open the doors.

Once we're inside, I can't deny the place is rather stylish. The foyer is decorated in festive, sparkly crap, but I know that crap was handpicked by Maddy to make her day as perfect as she is. We make our way through the double doors which lead out onto the beach. There is a huge white canopy a few yards away with white chairs lined up underneath, seating a few dozen guests.

As I look to the left, I see a red carpet extending out from a private room off the side. That's got to be Madison's room. I spin on my heel, but Hunter grabs my arm. "What happened to cool?"

"Cool can kiss my ass. Madison is in that room, getting ready to marry some asshole. I need to get in there."

A few guests standing near us and sipping champagne turn to look at the commotion, but I don't even bother to conceal the fact I'm moments away from going apeshit. I break from Hunter's grip and march over to the room, not caring who or what stands in my way. My eyes are glued to that room, and that room alone.

When I'm almost there, I can suddenly smell her. Her light vanilla scent catches on the cool breeze, fueling my hunger even further. "Madison," I say under my breath, quickening my pace to a run. However, what I never expected was to run into Madison…literally.

I collide with her tiny frame, which has her yelping and tumbling forward. My brain may be a jumbled mess, but my instinct to protect her is clear as day. I pounce out, my body singing at the possibility of touching her after so many months, but that happiness turns to rage when another hand gets there first.

A growl rumbles from my throat as I glare over to the left to see some wildebeest latching onto Madison's bicep. I'm… going…to…kill…him.

He saved her from falling on her ass, but now that she's standing, it's time to let her go. "Motherfu—"

"My Cherry Pie, Madison! Hi!" Hunter cuts in, stepping in front of me.

"H-Hi," she stutters. That simple word has my body salivating.

I step out to the left because I need to look at her. I need to ingest everything that I've been missing for almost three hundred long days. The moment she meets my eyes, I know I'm not leaving without her.

She looks older and wiser, but the innocence I fell in love with is still there. Her cheeks turn a lovely pink hue while she nibbles on the corner of her mouth, toeing the sand beneath her bare feet. She's wearing a silver anklet, the small star pendant catching the gentle sunlight. I work my way up, remembering how strong those legs were when they wrapped around my waist, riding me until I was milked dry.

She's wearing a simple white, over-the-knee silk dress, but nothing could ever look simple on her. I can't help but linger on her incredible breasts, which look just as delectable as the day I first tasted them in the flesh. Her long and flowing hair sits curled and draped across her shoulders. I want to reach out and touch it, sniff it like a creeper because I need to make sure she's real.

She's barely wearing any makeup, but she doesn't need it; her natural beauty makes her the most beautiful girl in the world.

But my illusion shatters in an instant when my gaze falls down to the hand, still clutching her bicep tightly. Is this Alex? Her betrothed? The thought has me raising my eyes and matching his heated stare.

Nothing is better than seeing your ex…with someone more unsightly than you. Alex is way too…smiley for Maddy. She needs a real man. She needs me. Not to mention he's short, and his face looks like it's gone a round or two with a frying pan.

"Dixon."

Her voice, her angelic voice brings back so many memories, but I suck it up and look at the reason I'm here. "Madison."

Nothing exists but us, just the way it should be. So much has changed, yet when I look into those big green eyes, I know that a lot has remained the same. She feels it. I feel it. The charged electrical current is still as strong as it was the day we first met.

But what does that mean?

I need to know.

A big, obnoxious hand comes into my line of sight, ruining my high instantly. "Hi, I'm A—" I cut off the fuckstick and focus my attention on Maddy.

"Can we talk?"

She blinks. "Now?"

I nod. When she appears torn, I add, "Please."

A the Asshole decides to intervene. "The ceremony is about to start, Maddy. We have to take our places."

If looks could kill, A would be dead and buried where he stands.

Maddy agrees with him, which makes me even madder. "He's right, Dixon. I have to go inside and get ready."

No, this isn't how it's supposed to be. I won't take no for an answer, and she knows it. "Madison "

"Okay, five minutes." She waves her hands, telling me to shut up.

I internally celebrate.

Before she has time to rethink her decision, I step forward and latch onto her bicep. I can feel her skin, actually feel her skin prickle the moment I touch her. I smugly look up at A, telling him to suck it. She's not impressed by our pissing contest and lightly removes her arm from my grip before walking off.

I'm like a fucking puppy dog, and I follow, unconcerned where we're going. She walks past the room where I originally thought she would be and stops when we round the corner. It's just open beach, but the seaside is ours.

She leans against the brick wall, folding her arms across her chest. "Four minutes."

Four minutes?

How do I sum up everything I want to say in four measly minutes?

"Three and a half."

Shit.

"How are you?" I cringe and run a hand down my face. I'm wasting precious time with this dribble. Grow some balls, Dixon, and tell her how you feel. "Why did you invite me?" I blurt out.

She shrugs. "I thought you'd want to be here."

"You didn't think that would be a touch awkward?"

"Of course I did. But I thought we could put our differences aside for one day."

"One day? And what about tomorrow? Am I just supposed to pretend today never happened?" I ask, spreading my arms out wide. I'm suddenly getting angry, which is what I wanted to avoid.

She lowers her eyes. "I'm sorry. I shouldn't have invited

you. This is just uncomfortable for everyone."

"Damn straight it is. Were you expecting it to be anything else?"

Meeting my heated gaze, she shakes her head. "I'd hoped we could have moved on."

"Moved onto what, Madison?"

She gasps, her arms slipping from their hold. "I don't know."

This conversational ping-pong is growing old. And my time is almost up. "You're the one who left me, remember? You're the one who told me to stay away. But then you invite me to this wedding, expecting me to be okay. How can I be?"

She bites onto her bottom lip, attempting to stop her tears. "I'm sorry, I didn't think. I thought…I wanted…"

"You wanted what?" I ask, stepping forward as she takes a step back.

"I-I…" Her chest begins to rise. "I thought I would be okay with this, but I'm not."

"What aren't you okay about?" I take another step forward while she bumps into the wall behind her.

Now that she's imprisoned, I have no intention of letting her go. I cage her with my arms, placing both my palms on either side of her head as she arches into the brick wall. Her warm, quick breaths lick my cheeks, and I close my eyes, inhaling her.

"Tell me, Maddy," I demand in a whisper, my eyes sealed shut.

"I thought that after all this time apart, things would be different. But…they're not." Her confession dances with sorrow but also relief.

I knew she felt it, too. But the question is, what are we going to do about it?

Fuck being coy, I need her to know how I feel. I need her to know that no matter what, she'll always be my girl.

"Madison…" Slowly opening my eyes, I drown in her. "*Angelo…*" I correct, pressing our foreheads together, our lips inches apart. "I still lo—"

"Maddy?"

That *motherfucker*.

Just like that, our moment is shattered. Maddy guiltily turns to look at the Asshole, gasping when she realizes how close we've grown. She gently pushes me away, but I stand my ground.

"Let her go." I'm seconds away from snapping this bastard's neck.

When I push off the wall angrily, Maddy latches onto my arm. "Don't!"

"Don't what?" I shout, pulling out from her clasp. "I can't believe you actually like this moron!"

"Moron? Excuse me, I'll have you know I'm a fully qualified nurse," Asshole retorts smugly. Is his comment meant to prove his smartness? Because from where I stand, that just cements that Maddy belongs with me.

"A nurse?" I can't stop the sarcastic laugh which thunders from my chest. "He's a male nurse, for Christ's sake, Madison!"

Which, in fact, is a wonderful profession. But who could be a fucking astronaut, and I'd still want to kick him in the balls.

Asshole steps forward, and Madison ducks between while I'm still cackling over the fact he just called himself a nurse. I know I'm being incredibly judgmental, considering I know a lot of intelligent male nurses, but they aren't trying to marry the love of my life.

"You're still a conceited bastard, I see," she snaps, glaring at me.

"And you're still a little girl playing games," I rejoin, sick of this bullshit. Her mouth hinges open in shock, and I see her palm twitch.

But what does she expect? She was seconds away from kissing me. Or at least confessing that she still feels something for me. Now her walls have been resurrected, and she's defending her male nurse *fiancé*.

She flies forward, pushing me in the chest. "You know what—" Her sentence is cut short when the air fills with a soft, gentle melody—a total contradiction to what was filling the air moments ago.

"What?" I challenge.

But she bites back her anger. "Forget it. I have someplace I have to be."

I can't believe she's actually going through with this. Do I not mean anything to her after all?

"You're really doing this?"

Her gaze never wavers when she replies, "Yes." Asshole smugly smiles, gently placing his arm on her shoulders.

I don't even know what to say. My heart is splitting into two for the hundredth time today. How can I fight for someone who doesn't want to be fought for? She's chosen who she wants, and it's not me. This wasn't part of the plan, but that serves me right for not thinking it through.

"I'll see you out there," she has the gall to say.

I don't even bother responding.

She leaves with the Neanderthal trailing close behind, asking if she's okay.

Well, if that wasn't completely fucked up, then I don't know what it was. This entire thing has just backfired, and I don't know what to do. I need to hit something, but the only thing around me is a brick wall and sand.

Too many emotions are plaguing my head. I love her, no, I hate her. I miss her. I'm better off without her. I cradle my head in my palms and let out a strangled, frustrated cry.

"Dix?"

"I need a scotch," I say from between my hands.

"What happened?" Hunter asks, his footsteps swishing in the sand.

"What happened is that this was a total waste of time. She's marrying that dickhead. And to make matters worse, he's a fucking nurse! That means he's kind, patient, and fucking smart. Something I clearly am not."

I look up to meet the concerned eyes of my friend. "It's not a waste of time. Go talk to her."

"I have talked to her. It made no difference. Actually, I'm pretty sure it made things worse. Let's just go."

I attempt to push past him, but he stands solid. "So that's it? You've giving up?"

"I'm not sure if you heard me correctly, but she's marrying the nurse."

"Were you really expecting shit to be easy? I mean, when have things between Madison and you ever been easy?" he asks, lifting a challenging brow.

"This is impossible," I correct, stubbornly.

"Nothing is impossible. You know that. You're proof of that. I thought it was impossible for you to ever settle down after Lily. But you did. You found someone better because you found yourself in her. Don't let that pass you by, you stubborn fuck." He lightly punches me on the arm while I stare at my best friend, wondering what the fuck just happened to him.

"What do you propose I do then, huh? Walk down the aisle and proclaim my undying love for her?" I ask jokingly.

Hunter's stern face and stance reveal that's exactly what he expects me to do. "What have you got to lose?" he asks, shrugging.

"My dignity," I counter.

He moves his lips from side to side. "That's where you're wrong. You do this and you're taking it back."

As the music gets louder and louder, I know that Madison is seconds away from making the biggest mistake of her life.

I've traveled over one hundred miles to see her, and I haven't even told her everything I came here to say. Until I have, until I really try, then I can't give up. I saw it in her eyes. I felt it on her skin. I heard it in her breathless whispers. She still loves me.

And I'm not leaving until she tells me otherwise.

My father didn't raise a coward. And my mother didn't raise a bastard. They taught me to fight for what I want, and I want…I've always wanted Madison Roberts.

"That's my boy." Hunter grins, slapping me on the back as I stampede past him and sprint around the corner.

The moment I see Madison is halfway down the aisle, my senses kick in, and I run like a star quarterback juiced up on his daily fix. I don't care that a hundred sets of eyes are on me as I sprint toward the red carpet. All I care about is…

"Madison!" I stop running, suddenly terrified to take another step.

She comes to an abrupt stop, her bare feet digging into

the carpet. She slowly looks around at the bewildered crowd, knowing that she indeed heard what she thought she did.

Turn around, I silently will her.

And she does.

She spins around gradually, as we both know what will happen when she does. Her eyes meet mine, a look of confusion, anger, and a hint of relief speckled in their depths. "Dixon... what?"

But I don't allow her to finish. She's done enough talking, and now, it's my turn. I'm about to tell the entire world something I should have done the moment she left me.

"I object!"

Thirty-Three

Dixon

ove makes you do stupid things. I should know. I've participated in my fair share of stupidity over the years, but stopping Maddy from walking down that aisle isn't one of them. This is the best kind of stupid.

The curious guests turn to look at one another, hushed whispers filling the air, asking exactly what I object to. But Maddy and I never break our connection because she knows shit is about to get real.

"Dixon…"

I storm forward, not allowing her to say a single word. "It's my turn to talk." She doesn't argue.

"Madison, I—" The pianist is still playing loudly, drowning out my confession. I turn to her. "Can it, sister!" The last note sounds like a strangled cry for help.

We have everyone's attention, but I don't care. I'm not ashamed of how I feel. "Madison, I'm sorry. I think I'll forever be saying sorry because I'm not perfect. I know I'm impulsive, stubborn, impatient, and most of the time, insanely jealous. But I'm also loyal, faithful, and completely and utterly…in love with you."

The guests gasp while Maddy's eyes dampen.

"I can't guarantee that I won't fuck up again, but I can guarantee that I'll love, honor, and cherish you for the rest of my life. These past nine months have been hell, but I'm glad they happened. I've finally become the man I've always wanted to be, and that's because of you."

Unfastening my bow tie and opening up the top button of my shirt, I reach inside and yank out my chain. "I've found the journey I want to be on. And that's the journey with you. I want you to know that I will always be your home. No matter how far you roam, I'll always be here, waiting for you to come home," I conclude, reciting the same words I said to her in Rome.

She covers her mouth, muting her cries, but the stream of tears betrays her anguish. I can only hope they are happy tears.

For some unknown reason, Hunter chooses this moment to intervene. "Ah, Dix. Can I have a word?"

Seriously? He wants to talk *now*? I ignore him, my eyes never leaving Maddy's. "I love you, Madison. I never stopped. Therefore, I can't stand by and let you make the biggest mistake of your life."

She wipes her eyes, sniffing. "Mistake?"

"Yes. I can't—"

"Dude, seriously, we need to talk."

"Not now, Hunter!" I snap, spinning on my heel to look at him. "I need to tell Madison she can't go through with this."

"Well, that's what I need to talk to you about," he quickly

rebukes. I stupidly ignore him once again.

"Go through with what?" Madison asks.

When I turn back around to look at her, I see that she's stopped crying. She now appears utterly confused.

"With this," I clarify, sweeping my hand out in front of me.

"Dixon! For fuck's sake!" Hunter presses, storming around me and standing near Madison. "Shut up."

I glare at him. What's the matter with him? "No, I won't shut up. This is the reason we're here. I can't allow Madison to marry that asshole!"

Madison pulls back, curling her lip. "What asshole? What are you talking about?"

Hunter slaps his forehead, shaking his head.

You'd think his reaction would alert me to the fact that something isn't right and shut me up. It doesn't. "I'm here to stop your wedding to Alex. I object to you marrying anyone but me!" There, I said it, and it felt damn good.

However, my high soon fades when Madison looks at me like I've gone insane. And when it appears everyone else is looking at me in the same manner, I know I've missed the memo.

Maddy blinks. "You object? What?" She pauses, processing what I just stupidly revealed. "Dixon…" A hint of a smirk pulls at her lips a moment later. "I'm…*not* getting married."

I arch my brow. "You're not?" She shakes her head.

My speech worked. *Boom!*

Or not.

"No. I never was."

My brain short-circuits. "You never…wait, hold up, what?" I hold up my finger, needing a minute.

"Whose wedding do you think this is?"

I scratch my head while looking over at Hunter. He waves me off, indicating I'm alone on this one. He takes a seat, getting comfy.

I take a stab in the dark. "Yours and the male nurse's?"

She laughs in disbelief. "Ashley?"

"Who the fuck is Ashley?" I sharply retort, as she surely cannot have another beau on the side.

"Ashley is my friend, and a work colleague. He's also an ex-pupil of Dr. Wellington," she explains clearly.

A friend? The way he was pawing her indicates he's more than a friend. And what's Max got to do with this? I'm so confused.

However, as I peer around, I see there are a lot of old people here. There are also a lot of my colleagues. Mine and Max's colleagues.

…Fuck.

As I desperately look over at Hunter for a little help, he sharply holds up the wedding program, which displays a picture of Max and Aiko. He taps the writing underneath their picture. The cursive font says, "We Still Do." It takes me all of two seconds to realize what's going on. When I do, Hunter throws the program up into the air, thankful I've finally caught on.

Although I think I know what's going on, I need to ensure I'm on the right page. "So you're *not* marrying Alex?"

Madison shakes her head.

"But the invite said Madison and Alex."

"Did you open it?"

I scratch the back of my neck. "Well, no."

"Open it."

"I...can't. It's sitting at the bottom on the Hudson," I explain sheepishly.

She lets out a small chuckle. "Alex, can you please wave?"

On her call, a familiar brunette, who is standing by the celebrant, waves.

"Hi, Alex," Maddy says, waving over her shoulder.

"*That's* Alex?" I ask, my mouth agape.

"Yes, I believe you met her in Boston. I also believe you flirted with her." She cocks her head to the side, challenging me to argue.

"That doesn't sound like something I'd do," I reply, tongue in cheek.

Suddenly, I remember where I've seen her. She was sitting at the breakfast table with Max and Maddy the morning I was a complete ass to Madison in Boston. And Maddy is right, I did flirt with her. But only to make Madison jealous.

As I study her, I notice she's wearing the same dress as Maddy—a bridesmaid dress. Holy shit, this is *Max's* wedding, or a renewal of vows ceremony, not Maddy's. She's the... bridesmaid.

Thinking back over my phone conversation with Max, I now know I misunderstood because I was convinced it was Madison who was getting married, not him. Well, don't I feel foolish.

"But why are you organizing Max's wedding? Or vow ceremony? Or whatever," I ask quickly.

She smiles. "Because Dr. Wellington is not only the best teacher I've ever had, he's also become a good friend. He's become a good friend to all of us," she adds, looking around. "When he let slip he always wanted to give Aiko the beach wedding she's always dreamed of, we all made it happen. I guess he touched the sappy romantic in me." She lowers her eyes for the briefest of moments before adding, "And besides, fifty plus years of marriage is something to celebrate."

My mouth couldn't fall any farther open. "Well, that's generous."

"It's the least I could do. Without him and his letter of recommendation, I wouldn't have got the job at New York Presbyterian."

I lie. My mouth just hit the ground. "*What?* You're coming back to New York?"

She nods. "Yes."

I need to sit.

I blindly slump down onto a chair, taking it all in. If this were a Shakespearean play, I would have kicked myself for swallowing the poison prematurely. But I would have never known the truth if I hadn't come. I would have forever believed she had married someone named Alex, who is in fact her classmate and a girl.

I have no idea why Max is renewing his vows, and I don't care. All I care about is the fact Maddy is not getting married.

"Dixon, my friend. Nice of you to come." I look up and see Max standing beside me.

"You know me," I reply, my voice parading my perplexity. "I just love weddings."

He laughs deeply, slapping me on the back. "Well, in that case, do you think I could get back to mine?" He cups his mouth brazenly. "They charge by the minute."

I shake my head, coming back down to earth. "Oh, of course. I'm sorry, Max. Forgive me." I stand, thankful my legs still hold me up.

"That's quite all right. I'm glad you're here." He gives me a knowing smile. Did he know I'd end up making a fool of myself this entire time? When he secretively nods, I know that he did indeed.

That meddling, conspiring so-and-so.

He walks down the aisle, leaving Maddy standing uneasily off to the side, fiddling with her bouquet. "I better stop making an ass of myself and let you get back to it." I've held up the proceedings long enough.

She nods.

I turn around, but she stops me mid-step when she proclaims, "You didn't."

I smile but don't say a word and take the spare seat next to Hunter.

Once everyone stops staring at me and whispering what a nutjob I am, the music resumes. My eyes lock on Maddy as she takes a deep breath and turns around. Once she looks as composed as she can be, considering the past five minutes, she continues her walk down the aisle. Aiko follows a moment later, while Max looks at her with nothing but love in his eyes.

As the ceremony commences and we take our seats, Hunter leans in and whispers, "And the award for the biggest dumbass goes to…"

"Shut up," I mumble. "By the way, you are the world's worst wingman. Where were you when I was making a complete fool out of myself? A heads-up would have been nice."

He raises his hands, brushing aside all blame. "Hey, I tried. It's not my fault you had verbal diarrhea."

I can't argue with that.

We watch the rest of the ceremony in silence, and I'm thankful for the distraction because I have no idea what comes next.

"So you think I should just go over and be like, Madison…I want you back?"

Silence.

Turning over my shoulder to see what has captured Hunter's attention, I spot a certain redhead. "Give it up, man. I'm pretty sure your staring is starting to creep her out. In fact, it's starting to creep me out." I flail my hand in front of his face, needing to ensure he's still breathing.

He dodges it, transfixing his gaze back on Mary. "Should I wave?"

"Sure, why not." Surely it can't hurt. I spin in my chair, curious to see how this pans out.

From the corner of my eye, I see his arm shoot up high, and he waves a little too zealously. He gains everyone's attention, which seems to infuriate Mary. However, when she gradually raises her hand, both Hunter and I gasp.

"Holy shit, Dix, are you seeing this?" I'm almost certain Hunter is about to rocket off his chair in excitement. "Should I go talk to her?"

The fact she acknowledges him is rather promising, but that hope nosedives a second later. I burst out laughing, turning back around to face my shattered friend.

"Well, at least she waved back," he defensively states, reaching for his beer.

"Yeah…with her middle finger. I'd give up, Hunt. She's not interested."

He slumps back into his seat, nursing his beer unhappily. "I don't get women," he gripes.

I match his pose. "Yup, you're preaching to the choir, my friend." We both drink to our sorrows while watching the surf through the window, as Budweiser has yet to let us down.

"Are you having fun?" Max has come to stand by our table, mineral water in hand. He looks beyond elated, while I'm wondering how long it'll take to drown.

"I'll get us another beer." Hunter stands, offering his seat to Max.

When he sits, I sigh because I know what's coming. "You knew, didn't you? This entire time you knew." I don't even have to clarify what I'm talking about.

He nods.

"Why didn't you stop me?"

Placing his mineral water on the table, he coolly shrugs. "Sometimes we need to believe we've lost everything to appreciate what we had."

Max and his damn philosophies.

"Well, I sure as hell have appreciated what a moron I am. I'm utterly embarrassed and sorry for ruining your day."

He's quick to reply. "You didn't ruin anything, Dixon. You just confirmed what this day is all about."

"And that is…?" I need him to fill in the blanks. But as usual, he doesn't.

"You know what. Don't be coy; we both know you're smarter than that." When he waves lovingly at Aiko, I know that it's a *who* he's referring to. Today is about unity and promise. It's about surrendering oneself to another to find the missing piece of the puzzle that is love. I've put off the inevitable for far too long,

"Congratulations, by the way. You're a lucky man." I too stand, offering my hand to Max.

But he surprises me as he draws me in for an unexpected hug. "We're all blinded at one stage or another in our lives, but now it's time to go find your light." He adds softly, "I saw her minutes ago, sitting by the shore. Alone."

With that, we break apart, and the wisest man I know goes in search of his light while I go find mine.

Hunter is lingering near Mary, so I gesture I'm going for a walk. He nods before raising his fist in the air. As ridiculous as we look, I fist-bump the air and so does he. But he gets it. He gets that it's finally time.

Without delay, I excuse myself through the sea of people, but most turn the other way when they see me coming, most likely afraid I'll speak gibberish and drool on their shoes. Once I step outside, I use my hand to shield the sunlight from my eyes, and just like always, I'm drawn to her.

I see her sitting along the shoreline, her knees drawn up to her chest. She appears to be lost in thought as she stares out into the ocean. Taking a moment to appreciate her beauty, I'm thankful for the day I met her. Even after everything we've been through, I'll never regret all the times, good and bad, that we've shared.

My pace is measured as I walk toward her, my palms sweating and my legs like lead. But I push on, needing this more than I ever have before. Needing *her*. That invisible, ever-present pull is like a whirlpool of emotions, and just as I swallow hard, she turns over her shoulder, her mouth parting.

She can see my resolve, and the trembling of her fingers as she brushes back her hair indicates she knows I'm not going anywhere until we talk. I stop a few feet away, interlacing my hands behind my back so she can't see my nerves. Our eyes connect, but no words are spoken. Not yet. We both need to regain our thoughts.

She digs her tiny feet into the sand, appearing to want to tunnel her way out of here as she turns her attention back to the water.

"Madison…" I finally speak, but my voice sounds unlike my own. She doesn't turn to face me, but that's okay. She will when she's ready.

Feeling ridiculous hovering over her, I sit, ensuring I'm not too close, not wanting to smother her. "I don't know where we go from here, Maddy. I meant every word I said. I still…love you. I never stopped. And the prospect of going home without you is an empty one." I exhale a deep breath, looking out into the clear water as I lean back on my hands.

Her unresponsiveness has me filling the silence. "Max just told me we have to believe we've lost everything to appreciate what we had. And he's right. But my question is, have I? Have I lost you…*angelo*?"

I'm too afraid to look at her; too afraid of what her answer will be because honestly, if she tells me yes, then I don't know how I'll go on. This isn't the way our story is supposed to end.

However, when one minute turns into two, I can't endure the silence any longer. I push off my hands, ready to stand and accept that this might actually be the end. But when Madison finally turns, I stop dead in my tracks. Her gentle eyes are puffy, and her nose is colored a bright red. She looks just how I feel—broken.

"No."

That one single word bears so much weight that I can't help but swallow. "No?" I question, unsure what no means.

"No, Dixon, you haven't lost me." Although those words were as soft as a feather, I know I heard them. I know I heard what I've been dreaming about since she left.

I take a second to process it all because although I haven't lost her, that doesn't mean she wants me back. Or does it?

"I miss you so much," she confesses on a strangled, defeated sob. "I don't understand. It's getting worse instead of better. I th-thought the distance would make it all go away, but it hasn't. The distance has just made me miss you more. I see you everywhere." Her lower lip quakes. "You're the store clerk at my local store; you're the mailman. You're even my damn dentist. Everywhere I look, I see you. I know it's just my mind playing tricks, but it's got to mean something, right?"

In an attempt to stop her cries, she places a fist in front of her mouth, but her cries—in a bittersweet, morbid way—are a balm to my blistering soul.

She's right. It does mean something. It means she's as miserable as I am. "Maddy, just come home. Come home with *me*. I don't know what's going to happen, but let's try to figure it out together. I don't want to live without you. I can't. I can't breathe without you, *angelo*. Please, breathe new life into me."

Tears cascade down her soft skin as she silently weeps. I want so badly to comfort her, but I don't.

"Do you still love me, Maddy?"

It's a simple question. One which will change how the next

thirty seconds plays out.

Her hesitation has me sucking in a choked breath. "Maddy...do you still love me?" I repeat, pinning her with my desperate stare.

"It's not that simple. What happened between us..." But she suddenly stops.

"I know that, and I would never expect you to forget what I did. But I need to know...do you...still...love me?"

She closes her eyes, lowering her chin to her chest.

The fact she can't answer this question kills me, and the waves crashing along the shore drown out the hammering of my heart. If she doesn't answer me soon, I'm sure to...

"Yes, Dixon..." she whispers, finally turning to look at me. "I still love you. I never stopped. I tried to, but it was like fighting nature—it's impossible. If possible, I love you more than I did the day I left. I've grown and changed, and so has my love for you. I'm so lost without you."

I... she-she loves me?

Those words are the best words I'll ever hear because those words are full of hope—hope for our future.

Max was right. We needed to believe we'd lost everything to appreciate what we had.

"I didn't know what was going to happen today, but I should have known."

"Should have known what?" I question, shifting closer, thankful when she doesn't shy away.

"I should have known that nothing will ever change between us. No matter how many miles, how many oceans or seas..." She places a hand on my cheek, her wavering touch kissing my heart. "Nothing will ever change the fact that I'm forever yours."

Turning into her, I relish the way she feels, the way she smells. I missed this. I missed all of this. But mostly, I missed us.

I'm not expecting things to go back to the way that they were right away. I want her to know I'm happy to take it as slow as she wants. Besides, in a way, we're getting to know one another again. "Madison Roberts, can I buy you dinner?"

She strokes over my scruff, choking on a laughing sob. "Dinner is provided tonight."

I smile, nuzzling into her hand like a docile kitten. "I know, but it's an open invitation. Whenever you feel like dinner, whether that be tomorrow, next week, month, or year, call me. Just know I'll be here waiting."

Not so patiently, but I'll try.

She appears to ponder over my promise, and I don't know which way she'll go. It's a painstakingly slow few seconds, and when she lightly brushes over my beard, appearing to weigh up what to do, I feel winded and am at her complete mercy.

The anticipation is almost too much to bear, but she cups my cheek with tender fingers before curling her hand around my nape. I freeze, unsure what happens next. She's in total control when she climbs into my lap, straddling me snugly.

The surprise is clear on my face, and she smiles, wiping her eyes. "How about you buy me dessert?"

Her lips, her smell, her warmth, her entire essence is within reach, but I restrain my need to hold, touch and kiss her. "Dessert isn't provided tonight?" I ask, feeling her rasping exhalations mingling with mine.

"Yes, it is. But I could always eat two."

I can't…this is too much. I need to kiss her. After so long, I need to feel whole again.

She senses my internal war, inching her lips closer and closer until our breaths become one. There is only one thing I can say to sum up how I feel. It's something I've said to her before.

Thumbing her lower lip, I roughly state, "If you kiss me, you can't take it back."

She smiles, and a sight has never looked more beautiful. "I don't want to take it back." Her warm breath caresses my cheeks, her eyes filled with molten desire.

"Good," I growl, before swooping forward and taking back what's always been mine. She groans into my mouth, tightening her hold around me while I clutch onto her waist, basking in what it feels like to come home.

This kiss is filled with so many emotions, so many months of longing, forlornness, and despair, but as her tongue duels with mine and she keeps up with my wanton pace, we fall back into sync, just how it's supposed to be.

She pushes me down and pulls away, placing frantic little kisses all over my face as I lie back in the sand. Tears wet my cheeks, but I know these tears are the happy kind.

We kiss like starved creatures for minutes, maybe hours, I don't know. And although we've shared countless kisses before, these kisses are my favorite kisses of all.

Epilogue

"**P**eek-a-boo."

Not in a million years did I ever think that the high-pitched squeal of a six-month-old drooling baby would be adorable, but as I tickle this little cherub's tummy, I know I'm a total convert.

Using my hands as a makeshift window over my eyes, I thrive on her giggles when I cluck, "Peek-a-boo," for the umpteenth time.

"Here, Dix, you want her?" teases Finch as he passes his baby daughter, Simone, my way. I happily accept her, laughing when her chubby little hands reach for my glasses.

"Who's a grumpy pants?" I coo, bouncing the bundle of joy in my lap. "It's your daddy, yes it is." I sound utterly ridiculous, using a high-pitched voice which should only be reserved for grandmas and clucky mothers, but this is the new me. And I'm not ashamed of it.

This crazy journey has taught me many things, but the most important is to be honest with the one person you should love the most, and that person is you. If you can do that, odds are your honesty and happiness will rub off on others.

Others like Hunter.

"More like who's a stinky ass?" He pinches his nose and shoots up off the couch like it's on fire. When I get a whiff of what he smells, I stiffly pass Simone back over to her daddy. Drool I can deal with, dirty diapers, I cannot. See, I'm all about the honesty.

Finch smirks and shakes his head as he grabs the pink-striped baby bag. "Who's a big pansy ass? Your uncles, that's who," Finch coos in a sweet voice as he walks to the bathroom with his babbling daughter.

Not so long ago, Hunter and I would be sealing the deal with some random barflies, while Finch would be going home, no doubt praying that we would stop with the man-whoreness and settle down. But those days are over, for the both of us.

Even though Hunter is still single, he's very much a one lady's man, and that lady is currently upstairs with my lady, getting ready to hit the town. Yes, I don't fail to see the irony in this situation—the boys stay at home while the girls have a few cosmos in town—but I wouldn't have it any other way.

My wild days are over and now I'm just boring Dr. Dixon Mathews—psychiatrist, lecturer, and lover.

After that day on the beach, things between Maddy and I changed dramatically. We agreed to take things slow, but after the first course I decided to skip mains and head straight for dessert—I'm sure you can guess what my dessert consisted of. I agreed to take things slow, but I'm not a damn saint, and it appears neither was Maddy.

She moved in with me and my dad a month later.

We easily fell into a simple routine. She loves her job at New York Presbyterian, and I can finally say I've become the psychiatrist who was worthy of winning the Gerald Harriet's Award. The shard sits on my mantel, a reminder of what I almost lost.

My life could have turned out so differently, and although I've endured some hardships I wish to never experience again, I've come to realize that I *am* the hero of this story and I'm *finally* the good guy—I'm Madison's good guy.

As they say, behind every great man lies an even greater woman, or, in Madison's case, the only woman I'll love for the rest of my life.

"Oh for fuck's sake, Dix, I can hear your balls rolling around in Cherry Pie's purse upstairs," Hunter quips, leaning against the mantel. He's privy to my obvious, soppy thoughts, but I don't care.

"She can do whatever she likes with my balls," I retort with a wink. "Come to think of it…"

Hunter swiftly places his hands over his ears while screaming, "I can't hear you!"

His obsession with Mary, who still hates his guts, has turned him into a monk. He's just waiting for her to turn around and see what a great guy he is. See that he's changed. It's yet to happen, but if Madison saw something in me that I didn't, then there's hope for my friend.

My father, who is sitting in front of the TV, snorts.

Maddy's Italian has improved vastly, thanks to my dad and his selective hearing. At times, he acknowledges her talking to him in English, but mostly he won't reply until she pulls out her little dictionary and repeats herself in his native tongue. He may be mute most of the time, but he conveys enough cheek in his silence.

All in all, it's just a typical day in the Mathews' household.

Finch returns with a freshly diapered Simone, who is sucking away on a bottle. The dad look suits him, and I wonder if it'll suit me too.

When the enchanting laughs of the girls trail down the stairs, my heart skips a beat. Heidi, Mary, and Madison have formed a little threesome, just like Finch, Hunter and I. If Mary didn't hate Hunter's guts, we could do the whole triple dating thing, but I see that ending with Hunter paying a trip to the emergency room. He doesn't allow her aloofness to deter him, and when she steps into the living room, his entire face lights up as he wipes his sweaty palms on his jeans. It's a look I know well because I'm wearing the same one.

Madison meets my eyes from across the room, smiling broadly as she shyly tucks a soft piece of hair behind her ear. She knows I am currently undressing her in my mind, and wondering what she's wearing underneath that tight black dress. Luckily for me, I plan on finding out tonight.

Heidi and Gabriella walk over to Finch, giving Daddy a hug goodbye, which leaves Hunter and I staring like lovestruck fools. A poised grin is plastered on Maddy's face the entire time she walks over to me, knowing what her long legs and pushed-up breasts are doing to me.

Her confidence is infectious. "One cocktail and then you're coming home." When she tweaks a brow at my bossiness, I add in her ear, "Because then I plan on giving you your own special cock…tail."

Her breath catches and she nods eagerly. "I'll take it straight up." Her bold comment has me wheezing like an emphysemic old man. God, I love this woman.

"C'mon, love birds," Mary groans, latching onto Maddy. "Enough with the PDA."

Her comment just confirms what a perfect match for Hunter she really is. "Hi, Mary," he nervously says. "You look nice." I bite my lip to stop my cackle.

She gives him a stiff upper-lip smile, which looks like a fuck you, but Hunter looks to be over the moon with the acknowledgment.

"All right, girls, let's go." Mary yanks on Maddy's forearm, but I scoop her up and kiss her quickly.

Well, it was meant to be quick, but the moment I sip on her sweetness, it's hard to let go. I feel dizzy, completely intoxicated with her, and I revel in the feeling of madness. Only when Mary clears her throat loudly do I slow down my assault and nip her bottom lip before pulling away.

Madison's flushed cheeks have me thinking of something else bearing a similar pink tinge, and when she casts her gaze downward, I know she knows it too.

This woman makes me insatiable and I love it. I love her.

"Have a good night, *angelo*. I love you," I say, stroking the length of her neck, brushing my fingers over my mother's chain, which she never removes.

I watch with envy as goose bumps lick every inch of her pale, supple skin. "I love you, too. Go Yankees," she cheers a second later, waving invisible pompoms.

Both Mary and Maddy turn to leave, while Hunter and I not

so discreetly check out their asses. Some things never change. Madison kisses my father on the head before her happy chatter follows her out the door.

Hunter and I casually walk over to the window and I draw back the curtain, watching Maddy stroll to my BMW while chatting merrily to her friends. She's come a long way and she deserves this happiness because she too has finally grown into the woman she's always wanted to become.

So this is what my Friday nights entail. The girls going out and letting their hair down while the boys stay home, drink beer, eat pizza, look after the kids, and watch the game. Nothing has felt more perfect.

Well, that isn't entirely true.

I dreamily toy with the small velvet box which currently sits in my pocket. Although it weighs close to nothing, symbolically, it weighs a thousand pounds.

"So you're really going through with it?" Hunter asks, his eyes never veering away from the scene in front of us.

My chest expands in pride, as I want nothing more. "Yeah, man. I am."

Hunter laughs happily, slapping me on the arm. "I think you mean I do."

We only step away from the window when the taillights of my car fade into the night. Yup, we're both completely and utterly pussy-whipped and proud of it.

As we sit watching the Yankees, I can't help but ponder how my life has changed. Once upon a time there lived a selfish, lonely man-whore with no regard for anyone other than himself. The man-whore took up with many witches, never believing that true love really existed. But one day in a kingdom

far, far away, that man-whore soon met a princess, one who showed him that underneath his beastly exterior...he was a prince after all.

Be all my sins remembered.
Hamlet, *William Shakespeare.*

Acknowledgements

My author family: Elle and Vi—I love you both very much.

My ever-supporting parents. You guys are the best. I am who I am because of you. I love you. RIP Papa. Gone but never forgotten. You're in my heart. Always.

My agent, Kimberly Brower from Brower Literary & Management. Thank you for your patience and thank you for being an amazing human being.

Sommer Stein, you NAILED this cover! Thank you for being so patient and making the process so fun. I'm sorry for annoying you constantly.

My editor, Jenny Sims. What can I say other than I LOVE YOU! Thank you for everything. You go above and beyond for me.

My publicist—Sarah Ferguson from Social Butterfly PR. Thank you for all your help.

Danielle Sanchez from Wildfire Marketing Solutions—You are amazing. I would be lost without you.

To the endless blogs that have supported me since day one—You guys rock my world.

My bookstagrammers—Your creativity astounds me. The effort you go to is just amazing. Thank you for the posts, the teasers, the support, the messages, the love, the EVERYTHING! I see what you do, and I am so, so thankful.

My ARC TEAM—You guys are THE BEST! Thanks for all the support.

My reader group—sending you all a big kiss.

Samantha and Amelia—I love you both so very much.

Michelle, you're my soul mate. I love you always. Thanks for saving me.

David—thank you for being a beautiful human—inside and out. I love you lots x

David and Michelle, you SLAYED this cover!

My fur babies—mamma loves you so much! Dacca, I know you're hanging with Jaggy, Dina, Ninja, and Papa.

To anyone I have missed, I'm sorry. It wasn't intentional!

Last but certainly not least, I want to thank YOU! Thank you for welcoming me into your hearts and homes. My readers are the BEST readers in this entire universe! Love you all!

About the Author

Monica James spent her youth devouring the works of Anne Rice, William Shakespeare, and Emily Dickinson.

When she is not writing, Monica is busy running her own business, but she always finds a balance between the two. She enjoys writing honest, heartfelt, and turbulent stories, hoping to leave an imprint on her readers. She draws her inspiration from life.

She is a bestselling author in the U.S.A., Australia, Canada, France, Germany, Israel, and The U.K.

Monica James resides in Melbourne, Australia, with her wonderful family, and menagerie of animals. She is slightly obsessed with cats, chucks, and lip gloss, and secretly wishes she was a ninja on the weekends.

Connect with Monica James

Website: authormonicajames.com
Instagram: @authormonicajames
Facebook: facebook.com/authormonicajames
Twitter: twitter.com/monicajames81
Goodreads: goodreads.com/MonicaJames
TikTok: @authormonicajames
BookBub: bookbub.com/authors/monica-james
Amazon: https://amzn.to/2EWZSyS
Join my Reader Group: http://bit.ly/2nUaRyi

www.ingramcontent.com/pod-product-compliance
Lightning Source LLC
Chambersburg PA
CBHW070158120726
47909CB00001B/158

* 9 780645 508222 *